"Clever, fast-paced and well-plotted, *Dead Canaries Don't Sing* stars an appealing heroine and furry sidekicks sure to enchant pet lovers."
—Carolyn Hart, Agatha, Anthony and Macavity awards winner

"*Dead Canaries Don't Sing* is top dog, the cats's pajamas, and the paws that refresh all rolled into one unfurgettable mystery entertainment."
—Sarah Graves, author of the *Home Repair Is Homicide* series

"Loads of fun! Baxter's veterinary sleuth and her menagerie of animal companions are a great way to spend an afternoon. So pull up a chair and dive in."
—T. J. MacGregor, Edgar Award winner and author of *Category Five*

"An auspicious debut . . . Messages, murder and a menagerie of odd animals are along for the fun."
—*Mystery Scene*

"Should be on your [summer reading list]." —*Newsday*

"Baxter's light-hearted, enjoyable mystery is an entertaining debut featuring a likable menagerie of characters, a few surprising plot twists and a touch of romance." —*Lansing State Journal*

"Charmingly humorous . . . [Baxter is] funny without being fussy. Along with lovable Jessica and her menagerie, the author has created a subtle yet creepy antagonist whose unmasking is as intense as it is surprising." —*Romantic Times*

"A truly refreshing read t
along. I'm looking forward
—*Rena*

D0181030

Hare Today, Dead Tomorrow

A Reigning Cats & Dogs Mystery

Cynthia Baxter

BANTAM BOOKS

HARE TODAY, DEAD TOMORROW
A Bantam Book / May 2006

Published by
Bantam Dell
A Division of Random House, Inc.
New York, New York

This is a work of fiction. Names, characters, places, and
incidents either are the product of the author's imagination or
are used fictitiously. Any resemblance to actual persons, living or
dead, events, or locales is entirely coincidental.

All rights reserved
Copyright © 2006 by Cynthia Baxter
Cover art by Robert Giusti
Cover design by Marietta Anastassatos

Bantam Books and the rooster colophon are registered
trademarks of Random House, Inc.

ISBN-13: 978-0-553-58843-9
ISBN-10: 0-553-58843-5

Printed in the United States of America
Published simultaneously in Canada

www.bantamdell.com

OPM 10 9 8 7 6 5 4 3 2

To Faith

Acknowledgments

In researching this book, I worked with several people who were unbelievably generous with their time and their knowledge. I would like to thank Ursula Massoud of Paumanok Vineyards, Ltd in Aquebogue, who taught me the basics about wineries and winemaking. I would also like to thank Martha S. Gearhart, D.V.M., as well as Marc A. Franz, D.V.M. and the entire staff at the Woodbury Animal Hospital in Woodbury, especially Wendy Niceberg, Kim Marino, and Joanne St. George.

The fascinating true story of Captain Kidd comes from an outstanding book, *The Pirate Hunter: The True Story of Captain Kidd,* by Richard Zacks. I would also like to thank Lisa Pulitzer and Kieran Crowley, my much-appreciated sources for information about police procedures.

And thanks to Caitlin Alexander for her invaluable help in pulling the whole book together, as well as Faith Hamlin, who is an ongoing source of encouragement and support.

A Note to Readers

Hare Today, Dead Tomorrow is a work of fiction, and all names and characters are the product of the author's imagination. Any resemblance to actual events, organizations, or persons, living or dead, is coincidental. Although some real Long Island places and some real people are mentioned, all are used fictitiously.

Hare Today,
Dead Tomorrow

Chapter 1

*"A man who carries a cat by the tail learns
something he can learn in no other way."*

—Mark Twain

What!?"

"Cassandra's cat. He just stared at me.... There was blood everywhere, and she was lying on the floor, not moving—" Suzanne Fox's voice broke off in a hoarse choke. We were sitting in her living room, less than forty-eight hours after she'd first called me with the news.

"Start at the beginning," I instructed her, struggling to keep my voice even. I'd done the same thing hundreds of times before—usually while trying to calm an alarmed animal owner. "Slow down, take a deep breath, and tell me exactly what happened."

She let out what sounded more like a desperate gasp than a deep breath. "Jessie, the police think I murdered my ex-husband's fiancée. Her name is—was—Cassandra Thorndike. What am I going to do?"

"Thorndike—as in Thorndike Vineyards?" I asked, naming one of the most successful and best-known wineries on Long Island.

"Exactly. She was found stabbed to death at her house in Cuttituck, out on the North Fork." Suzanne paused, as if she was trying to find the strength to go on. "Apparently her next-door neighbor dropped by for a visit. But Cassandra didn't come to the door, even though it was wide open. The neighbor noticed her car was in the driveway and the TV was on. So she dialed 911. The police showed up, expecting to find some senior citizen with an overly active imagination and too much time on her hands." In a strained voice, she added, "Except it turned out she was right."

"But why would the police think you had anything to do with it?" I asked.

"They have witnesses, people who live in the neighborhood, who claim they saw a car the same make and color as mine drive up to her house not long before her next-door neighbor called. They said the driver had bright orange-red hair."

"*Were* you there?"

"Yes." She let out a little choking sound before adding, "I—I saw her body, Jess. So I wasn't really surprised when the cops showed up on my doorstep a couple of days ago and said Cassandra had been murdered."

"You told them what happened, right?"

She waited for what seemed a very long time before answering. "Not exactly."

"What do you mean, 'not exactly'?" My mouth had suddenly become very dry.

"I—I told the police they had the wrong person. That I'd never even been to Cassandra's house." Before I had a chance to react, she cried, "Jessie, you've got to help me!"

It's not easy staying calm when you've just found out one of your best friends is a murder suspect. I liked to think my decade of working as a veterinarian had taught me to handle all kinds of situations, especially the past few years of traveling around Long Island with my clinic-on-wheels. But this...well, this was something new.

I just stared at Suzanne for a few seconds, not wanting to seem too horrified by her situation but not quite able to take it all in. Even though she sat in a wooden rocking chair, she remained motionless. The fact that I always think of her as one of those people who never sits still made the image especially peculiar.

It was late morning, yet the blinds were drawn and the lights were off, casting the room in shadow. Even in the dim light, I could see that her huge, round eyes, the same shade of blue as cornflowers, were swollen and rimmed in red, as if crying had become as much a part of her routine as breathing. Her nose and cheeks were also puffy, and they'd taken on a pinkish tinge. Her remarkable orange-red hair looked surprisingly lackluster. While she had tamed her wild, wavy mane during our college years by wearing it in a waist-length braid, she'd recently gotten it cut into layers. Somehow, through either physics or chemistry, she'd also made it dead straight. It was usually stunning. Today, however, it hung limply about her face, looking as dejected as she did.

"I'm still not getting this," I told her. "Why were you at Cassandra's house in the first place?"

She glanced at me warily. "You know how upset I was when I heard Robert was engaged. For heaven's sake, we'd only been divorced for a few months! The body that was our marriage was still warm."

I cringed at the metaphor. Somehow, the image of anything dead, even a relationship, hit a raw nerve.

"I do remember you telling me how painful it was for you," I commented.

"'Painful' is an understatement," she replied. "I felt

worse than I did when my impacted wisdom tooth got infected. Anyway, I decided that meeting her might make me feel better. I figured that once I saw for myself that she was just another person, maybe even someone I could be friends with, the idea that Robert had chosen her over me wouldn't hurt as much."

Frankly, I thought that sounded like a really bad plan. But at this juncture, it seemed kinder to keep my opinions to myself.

"So I found out where she lived," Suzanne continued. "On Tuesday afternoon, I went over to her house and rang her doorbell. I figured I'd introduce myself and that maybe she'd offer me coffee or something. I was hoping that by the time I got out of there, I'd have the closure I was looking for." She shook her head sadly. "I mean, she couldn't have been an ogre. She was probably a very nice person, someone I would have liked if we'd met under different circumstances."

"Probably," I replied unconvincingly.

"Anyway, when I got there, I was pretty sure she was home. But she wouldn't come to the door."

"Why did you think she was in the house?" I asked.

"Her car was parked in the driveway."

"How did you know it was hers?"

Suzanne rolled her eyes. "Jess, it was a red Miata with the license plate CASSLASS. Who else could it belong to?"

"Good deduction," I said, nodding.

"Besides, the front door was open. That wasn't surprising, since it was one of those gorgeous October days. And the TV was on."

"So you rang the bell?" I prompted.

"Two or three times. Then I knocked, really loudly." Frowning, she noted, "My first thought was that she knew perfectly well who was on her doorstep. I figured she'd looked out the window and recognized me from Robert's description, or photos he had.

"Anyway, the idea that she was holed up inside her house, hoping I'd just go away, got me mad." Suzanne hesitated. "Finally, I opened the screen door and walked in."

I guess a look of surprise crossed my face, because she quickly added, "It's not like I barged in or anything. I just stepped inside and called her name. You know, like, 'Cassandra? Are you here? Anybody home?'

"I could hear the television blaring from the back of the house. So I followed the sound. But I kept calling her name. I mean, I wasn't trying to sneak up on her or anything.

"Then I reached a room that looked like a home office. It had a computer and a fax machine and a little TV, stuck up on a shelf. I got as far as the doorway. And then, and then—" Her voice broke off. "I saw her."

"Exactly what did you see, Suzanne?" I asked gently.

She paused to take a couple of deep breaths. "She was...she was on the floor, facedown. But she was crumpled up, as if she'd fallen. There was blood everywhere. Most of it had soaked into the carpet, I guess. And there was plenty of blood on the desk. Everything on top was in chaos. Papers were lying all over the place, and the pencil mug was on its side with pens and pencils scattered.

"The whole scene was horrible, Jess! And what made it even more disturbing was the fact that, right in the middle of this grotesque scene, there was one single sign of life."

I blinked. "What are you talking about?"

"Like I told you: Cassandra's cat. He was lying on the floor next to her, acting as if he was just waiting for someone to come and help. He looked up at me and blinked, then let out a loud meow. It was really creepy. I almost got the feeling he was trying to tell me what had happened. Or that maybe he was asking me *why* it happened."

The idea of someone's poor pussycat witnessing such a horrendous event broke my heart. I immediately thought of my own two cats. Cat—Catherine the Great—was a longtime companion who had often picked up on my bad moods, everything from sadness to grumpiness. She seemed to have a sixth sense about what was going on with me, and she seemed to long to comfort me. Tinkerbell was still just a kitten, but I'd even caught her staring at me, wide-eyed, at times when I was upset, as if she had also noticed that something was amiss.

"Anyway, I panicked," Suzanne continued. "I just turned and ran. I got in my car and drove off." Her shoulders slumped. "That's what happened. But somehow, I couldn't bring myself to tell the police."

The face of Lieutenant Anthony Falcone, Norfolk County's chief of homicide, flashed before my eyes like one of the bursts of light that often precede a migraine. Even in my imagination, he didn't look happy.

"Why not, Suzanne?" I demanded, trying not to sound exasperated. "Why didn't you just tell them the truth?" I realized I was perched so far on the edge of the couch that I was close to toppling onto the floor. I also noticed that the brightly colored fabric, splashed with cheerful flowers, looked painfully out of place in the somber room.

"Jess, when they showed up at my house, I just freaked! All these thoughts started racing around in my head, like, *They're going to think I killed Cassandra Thorndike because I was jealous!* and *I can't let them know I was there!*" The tears that had pooled in her eyes began streaming down her cheeks. "I didn't want to get involved. I was afraid they'd suspect me."

In a choked voice, she added, "But I didn't do it, Jessie! You believe me, don't you?"

"Of course I do!" I cried.

In fact, I was one hundred percent convinced that she

was innocent. Suzanne Fox and I had been friends since our freshman year of college, when the fact that we both wanted to become veterinarians had instantly bonded us. We'd memorized the periodic table together, filled out our vet-school applications together, and even opened our letters of acceptance together. Even though we lost touch for a few years after she went to vet school at Purdue University and I went to Cornell, the previous June we had reconnected when I discovered that she, too, was living on Long Island. She was someone I'd been friends with for more than a decade and a half. As far as I was concerned, that was more than enough time to be certain of her true character.

"What did the police say when you told them it wasn't you their witnesses had spotted?" I asked.

Suzanne's lip trembled. "I'm not sure they believed me. When they left, they told me not to leave the New York area. In fact, they said I'd be wise to stay on Long Island."

"Suzanne, listen to me," I said, doing my best to remain calm. "You've got to tell them the truth. Sooner or later, the cops are going to—"

"Don't you see?" she cried. "I can't change my story now. It'll only make things look worse."

"But don't you think that sooner or later they're going to figure out you really were at Cassandra's house that day? That they'll find your hair or your fingerprints or . . . or some other proof?"

She shook her head hard. "I'm not even going to think about that right now," she insisted. "If that ever happens—and I don't see any reason why it should—I'll deal with it then."

Her capacity for denial was truly remarkable. Then again, she'd already astounded me with it through her choice of boyfriend.

I decided to try a different tack. "Have you contacted an attorney?" I asked. "Someone who can give you advice?"

She nodded. "Marcus put me in touch with somebody. A guy he went to college with. I think they were in the same fraternity."

Great, I thought as a wave of dismay swept over me. I hoped that, whoever he was, he'd turn out not to have gotten through school the same way as that boyfriend of hers, Marcus Scruggs: by majoring in Girls and Beer. "Who is he?"

"Jerry Keeler," she replied. "He's got an office right across from the Norfolk County Courthouse."

I made a mental note of his name.

"Is there anything *you* can do, Jessie? Can you talk to that obnoxious guy in homicide? You know him, don't you? What's his name—Vulture or something?"

"Falcone," I corrected her. "Lieutenant Falcone."

"If he hurries up and finds the real murderer, I'll be off the hook, right?" she asked anxiously. "Besides, aren't you two friends?"

I hesitated before replying, "Actually, he and I are not exactly on the best of terms."

That was an understatement. Not only was the man utterly convinced that I spent way too much time investigating murders; the fact that I occasionally turned out to be better at it than he was only furthered the damage. Given our history, I suspected that alerting him to my connection to this case would only aggravate what was already an appalling situation.

But I had to take action. Especially since Suzanne didn't seem to realize that she'd made a bad situation a hundred times worse by lying to the police about having been at Cassandra Thorndike's house the day she was murdered. Despite my feelings about Falcone, he was sharp enough that such a blatant lie was bound to raise red flags.

And when Falcone was seeing red, there was no telling what he might do.

• • •

Before I drove off, I took a long look at Suzanne's house, a small West Brompton Beach bungalow that had clearly been built as a summer home. It looked ridiculously cheerful and full of hope for the future, despite the fact that whoever designed it had clearly been influenced by the Shoe Box Movement. Suzanne had done a valiant job of making the best of it. Its white shingles had been painted recently, probably around the time she and her then-husband, Robert Reese, moved in two years ago, when they'd relocated to Long Island so he could open his own restaurant. Back then, of course, Suzanne didn't realize their marriage had already gotten to dessert.

Even though she'd been born and raised in the Midwest, she'd opted to keep the house, buying out Robert's share as part of their divorce settlement. She'd already set down roots in the area, establishing a veterinary practice in nearby Poxabogue. Somehow, the house suited her. The simple, one-story structure reflected her Midwestern practicality. Yet she'd added a few flashier touches—painting the shutters turquoise and lime green, for example, and putting out one of those cynical doormats that read *Go Away*—that I tend to think of as her ever-increasing New York–ness.

It was certainly true that Suzanne had changed a lot since our college days, when she'd arrived at Bryn Mawr literally right off the farm. But she was a long way from being tough enough to withstand something like this without completely crumbling beneath the stress.

When she'd first called me to tell me she was in trouble, I was lying in a hospital bed, recovering from having my stomach pumped. The entire thing was so surreal that I'd wondered if I was simply experiencing some bizarre side effect from the drugs the doctors had given me.

Unfortunately, the sick feeling that immediately lodged in my stomach told me it was all terribly real.

Of course, that feeling was probably also due to the fact that I'd been poisoned not long before. I still wasn't feeling even close to perky.

I didn't look particularly perky either, I realized as I climbed into my red VW and caught sight of myself in the rearview mirror. My face was pale and drawn, and my expression made me look like someone who had just received some of the worst news of her entire life. My dark-blond hair, badly in need of washing, was pulled back into an unflattering ponytail. And my green eyes had a dull look that I knew could only be cured with a cup of joe. I promised myself that I'd dash into the first Starbucks I spotted—whether my stomach agreed that it was a good idea or not.

At least locating some desperately needed caffeine wasn't likely to prove too much of a struggle. West Brompton Beach was like most of the other communities on Long Island's South Fork, the nickname for the bottom prong of the fish-shaped island's tail: It was filled with establishments that catered to the needs of individuals with more money than they could spend in several lifetimes. During the summer, swarms of ridiculously wealthy actors, writers, artists, pop stars, and rappers, along with the behind-the-scenes business moguls who'd made them all household names in the first place, moved the glitz and glamour of their Manhattan lifestyles one hundred miles east to the area known as the Bromptons. My mobile veterinary practice, a 26-foot van that serves as my office, frequently took me there to treat the dogs, cats, and other pets that belonged to both locals and summer residents. So I knew only too well that between Memorial Day and Labor Day, you couldn't find a parking space, buy a cup of coffee for under three dollars, or walk more than twenty feet without spotting someone you'd seen on the cover of *People* magazine.

But the seaside village had a split personality. September had just eased into October, and the summer playground of the rich and famous was already showing signs of rust. Many of the luxurious vacation homes were closed up for the winter season, along with some of the boutiques. As for the restaurants, maître d's who would laugh at anyone calling for a reservation less than a month in advance during the high season were now desperately pushing three-course prix fixe dinners for under thirty bucks.

Actually, autumn and winter were my favorite times of year on the island's East End. The beach towns took on a magical quality, thanks to the stark gray-white light of the luminescent sky. The endless white-sanded beaches, not a soul in sight other than the shrieking seagulls scavenging for food, always struck me as romantic. The same went for the beach communities' Main Streets, as crowded as cities during July and August but as deserted as ghost towns in the fall. It was easy to see why the Tile Club, the group of artists who had first trekked out to the South Fork from New York City in the late 1800s, had instantly fallen in love with the area's natural beauty. Famed architect Stanford White, painters Winslow Homer and William Merritt Chase, and the other members of their exclusive group published their drawings and paintings of the South Fork in a popular magazine, instantly creating a brand-new tourist destination.

Besides, Starbucks was open year-round.

Sure enough, I found one less than a mile from Suzanne's house. After I'd obtained a double grande cappuccino, enough industrial-strength coffee to jump-start an entire football team, I settled back into the front seat of my car and made a bunch of phone calls, rescheduling the rest of the day's appointments.

Then I dialed Nick's cell phone number. I only hoped he wouldn't be so involved in contracts and torts and whatever else he was learning about in his first year of law school that I wouldn't be able to reach him.

Relief washed over me when he answered on the second ring.

"Jess?" he asked eagerly. "Are you okay?"

"I'm fine, Nick," I assured him. "A little shaky, but that's to be expected." I paused before adding, "I wish I could say the same for Suzanne."

"What's going on with her?" He'd been standing right next to me when Suzanne had called me at the hospital. And when he'd driven me home earlier that morning before heading off to a full day of classes, her predicament was pretty much all we'd talked about. So I knew he was anxious for an update.

"It's as bad as it sounded on the phone," I told him, figuring there was no point in telling him the truth: that it was actually even worse. "Suzanne's in serious trouble. She's apparently a suspect in Cassandra Thorndike's murder."

"But that's insane!" he exclaimed. "Suzanne Fox is the last person in the world who would ever be capable of something like that!"

"My sentiments exactly." I paused for a few seconds before adding, "I have to help her, Nick, whether it means talking to the police or . . . or just holding her hand as she goes through this. . . ."

"I understand that, Jess. But if she's innocent—"

"There's something else." I took a deep breath, bracing myself before dropping the real bomb in his lap. "She lied to the police. Several witnesses saw someone who fit her description in a car that matches hers near the victim's house around the time of the murder. But when the police questioned her, she denied being there."

He let out a long, loud sigh. "Whoa, boy," he muttered.

"Nick, I can't just sit by and watch her go through this without doing everything I can. I know I'm supposed to give myself a few days to recover—but that also gives me an excuse to take a little time off to do what I can for Suzanne. I want to check out her lawyer and make sure he's the best guy she can possibly get and—and maybe talk to Lieutenant Falcone. I don't even know what else to do yet, but whatever it is, I have to do it." I hesitated before adding, "And even though you're busy with law school and all, maybe you could help me...?"

I really did need Nick's help in this. For one thing, the years of experience he'd racked up as a private investigator, back before he decided to change careers and go to law school, might come in handy. But even more important, helping to get Suzanne through this wasn't going to be easy, and I knew I'd need his moral support. Desperately.

"Okay, Jess," he said solemnly. "I hear what you're saying. And I promise I'll do whatever you need me to do."

"Thanks, Nick," I breathed. "You have no idea how much that means to me."

That last part was painfully true. I suddenly felt overwhelmed by Suzanne's situation.

One thing was certain: I was glad she hadn't wasted any time finding herself a lawyer, even though she'd had nothing more than Marcus Scruggs's recommendation to go by. At this point, making sure she had crackerjack representation appeared to be our best hope.

I just hoped that whoever Jerry Keeler was, he'd turn out to be really, really good.

Chapter 2

"A kitten is more amusing than half the people one is obliged to live with."

—Lady Sydney Morgan

The temporary lift that resulted from my caffeine orgy had all but faded by the time I maneuvered my Volkswagen through the congested streets surrounding the Norfolk County Courthouse. As if feeling both exhausted and overwhelmed weren't enough, a steady rain had begun to fall. I was glad I'd grabbed my navy blue polyester fleece jacket that morning before jumping into my car to drive to Suzanne's. It wasn't exactly the height of fashion, since it was embroidered with "Jessica Popper, D.V.M.," but it was perfect for weather like this.

The rain made it hard to read the numbers on the imposing glass and steel office buildings as I tried to find one that matched the address I'd found in the phone book. After half an hour of peering through the streaks the wipers made on the windshield, I decided it was time to stop and ask directions.

I pulled into the first parking space I saw and was nearly sideswiped by a Mercedes whose driver had decided it should belong to him—even though I got there first. I wasn't surprised that his license plate read ILL SUE 4U.

"Lawyers," I muttered, groping around the backseat for my umbrella. I only hoped somebody in one of the slightly seedy stores I'd parked in front of would be able to help me locate 1211 New Country Road. Between the bail bondsman, the pawnshop, and the delicatessen, someone was bound to know something.

Once I was out on the sidewalk, cowering under my umbrella and mournfully watching raindrops splatter over the one pair of good shoes I own, I realized I was only steps away from the very place I was seeking. While I'd just assumed that Marcus's college pal would have an office in one of the ultramodern buildings closer to the courthouse, he apparently ran more of a budget operation.

I stood outside the nondescript red brick building for a good five minutes, hoping against hope that I'd gotten it wrong. Surely the man in whose hands Suzanne Fox's entire future lay couldn't be based in a third-floor walk-up above a deli whose claim to fame appeared to be the $4.99 Al Capone Meatball Sub Special.

The peeling gold letters stuck on the third-floor window told me otherwise. I could see for myself that they spelled out Jerry Keeler's name. Right below were the words *Criminal, Divorce, Immigration, Bankruptcy*. In smaller letters, down at the bottom, were the phrases *Se Habla Español* and *Payment Plans Available*.

Not exactly in the same league as O.J.'s defense team, I thought, my spirits plummeting.

Give the guy a chance, I told myself. Maybe he'll turn out to be one of those dedicated types who'll do anything for his clients—the kind who doesn't give a hoot about fancy offices and other unnecessary niceties. Like functioning hardware, I thought, wrestling with a tarnished doorknob that didn't appear to have been updated since 1975.

When I finally managed to accomplish that feat, I stepped into a small foyer that was so dark that it took a few seconds for my eyes to adjust. Once they did, I cringed. The dull green linoleum in the hallway was cracked. So were the yellow plaster walls. I surveyed the row of mailboxes, noticing that the metal doors on two of them had been bashed in.

I walked up two flights of stairs. The hallway smelled funny, from something I couldn't quite identify. Frankly, I didn't try very hard.

On the top floor, I found several wooden doors, each one inset with a window made of frosted glass. Written on the one at the end of the hall were the words *Jerry Keeler, Attorney At Law.*

At least, that's what I thought it said at first glance. But something didn't look right. I moved closer and studied the letters more carefully.

What it *actually* said was *Jerry Keeler, Attorny At Law.*

The little bit of optimism I'd been clinging to was fading fast. I opened the door and found myself in a small waiting room. It was furnished with dark-red plastic chairs with chrome armrests and a coffee table made of Formica that was designed to look like wood. A few horrifying pieces of what I assumed was supposed to be artwork hung on the mint-green walls. The floor was covered in the same type of linoleum that was in the entryway. Same vintage, too. And condition.

The receptionist sitting behind a glass partition glanced up. She looked surprised, although whether that was because an unexpected customer had just walked in or because her eyebrows had been tweezed to form two unnaturally high arches, I couldn't say. Her hair was a startling coppery color, styled into a bubble that reminded me of the last Doris Day movie I'd seen. She also wore a great deal of makeup, including an electric-blue eye shadow that I suspected lit up in the dark. If the blue stuff smeared on her lids didn't, then the glitter in it had to.

"Can I help you?" she asked doubtfully.

"I'd like to see Mr. Keeler, please. And by the way, there's an *e* in *attorney*."

She just stared at me and blinked, her heavily mascaraed eyelashes creating a breeze that was nearly strong enough to knock me over. In fact, she was so shocked that she even stopped chomping her gum.

" 'Scuse me?"

"The word *attorney*," I said again. "There's an *e* in it. You might want to correct your sign."

She squinted at me suspiciously. "Who'd you say you were?"

"My name is Jessica Popper. Dr. Jessica Popper. I'd like to speak with Mr. Keeler."

"If ya don't have an appointment, I can't just let you walk in there," she insisted. She snapped her gum, which seemed to be back in operation. "This happens to be a professional office, not a drive-through."

I glanced around, wondering how long paintings on velvet had been considered appropriate décor for professional offices.

"I understand that," I replied patiently. "But if I could just have five minutes of Mr. Keeler's time—"

"Dottie, what the hell is going on out—oh, hello." A man in his late thirties had opened the door that led off the waiting area and stuck his head out. His demeanor changed the moment he saw me. Maybe he was pleased that a potential customer had entered the premises. Or maybe, like his buddy Marcus, he was simply impressed by the fact that I possessed two X chromosomes. "Is there something I can help you with?"

I composed myself quickly. "One of your clients is a

friend of mine. Suzanne Fox. I was wondering if I could talk to you about her case."

"Well, there is such a thing as attorney–client privilege," he said, chuckling.

"I understand," I told him. "I'm not looking for information. I just thought we might be able to...chat." Without me being billed, I was tempted to add.

"Okay, sure. We could do that." Jerry Keeler turned to Dottie. "Hold all my calls, will you?"

Given the fact that his phone wasn't exactly ringing off the hook, I thought he was being overly optimistic. But I followed him into his office and sat down.

The same decorator who had created the waiting room's distinctive look had obviously worked his magic in here as well. He had gone with the same refreshing mint-green walls—*refreshing* referring to the fact that it reminded me of breath-freshening chewing gum. The yellow linoleum floor not only set off the green walls; it also complemented the gunmetal-gray furniture. The artwork in here differed, however. Instead of the classic kittens-on-velvet motif, the walls were dotted with framed diplomas that celebrated the educational and professional accomplishments of Jerry Keeler, Attorny At Law.

At least he went to a real law school, I thought, instead of taking classes on the Web.

He leaned back in his chair, crossing one ankle over his knee and studying me. Meanwhile, I studied him. I didn't like what I saw very much. Whether it was the shine of his slicked-backed hair or the shine of his polyester suit, I couldn't say.

"First of all, how do I know you're who you say you are?" He picked up a ballpoint pen and began tapping it on the edge of his desk in a most annoying manner.

"I'll show you my driver's license."

"That's not what I mean. How do I know you're a

friend of Suzanne's and that you're not, you know, working for the prosecution?"

Does that kind of stuff really go on? I wondered. But I didn't ask.

Instead, I reached into my wallet and pulled out a photograph of Suzanne and me, taken the day of our graduation from Bryn Mawr College. After she and I had reconnected four months earlier while I was filling in for Marcus at a charity dog show in the Bromptons, I'd come across this photo and stuck it into my wallet to show her. We'd had a great time reminiscing about our college days—and marveling over how quickly the years since then had passed. I'd been meaning to put the photo back in the album where it belonged but had never gotten around to it.

I dropped it in front of Jerry Keeler. "Recognize us? That's Suzanne and that's me. This photo was taken at our college graduation."

He glanced at it, his face lighting up immediately. "Hey, you were both pretty hot back then! What were you, twenty, twenty-one?"

Whatever traces of optimism I'd still been clinging to vanished. In fact, I felt as if a wrecking ball had just landed on my stomach.

"You could call Marcus Scruggs," I told him. "He'd vouch for me—and the fact that Suzanne and I really are friends."

He leaned forward, stroking his ballpoint pen in a way I found most disconcerting.

"So you're a friend of Marcus's, huh?" he said, his expression definitely leering.

"Yes, as a matter of fact." I sat up a little straighter and folded my hands primly in my lap. "I'm a veterinarian, too."

"I see. You know, I've always wondered about female veterinarians and horses."

"Excuse me?"

"Veterinarians have to perform some pretty—shall we say *personal* procedures? I remember reading once that—"

I could feel my blood heating up. "I'm here to talk about Suzanne," I insisted. "I want to know if you think the Norfolk County cops have a case."

He slumped back in his chair and tossed his pen on the desk.

"Between you and me?" he said, not quite looking me in the eye. "I wouldn't bet any money on her getting off. I mean, the police got witnesses who saw Suzanne going to the victim's house shortly before she was found dead."

"But a jury would never convict her on something that shaky!"

He narrowed his eyes. "And what law school did you say you graduated from?"

It took all the self-control I possessed not to do him bodily harm. "I watch Court TV whenever there's a re-run on Animal Planet," I said dryly.

He actually seemed to accept that as a valid explanation. "Okay, then you'll understand that on top of all that, they also got a powerful motive: jealousy. This Thorndike lady was boffing Suzanne's ex."

"Actually, Cassandra Thorndike and Suzanne's ex-husband were engaged to be married," I pointed out.

"Yeah, I seem to remember something about that."

My blood quickly went from simmer to boil. "If you don't mind me saying so, you don't seem to be putting a lot of effort into this case."

He shrugged. "Look, I been doin' this a long time. It gets to be routine, y'know? I guess what I mean is, I don't sweat it the way somebody who's brand new at this might."

"Does that mean you can't be bothered to remember the facts of the case correctly?"

"Hey, when the time comes, I'll read through my notes. Right now, I got three different dope dealers, an armed robbery at a florist, and a guy running cock fights in the basement of the local elementary school. D'you believe that?"

"Quite an illustrious list of clients," I observed, already planning what I was going to say to Suzanne the moment I left Jerry Keeler's office. She simply had to listen to reason. "By the way," I asked, "how many murder cases have you handled?"

He squirmed in his seat. "You mean including this one?"

That wrecking ball that had started slamming against my stomach a few minutes ago was back in action. "Yes, including this one."

"Well, now, let's see." He screwed up his face as if he was thinking very, very hard. And as if he found the effort painful. "One, two...*three*..."

I stood up. "I think I'd better talk to Suzanne about finding another lawyer."

"Hey, I'm practically doin' this for nothing!" he cried, sounding hurt. "It's a real favor to Marcus, since we've been friends for so long!"

"I'm sure your intentions are good," I said, even though I didn't believe that for a minute. "I just want to make sure Suzanne has the best possible representation. And so it only makes sense that she consider more than one attorney."

"Whatever."

"Well, thanks for your time," I said.

A glazed look came into his eyes. "Listen," he said, his voice suddenly as smooth as chocolate pudding. "There's this great little Greek restaurant I know, not too far from here. You should see what they can do with their couscous." His eyebrows were jumping up and down as if he were the villain in a silent movie. "How about if, later on, you and I..."

I wondered if the college Marcus Scruggs and Jerry Keeler had attended offered a major in Hitting on Women Who Aren't the Least Bit Interested in You. Or maybe this particular skill was something their fraternity specialized in, like chugging beer and vomiting it back up again in an exceptionally short period of time.

"Thanks, but I'm involved with somebody."

"Too bad. For you, I mean!"

I considered forcing a polite smile, then decided it wasn't worth the effort.

"Well, if you ever change your mind, you know where to find me," he went on. Grinning, he added, "And if *you* don't, the cops do."

He leaned across his desk and handed me his business card. I took it reluctantly, then glanced down, just to check. Sure enough; like the sign on his door, it read, *Jerry Keeler, Attorny At Law.*

"You know, you really should fix your sign. And your business cards."

"Huh?"

"There's an *e* in *attorney.*"

"No shit. Hey, if you're accusing me of being a bad speller, then I'm guilty as charged!" Jerry shrugged. "But believe me, I got plenty of other assets—and being innocent isn't one of them!"

As I left his office, I could hear him guffawing over his own cleverness. I only hoped the steam that was coming out of my ears wouldn't make my hair frizz.

• • •

As soon as I got back to my car, I pulled out my cell phone and punched in Suzanne's number.

"Suzanne, it's Jessie," I said as soon as she answered. "I just paid a little visit to your lawyer. I thought it might be a good idea to check him out. You know, so you could get a second opinion."

"He's great, right?" she asked hopefully.

"Suzanne..." I realized it probably would be kinder to resist my natural inclination to tell her what I really thought. Somehow, words like *turkey* and *idiot* seemed so harsh. "I really think you need to find a new lawyer."

"But Marcus recommended him!" Suzanne insisted. "He and Jerry have been friends for years! Besides, he must know what he's doing. Otherwise, how would he have gotten through law school? How would he have passed the bar? How would he have kept his practice going for all these years?"

I suddenly remembered a lawyer joke I'd once heard. A lawyer goes to court to defend his client, who's found guilty. The client turns to him and says, "What happens now?" The lawyer shrugs and says, "You go to jail, and I go back to my office."

I'd never found that so-called joke particularly amusing. But today I found it downright chilling.

I burst forth with a long list of reasons why Suzanne would be making the biggest mistake of her life by putting all her eggs in Jerry Keeler's basket, meanwhile watching the rain streak down my windshield.

"Jess, I know you mean well," she finally said, sounding as if she was losing patience. "But I have to go with the lawyer Marcus thinks is best. He loves me. I've got to trust him!"

Her words—and the sentiments behind them—set my teeth on edge. The fact that *love* was a four-letter word wasn't wasted on me. It had the potential to be extremely dangerous. In fact, the longer I lived, the more I saw people doing all kinds of crazy things because of what they claimed was *love*.

As I hung up the phone, I was tempted to call Marcus

to beg him to change his mind—and Suzanne's. But I knew I wouldn't have any better luck with him than I'd had with her.

I was starting to suspect that if anybody was going to get Suzanne out of trouble, it was me. The frightening thing was, I had yet to figure out how I was ever going to accomplish such a daunting task. But I figured that going straight to the top wouldn't be a bad way to start.

I was sitting in my car, still watching the rain and trying to muster up the nerve to drop in on Lieutenant Anthony Falcone, Norfolk County's chief of homicide, when my cell phone rang. I glanced at the number that appeared on the screen but didn't recognize it.

"Dr. Popper," I answered.

"Dr. Jessica Popper?" a squeaky female voice inquired.

"That's right. Who's this?"

"Dr. Popper, my name is Marlene Fitzgerald, and I'm calling from Sunshine Media—"

Great. A telemarketer from the company that supplied my cable service, interrupting me with an annoying sales call at the least convenient time possible. "I'm sorry to be rude," I snapped, not trying in the least not to sound rude, much less even remotely sorry about it, "but I'm in the middle of something important and I really don't have time for this."

"But—"

I hung up before I had a chance to say anything even ruder. Then I turned the key in the ignition and drove off, wondering if I was making a huge mistake by not fortifying myself with the $4.99 Al Capone Meatball Sub Special before venturing into the belly of the beast.

• • •

I knew I was taking a chance by simply dropping in on Lt. Falcone at his office. Then again, it was raining, and

Falcone was the kind of guy who'd think twice about going outside on a day when he might ruin his shoes—even if they were probably pleather.

I pulled into the parking lot surrounding the intimidating complex of gray brick buildings that included the Norfolk County Police Department's headquarters and dashed into the lobby, where a uniformed officer sat at a high, imposing counter that practically had a moat around it. I nodded in his direction, then headed toward the metal detector that led to the elevators.

"Whoa, whoa, whoa," the officer at the desk sang out. "Where do you think you're going?"

"I have an appointment with Lieutenant Falcone."

"In that case, I'll check your ID, call upstairs to confirm your appointment, and *then* send you through the metal detector."

I slid my New York State driver's license across the counter, then stood calmly in front of him while he made the call. I half-expected a cauldron of boiling oil to be poured on me the moment I was found out.

"Hey, Joe. I got a gal here name of Jessica Popper who says she has an appointment with Lieutenant Falcone. No? Then I'll—sure, I'll hold." He glowered at me while he waited. It took every ounce of nerve I possessed to continue looking him in the eye.

"Yeah? Really? Okay. I'll send her up."

He hung up the phone and shrugged. "He says the lieutenant will see you. Fifth floor."

"Thanks," I told him, unable to keep either the triumph or the surprise out of my voice.

When I exited the elevator, I found Lieutenant Anthony Falcone standing in the doorway of his office. Whether he was waiting there to greet me or to bodily block me from entering, I couldn't say.

"Dr. Popper," he said. Only, thanks to his New York accent, the way he pronounced my name was more like

"Docta Poppa." Smirking as if he were about to say something terribly clever, he added, "The vet with a nose for murder. I see you're up and around again."

"Hello, Lieutenant," I said, trying to sound friendly. "Thanks for seeing me."

"Yeah, well, I figured this wouldn't take long," he replied gruffly.

Falcone stood only about five foot four, so even though I'm not exactly a giant, talking to him meant talking *down* to him. I was glad that he headed straight for his desk and sank into his chair. Today, as usual, he was wearing a cheap shiny brown suit that made him look like a fashion "don't." His equally shiny, blue-black hair was slicked back, giving the impression he was auditioning for *Grease*.

But it wasn't his fashion sense, or rather his complete lack of it, that irritated me. It was his cocky attitude. Maybe it came from being short and slight of build, factors that Dr. Freud could no doubt have gone to town with. Or maybe it stemmed from the fact that his line of work not only entitled him to carry a gun; it also allowed him to boss around other people who carried guns.

Even so, I was determined to act all sweet and gooey, hoping he'd forget some of our past history. Perhaps even all of it.

"I'd like to talk to you about a recent case," I began as soon as I sat down facing his desk, "though I know you haven't exactly been crazy about my past interest in murder investigations."

He grimaced. "Isn't that what more literary types call an understatement?"

Literary ... or literate? I thought dryly. Fortunately, this turned out to be one of those rare occasions on which I had enough self-control to keep my mouth shut.

"This is about the Thorndike case, right?" he added.

I nodded.

"I thought you and Suzanne Fox might be pals, since both you ladies are veterinarians and all. In fact, it wouldn't surprise me if it turned out you two were as thick as thieves. Of course, that may not be the best metaphor, given the situation."

"Simile," I muttered.

"Excuse me?"

"*As thick as thieves* is a simile, not a metaphor."

"What, you're an English teacher now?" Falcone said, scowling. "It's not enough that you're a veterinarian and an amateur detective?"

"You're absolutely right," I replied crisply, ignoring the last of his obnoxious comments. "About Suzanne and me being friends, I mean. We went to college together. We were lab partners in every single undergraduate science course we took together. We even applied to vet school at the same time and opened our acceptance letters in front of each other."

"Now, isn't that sweet," Falcone replied sarcastically.

"Lieutenant Falcone, I wish there was some way I could convince you that Suzanne had absolutely nothing to do with Cassandra Thorndike's murder. She told me that herself, of course, but she didn't need to. I've known her for more than fifteen years. There's no way she was involved." I hesitated before adding, "You have no real evidence to link her to the murder, do you? Aside from what a few witnesses might have said?"

He narrowed his dark, beady eyes. They reminded me of the black button eyes on stuffed animals—except those are usually cute and cuddly. There was nothing the least bit cute *or* cuddly about this compact bundle of polyester-wrapped testosterone.

"Surely you didn't come here thinkin' I'd be willing to discuss the details of this case with you."

I sat up straighter and looked him in the eye. "As a

matter of fact, I was hoping that you would. You and I have the same goal: making sure the person who really killed Cassandra Thorndike is caught."

"Oh, I intend to do exactly that," he returned. "And since you're so dedicated to finding the killer, maybe you'll pass along a few words of advice to your friend."

I held my breath.

"Tell her that when it comes to murder, honesty is the best policy," he said. "Especially since we got the best forensics experts in Norfolk County working on this case. If she had anything at all to do with Cassandra Thorndike's murder, we'll find out."

Any last lingering hopes that Suzanne wouldn't be implicated were now gone.

"But I also got a message for you, Dr. Popper," Falcone continued. "I hope the fact that you have a personal relationship with one of my suspects—and she *is* a suspect, or at least a person of interest—doesn't mean I'm going to be tripping over you every step of my investigation."

I held my head up a little higher. "Let's just say you probably shouldn't fall over in shock if our paths happen to cross every now and then. I'm not about to let an innocent person—especially a friend—be implicated in a crime she didn't commit."

"I was afraid of that." Smirking, he added, "Actually, maybe you can be of some assistance, since this is one of those rare cases where there's an animal involved."

Ha-ha, I thought, not the least bit amused by what I assumed was a reference to Cassandra's pet cat, who'd had the misfortune to witness his mistress's horrible death.

But I let it pass.

"What about her neighbors?" I asked. "Did anyone hear anything during the actual murder?"

Falcone shook his head in disgust. "The neighbors

aren't much good. The only ones close enough to have heard anything are the ones next door. And that's just an old lady who's hard of hearing and a kid who's barely out of diapers."

"Still, either one of them might have noticed something out of the ordinary or heard something that—"

"Look, Dr. Popper," Falcone said tiredly. "I got an important press conference to get to. So why don't you hightail it out of here—no pun intended—and go back to that animal hospital on wheels of yours."

From the twisted smile on his face, I could tell his bad pun was very much intended. But at the moment, that wasn't what had me so ticked off. It was the fact that he'd already determined that Suzanne was guilty—and that he wasn't even willing to seriously listen to input from someone who'd once solved a case he'd insisted wasn't even a murder! Besides, how could a photo op be more important than solving a murder?

"Lieutenant Falcone," I said, giving it one last try, "please let me help you with this. Surely there's something I can do to—"

His expression twisted into a sneer. "I mean it. You don't belong around a murder investigation. You're not a homicide detective. This isn't your business, and I intend to do everything I can to keep you as far away as possible."

"This isn't my business?" I repeated, doing my best to sound as condescending as he did. "The police think one of my best friends may be connected to the worst possible crime, and it's not my business?"

"I don't care if the investigation involves your own mother," he countered. "I don't want you stickin' your nose where it doesn't belong. And I meant what I said about telling your friend to come clean. She might think she's smart, but she's playing with fire."

I opened my mouth to reply, but I knew he was right. Falcone had been right about something else, too: that it was only a question of time before the cops gathered enough evidence to implicate Suzanne. In fact, if there was one thing I'd learned this afternoon, it was that her situation didn't look good.

Yet something positive had come out of this meeting. And that was that having the opportunity to once again experience Falcone's arrogance firsthand increased my resolve to wrench Suzanne out of his slimy grasp—even if it meant figuring out who killed Cassandra Thorndike myself.

• • •

I'd barely gotten back into my car when my cell phone trilled again. I was so busy muttering to myself about Falcone's obnoxiousness that I answered without bothering to check the caller ID.

"Dr. Popper," I barked. It was more of a Rottweiler bark than a poodle bark.

"Dr. Popper, it's Marlene Fitzgerald again. From Sunshine Media?"

I tensed, wondering how I'd let myself fall into this trap twice. I was about to growl that, *no*, I wasn't interested in adding the Arena Football Network to my cable service, but decided to go for a more direct approach.

"Please don't call me again. I really don't have time for—"

"This isn't a sales call," the young woman at the other end of the line insisted, sounding even more like Minnie Mouse than she had the last time she'd called. "Channel Fourteen is starting a new television show, and we're looking for someone like you to be on it."

I was still trying to digest the image of me on some ridiculous game show when she added, "We got your name and number from Forrester Sloan. He said he thought you'd be interested."

Forrester? Just hearing his name gave me pause. I'd met the *Newsday* reporter a few weeks earlier while treating a polo pony in the posh community of Old Brookbury. He'd been covering the murder of a handsome young polo player, and he'd enlisted my aid. I found the killer, all right, even though the investigation had landed me in the hospital.

But our relationship, at least from my perspective, would best be characterized as complicated. Okay, I had to admit he was mildly attractive. At least, if you like the preppy type. Still, there was something about him I found infinitely irritating. It was partly his self-assuredness-bordering-on-arrogance and partly his constant flirtatiousness—which I was certain I did absolutely nothing to encourage.

"Forrester was mistaken," I replied. "Thanks, but you've got the wrong person."

I switched off the call, stared at the phone for a fraction of a second, and then punched in a number.

"Forrester Sloan," a deep masculine voice announced.

"Forrester, what on earth is wrong with you?" I demanded.

"Hey, Popper!" he replied without hesitation. "But shouldn't I be asking you that question? After all, you're the one who's been in the hospital. Speaking of which, have they sprung you yet?"

He sounded genuinely happy to hear from me. Which only fueled my irritation.

"I didn't call to discuss my health," I replied impatiently. "I called to ask you where you came up with the bright idea of telling Sunshine Media to harass me!"

"Sunshine Media...Oh, you mean Channel Fourteen!"

"Whatever they're called, I don't need them calling me on my cell phone when I'm in the middle of something important."

"You mean the way I'm in the middle of something important right now?"

I instantly felt sheepish. It hadn't even occurred to me that he might be sitting in a meeting or interviewing somebody. Forrester Sloan was one of *Newsday*'s top reporters, so it was more than likely that, in the middle of a workday, he would be embroiled in something pressing himself.

"I'm sorry," I said begrudgingly. "I suppose I should have asked you if you were busy."

"Ha. If I were busy, I'd have turned off my cell phone. In fact, I'm driving to a ribbon-cutting ceremony for a new homeless shelter. True, every politician in Norfolk County will be there, not to mention a few other hangers-on. Hardly front-page news."

"You're not supposed to drive and talk on a cell phone at the same time," I grumbled.

"Headset," he informed me. "Besides, I've got an in with most of the cops around here. The last thing they want is for me to make them look bad in print.

"Speaking of cops, Popper," he went on breezily, "I've been thinking that you and I need to have a little talk, and this is probably as good a time as any. You had a close call the last time you got involved in a homicide investigation. From now on, it might not be a bad idea for you to leave the murder biz to the professionals."

"You mean like newspaper reporters?" I shot back.

"Touché," he returned. "Okay, so maybe I'm not a seasoned professional like our pal Falcone. But working for the press gives me certain protection. Maybe I'm naive, but I still believe the pen is mightier than the sword. And when you start thinking about the power of the word processor . . . But I'm sure you didn't call me so I could lecture you about how to conduct your life."

"No, I called to read you the riot act for giving my number to those annoying TV people. Who else are you giving it out to—or have you written it on a men's room wall somewhere?"

"Honest, Popper, the TV folks are looking for somebody like you who has star quality. You should talk to them. Who knows where it will lead?" He muttered something about a tailgater, then added, "So what's this important thing you were in the middle of? Some high-level veterinary procedure on a ridiculously expensive polo pony? Or a life-and-death situation involving the beloved pet of one of the Bromptons' rich and famous citizens?"

"It involves life and death, all right," I replied archly. A lightning bolt suddenly flashed through my brain. While I'd called Forrester to complain about giving my name and number out to media moguls, it occurred to me that he might have his uses, after all. "Not to change the subject, but I don't suppose you're covering Cassandra Thorndike's murder, are you?"

"As a matter of fact, I am. I was just over at her house yesterday, and I'm planning to head back there again later today." He paused, and I could practically hear the wheels turning in his head. "Wait a sec. I'm starting to put two and two together here. Does your interest in Cassandra Thorndike have anything to do with the fact that several witnesses reported seeing her fiancé's ex-wife—who just happens to be a veterinarian—at the scene of the crime? This is a hot story, since her family has mega-bucks—not to mention a well-known name. I don't suppose the vet is somebody you know, is she?"

"Actually," I replied, trying to sound casual, "Suzanne Fox and I went to college together."

"No *way*!"

"Would I lie?" As soon as I said the words, I gritted my teeth. All things considered, joking about telling lies probably wasn't a very good idea.

"In that case, you'll be interested in knowing the police aren't buying her story about all their witnesses being wrong," he went on. "Not for a minute. Sooner or later, they'll prove she was at Cassandra's house the day of the murder. And our buddy Falcone doesn't like being lied to. Especially when the person in question has the motive, the means, and the opportunity to commit the crime."

My stomach lurched in a most unpleasant way. "Forrester, if you're trying to make me feel better, it's not working."

"Sorry." He hesitated, then said, "Hey, the fact that you and this Suzanne character are friends could turn out to be very helpful. Maybe you could give me some insights into the insanely jealous ex, the redheaded vixen who lied about being at the scene of the crime—"

The temperature of my blood escalated so quickly it was as if somebody had sat me down on the power burner of a gas stove. "She's nothing like that, Forrester! And if you even *think* about characterizing her that way—"

"Relax! It's not like I write for the *Gossip Gazette* or one of those other supermarket tabloids. I'm a serious reporter. I try to be coldhearted and objective."

Objective sounded good. Coldhearted sounded decidedly *not* good. After all, the way the press portrayed her—especially if she was actually charged—would be crucial.

"Tell you what: let's make a deal," Forrester went on. "I'll tell you everything I learn about the investigation if you tell me everything you know about Suzanne. A background piece might make an interesting feature, you know?"

I hesitated. Forrester's offer to help was tempting. But my feelings of loyalty to Suzanne made the idea of working with a reporter seem risky. After all, he was trying to get a story, not prove her innocence. The last thing I wanted was to inadvertently do or say something that would make her situation even worse.

"Thanks, but no thanks," I replied.

He chuckled. "Think about it. In the meantime, I'm going to be in Cassandra Thorndike's neighborhood mid-afternoon. I want to knock on some doors and see what else I can learn from her neighbors. But I should be done by around three. Why don't you swing by her house and meet me there? The address is two-fifty-four Cliffside Lane."

I had to admit, the idea of visiting the victim's home sounded intriguing. Still, I'd only been out of the hospital for a few hours—and since then, I'd been on the go every minute. I'd planned to spend the rest of the day at home, curled up in bed with two dogs and two cats who were warm and fuzzy and ecstatic to have me back. That is, after I'd taken a steaming hot shower that would wash away the hospital smells that still lingered on my skin.

"I don't need your help," I told him crisply.

"I think you do. At any rate, I'll be there, if you care to join me, Popper. 'Later!'"

I clicked off the call, wondering why I found him so darned irritating and wishing I wasn't using a cell phone so I could have slammed the phone down in the receiver.

Yet I had to admit that the more I learned about Suzanne's plight, the worse it seemed. Falcone clearly had it out for her. And her poor excuse for a lawyer certainly wasn't going to be much help. On top of that, she wasn't improving things by continuing to lie to the cops. Her situation looked pretty bleak. I was slowly coming to the realization that the only way I was going to help my friend out of this mess was by finding out who the *real* murderer was. And given that fact, even I wasn't too pig-headed to recognize that Forrester Sloan had just made me an offer I couldn't refuse.

Chapter 3

"The way to get on with a cat is to treat it as an equal—or even better, as the superior it knows itself to be."

—Elizabeth Peters

Since Forrester Sloan was going to be helping me out—a sign of just how desperate I was to get Suzanne out of this jam, given the fact that the man had an ego the size of North Dakota—I figured I'd better check out what he'd already had to say about the case. I made my next stop the public library, bypassing the shelves lined with New Mysteries and Best Sellers and making a beeline for the periodical room.

Just as I figured, Wednesday's and Thursday's editions of *Newsday* were underneath today's edition on the circular wooden rack. I grabbed Wednesday's, figuring that since being in the hospital had cut off communications from the outside world, I'd start at the beginning.

I found Forrester's story on page 5. It was short and matter-of-fact. In fact, most of the full-page coverage was dedicated to photographs of Cassandra, her house, and her parents' winery. Her picture looked like a typical high-school yearbook shot: a dewy-eyed young woman with straight, neatly combed dark hair, dreamily staring off into space. She was wearing the usual high-necked sweater with a string of pearls that you just knew she couldn't wait to yank off.

Cassandra Thorndike, 29, was found slain at her home in Cuttituck yesterday, I read, trying to commit every word to memory. *Police reported to the victim's home at 254 Cliffside Lane at approximately 4:30 P.M. after Thorndike's next-door neighbor, Virginia Krupinski, called 911. Krupinski told police she had repeatedly rung the doorbell but received no response.*

According to Lieutenant Anthony Falcone, Norfolk County Chief of Homicide, the victim had suffered multiple stab wounds to the chest, which police believe was the cause of death. The victim had been dead for approximately two hours at the time she was found.

Police have not yet determined the murder weapon. According to Falcone, the investigation is ongoing and several suspects are being questioned. They found no signs of forced entry, and robbery is not believed to have been a motive.

Thorndike was employed as a sales representative who specialized in restaurant sales for Thorndike Vineyards, a Cuttituck winery founded by her father, Gordon Thorndike... The rest of the article was devoted to quotes from neighbors. They mainly commented on how shocked they were that such a brutal killing had occurred right in their midst. The impersonal nature of what they said gave me the feeling that none of them had actually known her.

Thursday's article was more detailed, although the number of photos had been reduced to one. It was the same high-school picture they'd run the day before.

Police are continuing to question suspects in the murder of Cassandra Thorndike, according to Lieutenant Anthony Falcone, Norfolk County Chief of Homicide,

I read. *The 29-year-old woman was found slain on Tuesday in her Cuttituck residence.*

"We believe the victim was home alone when some-one came to her house," Falcone said. *"It is likely that that individual was someone she knew. At some point, a disagreement may have broken out, although the perpetrator may have come to the house with the intention of killing the victim."*

Falcone stated that police found a large amount of blood at the crime scene, and much of the room, especially Thorndike's desk, was in disarray, indicating a struggle between the victim and her attacker.

The rest of the article was more of the same. It re-capped the basic facts, threw in a few quotes, and assured the public that the police were doing everything that could be done to solve the crime. To me, it said they may have had suspects but no hard evidence that pointed to any one person. At least, not yet.

•   •   •

I tried to take comfort in that fact as I drove along Route 35 later that afternoon, passing through Riverton on my way out east to Cassandra Thorndike's house. The rain had stopped a while ago, yet the day was still dreary and gray. It had gotten cooler, too, and I'd zipped my poly-ester fleece jacket all the way up.

As I checked out my surroundings, I was struck by how quickly the sprawling town at the juncture of Long Island's North and South Forks was turning into Anytown, U.S.A. Practically overnight, gigantic box stores like Home Depot and Linens 'N Things were springing up on land that just a few years earlier had been scrubby lots lining a sleepy country road. Yet after passing every chain store I could name, I noticed a large sign at the side of the road as I was about to veer off onto the North Fork.

Welcome...
To Long Island

WINE COUNTRY

Tour
The Vineyards

If the sign wasn't enough to tip people off that they were about to enter a special place, the countryside immediately went through a dramatic transformation. I felt as if I'd passed through a time warp and was suddenly driving through the Long Island of the 1950s—or even the 1930s. As I meandered along the two-lane road, relieved that the rain had finally let up and I could actually see where I was going, I took in one quaint country town after another. Each one consisted of a block or two of rustic wooden buildings that housed antiques shops, luncheonettes, and small grocery stores. In between were white-shingled farmhouses with large, friendly porches, often with weathered barns set even farther back from the road.

Farm stands were as abundant as telephone poles. The larger ones were already stocked with piles of pumpkins and huge terra-cotta pots of chrysanthemums, a clear indication that autumn was upon us. Others were tiny family operations consisting of a single cart at the edge of the road, offering bouquets of wildflowers, ripe red tomatoes, and bushels of apples. Most of them were unmanned, and customers were expected to pay by leaving the correct amount of money in the large jar that had been left for that purpose.

Beyond the houses and farm stands stretched the flat fields of rich soil that had attracted farmers to the North Fork in the first place. While housing developments were going up on some of them—a sign of modern times, and one that I didn't find particularly pleasing—most were still being used as farmland.

After I'd driven another mile, however, even that changed. The trees along the road, their leaves barely tinted with the fiery colors of fall, began to disappear. Here, the fields were covered with grapevines planted in perfectly even rows. Every mile or so, a sign with the name of a vineyard jutted up along the side of the road: Costello Cellars, Martin Creek Vineyards, Cuttituck Winery, Sophia Family Vineyards and Winery. There was almost always a visitors' center, and most advertised tours and tastings.

I finally trundled into the village of Cuttituck, periodically checking my trusty Hagstrom map to make sure I didn't miss the turnoff to Cassandra Thorndike's house. I'd never actually had a client in Cuttituck, but I'd driven through it a number of times. Like many of the towns on Long Island's North Fork, it was a charming little hamlet that looked as if it were stuck in time. A few of the businesses were geared to the locals, like the video store and the delicatessen housed in a tiny clapboard house. Some establishments clearly catered to the tourist trade, like Annie's Antiques and the Wine-Tasting Room, a tiny shop that featured the wines of several of the local vineyards.

One of my favorite roadside attractions was the ironically named Modern Café. The sign outside featured a woman with a 1950s-style pageboy, holding a tray of steaming hot biscuits. The Modern was frequented by both visitors and members of the community. In fact, on the few occasions I'd stopped in to chow down on some good old-fashioned comfort food, I'd been amused to find well-heeled Manhattanites dressed in Ralph Lauren and Donna Karan alongside farmers and winery owners. It was always fun to watch them wolf down house specialties like the meat loaf platter and the liver and onion special, as ecstatic as if they'd just discovered the new sushi.

I turned left onto the Northway Turnpike and headed north. The road remained straight and well-paved for a mile or two. But suddenly it branched off into a maze of narrow, unpaved streets that meandered toward the coast.

I braked heavily, not only for safety but also to allow myself a closer look at the residential enclave I'd just entered. Most of the houses had clearly been built decades earlier as summer bungalows. But interspersed among the boxy, one-story buildings were larger, more modern houses. These were at least two stories high, and many were perched atop hills that afforded them a view of the Long Island Sound, only a few hundred yards away.

I hadn't ventured far along Seashore Lane before I spotted a weather-worn sign that read CAPTAIN KIDD COVE. I had to smile. As most Long Islanders know, in the late 1600s the infamous pirate William Kidd buried booty that was reportedly worth a small fortune on nearby Gardiner's Island, marking the spot with a pile of rocks that still stood. Shortly afterward, he was arrested. He was eventually hanged, but not until the governor of New York had seized his treasure.

Yet the notorious pillager and plunderer was said to have buried some additional loot in this area, hidden treasure that had never been recovered. There was even a rocky spot known as "Kidd's Ledge" that garnered some coverage in the local media every now and then. The legend of Captain Kidd and his missing treasure had never been proven—nor had it ever been forgotten.

I checked my map one more time before turning onto Cliffside Lane. My poor little VW bumped along the gutted, muddy road, which ran parallel to the coast. On the sea side, the terrain dropped sharply. Forty or fifty feet below stretched a narrow strip of sand, edged with the calm, lapping waves of Long Island Sound. Most of the houses on that side of the street, particularly the newer, larger ones, had long wooden staircases leading down to the beach.

I focused on the six or eight houses that dotted both sides of the street, figuring their inhabitants were the witnesses who had noticed Suzanne in the neighborhood the same afternoon Cassandra had been murdered. On a quiet back street like this one, I could understand that a visit from an outsider was something they would have noticed.

At the same time, if Cassandra's killer had been someone she knew, her neighbors wouldn't have thought twice about the appearance of a vehicle and driver they recognized. It may not even have registered in their minds—which would have explained why they hadn't mentioned it to the cops.

I immediately knew which house had belonged to Cassandra Thorndike: the one with Forrester Sloan's dark-green SUV parked in front of it. I pulled up behind it. Before getting out, I took a minute to study the house with the faded 254 stenciled onto the mailbox and the red Miata with the CASSLASS plates parked in the driveway. It was one of the small houses that had originally been built as a summer place. It probably consisted of no more than a living room, kitchen, and a couple of bedrooms, all nestled together on the main floor. From the outside, its most distinctive features were its weather-beaten unpainted cedar shingles and the broken step leading up to the front porch. There were few signs that it was lived in, and even fewer that it was loved. No cheerful curtains in the windows, no flowerpots on the porch, no brightly painted birdhouses in the few scraggly trees that somehow managed to grow so close to the cliffs. While I had yet to learn a single fact about its owner, I already knew she hadn't possessed the Martha Stewart gene.

Of course, the yellow crime-scene tape stretched across the front didn't exactly scream Home Sweet Home.

I climbed out of my car, wondering if I'd get the chance to see if any more of Cassandra's personality was reflected on the inside, when I heard someone cry, "Hey, Popper!"

I whipped my head around and saw my host for the afternoon striding toward me.

"Thought you might turn up," Forrester said, grinning. "I guess I'm as irresistible as always."

I cast him the dirtiest look I could muster. "Hardly. I'm just trying to help Suzanne."

He laughed. "Seriously, Popper, it's good to see you. *Really* good."

He just stood there for a few seconds, staring at me and grinning. I couldn't help wondering if he'd gotten especially spiffed up for me. He smelled suspiciously like soap and men's cologne, as if he'd somehow managed to sneak a shower into the middle of his busy day. The fact that his thick blond hair looked slightly damp, especially the mass of tiny curls at the back of his neck, added weight to my theory.

Like me, Forrester was in his mid-thirties. He was tall with a sturdy build, his broad shoulders giving him the look of someone who'd played football in college. As usual, he was dressed as if he were posing for the cover of *The Preppy Handbook*. He wore a pink cotton button-down shirt, khaki pants with nary a wrinkle, tan loafers, and a sporty brown jacket made of a tweed fabric that probably had an English-sounding name like Harrington or Tatterbumper.

But it was the look in his gray-blue eyes that really got me. I was pretty sure that what I saw in them was real

concern, coupled with something that looked danger-
ously like fondness.

I looked away.

"You know I hate being called Popper," I reminded him.

"Precisely why I enjoy doing it so much," he returned
breezily. "There's just something about you that makes
me want to get under your skin."

Probably a few other places as well, I thought. I'd be
lying if I said that Forrester Sloan didn't have some appeal, at least on an intellectual level. He possessed something that wasn't quite charm, but close enough that he
deserved at least some credit for it. But given the situation, I had absolutely no patience for him—and no interest in fending off his flirtatiousness. The fact that we were
both standing outside Cassandra Thorndike's house was
a harsh reminder of the reason I was here in the first place.
A young woman had been murdered—and another
young woman was being unjustly accused.

"I talked to Falcone earlier today," I said, anxious to
bring the conversation back to the investigation. "He
wasn't exactly thrilled over my interest in this case."

"Even though you and Suzanne Fox are friends? I'd
have thought that would make him more willing to indulge your interest in the investigation."

"Except that he's trying to prove that she did it and
I'm trying to prove that she didn't. That kind of puts us
at cross-purposes, don't you think?"

"I see your point." Forrester only hesitated for a moment before saying, in that newspaper-reporterly way
of his, "So tell me more about your relationship with
Suzanne Fox."

"There's not much to tell," I replied with a shrug.
"We've been good friends for over fifteen years. We met
in college, at Bryn Mawr. We both wanted to be vets. She
went to Purdue and I went to Cornell, and we lost touch
for a few years. But this past June, I discovered that she'd

moved out to West Brompton Beach. She has a practice in Poxabogue." I shrugged again. "That's it in a nutshell."

"I see." I braced myself for a smart-ass comment. Thankfully, it didn't come. Instead, Forrester said, "So, Popper, what can I tell you about the case?"

"I already know the basics," I replied. "Cassandra was alone in her house on Tuesday when somebody came to visit. Somebody she knew. Or maybe that person sneaked inside without her realizing it. At some point things got ugly, and the visitor grabbed something sharp and stabbed her with it. Somewhere in there— probably after she'd been stabbed at least once—there was a struggle that left the entire room in disarray. Lots of blood everywhere, stuff knocked over . . . Cassandra tried to fight off her attacker but her attacker prevailed, and she fell to the floor, dead." As I outlined the scene, it played through my head with disturbing clarity.

"Give the girl a gold star!" Forrester replied. I was ready to slug him—with words, since they're much more stinging than fists—when he added, "It's probably worth mentioning that the police didn't find any signs of a forced entry—through the windows, for example—so they figure the killer came through the front door. Either it was open or Cassandra let the person in. There's a back door, too, but the only fingerprints and footprints that were found in the kitchen were Cassandra's, so that pretty much lets that out as a point of entry. Anyway, the police think the person who killed her was somebody she knew."

"Not surprising," I commented. "Especially since the North Fork isn't exactly a hot spot for random killings."

"There's one more really intriguing aspect to this case," Forrester went on. "Something that wasn't in the paper."

" 'Intriguing'?" I repeated. Usually, that was one of

my favorite words. But given the situation, just hearing it made me feel like someone had grabbed hold of my heart and was clenching it in his fist.

"That's the word I'd use," he said. "Apparently our murderer left behind a few clues."

I hope none of them have Suzanne's fingerprints on them, I thought.

Aloud, I asked, "What are you talking about?"

"Now, listen up, Popper." Forrester glanced from side to side, as if wanting to make sure no one was listening. "I'm sworn to secrecy on this. I'm about to tell you information the police aren't releasing to the public. I've got a friend in the department who told me this in the strictest confidence, and he made me swear on my BlackBerry that I wouldn't print anything about it."

My heart had begun to pound. Maybe, just maybe, whatever Forrester was about to reveal would get me closer to proving Suzanne innocent by finding the real murderer. "I promise I won't breathe a word to anyone."

"Aha!" He folded his arms across his chest triumphantly. "So I've finally got something that Popper wants. Maybe this would be a good time for me to do a little negotiating. I give you what you want, you give me what I want . . ."

"Just tell me," I insisted. "Look, we're talking about murder—and the fact that one of my closest friends is the primary suspect. If I wanted to flirt, I'd go home to my boyfriend. So let's hear it."

"Whoa." Forrester actually looked impressed. Which was fine, if it would get me what I wanted. "Okay, then. Here it is. The cops found three objects next to Cassandra's body. They think it might be the killer's signature. Or that maybe he or she was leaving some kind of message."

"What were they?" I demanded.

"A paperback novel, a small stuffed bunny rabbit, and a running shoe."

I just stared at him, too startled to speak.

"You're kidding, right?" I finally managed to say.

"As a matter of fact, I'm not. Neither the investigators nor the members of Cassandra's family have been able to figure out what it means either—that is, assuming it means anything at all. There could be several explanations for why those things ended up lying on the floor."

"Like ...?"

"Like maybe Cassandra was cleaning up when she was attacked and she was about to put those particular items away. Another theory is that her cat dragged them over."

"Yes, I heard she had a cat."

"His name is Beau," Forrester noted. "As in Beaujolais."

"Cute. Naming him after a type of wine, I mean." Frowning, I added, "I suppose the cat could have brought over the stuffed animal, if it was small enough. Especially if it was one of his toys. But a running shoe would be too heavy for most cats. Besides, why would he drag over a sneaker? The same goes for the paperback book. It doesn't make sense that a cat would be interested in something like that."

"One theory is that the cat knocked them off a shelf. You know, with his paw. Or maybe his tail." He shrugged. "Hey, you're the animal expert."

"Maybe he knocked off the book," I mused. "But who keeps sneakers on a shelf?"

"I'm just telling you what I heard. Doesn't make sense to me either."

"What was the title of the book?"

"The Scarlet Letter."

"The Nathaniel Hawthorne classic?" I asked, confused. "That's not exactly beach reading. I can't imagine why someone like Cassandra would even have a book like that in her house—unless it was one she'd saved from her college days. Or maybe the murderer brought it along...?"

"Nope. Her copy. The cops found her name inside. Her handwriting."

"Which makes it even more likely it was a book she'd gotten for a class. Not many people take the trouble to write their name in their books once they're out of school."

Forrester shrugged. "Like I said, the whole thing is a complete mystery. But why don't you wrap that pretty little head of yours around this puzzle, and maybe you can come up with the answer."

I opened my mouth to lambaste him for using a phrase that I hadn't heard since the last time TNT ran a Dean Martin movie. Then I noticed the twinkle in his eyes and realized that, once again, the man was playing with me.

"Maybe I'll do just that," I returned loftily. "Especially since the cops haven't managed to wrap their ugly little heads around it and come up with anything at all."

He laughed. "You're fast, Popper; I'll give you that. And you know, I've always liked fast women—"

"What else did the police find at the crime scene?" I interrupted. "Were there any hairs, fibers, fingerprints, footprints...anything at all?"

"All of the above, actually. Over the next few days they'll be analyzing the forensic evidence and putting together a list of all the people who were recently in that room."

I nodded. "Have the police determined what the murder weapon was yet? Was it a knife or some other sharp object—a letter opener, maybe? Have the cops found it? Does it have fingerprints—"

"The police still haven't located the weapon."

My mind raced as I tried to consider every possible angle and every possible detail. I could picture driving away from Cassandra's house and slapping myself on the head for forgetting to ask Forrester for some key piece of information. "Was the phone in her home office off the hook?" I asked. "A sign that she'd tried to call for help?"

"There was no phone in the room. In fact, the only land line in the house is in the kitchen. A leftover from the old days, before cell phones."

"Speaking of cell phones..."

"The police found Cassandra's cell in her purse, in the living room."

"So the murderer didn't take her purse."

"Or anything else, apparently. At least, not that the cops have noticed. The TV, the DVD player, jewelry, some cash that was in a drawer—all untouched."

"So robbery was not the motive, just like it said in your article." My head buzzed with all the bits and pieces of information Forrester was handing me. "Are there any theories about whether Cassandra's attacker was someone she knew or if he—"

"Wait a sec. You referred to the murderer as a 'he.' How do you know it wasn't a 'she'? In fact," he went on, a strange look crossing his face, "how do you know it wasn't your pal who killed Cassandra? Just because you and this Suzanne used to play field hockey together at Bryn Mawr—or whatever you two did—doesn't mean she didn't off her ex's new flame."

Once again, I could feel a wave of fury rising up inside me. "Look, Forrester. I've known Suzanne Fox for a very long time. And I would bet my life on the fact that there's absolutely no way she had anything to do with this!"

"I hear you," Forrester returned, holding up his hands. "I'm just raising the question, that's all. I mean, when you come right down to it, how well do any of us really know each other?"

I had no interest in pursuing *that* line of discussion. Pointedly, I changed the subject, saying, "Falcone made a rather snotty remark about the possibility of me being of some use because there was an animal involved in the case. I just assumed he meant Beau, Cassandra's cat. But now I'm wondering if he meant the stuffed bunny." I couldn't resist muttering, "That idiot." Actually, I was thinking of some much more colorful comments I could make about Lieutenant Falcone, including some that used variations on the word *stuffed*.

"If I were you," Forrester said mildly, "I wouldn't go out of my way to aggravate Falcone."

I stared at him in disbelief. "Since when are you the diplomat?"

"Since always. I'm a reporter, Popper. And one of the first lessons I ever learned is that you don't get people to help you by pushing their buttons."

"But—"

"I suggest that you stop and ask yourself a very simple question: What matters more, your ego or your friend Suzanne?"

I had to admit that he had a point.

"Look, Popper," he said. "If you want to help your friend, you don't need Falcone, okay? In the end, it won't matter whether or not he has witnesses and forensic evidence that put her at the scene of the crime. This is one of those cases that's not going to be solved with physical evidence. The answer's going to come from the people who knew Cassandra. If you want my advice on how to clear your friend's name and find the real murderer, I'd say go ahead and ask as many questions as you want—and meanwhile stay out of Falcone's way."

I jammed my clenched fists deep into the pockets of my polyester fleece jacket, biting my lip and thinking hard. I could tell from how hot my cheeks were that they had turned beet red.

"Hey, think about it, okay?" Forrester finally said. "That's all I'm asking. You've got a good head on your shoulders. Use it to insinuate your way into Cassandra's world. Get to know the people she knew. Find out which ones were her true friends—and which ones just pretended to be her friend. And try to re-create, in your mind, exactly what happened on Tuesday. That's where the answer lies, not in the hairs on her carpets and the fingerprints on her front door.

"Besides," he added in a voice that was only half-teasing, "maybe you can help me scoop the other news mongers by finding the real murderer and giving me an exclusive. I'm telling you, this looks like a case you can crack."

He turned and began walking back to his own car.

"Forrester?" I called.

He glanced back over his shoulder, raising his eyebrows.

"Thanks."

His face melted into a grin. "That's the spirit, Popper. Later."

● ● ●

I stood in front of my car, watching him drive away. The anger that always seemed to arise simply from being in Forrester's presence was already dissipating—largely because I realized he was right.

Of course, the fact that the answer to the riddle of who had killed Cassandra Thorndike probably didn't lie in fingerprints and fibers wouldn't make it any easier to solve—especially since Suzanne's were guaranteed to be among them. But at least it didn't put me at a major disadvantage by not having Lieutenant Anthony Falcone and his staff of forensics experts on my team.

I glanced up Cliffside Lane one last time, making doubly sure that Forrester was gone. Then I wandered up the front walk, back toward Cassandra's house. Even with the yellow crime-scene tape, it looked tempting. But at the moment, it wasn't number 254 I was interested in. It was the charming if somewhat dilapidated house next door, the home of the woman who'd found Cassandra's body.

The good news was that someone had painted it a cheery yellow. The bad news was that it looked as if that had happened about thirty years ago—without a single touch-up since. The front porch sagged, the grass badly needed cutting, and the black paint on the wooden shutters was peeling. The old car parked in the driveway fit right in. Its fenders and doors were bumped and bruised, and it was in dire need of a day of beauty at a local car wash.

Still, the little house looked like it was loved. Pots of chrysanthemums, bright yellow and deep purple, stood on each wooden step, and a wreath made of dried flowers hung on the open front door. White lace curtains covered the large living-room window, and a row of ceramic figurines lined the windowsill.

The afternoon had warmed up enough that whoever lived there had left the front door open. A television blared through the screen door. It sounded like it was tuned to one of those home-shopping channels, since an unusually seductive woman's voice was insisting there were only three left and that $49.99 was the deal of a lifetime.

I studied the porch, noticing that a wooden swing, one of those old-fashioned ones that hold two people, was hung at one end. I also spotted a tricycle, and a red plastic bowl was placed on the porch's top step so a pet could easily drink from it.

I peered through the screen, but all I could see was a

small living room. Along the back wall was a large sagging couch decorated with four needlepoint throw pillows. Two matching upholstered chairs, covered with dark green chenille slipcovers, were draped with crocheted armrest covers the color of limes. A beige pole lamp was topped with a fringed lampshade that was still encased in clear plastic. Yet aside from the noise from the TV, there were no signs of life.

At least, none that I could see. I raised my arm to knock on the screen door, then froze. Even though I was the one who was sneaking around, I couldn't shake the sudden feeling that I was being watched. I turned and scanned the yard but didn't see a soul.

As I started walking toward Cassandra's front door, trying to act as if I actually had a reason to be there, I heard a twig snap. This time I whirled around quickly, trying to catch whoever was spying on me. Yet I still didn't see anyone.

So I jumped high enough to qualify for the Olympics when I heard a high-pitched voice demand, "Are you looking for Cassie?"

I turned around once more and saw that the person who'd been watching me was a little girl no more than four or five years old who had suddenly appeared in the front yard of the house next door. She had the angelic face of a cartoon character—one of the Rugrats, maybe—and was dressed in kelly-green corduroy pants, orange high-top sneakers, and a red shirt printed with a faded picture of Big Bird. Both her pants and shirt looked about two sizes too large. Wisps of dark brown hair curled around her face, which featured the biggest brown eyes I could remember having seen in a long time.

"Uh, no," I replied. "I don't think she—"

"'Cause Cassie's not here anymore. Grammy says she's not coming back, not ever. But we got her cat! He's *my* kitty now!"

Her last comment really caught my interest. After all, Cassandra Thorndike's cat was the sole witness to her murder. Even though we couldn't put him on the stand, the idea that the feline had probably watched the entire crime unfold intrigued me to no end.

"I'll show you my cat," the little girl continued, as if my silence had been an indication of disbelief over her good fortune. Wandering around the side yard that separated her house from Cassandra's, she called, "Come here, Beau. Beau, where are you? Nice kitty..."

Just as I was beginning to doubt the little girl's claim, a cat darted out from underneath some bushes that ran along the two backyards, edging the cliff. The sleek animal was completely black. In fact, with his wide green eyes, he could have posed for Halloween decorations.

"Hey, pussycat," I called in a soft voice.

"Meow!" he yowled angrily, pausing only long enough to glare at me. Then he dashed toward the small yard behind Cassandra's house, which ended in a sharp drop down to the sea. Ignoring the yellow tape reading *Crime Scene—Do Not Cross*, he darted inside through the cat door set into the back door.

"Beau keeps going back to Cassie's house, even though he's supposed to be *my* pussycat now," the little girl pouted. "There's a teensy-weensy door in back, just for him, and he goes in and out all day." With the feline no longer around to distract her, she turned her attention back to me. "Are you a policeman?"

"No, honey. I'm a doctor. I take care of animals. Cats and dogs, mostly, but also horses and all kinds of other animals."

She brightened. "I love animals! Doggies and kitties and bunnies and goldfish... but I was never allowed to have a pet before. Mommy works all day, so Grammy takes care of me. And she's too old to take care of animals. She's not really my grandma. She's Mommy's grandma, so she's *really* old." Pensively, she added, "I hope she lets me keep Beau. 'Cause he doesn't have anybody else to take care of him. Not since Cassie left."

"I hope you can keep him too," I told her. "I can tell you're really good at taking care of animals."

She accepted the compliment with a shy smile. "What's your name?" she asked.

"Jessie. What's yours?"

"Maggie Rose."

Before I had a chance to reply, a woman's scratchy voice interrupted, "Come away from there, Maggie Rose! Stop bothering the lady!"

"She's not bothering me in the least," I assured the elderly woman who had just come out to the porch and was making her way down the uneven wooden steps, clutching the rickety wooden railing. "In fact, I've been enjoying talking to her."

Like the little girl, her caretaker was dressed in clothes that didn't quite fit and didn't quite match. A pair of lemon-yellow stretchy pants with an elastic waistband was pulled up high around the woman's thick torso, the pale blue T-shirt she wore with it carefully tucked in. She also wore a bulky sweater that looked hand-knit, made of puffy salmon-colored yarn and containing an impressive number of different stitches. Like the little girl, her hair was a halo of wisps, although time had turned hers gray. There was one major difference between her and her great-granddaughter: Her eyes were a pale shade of hazel, as if time had faded them as well.

"You a friend of Cassie's?" she asked, peering at me over her glasses.

"Not exactly. It's more like I know people who knew her."

"What's that?" she asked, squinting at me and leaning her head forward.

"I said I know some friends of hers," I repeated, this time more loudly.

"Terrible thing, isn't it?" She shook her head slowly. "So young. A person's not even safe in their own house anymore. Somebody shows up at your front door, and the next thing you know—"

She stopped herself, glancing at the little girl beside her. Maggie Rose, however, looked much more interested in the butterfly she had just noticed hovering above a shrub.

"Yes, it's extremely sad," I agreed. "By the way, I'm Jessie Popper."

"Sorry?" She leaned forward. "I'm afraid I don't always hear so good these days."

"My name is Jessie Popper," I repeated, speaking up.

"Pleased to meet you, Jessie. I'm Virginia Krupinski. This here's my great-granddaughter, Maggie Rose. But I guess you two already met."

"We're practically old friends by now."

"I watch her during the week," Virginia explained. "My granddaughter works up at the big outlet mall in Riverton." Proudly, she added, "She's assistant manager at the Liz Claiborne outlet."

"I love Liz Claiborne!" Not that you'd ever guess by looking at me, I thought, glancing down at my less-than-stylish black jeans and my polyester fleece jacket in a classic shade of navy blue. Then again, I figured that a woman who still considered the popcorn stitch the height of fashion wasn't exactly in the best position to judge.

"How long have you lived here?" I asked. After all, there was no time like the present to pump her for every bit of information I could get.

The woman let out a loud, coarse laugh that sounded like a cough. "Longer than you can imagine. Since way before the war—the big one, that is."

I did a quick calculation. If she'd been in this house

since a few years before World War II, she was at least in her seventies—which sounded about right.

"How about Cassandra Thorndike?" I asked. "How long did she live here?"

"Oh, not long." She frowned, as if she was thinking hard. "Not even a year. Eight, ten months, maybe."

"Did you get to know her at all?"

"Sure did. Lovely girl, that Cassie. She always had time for Maggie Rose here. They'd play games or read stories. She was good to me too. That girl was always coming home with candy and things, since she worked in the restaurant business and all. One sales rep, who I guess was sweet on her, was always giving her these special chocolates his company made. Those were my favorites, and I never found any stores that sold them. She was always happy to share them with me.

"And of course the dessert chef at her boyfriend's restaurant—John something, one of them funny French names—he was always making her special desserts and things. Being a young girl and all, she was always worried about keeping her figure. So she'd invite me over to help myself. One of the few good things about being my age is that I stopped worrying about keeping my figure ages ago!"

"What about the day that she—what about Tuesday?" I eyed Maggie Rose, who still didn't appear to be paying attention to what the grown-ups were saying. Even so, I knew perfectly well that little girls often had big ears. "Were you home when...you know?"

"Sure was. I don't go out much these days. Especially when Maggie Rose is here. I'm getting too old to take her to some shopping mall where I'd have to chase after her."

"I'm sure the police already asked you this," I continued hesitantly, "but did you hear anything out of the ordinary that day?"

"The police?" She waved her hand dismissively, letting out another cough-style laugh. "They don't take somebody like me very seriously. They think I'm too old to know anything."

Maggie Rose trotted over from the backyard, having apparently lost interest in the butterfly. "Grammy says Cassie's not coming back here ever again," she announced.

"That's right, honey," Virginia agreed, glancing at me sadly.

"I'm gonna miss her. She was my friend." The little girl's face crumpled, and she looked forlorn—but only for a few seconds. Breaking into a sunny smile, she asked, "Do you ever take care of sick butterflies? Like if they break their wing or something?"

I laughed. "I'm afraid we didn't learn much about butterflies in veterinary school."

I turned back to Virginia, meanwhile fishing through my pocket. "Let me give you my business card, Mrs. Krupinski. As I mentioned, I know people who knew Cassandra. I'd be very interested in anything at all you can remember about Tuesday. If you think of something, even something that you think is insignificant, don't think twice about giving me a call. If you have access to the Internet, you can also e-mail me through my Web site. The address is at the bottom of the card."

"Maybe I'll call you if Beau here needs some medical care," Virginia said, taking my card and squinting at it.

"Please do." Sincerely, I added, "I enjoyed meeting you both, and I'd be happy to be Beau's doctor."

When I got back in my car, I slammed the door extra hard. I was trying to shut out the sound of Falcone's voice, which kept replaying in my head. As much as I hated to admit it, he was probably right when he concluded that Cassandra's neighbors weren't likely to be very useful in figuring out who had killed her—even though they'd both been right next door at the time she was murdered.

The clock was ticking—and with every passing second, Falcone was undoubtedly becoming more and more anxious to make an arrest. With Suzanne high on his list of suspects, I couldn't afford to waste time.

But at the moment, I was bleary-eyed from all the running around I'd done that day, especially since it wasn't quite what the doctor ordered. It was hard to believe that it was only that morning that I'd been released from the hospital. Since then, I'd visited Suzanne, met her incompetent lawyer, endured Lieutenant Falcone, and snooped around Cassandra Thorndike's neighborhood.

As I turned the key in the ignition, a sharp pain shot through my neck. The effort required to reach up and massage it made me realize just how tired I was. All at once, the long, stressful day seemed to be catching up with me. On top of that, it was already getting dark, and I still had a long drive back home.

Yet home was suddenly the one place I longed to be.

Chapter 4

"As every cat owner knows, nobody owns a cat."
—Ellen Perry Berkeley

Just pulling into the long, winding driveway that led to my cottage was usually enough to relax me. Today was no exception. As I veered off Minnesauke Lane, I could feel the tension draining out of my neck and shoulders. As always, the charming little house in Joshua's Hollow that I had the good fortune to call home seemed like a refuge from all the terrible things that were going on in the big, bad world.

True, my cottage was dwarfed by the other house on the property, a dignified mansion built in the mid-1800s by the estate's original owner, a successful industrialist named Tallmadge whose grandfather had been part of a famous spy ring during the Revolutionary War. But its grandeur only made my little abode seem cozier. Besides, my friend and landlady, Betty, lived in the Big House. Having her right on the premises was like having friendship on tap.

As I climbed out of my car, I noticed that a familiar cream-colored Rolls Royce was parked outside her house, a sign that she was spending this Friday evening entertaining. That was fine with me. At the moment, it wasn't companionship of the human variety I yearned for.

As soon as I threw open my front door, I was greeted by two leaping, barking canines who were so happy to see me you would have thought I'd been gone forty-eight years rather than forty-eight hours.

The feeling was mutual.

"Hey, you guys!" I cried, crouching down. "I am *so* glad to see you!"

My Westie, Max, bounced up and down, his dark brown eyes bright as he pawed the air with his fluffy white feet. As always, my adorable little terrier looked like a cuddly stuffed animal come to life, a cloud of white fur with a black nose that reminded me of the cherry on top of an ice cream sundae. Even though my Maxie-Max had lost his tail while living with his previous owner, he shook the stub that remained so hard he conjured up the image of a hula dancer who'd had too much caffeine.

Lou, my Dalmatian, was also beside himself with glee. My gangly charge with sleek white fur dotted with black and only one eye was unusually assertive, a sign that he'd really missed me. While he usually deferred to his canine brother—even though Max weighed a third of what he weighed—today was one of the rare occasions he took advantage of his greater size to shove Max out of the way. Terriers don't usually take no for an answer, so the two of them were having a grand old time slamming against each other, each one trying to prove that Mom liked him best.

"Who's the pretty birdy? *Awk!* The pirate's life for me!" Prometheus screeched from his huge cage in the corner of the living room. The sound of his shrill voice cutting through the barking, the panting, and the clicking of doggy toenails against the wooden floor made me laugh. My blue and gold macaw with his glossy, brilliantly colored feathers was also glad I was home, as evidenced by his confusion over which of his favorite phrases to screech next.

"Prometheus is the pretty birdy," I replied, as if I were the one who'd been well-trained.

"*Awk,* shake your booty!" he returned happily.

Amid the happy confusion, I noticed Catherine the Great emerging from the kitchen, leaving her favorite warm spot on the rag rug in front of the refrigerator to greet me. My gray cat with the dignified carriage of the empress who was her namesake moved slowly, her arthritic joints limiting her movements more and more every day.

But even before she'd made it across the living room, the commotion stopped. The newest member of my menagerie had just come in from the back of the house—and Max and Lou acted as if their boss had just entered the conference room and caught them throwing paper airplanes. The dogs moved aside, suddenly looking sheepish, as if they realized they'd overstepped their bounds. Even Prometheus quieted down, lowering his voice from an ear-splitting shriek to a parrot version of muttering.

Tinkerbell was in the building.

The little tiger kitten had only recently become part of my family. Even though she was just a few weeks old and still small enough to fit in the palm of my hand, it was already clear that she had the personality of a diva—and that she just assumed she was in charge.

"Hey, Tink!" I cried, scooping her up and nuzzling her amazingly soft fur against my cheek. Still cradling her in my hand, I gently picked up Cat and sank onto the couch, lowering both felines into my lap. Tinkerbell immediately attacked the button on my jeans, while Cat looked up at me as if to say, "Kids." The dogs followed, romping around my feet as Prometheus squawked a long string of nonsensical phrases that made it hard to keep a straight face.

"There's no place like home," I said with a sigh, nestling back against the soft cushions and relishing the moment. "Especially when it's obvious you guys missed me as much as I missed you."

"Hey, I missed you too." Nick emerged from the bedroom, lugging a thick textbook and grinning.

He was wearing what I'd come to think of as his law student outfit, which I had to admit looked a lot like what had been his private investigator outfit before he'd decided to go back to school. It consisted of a button-down shirt—pale blue today—with khaki pants that were invariably a little wrinkled. He'd been working so hard lately that he hadn't had time for a haircut, meaning his dark brown hair looked a tad shaggy and the poorly behaved lock in front had even more of a tendency than usual to fall in his eyes.

While I was used to my animals acting absolutely thrilled that I was home, I wasn't as accustomed to finding Nick waiting for me. Of course, I'd been tipped off by the music of the '60s rock group Cream that filled the room, with Eric Clapton mournfully singing, "In a white room..." accompanied by a twangy guitar.

"But I'm not going to jump all over you, like the rest of this group. At least, not until later." Nick strode over to the stereo, turning the volume down from earsplitting to merely numbing.

I had to admit that coming home to Nick felt kind of nice. The fact that a big shopping bag with the Szechuan Palace menu stapled to it was sitting on the dining-room table didn't hurt either.

"You read my mind," I said, gesturing toward what could only be dinner.

He grinned. "I knew that by the time you got home,

you'd be starving. Do you think your stomach can handle Szechuan Garden's finest?"

"I could be wrong, but I believe my doctor specifically said I should drink plenty of fluids and eat lots of Chinese food. You did good."

"Then do I get a kiss?" he asked.

"Did you remember the spring rolls?"

"Would I forget the spring rolls?"

"Garlic triple crown?"

"Would I dare show my face without it?"

"Then you get more than a kiss. But you have to wait until I've satisfied my most basic urges—like scarfing down all the food I can get my hands on."

As usual, I enjoyed the ritual of setting out plates and chopsticks, boiling water for tea, and opening all the waxy white containers and the rectangular plastic dishes. I always think of eating Chinese food as one of the special things that Nick and I do together, even though millions of people do the exact same thing. Billions, if you count all the people who are actually Chinese.

Predictably, Max and Lou both picked out a choice spot underneath the dining-room table. It wasn't my habit to feed them people-food, but every once in a while the force of gravity carried some tasty little morsel down to their level. They'd learned that it didn't hurt to be ready, just in case. Cat hovered nearby, slightly more reserved, while Tinkerbell was too distracted by a spider crawling up the wall to notice it was dinnertime.

Nick and I didn't do a much better job of controlling ourselves. We pounced on the food as if we were field hands who'd just come in from a long day of clearing the back forty. Frankly, I would have loved it if we had nothing more important to talk about than how wiped out we were, filling each other in on details like the most interesting medical case I'd seen that day or the latest intrigues of his study group. Unfortunately, that wasn't the case.

"So how's Suzanne holding up?" Nick asked as soon as we'd both piled our plates high.

The feast before me suddenly looked a whole lot less appetizing.

"I'm really worried," I told him. "She's not handling this well at all."

"Not surprising. And you didn't make any headway in convincing her to tell the police what really happened that day?"

"She still doesn't seem to get it," I said, shaking my head. "At least, not at this point."

He grimaced. "Bad move on her part."

"Nick, Suzanne is in serious trouble," I said somberly. I paused for a few seconds before adding, "If I'm really going to help her, I've got to find out who murdered Cassandra Thorndike."

I braced myself for his reaction. After all, I was well aware of his feelings about my nasty habit of sticking my nose into the shadowy nooks and crannies that surround murder investigations. And the fact that I'd just been released from the hospital, thanks to my latest escapade as veterinarian-turned-Nancy Drew, didn't exactly strengthen my position.

Sure enough, his response was a mild explosion. "Correct me if I'm wrong," he cried, "but didn't you and I recently agree that you might be better off pursuing a hobby that's less dangerous than homicide investigation? That maybe you should consider something along the lines of stamp collecting or basket weaving or . . . or classic rock?"

"But this is different!" I exclaimed. "This is *Suzanne*! Nick, I talked to Falcone today, and he really has it out for her. He's anxious to pin this murder on somebody, and he's decided she's the most likely target. I have to help her, no matter what it takes. And the only way I can clear her name is by finding the real killer. You understand, don't you?"

Anxiously, I waited for his reaction. And I was as startled as I was relieved when he finally said, "You're right. You have to do it. There's no other way to get her out of this."

"Thank you, Nick," I said breathlessly. "For understanding, I mean."

"But Jess?" Nick added. "Please do me a favor."

"What is it?"

"Be careful."

"I will," I croaked, suddenly having a hard time speaking. No one knew as well as I did that murder investigation was serious business.

"So what did Falcone have to say?" Nick asked earnestly. "Was the Norfolk County Police Department's answer to Columbo his usual charming self?"

"He said what he always says: that I should butt out and mind my own business. But I also talked to Forrester Sloan. Remember him?"

"The guy you claim I met at the hospital," Nick said. "But I barely remember him." Frowning, he added, "He's also the person who got you involved in your last foray into the fun and frolicsome world of homicide."

"That's the one," I replied. "He was at Cassandra's house this afternoon."

His eyebrows shot up to his hairline. "You were at the murder victim's *house*?"

"Nick, how else am I going to help Suzanne if I don't check out the scene of the crime? I have to learn everything I possibly can about the murder."

He gave a grunt that said that, even though he didn't like it, he understood. "Was this reporter guy helpful?"

"Yes, as a matter of fact. Turns out he's covering the case, so he told me everything he knows." I hesitated, wondering if I should mention the three clues the murderer had left behind. Given Forrester's vehemence about keeping it a secret, I decided there was no reason to let anyone else in on it at this point—not even Nick. "Forrester is convinced this isn't a case that forensics will solve. He thinks I have a good chance of finding out who murdered Cassandra just by talking to the people who were in her life and piecing together the story of what was going on—especially the part about why somebody wanted her dead."

"What about her lawyer?" he asked. "Who is he—or she—and what's his take on this?"

"It's a he," I replied. "Jerry Keeler. The guy's a disaster."

"Then why is Suzanne using him?"

I hesitated before answering. "Marcus recommended him. Apparently they went to college together."

"Marcus?" Nick cried. "That jerk?"

I had to admit that Marcus Scruggs was a pretty good veterinarian. But that was about the only positive thing I could say about him. In fact, whenever I thought about Marcus, the word *lout* always came to mind.

I'd met him back when I was applying to veterinary school. But I'd realized from our first interaction that he was one of those men who made most decisions with the part of his body that was covered by his pants, not his hat.

Introducing the two of them three months earlier had been Suzanne's idea, not mine. I'd made the mistake of mentioning him in the same conversation in which she told me about her divorce, and before I knew it, she was insisting that I bring him along to dinner. From the moment they met, so many sparks flew that I hoped the restaurant's smoke detectors were up to code.

"If Marcus recommended this Jerry Keeler, no wonder

he's a disaster!" Nick grumbled. "What's wrong with that woman? How can Suzanne trust a guy who insists on referring to himself as 'the Marc Man' with something this important?"

I cringed, even though I felt exactly the same way. Somehow, hearing Nick express the same feelings of alarm that had gripped me since I'd met the man who was supposed to be getting Suzanne out of this mess made the whole situation seem even more horrifying.

"I tried to change her mind," I told him. "She won't budge."

"Great, just great," Nick muttered. "If you don't mind, let's not talk about Marcus while we're eating. This topic of conversation is giving me indigestion. Besides, you and I have something important to discuss."

It took me a few seconds to figure out what he was talking about. "Oh," I finally said. "Right."

Our future. At least, our immediate future. The fact that Nick was on the verge of being thrown out of his apartment, an illegal rental on the second floor of a charming Victorian house in nearby Port Townsend. And that his sudden and unexpected lack of a place to reside made this a good time for the two of us to consider living together.

At least, that was how Nick saw it.

"Can we be perfectly honest with each other?" he continued.

I gulped like a Looney Toons character. Even though I've always considered honesty one of the Top Five requirements for a solid relationship, I suddenly felt as if someone had turned the thermostat up about twenty degrees. I had to fight the impulse to run over to the front door, fling it open, and stick my head out into the cool night air—the best way I could think of to start breathing normally again.

"Let's face it, Jess," Nick went on. "You have some major commitment issues."

"I have pets," I pointed out feebly. "That's a commitment."

He nodded, but I knew he was just being polite. "That aside, I think you recognize how special our relationship is."

That was true enough. Nick Burby was one of a kind. He was intelligent, funny, patient, sensitive...and willing to put up with a mouthy parrot, a needy senior citizen of a cat, a tiger kitten who was the size of a coffee mug but firmly believed she was the successor to the Lion King, and a couple of canines who made the Three Stooges look as dignified as Belgian royalty.

He even accepted my obsession with investigating murders. More or less.

"At any rate, there's absolutely no doubt in my mind that nothing would make me happier than us living together," Nick went on. "Especially since our schedules have become so insane. Between the crazy hours you work and the time demands of my first year of law school, you and I hardly see each other. If we were sharing the same bed and the same breakfast table and the same bathroom, at least we'd have some semblance of a relationship. And since we'd be splitting expenses half and half, think of all the money you could save."

I took a particularly large bite of a spring roll, which I considered to be an effective way of buying time. He was right about the practical aspects of him moving in with me. Our crazy schedules aside, his landlord wanted him out by the end of the month. Apparently the landlord's newly divorced daughter who'd moved back home was getting tired of living with the Peter Frampton and Boy George posters in her old room. The idea of forcing Nick to scramble around to find a new place to live, especially given the demands of his course load, seemed kind of coldhearted.

I had to admit that I'd run so hot and cold with Nick over the years that he practically needed a plumber. True, I'd fallen for him hard almost right from the moment we met, back in the days when he was still a private investigator and I was helping him out with a case that involved pit bulls. But even my strong feelings for him weren't an effective antidote to my so-called "commitment issues."

Who knows? I thought. Maybe it's time to take a deep breath, hold my nose, and jump into the commitment pool—for lack of a more graceful metaphor. There were certainly some definite pluses to being in a serious relationship, ranging from having a wonderful man around to sneak up behind you and give you a hug while you were brushing your teeth to being able to complain about the electric bill to somebody who cared as much as you did because he was paying half of it. I could handle that part.

The feeling that I was giving up something precious and hard-won—namely, my independence—was more complicated. And that was where the attacks of claustrophobia came in.

But Nick was waiting for an answer. As I was teetering between "Sure, why not?" and "Help!" he suddenly said, "You know, Jess, we could consider this a trial. Decide that we'll try living together for three months— let's say until the New Year. At that point, we can step back and reevaluate. You know, look at all our options."

It occurred to me that Nick was already starting to talk like a lawyer—even though he'd only been a law student for a few weeks. But what mattered here was that he recognized my apprehensions and, even more important, that he was leaving me a way out. An escape clause, for lack of a better expression.

That alone was enough for me to say yes.

"Nick," I told him, putting down my chopsticks, "I think it's a great idea. Let's do it. On a trial basis, the way you suggested."

A big grin spread over his face. He put down his chopsticks, came over to my side of the table, and put his arms around me.

"I love you, Jess."

"I love you, too, Nick."

I meant it. I really did. But that didn't mean I wasn't picturing a giant calendar in my head, with the pages for October, November, and December looming in front of me.

At least there was an upside to my deep feelings of apprehension: they made focusing on a murder investigation a whole lot easier, by comparison. And while I was already exhausted by all the ground I'd covered that day, not to mention a little overwhelmed, it was clear to me that I was going to have to dig even deeper into the details of Cassandra Thorndike's life.

My "To Do" list already had two items on it. The first was taking that long, hot shower I'd been fantasizing about and the second was enjoying a good night's sleep cuddled up next to Nick. But I'd just added a third: visiting the wineries that dotted Long Island's North Fork.

And I knew exactly where I'd start.

Chapter 5

"The cat, having sat upon a hot stove lid, will not sit upon a hot stove lid again. Nor upon a cold stove lid."

—Mark Twain

As I drove out to the island's wine region Saturday morning, retracing my steps of the day before, I was once again struck by how beautiful this part of Long Island was—especially on a sunny, crisp fall day like this one. There was one major difference between my last foray and this one, however: the traffic. Even though it was barely 11 A.M. on a weekend, a steady stream of cars was heading east along Route 35, a strange twist on the rush-hour concept.

At first, I thought there must be road construction up ahead. Then I realized the reason for the congestion was that plenty of other people had discovered the East End wineries. While I was seeking information, however, they were driving to the North Fork on a quest for the perfect chardonnay—or at least a relaxing day of tasting wine and enjoying the scenery.

For today's expedition, I'd opted to take my van. The 26-foot white monster had everything I needed to treat animals right inside. Stenciled in blue on the door were the words,

REIGNING CATS & DOGS

Mobile Veterinary Services
Large and Small Animals
631–555–PETS

During the other murder investigations I'd found myself involved in, being a veterinarian who traveled around with her own office-on-wheels had enabled me to gain entry to people's homes, meanwhile sneaking in a few questions without being too obvious. Since that was precisely what I hoped to do today, I figured I might as well come armed with everything I had.

I recognized the entrance to Thorndike Vineyards by the huge white sign at the edge of the road. In the center was a large gold T surrounded by a ring of dark-green vines. I pulled into the parking lot, where sightseers were already vying for parking spaces. Of course, the two big tour buses that took up a good chunk of the pavement didn't help. I lucked into a spot when a couple who'd just filled the trunk of their BMW with two cases of wine backed out hurriedly, probably rushing off to the next winery on their list.

The day was surprisingly cool for early October. I was glad that, once again, I'd remembered to bring my navy-blue polyester fleece jacket. I was equally glad the Thorndike Vineyards Visitor Center was just a few steps away. It was a large, barnlike building that looked at least a hundred years old. At least on the outside. Stepping inside, I saw that the interior had been completely renovated, with high white walls and sleek wooden fixtures that gave it the look of a Manhattan boutique—one that just happened to have a bar running along one wall. Even though it wasn't yet noon, it was lined with wine lovers who were taking advantage of the opportunity to taste.

All manner of wine-related paraphernalia was displayed on tables and shelves. Bottle stoppers topped with bunches of purple grapes or chubby sommeliers. Glittery gift bags designed to hold a single bottle of wine that would serve as a hostess gift. Fancy snack foods like paper-thin English crackers and obscure French cheeses, along with ceramic plates hand-painted with vines to serve them on. Most people were just browsing, although a few were filling the straw baskets the shop supplied with the frenzy of last-minute Christmas shoppers.

Then there were the wines themselves. Two of the room's walls were lined with shelves, displaying bottle after bottle of Thorndike wines. I saw chardonnays, pinot noirs, merlots, and a half dozen other varieties. Every label had the same elaborate letter *T* in shiny gold, encircled with dark-green vines, that was on the sign outside.

A large white sign proclaimed that Thorndike Vineyards had been named *Winery of the Year* at the previous year's *New York Wine Classic,* along with winning gold medals for its 1999 Merlot Grand Vintage and its 2002 Barrel-Fermented Chardonnay. Pretty impressive, especially to someone like me, who had always thought there were basically two varieties of wine: white and red.

"The eleven-thirty tour is about to get under way," a woman's voice announced, cutting through the din. "We still have one or two places available, if anyone is interested in touring the winery."

I thought you'd never ask, I thought, heading over to the small group gathered by the back door.

"...Six, seven, eight," a pleasant-looking middle-aged woman, whose blouse had the familiar *T* embroidered on it, counted aloud. "I think that should do it. If you'll please follow me..."

Our tour guide—Marian, according to her name tag—led us through double doors at the back of the tasting room. We were suddenly in a warehouse-type area, except that it was very well ventilated, with walls that didn't quite reach all the way to the roof. Every inch was immaculate, from the huge, shiny vats that lined one long wall to the concrete floor.

"Thorndike Vineyards started twenty-five years ago with the first planting of vinifera," she began after shepherding us into a cluster. "They're the grapes that are planted in France and California. We began with only forty acres, then acquired more land in the years that followed. Today, we plant a total of ninety acres and produce nearly twenty thousand cases of wine annually.

"The key to making good wine is using sweet grape juice," she continued, "which means starting the process with ripe fruit and good sugar." She pointed to the wall of vats. "We begin the process by crushing the fruit in these vats. We use stainless steel because, unlike wooden vats, they don't impart any flavor to the wine. We use wooden barrels at this stage only if we specifically want to flavor the wine.

"Inside each vat, there's a membrane that inflates and deflates like a balloon, pressing the fruit against the outer wall and causing the juice that's released to drip down into a receiving container. From there, we use a hose to pump the juice into a different set of stainless-steel tanks that hold two to three thousand gallons. At that point it's still fleshy, because it's filled with protein particles. We let it sit for twenty-four hours to allow the solids to settle at the bottom."

Marian led us farther into the drafty room. "Fermentation is the next stage," she continued. "We put the juice into wooden barrels, and we inoculate it with a special strain of yeast we get from a wine lab. Basically, the yeast feeds on the sugar in the juice, and when it digests it, it creates carbon dioxide—which escapes into the air—and alcohol.

"The winemaker's task is to create just the right conditions so the natural process can occur. The ideal temperature for fermentation is fifty-five degrees Fahrenheit for white and eighty degrees for red. This is the point when the yeast begins feeding on the sugar in the juice, and yeast cells soon line the barrel. The result is a harmony between the fruit and the oak."

"How long does the wine fermentation take?" a man in a New York Islanders T-shirt asked.

"From ten days to three weeks," the guide replied. "The sweetness or dryness of the wine depends on the sugar content of the grape and whether the winemaker arrests fermentation before all sugar is converted or just part." Pointing at the plastic tubes protruding from the top of each barrel, she added, "These tubes are called 'fermentation locks.' They let the fermentation gases escape. In the beginning, we stir every two days, but eventually we stir only once a week."

"What about all those crazy adjectives people use to describe wines?" another man asked. "Do those words mean anything or are they just showing off?"

A few members of the tour group chuckled. "The wooden barrels are made of French oak," the tour guide explained patiently. "The wood, which is made of starch, has its own distinctive flavor, which it imparts to the wine. For example, if someone describes a wine as having 'a hint of vanilla and butterscotch,' that comes from the barrel.

"By the end of May or early June, we return the wine to stainless-steel tanks for blending. We use sterile filtration to get it into bottles, and then we cork it, cap it, and label it. The wine is loaded onto pallets and moved to a separate building out back. Until it's sold, we hold it there in a separate temperature-controlled building that's kept at fifty-five to fifty-six degrees. By the way, it's also called the 'tax room,' because state or federal agents are free to inspect it. Wineries pay tax on every bottle of wine they produce, so it's important that we keep good records."

"How many grapes does it take to make a bottle of wine?" a teenage girl asked.

"One ton of grapes yields seven hundred sixty bottles of wine," she replied. "If you do the math, that translates to roughly two and a half pounds of grapes per bottle."

"I thought you were supposed to serve red wine at room temperature," a woman interjected, "but I read somewhere that the French keep their rooms cooler than we do. What's the best temperature?"

With our guide distracted by questions, I figured it was a good time to do a little touring of my own. I was anxious to find out whatever I could about Cassandra Thorndike's family and their flourishing enterprise. I edged my way toward the back of our group, then slipped behind a giant vat. I headed back into the main building but this time found myself in a different section.

No tourists here. In fact, the hallway was blocked off by a sign atop a freestanding metal pole. It read, *Employees Only.*

After glancing from side to side to make sure no one was watching, I ducked down the private corridor. When I reached the end, I found myself in a cavernous room that looked like a gigantic wine cellar. It served as a foyer, with several doors leading off it. From the name plates affixed to most of them, I surmised that they were offices. The walls were made of red brick, the temperature was cool, and there was only one lighting fixture, hung high on the back wall.

As soon as my eyes fully adjusted to the dim light, I saw that the lamp had been placed so that it illuminated a huge oil painting, over six feet high, in an ornate gilt frame. It faced the entryway, making it the focal point for anyone who entered.

The painting was a portrait of a tall, slender young woman with pale, luminescent skin and large blue-green eyes, their startling color emphasized even further by her thick, dark eyebrows. Gleaming, straight black hair spilled down her back, the ends curving gently around her shoulders like a shawl. She stood erect, her chin held at a slightly defiant angle, as proud and as graceful as a gazelle.

She wore a long gown made of rich purple velvet and flowered gold brocade. The theatrical garment gave her the not-quite-of-this-world look of a woman in a pre-Raphaelite painting. The wreath of white and lavender flowers that encircled the crown of her head made her appear even more ephemeral, as if she were a goddess or an angel that some artist with an overly developed sense of drama had conjured up.

"Can I help you?"

I whirled around, surprised by the unexpected sound of a sharp voice. I hadn't realized that anyone else had come into the foyer, probably because I was so absorbed by the painting.

The man glowering at me looked as if he was in his late sixties or early seventies, with a deeply lined face but a full head of thick silver hair. He appeared to be of medium height, although his slightly stooped posture made it a bit difficult to tell. He was also portly—a word that suited him well, not just because of his slightly rotund build, but also because he seemed as old-fashioned as the word. He was dressed in a well-worn, slightly faded blue plaid flannel shirt that stood in sharp contrast to his pants, a pair of those crisp, brand-new-looking jeans that older men tend to wear even though they emphasize how flat their behinds are.

"This is a private area," he added, using the same cross tone.

"I was looking for the restroom," I lied, resorting to my favorite fallback excuse.

He cast me a skeptical look. All right, so maybe it was hard to believe that a grown woman couldn't tell the difference between a sign that read *Employees Only* and one that features male and female paper cutouts, the international symbol for people who have to pee.

"Okay, that's not exactly true," I admitted. "The truth is that I noticed this portrait as I was walking by, and I just had to get a better look."

"Ah. Well." That excuse seemed to placate him. He gazed up at the painting, the corners of his mouth drooping and his eyes dampening. "She was beautiful, wasn't she?"

"Who is she?" I asked, even though I was pretty sure I already knew, thanks to the photo I'd seen in *Newsday*.

"Cassandra Thorndike. Gordon's daughter." As if he suddenly remembered that I was nothing more than an intruder, and therefore unlikely to know the people he had named, he added, "Gordon Thorndike founded Thorndike Vineyards."

"I see. Are you a member of the Thorndike family?"

"Me? No. I own Simcox Wineries, right next door." I guess he figured he'd already told me enough that it was time for an official introduction. "I'm Theodore Simcox," he said, extending his hand.

"I'm Jessica Popper," I replied as we shook hands.

"I'm actually a very close friend of the entire Thorndike family." Raising his eyes to the portrait once again, he added, "Cassandra was like a daughter to me. You may have heard about the recent tragedy. She passed away earlier this week—"

We both jumped a little as the subdued atmosphere of the foyer was broken by the sound of footsteps traveling briskly across the terra cotta–tiled floor. A short, plump woman in a gray wool skirt and a black sweater bustled into the room, closing the doors of one of the offices behind her. Her hair matched her outfit, I noticed, black with gray accents. It was also just as severe, pulled back tightly into a low ponytail.

"Theodore, I really can't tell you how much I appreciate you—" She stopped abruptly. "I'm sorry. I didn't realize you had a guest."

"I'm not a guest," I explained. "I just stepped in here to get a better look at this painting."

The woman drew her lips into a thin, straight line, as if she were trying to maintain her composure. Even so, her eyes filled with tears so quickly that I figured she'd been doing a good deal of crying over the past few days.

"You really shouldn't be in here," she said without much conviction.

"This is Mrs. Thorndike," Theodore Simcox said meaningfully.

"Oh! Mr. Simcox told me about your daughter. I'm so sorry."

She acknowledged my expression of sympathy with a nod.

In addition to being completely caught off guard by the realization that I'd just met Cassandra's mother, I also experienced a whole new level of understanding. Up until this point, I'd been so wrapped up in worrying about Suzanne that I'd barely thought about the people who had known and loved Cassandra Thorndike—and how much they were suffering. A young woman was dead. And that meant her parents would have to live with the terrible sadness of having lost their daughter for the rest of their lives. I felt a surge of determination to find out who had killed Cassandra Thorndike—not only for Suzanne's sake, but also for the people who had loved the poor young woman.

Mrs. Thorndike turned her attention back to Theodore. "Thanks again for running the show for us for a few days, Theo."

"I'm glad there's at least something I can do, Joan," he replied earnestly.

"You've lifted a tremendous burden off my shoulders. I need to be at home. I just don't feel right, leaving Gordon on his own. He's devastated." Glancing back at me, she added, "Right now, all the wineries on the East End are gearing up for the busiest time of the year. Not only is autumn the time of the harvest; it's also the height of tourist season. From September through November, I think most of us feel that our business is orchestrating tastings and hayrides instead of turning grapes into wine."

For a moment a small smile lit up her face, and I could see a trace of liveliness I hadn't noticed before.

The smile quickly disappeared. "But right now, my husband and I simply can't cope with the day-to-day operation of the winery. In fact, the only reason I came in today is that one of our employees called to tell me that my cat, Coco, is ailing. I brought her here a few days ago to help with a mouse problem we've suddenly developed. But she's apparently been acting strange, dragging around like she has no energy and squatting down in a weird position. They also said that for the last day or two, she hasn't been eating or drinking. So I came to pick her up and take her to the vet."

"If you'd like, I could take a look at her." In response to her puzzled look, I added, "I'm a veterinarian with a mobile services unit. You might have noticed my van on your way in; it's right in your parking lot. I'd be happy to treat your cat."

"Oh, *would* you?" she asked gratefully. "It would make things so much easier. But could I trouble you to drive your van to my house? It's not far, and I really want to get home to Cassandra's father. He's having such a difficult time coping with his daughter's death, and every minute I'm away seems like too much."

I guess my expression reflected my confusion, because she added, "I should probably explain that I'm actually Cassandra's stepmother. Her real mother passed away when she was a little girl. At any rate, would you mind coming over? I know it's a lot to ask."

"It's no trouble at all," I assured her.

"Terrific. I'll just grab Coco and meet you at the house."

She began giving me directions, then decided it would be simpler for me to follow her home.

Turning back to Theo, she said, "Feel free to close up early. I know you've got enough to take care of without doing double duty by running my vineyard as well as your own."

"Now, Joan, don't even think about it," he insisted. "You know that a lonely old bachelor like me doesn't have anything else to do on a Saturday. There's nothing on my schedule for the rest of the day except the roast-beef special over at Clyde's."

She smiled gratefully. "Thanks, Theo. You're a real friend."

As I pulled out of the Thorndike Vineyards' parking lot, I could scarcely believe my good fortune. I'd been wondering how I'd ever manage to get inside the world that Cassandra Thorndike had occupied, and here the perfect opportunity had just fallen into my lap.

Right, I thought. Nothing but pure luck. That—and a little scheming, a bit of acting, and the good fortune to own a clinic-on-wheels that gave me the perfect excuse to visit people's homes.

• • •

I'd been following Joan Thorndike's pickup truck farther east along Route 35 for less than a mile when her right-hand turn signal began blinking. As soon as I made the turn, I began bumping along an uneven dirt road. I slowed down, not wanting to damage anything internal—either inside the van or inside me.

By the time I reached the house, Joan's truck was already parked near the back door. She'd left the door open, as if she'd gone inside and expected me to do the same.

When I did, I found myself in a large, sunny farmhouse kitchen that combined modern appliances with old-fashioned touches like colorful braided rag rugs and wooden shelves instead of sleek cabinets for storing dishes. Cheerful yellow-and-white-checked curtains framed a large window that overlooked a dilapidated barn.

"Sorry about the state of our driveway," Joan apologized, distractedly petting the cat cradled in her arms. "I probably should have warned you."

"I've seen worse," I assured her. "In fact, I consider the occasional broken muffler an occupational hazard."

She barely seemed to be listening. "Gordon must be upstairs or outside," she mused, more to herself than to me. "His car's here."

"This is Coco," she said, slightly lifting the cat she was holding in her arms. "That's short for Minou Chocolate, which, in simple English, is 'chocolate pussycat.' You can probably tell she's half-Siamese."

The tiny cat couldn't have weighed more than five or six pounds. She had large green eyes and a pure brown undercoat with a black finish, except for a thin white stripe that looked like a surgical scar along her belly.

"Where did she get this scar?" I asked.

"Poor Coco!" Joan replied. "She swallowed a long

blue thread once and had to have surgery to untangle her intestines."

"Tell me more about her symptoms."

"As I mentioned, she hasn't had much energy, and she's been squatting a lot," Joan said. "She's also been vomiting a little."

"Let's bring her into the van," I said. "Do you have a toy or something to distract her with while I examine her?"

"Here, this one's her favorite." She grabbed a small red clown head off the kitchen counter. It looked as if it was so well-loved that its various pieces had been glued together, probably more than once. With the toy in her hand and the cat in her arms, she followed me into my van.

As I took Coco and placed her on the examining table, the cat kept looking over at Joan. "She seems very attached to you," I commented.

She beamed. "She's very loyal—aren't you, Coco? In fact, I think of her as my 'watch cat.' Once, my five-year-old niece was visiting, and Coco jumped a full eight feet, glomming onto my hip. It was her way of saying, 'Hands off.' The strange thing was that, up until that point, she'd always been afraid of kids. But it was clear she was ready to go hand to hand with this poor little girl."

Suspecting a bladder infection, I began by palpating her bladder, squeezing it gently and trying to express urine. A small amount passed through the urethra, so I knew we weren't dealing with a blockage.

"I'm going to take a urine sample," I told Joan, who was looking on anxiously. "I can collect it directly from her bladder with a syringe."

Joan grimaced. I suspected this was going to be harder on her than it would be on Coco. To distract her while I worked, I said, "Coco seems like a very sweet cat."

"She's amazingly affectionate," she replied. "Whenever she wants attention, she comes over and butts me with her head. Sometimes she offers to shake a paw, a little trick I taught her. And even when we had other cats over the years, Coco made no bones about the fact that she was the only one who was allowed to sit in my lap. All it took was a few strikes to the nose before the other cats got the message."

"I have a brand-new kitten who's laying down the law in my house, too," I told her, chuckling. "She has no qualms about bossing my two dogs around either."

Given the strain the entire Thorndike family was under, I was glad Joan had a chance to focus on something else, at least for a little while.

"It will take a week to culture Coco's urine sample," I told her. "In the meantime, I'm going to put her on an antibiotic. Her behavior suggests that she has cystitis—a bladder infection. But even if it's just an inflammation, the antibiotic will kill the bacteria that are causing it."

I set her up with amoxycillin, instructing Joan to give Coco two 15-ml doses a day with an eyedropper and urging her to make sure the cat drank sufficient amounts of water. I also mentioned that recurrent bacterial infections could be a sign of bladder stones, diabetes, or several other illnesses, and that it was therefore important to monitor her health.

"Thank you," she said gratefully as I handed Coco back to her. "I don't know about you, but after that ordeal, I'm dying for some coffee. Could I interest you in a cup?"

She'd just said the magic word. I'd been experiencing my usual early-afternoon droopiness, my body's way of screaming for a hit of caffeine.

"Thanks, Mrs. Thorndike. I'm pretty desperate for caffeine, too."

"Please, call me Joan. Especially since we seem to share the same addiction."

Once she and I had settled in at the large rough-hewn wooden table that seemed perfect for the kitchen, she commented, "I've never seen a 'vet on wheels' before. What an interesting way to make a living! Driving around Long Island, going to people's homes and taking care of their animals..."

"I love it," I replied. I took a sip of coffee, sighing as I felt a surge of energy flood my veins. "In addition to the rewards of working with animals almost every day of my life, I adore the freedom and the flexibility—not to mention the fact that no two days are ever exactly the same."

"Sounds like the wine business," Joan observed with a smile. She lifted Coco into her lap, stroking her soft fur distractedly as she spoke. "Of course, I've only been involved in it for the past fifteen years or so. Gordon started Thorndike Vineyards a good ten years before that, so I'm a relative newcomer."

As soon as she mentioned her husband's name, her smile faded. "That poor man. He's having such a difficult time. I don't think he can process the fact that his daughter is gone. He's fallen completely apart."

"I can't imagine how hard this must be for him," I said softly. "I didn't know her, of course, but I saw her portrait at the winery. She looked like an angel."

Joan set her coffee cup down on the table with such a bang that I jumped. "Believe me, Cassie was no angel."

My surprise must have registered on my face, because she immediately added, "I know; that probably seems like a mean thing to say, given all that's gone on. But anyone who's ever known either of us will tell you that Cassie and I never got on all that well, even though I spent years doing my darnedest to turn things around."

"I guess some kids are just never able to accept a stepparent," I commented.

"That was a big part of it. Cassie was twelve when I came on the scene. Fourteen when Gordon and I got married." She sighed. "Even though I knocked myself out trying to be the ideal stepmom, somehow I never figured out the right formula. Not with either of Gordon's kids."

"He has other children?" I asked.

"A son. Ethan. He's three years younger than Cassie. He's still living with us." She hesitated before adding, "He's also...troubled."

I decided to leave that comment alone, at least for now.

"From the time I first came on the scene, Cassie was a very angry child. I hate to say anything negative about her, especially after what's happened, but the truth is that she grew up to be a very angry adult."

Joan held Coco a little closer. I got the feeling that, over the years, her loyal, loving cat had played a major role in compensating for the rejection she felt from her stepchildren, something she lived with every day of her life.

"Do you think her anger was rooted in the fact that her mother died when she was still so young?" I asked gently.

Joan shrugged. "Who knows? Maybe that, maybe a dozen different reasons. Or maybe nothing logical at all. Right after she turned thirteen, she really started acting out. You know, doing all the normal teenage girl things. Boys, smoking, drinking, drugs, cutting school, staying out all night...Poor Gordon! When I think of what he went through with her. Frankly, I was never sure if me being around helped him or made things more difficult."

"I'm sure it helped," I said politely. "He probably found having you in his life a great source of support."

"That's what he always said." Joan stared off into the distance. "But I always wondered if—well, there's no point making myself crazy about it all. Especially since Cassandra finally seemed to be getting her act together."

"By meeting Robert?"

"That, and deciding once and for all that she wanted to get involved in the family business. Gordon was so pleased about that. And he was positively thrilled that she wanted to come back to the area where she'd grown up and start working for him. He was so relieved that she finally seemed to be settling down and that all the craziness of the past seemed to be over."

In my mind, I replayed Virginia Krupinski's description of her next-door neighbor. Her report that Cassandra was warm and friendly, sharing her special chocolates and pastries and finding time to read to Maggie Rose, implied that she had matured in other ways, as well.

"But I knew Cassie. I also knew we'd been through this before. Thinking the worst was over, I mean. Like the time she came home and announced she'd decided to go to art school. Gordon rented her an apartment in Manhattan, paid her tuition, bought her every kind of paint and brush and easel that had ever been invented— and within a month she announced that it wasn't for her and she was dropping out. Then, a couple of years later, she decided she was destined to be a great actress. Once again, Gordon knocked himself out to help her. Another apartment in the city, tuition at an acting institute...At least that one lasted a little longer. I think she stayed in the program for about three months before she gave up."

She shook her head sadly. "I guess I was afraid her sudden interest in the wine business wasn't going to pan out either."

"What about the fact that she was engaged to be married?" I asked. "Surely that was a sign that she was finally finding her way."

Joan grimaced. "I might have been less skeptical if she

hadn't been engaged at least twice before. Cassandra's attitude toward relationships had always seemed to be just like her feelings about careers. You choose one and try it for a few weeks, and if it doesn't immediately turn out to be exactly what you wanted, you chuck the whole thing."

We were both silent for a few minutes, pretending to be busy drinking coffee but each of us lost in our own thoughts. I had no idea what Joan was finding so absorbing, but I was mulling over what she'd told me about her relationship with Cassandra. She had openly admitted that she and her stepdaughter had never gotten along very well, and her honesty made her less of a suspect in my eyes. Still, she didn't seem particularly saddened, aside from the effect the young woman's death was having on her husband, about whom she clearly cared deeply. The idea that she would ever do anything to cause him pain struck me as remote.

Still, I'd misjudged people before.

"What about the last few months?" I finally asked. "What was going on with her? Who was she seeing, what was she doing...what was her life like?"

"Gordon and I only saw what she wanted us to see," Joan replied. "Cassie was an expert at hiding things. As far as we knew, everything was going just swell. She was working for Thorndike Vineyards, selling our wines to high-end restaurants on Long Island and in New York City.

"She and Robert were planning their wedding too. At first, Robert wanted a big, fancy wedding, just like his first marriage. But Cassie insisted on a modest affair, just family and a few friends, and he finally came around. They'd even picked a date: a Sunday afternoon next July. They wanted to get married at the vineyard, under a big white tent. The whole thing sounded absolutely lovely." She sighed deeply. "Somehow, even when she was talking about it—and she talked about it endlessly, in that very intense way she had—there was always this feeling gnawing at me that it would never really come to pass."

As if Coco had been listening in on our conversation and found it completely uninteresting, she suddenly yawned.

"Are you bored, Coco?" Joan asked in soft, cooing voice. "Have we been ignoring you?"

"It looks as if she thinks so," I observed with a smile.

"I can probably get her to do some of her tricks for you," she offered proudly. "At least, if she's in the mood. Let me see if I can get her to cooperate...." She placed the cat on the kitchen floor. "Come on, Coco! Shake a paw!"

I was amazed to see the cat actually extend her paw. I'd rarely seen a feline that eager to please.

"Stand up!" Joan commanded, and Coco balanced on her hind legs like a begging dog.

We were so busy enjoying the cat's antics that we didn't notice that someone else had come into the kitchen until he cleared his throat.

"Gordon!" Joan exclaimed, jumping out of her seat. "I was wondering where you'd gotten to."

She went over to the tired-looking man who was dressed in a faded blue T-shirt and khaki pants, both hanging loosely on his tall, gaunt frame. She planted a kiss on his cheek, then rubbed his back affectionately.

He didn't seem to notice. "Looks like you made coffee," he said flatly. "I was lying down and smelled it all the way upstairs. Mind if I help myself?"

"Please do," Joan replied. "Here, let me get you a mug."

I immediately saw the family resemblance. Gordon Thorndike had the same distinctive blue-green eyes as his daughter. He also had straight black hair, but his was streaked with gray. I wondered how much of the color change had occurred in just the past few days.

"I hope we didn't wake you," Joan said anxiously, handing him an empty mug.

He shook his head sadly. "I wasn't really asleep. Just trying. But I haven't been able to..." His voice trailed off. He leaned forward to pour himself some coffee, his stooped shoulders creating the very image of despondency.

"Goodness, I didn't even introduce our guest," Joan said brightly. "Gordon, this is Dr. Popper. She's a veterinarian who makes house calls. She stopped by to look at Coco. You know she hasn't been herself for the past couple of days."

He didn't respond or even look up. Instead, he shuffled across the room toward the door. "I'll just leave you two to whatever you were doing."

"You're welcome to join us," Joan said hopefully.

He was already on his way out, however, disappearing with as little fanfare as when he'd arrived. In fact, it was almost as if he were fading from the room rather than leaving it.

When I glanced at Joan, I saw that her expression had grown sorrowful. Gazing off into the distance, she said, "I'm really worried about Gordon. You should have seen him at the funeral! If his doctor hadn't pumped him full of Valium, I don't know how he would have gotten through it. He's taking this really hard. Cassandra was the apple of his eye. And having a child die before her parents—well, it's just not what nature intended."

"I can hardly imagine what a terrible time this must be for all of you," I said softly.

My comment seemed to remind her that I wasn't a member of the Thorndike family.

"Oh, dear, I've kept you here much too long," she said. "And you've been too polite to say anything about it. Here, let me write you a check..."

After we'd settled up, she said, "Before you go, could I ask you for one more favor?"

"Of course."

"My stepson has a cat too. But Ethan is really bad about bringing Jenny to the vet. Of course, the fact that she's ridiculously afraid of veterinarians doesn't help. Anyway, since you're already here, I wonder if you could—"

"Just point me in the right direction."

"Thank you so much," Joan said gratefully. "He lives in a small apartment above the garage. Maybe you could just go over and knock on his door. I'm sure he's there."

"Actually, animals are frequently less afraid of women than they are of men," I told her. "So having her treated by a female vet might not be such a bad idea."

"We'll have to see how Ethan feels about that," Joan muttered, more to herself than to me.

She walked me over to the back door and pointed. At the end of the driveway, a few hundred feet behind the house, sat a tired-looking white-shingled building. "Go in through the side door and you'll see a set of stairs," Joan told me. "Ethan's place is at the top. You can just knock. Or yell."

I made my way up the driveway, meanwhile studying the garage. The sagging building appeared to have once been a barn, or maybe a carriage house. At ground level were three garage doors, painted black. Above them, two eaves protruded from the dark-shingled roof, inset with small windows.

Yet there was no indication that anyone was home. No open windows, no blaring music, not even the clinking of dishes. I hoped Ethan wasn't sleeping, since I was about to interrupt him without any warning.

As Joan instructed, I pulled open the side door and stepped inside the garage. Unfortunately, she hadn't mentioned the location of the light switch. The one window I could see was covered with a dark flowered cloth that had been tacked up haphazardly, as if to keep anyone from looking inside. The only other illumination came from dim bands of light shining through the loose slats of the walls.

I blinked a few times, trying to adjust to the gloom. Once I did, I saw several cars lined up inside the long, low interior space: a battered Volvo, a shiny new SUV, and a red pickup truck streaked with rust. Around the edges, the usual assortment of garage paraphernalia was piled up. Lawn furniture, bicycles, an archery target with its stuffing poking out in several spots, sealed-up cardboard cartons whose contents were probably a mystery even to the Thorndikes themselves.

But no staircase. At least, I hadn't located one yet. I stood at the entryway, trying to spot it.

I'd thought I was alone. So I whirled around at the sound of a door slamming.

"Hello?" I called. "Is someone there?"

I'd barely gotten the words out before a head popped into a doorway I now realized opened onto the staircase leading to the apartment above the garage.

"Trespassers aren't welcome here," a strange-sounding voice said.

"I'm not exactly a trespasser," I returned crossly. "In fact, Mrs. Thorndike—Joan—specifically asked me to come out here and find Ethan. Are you Ethan?"

"Now, that's what you call a tricky question."

I took a few steps closer—and realized that the person I was talking to seemed to have an unnaturally small head. Something else struck me as odd: His ears stuck out almost at right angles to his head and his forehead was completely smooth. In fact, the little bit of light that managed to sneak into the garage reflected off it.

"Are you a dummy?" The words popped out before I had a chance to think about what I was saying.

"I don't think there's any reason to be so rude," he replied indignantly. "Maybe we all aren't smart enough to have earned a medical degree, but that doesn't mean other people have a right to call us names."

"I didn't mean—you *are* a dummy!" Now that I'd gotten even closer, I saw that I was right: The person I was talking to wasn't a person after all. It was a large wooden ventriloquist's dummy, his cheeks painted an unnatural shade of pink and his eyes fixed in a frighteningly steady stare. He was dressed in a tuxedo, complete with a bright crimson bow tie and a matching cummerbund.

I was even more astonished when he cried, "Ethan! I could use some help here!"

I jerked backward as a tall, lanky young man joined the dummy in the doorway. In the shadowy darkness, all I could make out was his silhouette.

A chill ran through me at the sound of a click. But it turned out to be nothing more onerous than a flashlight being turned on.

The man's face was now illuminated. However, the fact that he held the light under his chin cast spooky shadows over his face, giving him a ghoulish look. Only his mouth, nose, and the corners of his eyes were lit, making him look as if he were wearing a mask.

Suddenly he moved the flashlight, casting a spotlight on his face. I let out a little gasp. Ethan Thorndike could have been Cassandra's twin, except that he was a slightly more exaggerated version of his sister. While her face was narrow, his was positively gaunt, with a thin, straight nose and pronounced cheekbones. He had Cassandra's dead-straight black hair, which was as sleek and glossy as hers was in her dramatic oil portrait. He also had the same startlingly blue-green eyes as both his father and his sister.

But Ethan's right eye was crossed, making him look a little off. Of course, the fact that he'd chosen such a creepy way to introduce himself added to that impression.

"So *you're* Ethan," I said, not sure whether to laugh or feel annoyed. I turned to his wooden companion. "And *you* . . . you really are a dummy!"

"We don't like visitors," the dummy said rudely.

"This isn't a social call—" I stopped mid-sentence, realizing I was defending myself to Pinocchio. Turning back to Ethan, I said, "Your mother asked me to look at your cat. You already seem to know that I'm a veterinarian."

"Mr. Ed and I like to keep track of who comes and goes," Ethan replied. "We find it . . . *comforting.*"

Mr. Ed? I thought. Why would someone name a dummy after a horse from a classic television series of the 1960s? I'd barely asked myself the question before I realized that a talking doll wasn't that different from a talking horse. So maybe Ethan had a clever streak, after all.

"Now that we've introduced ourselves," I said, trying to reestablish something along the lines of normal conversation, "maybe you can bring your cat—"

"Why are you here?"

"I told you," I said, trying to keep the irritation out of my voice. "Your stepmother asked me to—"

"On our property. Why did you come here today?"

"I ran into Joan at the vineyard, and she asked me to stop by with my clinic-on-wheels." I added, "I'd also like to say that I'm extremely sorry about your sister. What a tragedy that someone so young—"

"You didn't know Cassie, did you?"

His question startled me. "Well, no. Actually, I never—"

"Then you don't know she was a little bit crazy."

"Excuse me?" I asked, not knowing how literally to take him. For all I knew, he was simply playing the role of annoying little brother.

"Craziness runs in our family." In a matter-of-fact tone, he added, "On my mother's side of the family. Not my father's. In fact, my father is about as un-crazy as you can get."

I filed away his comment, wondering if he, too, had inherited what he considered the Thorndike family trait.

"But it's my cat you're interested in, not my family," he continued. "So why don't you come up to my apartment?"

Somehow, that didn't strike me as a particularly good idea.

"Tell you what," I told him evenly. "Why don't you bring your cat out to my van? It's parked right outside. That's where I always examine my patients, unless there are special circumstances."

A few minutes later, Ethan joined me in the driveway—this time, without his doppelganger. Instead, he carried a large calico cat in his arms. I estimated that she weighed at least ten or twelve pounds, a good size for a cat. She had long, fine fur, a beautiful mixture of gray, white, and orange.

"Hey, Jenny," I greeted her in a soft voice.

Ethan looked surprised. "How did you know her name?"

I was tempted to tell him I was as much a master at eavesdropping as he was. Instead, I told the truth. "Your stepmother told me."

"Ah, yes. Leave it to Joan to make sure everyone knows everybody else's business."

So she wasn't exaggerating when she said that Gordon's children had never stopped seeing her as the wicked stepmother.

"Her name is actually Pirate Jenny," Ethan noted as he followed me into my van, sounding a trifle indignant. "You know, from *The Threepenny Opera*? The play by Bertolt Brecht?"

I'd only known Ethan Thorndike for ten minutes. Yet somehow, naming a pet after a character in a musical satire of bourgeois society seemed to fit perfectly. I seemed to recall from my Twentieth-Century Theater class at Bryn Mawr that Pirate Jenny was a prostitute, the merciless Mack the Knife's girlfriend. Pretty heavy stuff for such a cute little kitty.

"Beautiful fur," I commented. "But I bet it mats easily."

Ethan looked surprised that I knew anything at all about cats. "I guess I should tell you that she has a heart murmur," he mumbled.

"Yes, that's important for me to know. Why don't you put her down on the examining table—"

"I suppose you should also know that Jenny isn't particularly fond of veterinarians."

While Joan had mentioned that fact, it was also something I could see for myself. As Ethan lowered her onto the table, she was already doing her best to lean over and bite me.

"Whoa, Jenny. Calm down." Glancing at Ethan, I said, "I don't suppose you brought a toy to distract her with."

"Didn't think of it. She has this furry squirrel toy, with catnip inside, that she spends hours trying to tear apart." He smiled condescendingly. "The vet that usually treats her has been known to sedate her."

"I have a better idea," I told him. I pulled off my polyester fleece jacket and draped it over her head. As soon as I blocked her vision, she quieted down.

"Good trick," Ethan offered begrudgingly.

"You pick up a few if you do this long enough," I replied. I reached over and grabbed the clipboard I kept well-stocked with information forms. "Why don't you fill this out while I get started? Just the usual questions, like name, address, and the animal's medical history."

Ethan took the clipboard but continued to watch what I was doing.

"How does Jenny act around other people?" I asked, partly because I found the way he kept staring at me so unsettling.

"What other people?"

"How about your friends?"

He looked at me strangely. "I don't have a lot of friends. I find that I prefer my own company to most other people's."

"I see," I replied noncommittally.

As I began palpating her organs, he commented, "Jenny hates other cats, too. In fact, we have to make sure we keep her away from Joan's cat. She's done some pretty vicious things—not with Coco, which would totally have freaked out Joan—but with other cats who've come around. She practically killed one. I'm talking ear-tearing, skin-breaking, fur-flying damage. All out war."

"Hmm," I said, making a mental note to put a huge "Caution" tag on Pirate Jenny's chart.

Not that making a follow-up visit was high on my list of priorities.

After finishing my second house call at the Thorndikes', I wasn't feeling particularly encouraged about the progress I was making. True, I'd managed to get my first peek inside Cassandra Thorndike's world by meeting her family. And like many families, hers was fraught with loyalties, rivalries, and tense undercurrents. Joan appeared to mean well, yet it looked as if she'd been cast into the role of Wicked Stepmother from the start. But she'd stuck it out because of her devotion to Gordon, which certainly seemed sincere.

And it was clear to me that Gordon had adored his daughter. His grief further highlighted the tragedy of a young woman who was just getting started with her life being killed. I suspected he'd never recover.

As for Ethan, he was harder to fathom. Was he playing a role for my benefit or was he really as creepy as he seemed? From what Joan had said, I had a feeling I wasn't the only person who was reminded of Norman Bates.

Welcome to another dysfunctional family, I thought ruefully.

My first impressions of the Thorndikes were reinforced by my years as a veterinarian, which had taught me that you could learn a lot about people by their pets. Again and again I'd observed that humans are frequently drawn to animals with personalities that are similar to theirs.

For example, Joan's beloved cat, Coco, was as loyal and affectionate toward her as Joan appeared to be toward her husband. Meanwhile, Ethan's cat, Pirate Jenny, clearly wanted as little to do with both cats and humans as possible. She seemed to prefer being alone— or at least in the company of the one person she felt understood her. And that happened to be someone who, like her, was happy living a hermit's life in a small apartment above a garage.

Yet I still didn't feel I'd learned much about Cassandra herself. Maybe that was because I'd only gotten as far as her roots, without yet finding out much about the direction in which she'd chosen to branch off.

But I had another trick up my polyester sleeve.

Before leaving behind the Thorndikes' homestead, I sat in my van in the driveway for a minute or two, consulting

my trusty Hagstrom map. Once I'd deciphered the maze
of meandering back roads that would serve as a short cut
to the South Fork, I turned on the ignition and veered
back onto Route 35.

It was time to meet Cassandra's fiancé.

Chapter 6

"Thousands of years ago, cats were worshipped as gods. Cats have never forgotten this."

—Anonymous

Thanks to a bit of Web research I'd done early that morning before setting off, I'd learned a few facts about Robert Reese, Suzanne's ex as well as the man Cassandra had decided to settle down with. He had opened his high-end restaurant, Granite, in a building that had already housed a string of similar establishments.

Even though feeding people for profit was a notoriously difficult business, one entrepreneur after another had moved into the same East Brompton location, tried, and failed. Yet there was apparently an endless supply of optimists, including Robert, who knew that the odds were stacked against them but still remained convinced that they could come up with just the right concept, just the right chef, just the right menu, and just the right ambiance. They were certain they could create a restaurant that was so desirable that sophisticated diners from New York City and Long Island would gladly wait five weeks for a reservation, then whip out their charge cards and pay whatever exorbitant sum they were asked to cough up.

It wasn't until I'd pulled my van into a parking lot off Windmill Lane that it occurred to me that I wasn't exactly dressed for the chic Bromptons—even if it was off-season. My black pants were covered in cat hair and my chukka boots looked as if they'd been dipped in mud. The *pièce de résistance* was my navy-blue polyester fleece jacket, which was embroidered with my name instead of some designer's.

Still, I'd come this far. I wasn't about to turn back, especially since I couldn't get the sound of that ticking clock out of my head.

In fact, that relentless *tick-tock, tick-tock* made the fact that I couldn't figure out which of the similar-looking brick buildings surrounding the parking lot was Robert's restaurant even more frustrating. One was clearly a bank, and another housed professional offices. That left two choices. Either they were both guilty of poor signage or I was guilty of extreme denseness.

"Eenie, meenie, miney, mo, catch a monkey... Oh, what the heck." With a shrug, I strode toward the one that happened to be closer to my parking space.

Frowning, I stood outside a windowless wooden front door that was painted black and sealed up tight. I tried the doorknob, not expecting to get very far. Yet while the front door looked like the gates of the Castle of Mordor in *The Lord of the Rings*, it turned out to be unlocked.

I pushed it open, surprised at how heavy it was and thankful that regularly lugging around mastiffs and even the occasional St. Bernard was part of my job description. As I did, I noticed a small black *G* on the front door. It looked as if it had been written by hand, possibly with a pencil.

Looks like understatement is in, I thought wryly. Always something new in the Bromptons.

I stepped inside, blinking a few times before my eyes adjusted to the darkness. Either the restaurant wasn't open for dinner or the décor had been inspired by Dracula. When a meticulously dressed gentleman in his mid-forties rushed over to me, I figured it had to be closed. This struck me as the kind of place that generally ignored whoever came inside for at least a respectable ten minutes or so.

"May I help you?" The man who approached me seemed unable to keep his slender hands from fluttering. He also couldn't stop running them through his spiky hair, which was dark at the roots but had tips that were bleached white. I guess I was getting hungry, because his hairdo reminded me of chocolate and vanilla ice cream. The way his nails caught the light indicated that they were lacquered with clear nail polish. Either that or olive oil played an unusually large part in his diet.

"Is this Granite?" I asked.

He looked stricken. "G," he replied.

I waited politely for whatever would come next: "Gee, yes," or "Gee, no," or even "Gee, willikers." But he just stared at me expectantly, as if it were my turn to speak.

"So this *is* Granite?" I repeated.

"G."

I was losing patience. Either I was missing something or this guy had major communication issues.

Then, sniffing the air in a way that made me stop and think about whether I'd taken the time to shower that morning, he added, "I can see you've never heard of us. It's G—as in the letter *G*. That's our name."

"G is a restaurant?"

He raised his chin a little higher. "G is *the* restaurant. I should know. I own it."

"Sorry. I'm in the wrong place." Deciding to test his reaction, I added, "I'm looking for Granite."

The expression on the man's face became even more disgusted. "Gra—Gra—that *other* place is next door. Gra—that *other* place and our establishment have the terrible misfortune of sharing a parking lot."

"So I noticed."

I looked past him, surveying the restaurant's interior. Now that I'd had a minute or two to fully adjust to the darkness, I could see that it wasn't my eyes that were the problem. It was the fact that just about everything in the place was black. The walls, the wooden chairs, even the fabric on the banquettes. By contrast, the white linen tablecloths were positively blinding. Of course, the tables were set with black dishes, with a black linen napkin neatly folded at each place.

What's on the menu? I wondered. Black bean soup? Blackened catfish? Blackberry tart?

I was tempted to share my cleverness with my charming host, but I got the feeling he didn't possess a particularly well-developed sense of humor.

Besides, he clearly wanted me out of there. "Is there anything else I can help you with?" he asked sharply. His hands still in constant motion, he added, "I'm extremely busy."

"I can see that," I couldn't resist replying, glancing at the rows of empty tables.

"In back," he explained haughtily. "We're preparing for dinner."

"Then I'll leave you to it and let myself out. Thanks for all your help."

Instead of taking me at my word, the owner of G followed a few paces behind. When I opened the door to leave, he let out a yelp. He sounded like he was in pain.

Before I had a chance to say something polite like, "Should I administer CPR?" he moaned, "What is *that*?"

I glanced out the front door, expecting to see something horrifying like a mugging or a carjacking or someone carrying a fake Prada pocketbook. But all I saw was my van. It took me a second or two to realize that was exactly what had elicited his horrified reaction.

"My place of business," I replied coolly. "I'm a veterinarian. See?" I reached into my pocket and pulled out one of my business cards. When he didn't seem the least bit inclined to take it from me, I deposited it on the front desk. "That van out there serves as my clinic."

"Surely you're not planning on keeping that—that *thing* in my parking lot?" he huffed. His face had turned an interesting shade of red, making it the most colorful thing in the entire room. "I don't want it scaring my customers away!"

"I won't be here long," I said crossly. I couldn't resist adding, "Thanks again, pal."

I hurried off, glad to be out of there. Unfortunately, I didn't expect to get any warmer a reception at my real destination.

Granite, I discovered as I stepped into my second restaurant of the day, was well-named. As soon as I walked in, I was confronted with huge slabs of slick, glossy stone. The floor was black granite, streaked with silver and white in a wave pattern, and the walls were speckled gray. Even the front counter was made of granite, making it a formidable fortress that separated the maître d' from the huddled masses yearning to be fed.

The effect was dramatic, but cold. And very primitive. In fact, I half-expected Fred Flintstone to come out of the kitchen hauling a tray of brontosaurus burgers.

Unlike its competitor, Granite was buzzing with activity. A man who was presumably the bartender stood behind the speckled rose-and-gray-granite bar, cutting lemons and limes into neat wedges. Meanwhile, a young woman busily filled each of the vases centered on the tables with three fresh blossoms. From the back, I could hear the kitchen staff bustling around, no doubt engaged in all manner of slicing and dicing as they prepared for the onslaught of the dinner crowd.

Almost immediately, a man about my age strode toward me, the heels of his highly polished shoes clicking purposefully against the smooth, hard floor. He was dressed in a gray suit that looked hand-sewn, if the tiny stitches around the collar were any indication, and his shirt was a dazzlingly bright shade of white. His hair looked painted on, thanks to some kind of hair gel that held each dark brown strand in place.

"How may I help you?" he asked cordially.

"I'm looking for Robert Reese," I said.

"I'm Robert Reese," he said. Just by uttering those simple words, he exhibited a pompousness that made the proprietor of G look like an amateur. Then again, I figured, maybe the ability to make others feel as if they should have slunk in through the service entrance was a qualification for the job.

"My name is Jessica Popper," I said, standing up a little straighter. "I was wondering if I could have a few minutes of your time."

He peered at me more closely, as if he might be trying to figure out just how many minutes of his precious time, if any, I deserved. "You're from ... where?"

I took a deep breath. "I'm a friend of Suzanne's."

His expression instantly changed from aloof to outraged. He grabbed my arm and maneuvered me into a short hallway that, from the looks of things, led to the kitchen.

"How dare you come here!" he cried. "How dare you even speak to me!"

"Mr. Reese—Robert—I understand that you're upset," I said, struggling to keep my voice from wavering.

"But you must listen to me. She is not in any way responsible for what happened to Cassandra. You know Suzanne. You were married to her, for heaven's sake! Surely you must realize there's absolutely no way she could have been involved!"

He stared at me coldly. "I might actually have believed that, at one time. But you're absolutely right when you say that I know Suzanne. We have a long history together, and I'm completely aware of exactly who she is and what she's capable of." He sniffed. "I had my moment of truth, all right—at the expense of my Starsky and Hutch lunch box."

I blinked. "Excuse me?"

"Suzanne knew how much I loved that thing," he said in a low, icy tone. "I carried my lunch to school in it every day from second grade until fifth grade, when lunch boxes became socially unacceptable. When I think of all the peanut butter and Marshmallow Fluff sandwiches my mom made, all those little packets of elf-shaped cookies she tucked in there, just for me..." His voice became too choked to go on. He took a deep breath before adding, "It was one of the few things in my life I've truly treasured."

I just listened, curious about where he could possibly be going with this. But the fire in his eyes told me that, sooner or later, I'd find out.

"And then...and then...when we were almost through with the divorce proceedings and we were dividing up all our stuff—in an extremely civilized manner, I might add—I suddenly remembered it. I'd stored my beloved lunch box in a carton with some of my other valuables."

Like your KISS and Alice Cooper records? I wondered. Or maybe your stash of Pop Rocks?

"I looked for it, but it wasn't where it was supposed to

be," he went on bitterly. "So I asked Suzanne, very calmly, where it was. Do you know what she did?"

I didn't, but I would have bet my clinic-on-wheels that she hadn't whipped out a sharp object and gone berserk.

"She *laughed*! And not just any laugh either. It was a cruel, high-pitched laugh! 'I gave it away,' she said. *She gave it away!*"

I cleared my throat. "Well, obviously that was rather... vengeful. But she was undoubtedly going through a difficult time, with the stress of the divorce and all, and—"

"But that's my point!" Robert insisted. "Suzanne can be vicious! She's capable of things I never would have thought possible! There's no limit to what she can do!"

"Surely you must see there's a difference between getting rid of a lunch box and committing murder!" I cried.

"Is there?" he replied coldly. "Cassandra was my life. I adored her. I loved her like... like no man has ever loved a woman. The two of us clicked the very first time she walked into my restaurant, not long after I told Suzanne I'd had enough of her extreme behavior and wanted out of our marriage.

"I remember meeting Cassandra like it was yesterday. She showed up here wearing a black suit and carrying a briefcase, looking like she was working for Donald Trump instead of her family's winery. Then she launched into her sales pitch, trying to convince me to add Thorndike Vineyards' entire line to my wine list, instead of just their chardonnay and merlot..."

He sighed wistfully. "I even remember every word of our first conversation. We talked about how important it is for restaurants to offer really good wines by the glass, instead of just by the bottle. We agreed on that point one hundred percent. It was clear from the start that we were made for each other."

Funny; I didn't recall the "good-wine-by-the-bottle-versus-by-the-glass" discussion ever being part of my dating history.

"Cassie and I were about to begin a life together as husband and wife," Robert went on with the same intensity. "Don't you see that Suzanne had already demonstrated just how far she was willing to go to hurt me?"

An icy glaze covered his eyes, one that told me he'd frozen me out. "I think you should leave," he said. "Now."

"But Suzanne's entire future is on the line!" I protested.

"I have nothing more to say to either you or Suzanne. Except that I hope she gets exactly what she deserves."

He turned abruptly and stalked off, the staccato clicking of his shoes punctuating his exit. I stood watching him, my head spinning over his unwillingness to even consider the possibility that Suzanne was innocent.

Still, now that he'd made his position clear, I knew I couldn't expect any help from him.

Struggling to catch my breath as a crushing wave of defeat washed over me, I turned to leave. In fact, I'd almost made it to the door when I heard, "Mademoiselle! Wait!"

At least, I thought that was what I heard. Glancing around, I didn't see a soul aside from the members of the restaurant's staff who were focused on setting up for dinner.

"*Attendez*-wait!" This time, I knew I wasn't imagining things. Even I didn't make up voices that spoke in French.

Sure enough—this time, when I looked around, I spotted a stout, fortyish man with the same chubby cheeks and soft tummy as the Pillsbury Doughboy peering out at me from the door that opened into the kitchen. He was also wearing the same kind of chef's toque the little guy from the TV ads wore, along with a crisp white apron.

"Come inside," he insisted, beckoning with his hand. "I would like to talk weeth you."

I scanned the restaurant, making sure Robert Reese was nowhere in sight. Then I ducked into what turned out to be the back of the kitchen. Because the spacious cooking area was L-shaped, the rest of the staff couldn't see us.

"Are you the chef?" I asked, noticing that he seemed to have staked out this part of the kitchen for himself. A huge stainless-steel bowl was filled with flour. A second one, not quite as large, contained a mountain of eggs. In between, rolled out on the counter, was a thin circle of dough as big as a pizza. Other ingredients—a mound of cocoa, a basket of plump red strawberries—sat in wait.

"I am zee pastry chef," he replied in a thick French accent. "Jean-Luc Le Bec. But please, call me Jean-Luc." He picked up a tray of the most delectable pastries I'd ever seen in my life. "Napoleon?"

"Thanks, but not before dinner." I was tempted, but somehow, I had the feeling that one of Robert Reese's key employees hadn't sneaked me into his kitchen for the sole purpose of impressing me with his puff pastry.

He glanced around nervously. "I overheard what Robert said to you about hees great love for Cassandra."

Eavesdropping? I liked this man already. "Yes?" I prompted.

"Perhaps thees is not my business, but I cannot stand by while terrible lies are being told." He leaned closer, lowering his voice to a hoarse whisper. I was pretty sure I could smell chocolate on his breath. "The truth is that Robert and Cassandra, they would fight like—how do you say—cats and dogs. *Sacré bleu*, they break up all the time! The wedding ees on, the wedding ees off..." He shrugged helplessly. "Those of us who know them both, we are never sure eef they are madly in love or the worst of enemies. And we are certainly not one hundred percent certain that thees wedding will really take place."

"I see." And I did see. While it had occurred to me before that Robert Reese could have had something to do with his fiancée's murder, he'd suddenly moved into a *primo* spot on my list of suspects. "Monsieur Le Bec, do you remember—"

"Jean-Luc," he insisted.

"Jean-Luc." Just saying his name required using muscles in my cheeks I hadn't even realized I possessed. "Jean-Luc, do you remember any conversations Robert and Cassandra had right before she was murdered? Did they argue? Or talk about the wedding or . . . or their relationship?"

He frowned pensively. "I know they recently had a terrible fight about what kind of icing to use between the layers of the wedding cake. *Moi*, I refused to get involved. When the bride wants whipped cream and the groom prefers buttercream, there ees no doubt that the situation is going to become—how do you say—zee explosion!"

Maybe in your world, I thought, careful not to let my disappointment show. "Was there anything else you heard them talking about—perhaps last weekend?"

Once again, he glanced around. My heart began to pound. I was sure the happy couple had to have disagreed on *something* a little more important than which combination of fats and carbohydrates would be most appropriate for celebrating the beginning of their life together.

"Last Sunday, I overheard Cassandra arguing with Robert." Jean-Luc pronounced the name the French way, with the accent on the second syllable: Ro-*bear*. "They were fighting about the best way of dealing with Preston DeVane."

"Who?"

Jean-Luc sniffed. "Preston DeVane, the owner of G."

Aha! I thought. So I wasn't the only one who found the restaurateur next door to be less than neighborly.

"The man ees a total fraud," Jean-Luc hissed, waving his arms in the air histrionically. "He tells everyone he studied cooking in Paris. He forgets to add that he's referring to Paris, Texas, and that his training consisted of taking a class in—how do you say—zee adult education."

I could understand how such a misrepresentation could be a serious threat to the public's confidence in the man's meringues. But I didn't get how Cassandra and Robert fit in.

"But what did that have to do with Granite?" I asked.

"Cassandra was insisting that Robert should sue him. But Robert, he said that fighting him in the courts would only—how do you say—aggravate zee situation."

"And what exactly was 'the situation'?" I asked, my curiosity piqued.

Jean-Luc shook his head and clucked in a way that only a Frenchman can cluck. Or a chicken. "Preston DeVane is a truly wicked man."

My ears pricked up like Max's when he hears me use the word *ride* in a sentence. Calling someone "wicked" was fightin' words, at least where I come from. I had the feeling it was pretty much the same *en France*.

"Do you mean... he's rude?" I already knew the answer to that question.

"*Nom de dieu*, eet is much worse than that! He has done the *most* unethical things," Jean-Luc sputtered. "I have actually seen him—weeth my own eyes!—standing outside as our waitstaff was leaving za building late at night. I see heem in our parking lot!"

"To scare them?" I asked, confused.

"To offer them more money! He has stolen from us two of our best waiters...and...and..." He stopped, closing his eyes and drawing his puffy lips into a straight line. "He stole our sous-chef!"

"Shocking," I said, giving a little cluck of my own. While I recognized that the restaurateur next door was guilty of unethical behavior, I was disappointed that his past crimes weren't a little more extreme.

"And that ees not all!" Jean-Luc continued. "He has come here, acting as eef he were just another customer!"

No law against that, I thought. But I could see from the crazed look in Jean-Luc's eyes that, to him, this was a major infraction.

"He has ordered everything on the menu, and then tasted...just a leetle! Just enough so he can steal all our ideas!" A venomous look crossed his face. "Even my signature dessert, my crème brûlée with chocolate drizzle and raspberry compote. The next thing you know, I read in the *New York Times* that G is now featuring an innovative new dessert, crème brûlée with chocolate drizzle and *strawberry* compote. I am telling you, there ees no end to what Preston DeVane will do to destroy Granite!"

"That's horrible!" I exclaimed, doing my best to sound sympathetic.

I had to admit that I'd never really thought of the restaurant business as dog-eat-dog. But Jean-Luc's comments were putting it in a whole new light. The industry was apparently fraught with pressures, from impressing reviewers to pleasing demanding customers to coming up with unique ways of combining sugar and fat. And here I'd thought all a restaurant had to do to succeed was serve up a decent meal.

And given this cutthroat climate, Preston DeVane certainly sounded like trouble. Deciding that it made sense to take a closer look at him and his restaurant, I added *Have dinner at G* to my mental To Do list.

Still, pouring a little chocolate syrup over crème brûlée and tossing a few strawberries onto the plate was a far cry from murdering your competitor's fiancée.

• • •

As I turned off Minnesauke Lane and onto the long driveway that led to my cottage, I realized that my foray to the East End had left me exhausted. My head was spinning from all the people I'd met and the conversations I'd had, first at Thorndike Vineyards, then at the Thorndikes' home, and finally at the two restaurants I'd visited in East Brompton. I couldn't wait to share it all with Nick—not only everything I'd learned, but also the big white box of pastries that Jean-Luc had insisted on sending home with me, enough napoleons and éclairs and other luscious-looking pastries to keep my late-afternoon cup of coffee from getting lonely for a long, long time.

It felt surprisingly good to walk into my cottage and find him sitting on the couch, looking very much at home. The prospect of us living together, which I would have expected would make me break out in hives, was turning out to seem less terrifying than I thought. After all, it seemed like such a practical solution to the crisis surrounding Nick's living arrangements, especially since it was only temporary.

Besides, there was something to be said for having a human being excited about me coming home, instead of just members of the canine, feline, and avian groups.

Of course, officially saying hello to Nick had to wait until I'd gone through Max and Lou's usual greeting. As always, they both stuck their noses through the front door even before I'd gotten it open, so anxious to give me the greeting they felt I deserved that they fell all over each other, their paws skittering across the wooden floor. Lou had an advantage, since his gangly legs were so much longer than Max's. But Max was a terrier, and terriers never give up.

"Hey, you guys!" I cooed. "I missed you, too!" I crouched down to give them each equal attention, glad I had two hands. They jumped all over me, covering me with wet doggy kisses and nearly knocking me over.

"Back so soon?" Nick asked, glancing up from the huge textbook that sat in his lap along with Tinkerbell. Cat lay on the couch beside him, her body pressed against his thigh. He glanced at his watch, then let out a surprised yelp. "Whoa! Is it that late already?"

"Don't tell me you've been sitting in that spot all day, studying!" I cried.

His bleary eyes told me that he'd done exactly that.

"I bet you didn't even stop for lunch," I accused, holding the cardboard box high in the air to keep my Dalmatian from leaving nose prints in the whipped cream. "Fortunately, I brought provisions."

Nick placed Tink on a cushion, stood up, and stretched. "What have you got there?"

"Enough goodies for a garden party. I met a very friendly pastry chef."

I was about to put my calorie-laden booty on the table, but Nick was only too happy to relieve me of it. As soon as he opened the box, his face lit up like it was Christmas morning.

"Whoa! Have I died and gone to heaven?"

"No, but if you eat all these, you might do exactly that."

"St. Peter, here I come!" He plopped back down on the couch and put the box on the coffee table, studying its contents as intently as if they were torts, not tarts.

While I retrieved a couple of forks from the kitchen,

Nick reached for a slice of cheesecake swirled with what looked like blueberry and raspberry purees. "Check this out," he said gleefully. "Red, white, and blue cheesecake. Who thinks up these things?" With one bite, he reduced it to half its size. "Wow, this is amazing stuff. So where did you meet this pastry chef?"

I had a feeling he wasn't going to like my answer nearly as much as the doggy bag I'd come home with. "I stopped by Granite today. Robert Reese's restaurant."

His eyebrows shot up to his hairline.

"I knew I was taking a chance," I added quickly. "But I figured I'd lay my cards on the table. I told Robert I was Suzanne's friend and that I was absolutely convinced she had nothing to do with Cassandra's murder."

"And?" Nick asked.

I took a deep breath. "He's absolutely convinced that she did. In fact, he practically threw me out."

"Before or after you raided his dessert cart?"

"These were a gift from Jean-Luc Le Bec, his pastry chef."

"And what made him so friendly?"

"Apparently Jean-Luc overheard my conversation with Robert. He wanted to set me straight on the realities of the happy couple's relationship."

"You mean they weren't such a happy couple, after all?"

"Exactly. To use Jean-Luc's words, Robert and Cassandra fought like cats and dogs."

"Interesting. Since you're a vet, he probably wanted to explain it in terms he knew you'd understand." By this point, the cheesecake confection was history. Grabbing a fork, Nick started to attack the coffee-colored crème brûlée dotted with chocolate-covered coffee beans, then reconsidered. Instead, he took an impressively large bite out of a small foil dish of bread pudding smothered with cinnamon and dripping with whipped cream.

He'd barely licked the surplus gobs of cream off his lips before he asked, "Was it your impression that these little spats of theirs were intense enough that, oh, I don't know, one of the puppies or kittens in question finally whipped out a knife and did the other one in?"

"It certainly makes you think," I replied. "But Robert's not the only person I've added to my list of suspects. Jean-Luc also gave me an earful about the restaurateur next door, Robert's number-one competitor. His name is Preston DeVane—and apparently he isn't exactly in the running for Businessman of the Year. It seems Cassandra was angry enough with him that she was trying to talk Robert into suing him."

"In other words," Nick interjected, "this DeVane guy has become a person of interest in your eyes."

"Or at least warrants closer investigation," I said. "I'd like to check out DeVane's restaurant, G, a little more closely. And I know the perfect way to do it. I've been trying to come up with a way of getting Suzanne's mind off her troubles, and I think a night out at G may be just the thing. She deserves a break."

I was silent for a few moments as I worked on the crème brûlée. But instead of thinking about DeVane and Jean-Luc, my thoughts drifted to another aspect of the case that raised a lot of questions: the three clues the murderer had left behind. A classic novel, a stuffed animal, a sneaker...

It occurred to me that Nick could have insights into what the book might mean. After all, he hadn't only majored in English in college; he'd earned a master's degree by writing a thesis on Edgar Allan Poe. The man knew American literature in a way I never would.

"Nick," I began, choosing my words cautiously, "what do you know about *The Scarlet Letter*?"

"The Nathaniel Hawthorne novel?"

"One and the same."

"It's about hypocrisy, for one thing. And adultery, of course. It's the story of a minister, Reverend Dimmesdale, who fathered an illegitimate child but remains silent while the mother of his child, Hester Prynne, is shunned by Puritan society. She has to wear a scarlet *A* for *adulteress*, while he merely suffers in silence."

Hypocrisy. Adultery. Maybe that was what the murderer was alluding to by leaving the book for the police to find.

But no matter how hard I tried to picture a cold-blooded killer scanning the shelves, searching for a book with a particular theme, I couldn't do it. It just didn't make sense. Even if he or she was exceptionally calm and calculating, the idea of lingering at a crime scene long enough to assemble a group of objects after committing a brutal murder just didn't sound plausible.

I could feel the gears in my brain grinding away madly. And then something that felt very much like a jolt of electricity shot through my entire body.

"Wait a minute!" I cried. "What if it wasn't the murderer who left those three clues? What if it was Cassandra?"

Nick frowned. "I'm not following. *What* three clues?"

I decided it was time to spill the beans. Or at least to explain the beans I'd already spilled. "Forrester—the reporter—told me the police found three clues arranged together at the crime scene: a copy of *The Scarlet Letter,* a stuffed rabbit, and a running shoe. They assumed the murderer had left them behind.

"But maybe it was Cassandra who grabbed the sneaker and the book and the bunny and made sure the cops would find them at the crime scene," I went on, speaking just a little too fast. "And maybe the message she was trying to send us had something to do with adultery or hypocrisy, since they're the two main themes of the book. Maybe she'd had an affair and her lover had something to do with her being murdered. Or maybe someone who knew about the affair, or who had been hurt by it in some way. Robert is the most likely candidate, of course, but what about the spouse or girlfriend of whoever she was carrying on with?"

"The lover's jealous lover," Nick commented. "Now this is starting to get interesting." He paused. "But wasn't she about to marry Suzanne's ex?"

"Yes," I replied. "Robert Reese."

"Then how likely is it that she would have been having an affair?"

I thought about Joan Thorndike's characterization of her stepdaughter as someone who flitted from one thing to another whenever the going got the least bit tough. I also remembered Jean-Luc's comments about her tempestuous relationship with Robert. "From what I've learned about Cassandra, I don't think it's out of the question. She might have seen it as simply enjoying one last fling before settling down."

"Assuming she even viewed marriage as 'settling down,'" Nick noted. "Not everyone sees it that way."

"Good point. It could also have been a past affair," I mused. "Something that happened a while ago. Maybe the guy's wife or girlfriend just found out."

I was growing increasingly excited over the possibility that Cassandra had had an illicit liaison at some point, which would have explained why she'd left behind a copy of *The Scarlet Letter* to link her murder to the affair.

And she certainly wouldn't have been the first person to have a secret relationship turn around and bite her in the butt.

"But why wouldn't she have just written it down?" I mused. Almost instantly, I answered my own question.

"The desk! The chaotic condition of the desk! Maybe the clutter wasn't the result of a struggle between Cassandra and her attacker, the way the police assumed. Maybe after her attacker left her for dead, she pulled herself up, made it over to the desk, and tried to grab paper and a pen. But she was too weak or . . . or too disoriented, and the more she flailed around, the more impossible it became for her to put her hands on writing supplies. So she grabbed those three items instead." I could picture the whole scene in my head.

"Makes sense," Nick said earnestly. "And if you want my opinion, it's that her fiancé killed her. When I was in the P.I. business, I can't tell you how many cases I worked on that involved a husband or wife trying to find out if their spouse was having an affair. Sometimes the person who hired me was so furious over the prospect of being cheated on that I was reluctant to give them a definitive answer."

Grimacing, he added, "One more reason I decided to get out of the business. But from what I saw in the days I was poking around in other people's personal lives, my theory is that Robert found out about that 'one last fling'—or maybe the past affair, which pushed his buttons, for some reason—and went nuts."

His theory certainly made sense. The problem was, so did a lot of the other theories that had been slowly forming in my head.

"Enough!" Nick suddenly cried, pushing the pastry box out of the way. I wasn't sure if he was talking about murder or butterfat. "I put in a long, hard day of studying, and I need a break."

"Oh, yeah?" I asked flirtatiously. "What have you got in mind?"

"Come a little closer and I'll show you."

I kicked off my shoes and curled up next to him. "Is

that before or after you wipe that whipped cream off your cheek?"

"Funny you mentioned whipped cream," he said, reaching for me, "because I've got a few ideas about how we can put some of it to good use."

"Sweet," I murmured. My remark had nothing to do with Jean-Luc's desserts.

• • •

"I hope this wasn't a mistake," I commented nervously the following evening, scanning the crowd that had converged upon G. Most of them fit right in with the depressing décor, since dressing in black seemed like a requirement—a little piece of the Manhattan lifestyle that had apparently drifted east. By comparison, my outfit of a lavender silk blouse and dark purple pants was positively garish. "For all I know, they're not even going to show up."

When I'd first come up with the idea of Suzanne, Marcus, Nick, and me going out to dinner, getting Suzanne out of the house for at least a few hours had seemed like a real brainstorm. I couldn't forget the image of her all alone in her dark living room, sitting in a rocker without rocking.

But now, as I took in all the chaos of the restaurant—the waiters and busboys whirling by, the deafening chatter and laughter and clinking of glasses, the aroma of the other patrons' perfume mixed in with food smells—I wasn't so sure. It all seemed so overwhelming.

"Relax, Jess," Nick insisted. "I think this was a great idea. They're probably just running a little behind schedule. You said yourself that Marcus warned you that he probably wouldn't get here on time. Here comes our waiter. Let's order a bottle of wine."

As I was telling myself that the worst that could happen was that Nick and I would simply have dinner alone,

I noticed Suzanne weaving her way through the crowd toward our table.

"Sorry I'm late," she said breathlessly.

Nick glanced up, his polite expression instantly morphing into a look of astonishment. "Wow!"

I had to agree. Here I'd been worried that if Suzanne showed up at all, she might be wearing a bathrobe and a pair of bunny slippers. Instead, she looked as if she'd gone all out for our little night on the town. Her flamered hair had been brought back to life, or at least washed and styled by a professional. From the looks of things, the pros had also worked on her hands, creating ten perfect scarlet tips so shiny they still looked wet. Her makeup was a bit on the heavy side, by my standards—the luminous lip gloss, the thick coating of mascara—yet even I had to admit that the effect was dazzling. Then there was her dress, a clingy emerald-green number that fit her voluptuous curves the way a casing fits a sausage. The strappy black patent leather high heels were just the right touch.

Yet one element of her outfit struck me as out of place: a small gold heart-shaped locket that I'd never seen before. It looked like something a little girl would wear. A present from Marcus, I suspected.

"You look great!" I told her sincerely.

She forced a little smile as she sank onto the banquette next to me. "Thanks. I figured I'd go all out. That maybe looking good would help me feel better."

I didn't have the courage to ask if it was working.

"How are you doing?" I asked solicitously.

She responded by shaking her head. "We're not talking about any of that tonight. For once, I'd just like to take a break from—" She stopped mid-sentence and glanced around the restaurant. "No sign of Marcus?"

"Not yet." Quickly, I added, "He probably hit traffic."

"Right." Suzanne grabbed her napkin and, with a snap, flattened it and spread it on her lap. "So, Nick, how's law school?"

"It's great—especially if you're the kind of person who enjoys having surgery done without an anesthetic."

I laughed, glad that the tension was dissipating. Maybe this really is what the doctor ordered, I thought.

Good old Nick. He launched into one hilarious anecdote after another, describing his quirky law professors, the details of some of the more bizarre cases he'd studied, and the eccentric people in his study group. I laughed along with him and Suzanne, but kept sneaking peeks at my watch.

Where is Marcus? I thought, noting that he was over half an hour late. At the very least, doesn't the man own a cell phone? The three of us had already gone through a bottle of wine. The waiter, meanwhile, kept hovering near our table, no doubt agonizing over how he'd ever manage to squeeze in a second seating.

My annoyance was forming a knot in the pit of my stomach. Still, it was better than the other emotion I was trying hard to suppress: the fear that Marcus was about to disappoint Suzanne, big time.

When I finally heard his familiar voice booming, "…I'm meeting some friends, including an incredibly foxy lady—oh, there they are!" I didn't know if I felt like throwing my arms around him in relief or reading him the riot act.

I did neither. "Hey!" I called, plastering on a big smile. "We were about to send out a search party!"

"Tell me about it," he replied, pulling out his chair. Like Suzanne, Marcus had pulled out all the stops this evening. Then again, he always looked pretty well-groomed, a by-product of his vanity. The fact that he was exceptionally tall helped, although I always found him to be pretty gawky—if not out-and-out geeky. He was wearing what I knew he thought was his "cool" outfit: jeans and a white T-shirt, along with a sports jacket. His blond hair was cut short, little more than stubble.

"Parking in this town's an absolute bitch," Marcus grumbled as he sat down. "You'd think that now that all the tourists have gone home..." He leaned forward and gave Suzanne a perfunctory peck on the cheek. "Hey, babe. How's it going?"

My eyebrows jumped. Was I just imagining that there was a distance as wide as the Grand Canyon between them? I glanced over at Nick, anxious to see if he was reading what I was reading. At the moment, however, the only thing he seemed to be reading was the menu.

"Hey, this appetizer sampler, the Seafood Sonata, looks good," he said. "Lobster, shrimp, scallops...four different dipping sauces...I say let's go for it."

Thank goodness for food, I thought. The ultimate distraction. And the four of us actually managed to get through another bottle of wine—with most of the credit for our accomplishment going to Marcus—as well as our salads and appetizers before any mention of Suzanne's situation snuck into the conversation.

I was telling a story about a dog I'd recently performed surgery on after he'd eaten bread dough—the yeast ferments in the animal's stomach, causing alcohol toxicosis—when Nick turned to Suzanne and asked, "How's the vet business?"

Instead of answering, Suzanne glanced at Marcus. From the look on both their faces as their eyes locked, I knew we'd just crossed into dangerous territory.

"I've closed my practice," Suzanne said somberly.

"No!" I cried.

"It's only temporary," she replied, sounding strangely matter-of-fact. "Just for now, I'm referring all my clients to Marcus. There's no way I feel up to working. Ever since the police showed up at my house last week, acting as if I were the murderer, I've just been too upset. So I decided to take a little time off."

I glanced over at Nick. He looked as horrified as I felt. If something as dramatic as closing down one's place of business didn't spell guilt, especially in the eyes of the police, I didn't know what did.

"Does your lawyer think that's a good idea?" I asked cautiously. "It might be better to act as if nothing in your life has changed."

"I agree with Jessie," Nick added. "Proceeding with your life the way you normally do might be the best thing."

"Jerry didn't really seem to have an opinion," Suzanne said uncertainly. She grabbed a roll. With nervous, jerky movements, she began pulling off piece after piece and stuffing them into her mouth.

"Hey, Jerry's the best lawyer there is," Marcus insisted. "If he thinks it's okay, then I'd go with that. You gotta trust the guy's instincts. I mean, he's been doing this for, what, ten or twelve years?"

Personally, I'd have preferred a lawyer who'd been "doing this" for twenty or thirty. Not to mention one who actually had a track record as a criminal lawyer. Helping immigrants with the paperwork required for a green card was fine. Defending an innocent woman who the police suspected of murder was something else entirely.

Still, I knew that Jerry Keeler was here to stay, at least for now. I grabbed a roll of my own and began scarfing it down. When the going gets tough, I always say, go for the carbs.

"Besides," Marcus went on, speaking a little too loudly for the intimate space we were in, "I don't think there's anything to worry about. We all know that Suzanne's innocent. There's no way she had anything to do with what happened to Cassandra Thorndike. So I think we should all relax. After all, why shouldn't justice prevail? Why should we believe for even a moment that anyone would ever be capable of convincing a jury of twelve clear-headed, objective, intelligent individuals that Suzanne did something she's obviously incapable of even *thinking* about doing?"

Dead silence fell over our table. When I dared glance over at Nick, I saw that he was poised to speak. But then he snapped his mouth shut, as if he knew only too well what he was dealing with. Suzanne, meanwhile, had tears in her eyes. Tears of joy or maybe even gratitude, I surmised from the way she was looking at Marcus.

My hero! she seemed to be thinking.

I was glad that our waiter chose that moment to come over with our entrees. Focusing on who'd ordered the Thai Pepper-Crusted Ahi Tuna with Wasabi Ginger Ponzu and who got the Fettuccine Jambalaya in Cajun Tomato Cream Sauce was much easier than listening to Marcus Scruggs's diatribe on the effectiveness of the American judicial system.

Especially since the question of whether or not justice was likely to prevail loomed so dreadfully close to home.

In fact, it wasn't until I'd eaten my way through what I had to admit was probably one of the best meals I'd ever encountered that I remembered that I'd dragged my posse to G for more than the Wasabi Ginger Ponzu—or even to get Suzanne out of the house. The dessert list that the waiter presented to us with high drama was a great reminder. In fact, as I scanned it, my blood ran as cold as the strawberry drizzle that apparently accompanied the vanilla bean gelato.

I waited until Marcus was monopolizing Suzanne's attention with a long, detailed anecdote that, not surprisingly, centered around him. Then I whispered, "Nick, do you notice anything interesting about the dessert menu?"

"You mean aside from the fact that it doesn't include a warning from the Surgeon General?"

"Look at it carefully," I insisted. "Does it sound familiar?"

"Raspberry–Blueberry Swirl Cheesecake," Nick mumbled, reading aloud. "Cinnamon Brioche Bread Pudding. Espresso Crème Brûlée with Chocolate Coffee Beans." Slowly, a look of comprehension crossed his face. "Now that you mention it, this list does sound a lot like an inventory of the box of goodies you brought home yesterday."

"Exactly what I was thinking."

"So there's one of two things going on here," Nick said. "Either your friend Jean-Luc is in cahoots with the pastry chef here at G—"

"Impossible!" I interrupted. "Jean-Luc told me Preston is a fraud—not to mention a thief who steals his competition's recipes, employees, and anything else he can get his hands on. He hates Preston's guts. Although, being French, I suspect he'd put it more delicately."

"Okay," Nick said. "Another possibility is that every restaurant on the East End has pretty much the same repertoire."

"There *is* a third possibility," I told him. "The one Jean-Luc complained to me about. And that's that Preston DeVane has been robbing him blind. Not only has he been stealing his staff; he's also been stealing his desserts. Jean-Luc told me he'd co-opted one recipe, but I had no idea he'd stolen all of them."

"Hmm," Nick said thoughtfully. "Sounds as if there may be a dessert war going on."

I had to agree that that sounded like a distinct possibility. In fact, I was starting to see Dr. Atkins's warnings about the dangers of carbohydrates in a whole new light.

•　•　•

"What did you think?" I asked Nick as we drove west along Sunset Highway, leaving the East End behind.

"The food was great, but I shouldn't have had the appetizer. It was too much, even though that was the most incredible shrimp—"

"Not the restaurant," I interrupted. "Suzanne. And Marcus."

Nick cast me a wary glance from the driver's seat. "You know I'd rather have a root canal than spend an evening with that guy. As for Suzanne, she seems to be holding up okay. Why? What did you think?"

I remained silent for a minute or two, thinking. On the surface, the evening appeared to have gone just fine, although Nick was right about eating too much. Yet I'd definitely picked up on an undercurrent between Marcus and Suzanne. Or, more accurately, from Marcus to Suzanne. Something was going on from his end, and I suspected that it wasn't good.

"I guess it went okay," I finally said in response to Nick's question. It was easier than getting into a long explanation—and safer than voicing my fears.

"I'm pooped, and I've got to get to school early tomorrow," he announced after we'd gotten home and performed the usual ritual of greeting each of my pets, letting the dogs out, and checking all the water bowls. "I'm going to bed. Care to join me?"

"In a few minutes. I'm still wound up from the evening. I think I'll check my e-mail."

"Don't hesitate to give me a poke," Nick offered. "Just because I'm snoring, that doesn't mean I'm not available for entertainment purposes."

His eyes were so bleary and he was yawning so much that I already knew I wouldn't take him up on his offer. "Okay, hot stuff. I'll be in soon."

I scooped up Cat before sitting down at my desk, then

gently positioned her in my lap. She purred, letting me know she was grateful for the company.

"How's my favorite pussycat?" I asked, stroking her soft fur as my computer booted up. Tinkerbell didn't seem to mind. She was too busy rolling around at my feet, batting a thread that had come loose from my sock. I was noticing that while Tink had absolutely no problem bossing the dogs around, there was clearly no doubt in her mind who was top cat. She also kept her distance from Prometheus. I didn't blame her. The mere sight of his no-nonsense beak was enough to keep anybody in line.

I scanned the list of new mail in my in-box, noting that I'd received a few messages from the usual array of friends, veterinary organizations, and purveyors of various drugs and devices designed to work wonders on any substandard body parts I might own.

But there was one name I didn't recognize. The e-mail address was intriguing: AGoodFriend@emailsystems.com.

I checked the subject line. It read, *Hey, Jess. Thought you'd enjoy this.*

Somebody I know? I thought, grabbing the mouse and moving the cursor to that line. Or some clever Web marketer trying to get my attention?

When I double-clicked, the computer paused to load what looked like images of some kind. The text was already visible, however.

Hey, Jessica Popper!

Sorry we didn't get a chance to speak the other day. But I thought you'd get a kick out of these.

You'll hear from me again. I promise.

Odd, I thought, wondering who'd written such a strange e-mail. I waited while the graphics loaded, figuring this would turn out to be from some obvious person like Suzanne or even Marcus who was sending me a list of the Top Ten something or other.

But when the images finally finished loading, I was simply confused. And then my stomach lurched as I realized what I was looking at.

The photographs were of me. I was wearing my navy-blue jacket, just as I had every day this week. From the small amount of scenery I could make out in the background, they looked as if they'd been taken somewhere on the East End.

And I'd had no idea they were being taken.

"What *is* this?" I asked aloud, even though no one around me was likely to answer, aside from Prometheus.

I quickly clicked down past the three photographs, hoping to find a name at the bottom of the page. Nothing. I still had no clue as to who had sent me this e-mail. My mouth uncomfortably dry, I scrolled back to the top to study the photographs more carefully.

The first one was a close-up of my face, taken in profile. Whoever took it had been standing behind me, since most of the shot was of my back. Still, the top half of my body pretty much filled the frame.

Which meant the photographer either had a good zoom lens or had been standing very close to me.

In the second one, my mouth was open and I wore a peculiar expression, since I'd apparently been caught mid-sentence. I was talking to someone, although whoever it was hadn't been included in the picture. Just me.

Nothing wrong with that, I insisted to myself, trying to ignore the gnawing in my stomach.

It was the third one that made me gasp. Me again, standing in front of my van. I recognized the setting as the parking lot outside both G and Granite, which meant it had been taken yesterday. In the photograph, I was pulling my keys out of my pocket, getting ready to leave.

I remembered that moment clearly. I'd thought I was alone. Obviously, I was dead wrong.

Somebody was watching me.

Chapter 7

"Cats are smarter than dogs. You can't get eight cats to pull a sled through snow."

—Jeff Valdez

The uneasy feeling that came from having discovered that someone was keeping tabs on my comings and goings lingered into the next morning. And the fact that that person had managed to get to me in my own home as I sat alone in the wee hours increased the creepiness factor by about a hundred.

I replayed the last few days in my mind, trying to remember who I'd given my business card to. But then I realized my cards weren't the only way someone could get hold of my e-mail address. All they had to do was enter my name into a search engine like Google or Yahoo!, and my Web site address would come up. Then, they could click on *Contact Us* and, as Jean-Luc would say, "Voilà!"

Still, I decided not to say anything to Nick. At least, not yet. I knew perfectly well that he wasn't crazy about my involvement in investigating Cassandra Thorndike's murder and that the only reason he was being at all supportive was that he recognized the importance of proving Suzanne's innocence. The last thing I wanted was for him to worry any more than he already had. Especially since he was under so much pressure himself, thanks to the demands of law school.

As I drove to the North Fork to make a few calls and do a little more nosing around, I ruminated over who my secret friend might be. Driving on the Long Island Expressway was pretty monotonous at times like this, when mercifully little traffic clogged the three eastbound lanes of the dead-straight highway. It afforded me the perfect opportunity to consider each of the members of the murder victim's circle I'd already met, one by one.

I started with her family, even though I found it hard to believe that any of them could be involved. Joan Thorndike, Cassandra's stepmother, made no bones about the fact that she and her stepdaughter hadn't been on the best of terms. Even though I liked her, I couldn't completely discount her as a possible suspect. I couldn't say the same for Gordon. He was clearly distraught over his daughter's tragic fate. As for Ethan, he struck me as weird enough that anything was possible.

Next on the list were the people Cassandra knew through her fiancé—starting with the man himself. While I tried to remain open-minded about Robert Reese, now that I'd met him I couldn't help suspecting him. Anyone who could get that upset over a lunch box—a Starsky and Hutch lunch box, no less—had to possess at least a few screws that were badly in need of tightening. Besides, spouses and boyfriends were always key suspects in situations like this.

Then there were the other people Cassandra had associated with through her involvement with the family business, as well as through her relationship with Robert. According to Jean-Luc, Preston DeVane, the arrogant owner of G and Robert's number-one competitor, was pretty much capable of anything. Just how big a leap was it from stealing crème brûlée recipes to bumping off a business rival's fiancée?

Even Jean-Luc could have done it, I mused, instinctively stepping on the brake as I noticed a cop car by the side of the Expressway, lying in wait. Maybe all that sugar in his bloodstream got him a little too hyped up during an argument with Cassandra over how much raspberry drizzle was *too* much raspberry drizzle.

My list of suspects was already fairly long. And at this point, I simply didn't know enough about Cassandra or the people in her world to know who else to add. Virginia Krupinski, Theo Simcox, even someone I hadn't actually met but who had noticed what I was up to—any one of them could have sent me that eerie e-mail.

Fortunately, a morning filled with house calls took my mind off Cassandra's murder, at least for a few hours. It felt good to lose myself in treating animals, since I never failed to find it endlessly rewarding. As usual, it was refreshing to throw myself into the absorbing task of dealing with one patient after another. While being in the company of humans has its rewards, I've always found that surrounding myself with animals provides me with a level of emotional fulfillment that I can't get anywhere else.

It wasn't until I glanced at my watch and saw it was almost one that I realized how hungry I was. I also had a long break in my schedule, which I'd built in to allow for a bit of exploring on the North Fork.

For all I know, I thought as I turned into Clyde's Roadside Inn, I might stumble across Captain Kidd's treasure. Of course, I'd be much happier finding Cassandra Thorndike's killer.

It wasn't coincidence that my grumbling stomach prompted me to pull into Clyde's. Theo Simcox's comment about his plans to spend his Saturday night there gave me the impression he was a regular. I figured a man who described himself as a "lonely bachelor" could well have staked out a neighborhood eatery as a place where he could regularly find a little homeyness. With a little more of that "luck" that seemed to be going around, I might even run into him. I hoped he might be able to help me learn more about Cassandra's involvement in the family business.

Clyde's did, indeed, look every inch the roadside inn. Unpainted cedar shingles that had been darkened by weather and time covered the small, oddly shaped building. A red neon sign lit up the single tiny window that faced the road, boasting that Budweiser was on tap.

Inside, a long, narrow room lined with dark wood paneling stretched toward the back. Actually, the walls were covered with some synthetic material that simply looked more or less like wood. Still, the effect was the same as if it had been the real thing: dark and claustrophobic.

The bar that ran the entire length of one long wall—and was separated from the dining area by a wooden divider decorated with nautical paraphernalia like plastic starfish and fishing nets—made the space feel even more closed in. Yet there was news from the outside world, thanks to the television positioned above the bar. It was broadcasting the local channel, Channel 14 News. For a few seconds, I watched a segment on a Girl Scout troop that was introducing the residents of a senior center to the joys of rap music.

Clyde's looked like the perfect place to grab a cup of clam chowder, which, at the moment, was high on my list. In fact, I'd had about all I could handle of pretentious, overpriced restaurants that offered ambiance instead of mere atmosphere. At the moment, atmosphere suited me just fine, even if it did involve a few crumbs that the last patrons had left behind on the plastic red-and-white-checked tablecloth.

"Just one?" the waitress asked as I lurked in the doorway, honoring the *Please Wait to be Seated* sign. She glanced behind me anxiously, as if she were certain there just had to be somebody in the world who was willing to have lunch with me.

"Just me," I told her, smiling.

She led me to a back table and left me with a laminated menu. I was marveling over the fact that you could actually get a turkey club for under five dollars—and that the $7.99 Fish o' the Day Dinner Special included soup, salad, Jell-O, *and* tea or coffee—when I happened to glance up at the bar.

The image on TV was enough to take away my appetite.

Lieutenant Anthony Falcone's face covered the screen, his dark, piercing eyes staring straight at me. He looked as if he'd combed an unusually large amount of gel into his hair, even for him. His suit was at least as shiny. He kept pointing his finger at the camera to emphasize what he was saying.

I got up from my seat, edging toward the TV until I was close enough to hear him.

"... assure the people of Norfolk County that the police department has made finding the person who's responsible for the brutal murder of Cassandra Thorndike our number-one priority. This is truly one of the most heinous crimes that has occurred here in a very long time. Right now experts are collecting and analyzing forensic evidence, and we're interviewing several suspects. We're keeping a close eye on one particular person of interest, and we expect to make an arrest soon."

Falcone made his last statement with remarkable assuredness, even though he managed to pronounce the word *particular* without hitting either one of the *r*s. In fact, he sounded as if he were bragging rather than reassuring Norfolk County's citizens.

But it wasn't his Long Island accent or his self-important posturing that was making my stomach churn. It was his claim that he expected to arrest someone soon. I had a strong suspicion that the person he was referring to was Suzanne.

"You ready to order?" the waitress asked, clearly concerned that I was out of my seat.

"Um, no. I need another minute." I glanced back at the television screen and saw that Falcone had been replaced by our local weatherman, who was grinning so broadly I suspected we were in for a few days of sunshine.

I slunk back to my chair and studied my menu, pretending I was frowning because of indecisiveness rather than the giant rock that was now lodged in my stomach. In fact, I was so focused on trying to hide how upset I was that it took me a few seconds to realize that somebody was saying my name.

"Dr. Popper?" I heard again. I glanced up, surprised to discover that a man was standing next to my table, grasping a straw hat in his gnarled hands. "I thought that was you. But, well, my eyesight isn't that good, especially without my glasses."

"Hello, Mr. Simcox," I said. I was right about the likelihood of running into him—and pleased about the possibility of gathering more information. "It's nice to see you again. In fact, would you care to join me?"

He looked startled. Even I had to admit that our previous encounter at Thorndike Vineyards on Saturday hadn't exactly been what you'd call a bonding experience.

"I was just going to grab a quick bite before heading back to my own neck of the woods," I added. There was something about being on the East End that prompted me to talk like an old cowhand.

He hesitated. "Well...I don't want to intrude."

"Not at all," I insisted. "I'd enjoy the company."

He hesitated, then pulled out the chair opposite me and sat down. Just like the first time I'd met him, he was dressed casually in his new jeans and a comfortable-looking blue chambray shirt that was just a tiny bit frayed at the collar.

"Do you eat here often?" I asked.

"All the time. In fact, I suppose I'm what you'd call a regular." With an apologetic smile, he added, "Eating out all the time can add up. But sitting at a kitchen table alone gets pretty depressing, so coming here for most of my meals is my one indulgence. Besides, the prices aren't too bad."

Having scanned the menu, I had to agree. "So what's good?"

"Just about everything," he assured me. He perched on the edge of his chair awkwardly, as if he still wasn't convinced he wasn't making a bad move. "Except the chicken pot pie. I'd steer clear of that, if I were you."

"Thanks, Mr. Simcox," I replied, smiling. "Sounds like advice worth following."

"Please, call me Theo."

After we'd ordered—me, clam chowder and one of those underpriced turkey sandwiches, Theo, the tuna salad on white toast—we both settled back in our chairs.

"So," he began, spreading his paper napkin out in his lap, "what brings you to the North Fork? Seeing patients, I imagine." Thoughtfully, he added, "You do call the dogs and cats you treat 'patients,' don't you?"

"The animals are the patients. Their owners are the clients. And yes, that's why I'm in the area today. I had some patients to see." I hesitated, then said, "I thought I might stop in at the Thorndikes', too. Just to say hello and see how they're doing."

"Hmm. Yes." Theo's expression darkened as our waitress plunked a cup of clam chowder down in front of me. Maybe I was just being overly sensitive, but I was pretty sure she looked relieved that I wasn't going to have to eat my lunch alone like Charlie Brown after all.

"Poor Gordon," he continued. "He's not doing well, I understand. Not well at all. In fact, he's having such a hard time dealing with what happened that he's leaving all the details to Joan. Not only did she plan the entire funeral; she's started to pack away Cassandra's things. As if that weren't heartbreaking enough, she's also been trying to arrange for a cleanup crew to take care of the room where...Cassandra's home office."

"How well do you know the Thorndikes?" I asked, doing my best to sound as if I were simply making conversation instead of pumping him for information.

"Quite well, actually. I've lived on the property next to Gordon's vineyard for close to two decades. In fact, he and I have been friends since the early days, back when we were both starting out in the business. I've known Joan almost as long as Gordon has."

"It's wonderful that they both work in the family business together," I commented.

"And they complement each other beautifully," Theo added. "Gordon is the genius behind the winemaking, and Joan helps him with the marketing. And Cassandra, of course..." He cleared his throat, as if trying to banish the thickness I could tell was lodged there.

"It must be nice to have neighbors you have so much in common with," I said, doing my best to brighten up the conversation.

"Many of us who live here on the North Fork are in the same business, and it's certainly been a big factor in my friendship with Gordon. Still, he and I are different in a lot of ways. Our approach to the business, for one thing. For me, it's just that: a business. For him, it's a calling. Of course, he had the luxury of going into it with an entirely different perspective."

I shook my head to demonstrate my confusion.

"Gordon's one of the lucky ones who started out his operation with a lot of money."

"Investors?" I asked politely.

"Family money. Quite a bit, from what I understand. Not that you'd ever guess by looking at him. Gordon's a quiet, low-key guy. But he's steady. And he's passionate about wine. Has a real gift, too. A talent, I guess you'd call it."

"You must have it, too," I observed.

His response was a shrug. "Me, I learned the wine business by reading books and studying, not by instinct. Sure, I know all the facts. But as much as I've always wanted to master the wine business, I've never had Gordon's magic touch."

"You've certainly done well, though," I said.

"I suppose I can't complain," he admitted. "I've even won a few awards. Still, I'm not in the same league as Gordon. Never will be either."

I suspected he was just being modest. And very loyal to his friend, a trait I found endearing. Especially because of what life had recently thrown Gordon Thorndike's way.

"Since you've known Gordon so long, I guess you knew Cassandra since she was a little girl." I lowered my eyes, concentrating on excavating a particularly large chunk of clam with my spoon.

"Yes, I did. Ethan, too." He shook his head sadly. "I'm sure he's taking it hard."

"Were Cassandra and Ethan close?" I asked.

"Like cats and dogs, if you'll excuse the expression."

Not only did I excuse it; I recognized that I'd heard it before. From the looks of things, the list of people Cassandra had had trouble getting along with was long indeed—and it included blood relatives as well as her fiancé.

Theo attempted a smile but didn't get very far. "Although I suppose that when you came right down to it, Cassandra and Ethan were too much alike to have a close relationship."

I hesitated, wondering how far I dared push the conversation. Doing my best to sound casual, I said, "Joan mentioned something about Cassandra being...difficult."

My words seemed to turn Theo's face into stone. "I thought the world of that girl," he said in a low, controlled voice. "It's true she was independent. Strong-willed, even. But while I'm extremely fond of Joan, I'm not about to allow whatever difficulties the two of them might have experienced as stepmother and stepdaughter to smear Cassandra's name."

The vehemence of his reaction startled me into silence. I'd taken a chance—and it had backfired. Clutching my spoon, I started shoveling in clam chowder, desperately trying to come up with a less incendiary topic of conversation.

"I always enjoy making calls on the North Fork," I said, deciding that talking about work would provide a convenient segue. "It's so peaceful—and it has such an interesting history. Speaking of which, where do you stand on the issue of whether Captain Kidd's treasure still lies buried out here?"

He raised his eyes from his plate. "Oh, there's treasure out here, all right."

"Really?" His response surprised me.

"Sure." He gestured toward the window. "You're looking at it." My confusion must have shown on my face, because he added, "The land."

"Of course." Glancing out, I saw the fields of a neighboring farm stretching out, the rich soil nurturing apple trees, endless rows of cauliflower and broccoli, and of course pumpkins, a sure sign that Halloween was getting close.

"We've got some of the most fertile land you'll find anywhere," Theo continued with more than a trace of pride in his voice. "In fact, when the English settlers first arrived on the North Fork in the 1600s, they could hardly believe their good fortune. They found an unbelievable abundance of wildlife to hunt, fish to catch, and top-quality soil just waiting to be planted. In fact, the farming conditions here were far superior to what they found in the New England colonies like Connecticut and Massachusetts. And our growing season is substantially longer.

From what I understand, back in those days, the English grew a little bit of everything. Of course, that changed in the late nineteenth century when immigrants from Poland and Ireland started coming in. They planted the crops they were familiar with, like cauliflower, cabbage, and the one Long Island became most famous for: potatoes.

"Today, Long Island's farms are the most productive in New York State. Of course, farming has diminished significantly over the last decades, and these days most of it is dedicated to flowers and ornamental shrubs. But the region still produces fruits and vegetables, mostly tomatoes, corn, and, yes, potatoes. If you ask me, that's a treasure more valuable than anything Captain Kidd could have left behind."

"I suppose there are all kinds of treasure," I agreed.

"Besides," he continued, "there's more to the story of Captain Kidd than most people know. The truth is that he wasn't a bad guy at all. In fact, he was merely a pawn in a rich man's game."

"Tell me more," I said, genuinely intrigued.

"Kidd was originally a Scotsman, the son of a minister.

But he made a name for himself as a skilled sea captain early on. He moved to New York City in the 1680s and married a wealthy widow. The following decade, England and France went to war, and Kidd forged a successful career as a privateer. Privateers were basically freelance sailors who provided support to the British Royal Navy. Ironically, Kidd's job was defending British and American trade routes in the Caribbean against pirates.

"Then the newly appointed governor of New York City, Lord Bellomont, and three other well-to-do individuals commissioned him to lead an expedition in the Indian Ocean. His official duty was to protect his ship from pirates. But his backers made it clear that he was welcome to capture any French ships he came across and help himself to their cargo—with the understanding that he'd share the spoils with them, of course.

"Captain Kidd had a difficult time finding men, though, since the British Navy had just drafted most of them. He was so desperate to put together a crew that he ended up promising to pay them an unusually large percentage of the booty. In fact, by the time he embarked on his journey, he'd promised well over one hundred percent to his crew and his backers. He also ended up signing on some men who were known to be pirates.

"The voyage began like any other. But the crew became restless. Too many ships that weren't French were getting past them, and they revolted. In the midst of the melee, Kidd hit a gunner in the head with a bucket. The man—William Moore, I believe his name was—died of a fractured skull soon afterward.

"From then on, the members of Kidd's crew considered themselves pirates. When they neared India, they attacked a ship called the *Quedah Merchant*. They stole her cargo—sugar, opium, silk, spices, and gold—which was supposedly worth the spectacular amount of seventy thousand pounds.

"But the real problem for Kidd was that while he was on his two-year voyage, things changed back at home. The English had begun clamping down on piracy. When he reached the West Indies, he learned he was now considered a pirate—and that he was a wanted man. He managed to obtain a pardon by bribing a few corrupt politicians, as was the norm in those days. He then buried some of his booty on Gardiner's Island—and, some people believe, a few other places along the North Fork."

"So the story has a happy ending," I commented, "at least for Captain Kidd. Thanks to those corrupt politicians, he was pardoned."

"Not quite. He sailed home, thinking all was well. Instead, he was arrested and sent back to England. He was held in Newgate Prison for a year, where he was forbidden to communicate with his wife or anyone else. When he finally stood trial, he was never given a fair chance to defend himself. Of course, the fact that his backers withheld the documents that might have proven his innocence didn't help his case. He wasn't allowed to take the stand to defend himself, and neither were any members of his crew, aside from two deserters.

"Captain Kidd was found guilty of both piracy and the murder of William Moore. As was the tradition in those days, he was executed by hanging and his corpse was put in a harness made of hoops and chains and covered in tar to keep the skeleton together. Then it was put into an iron cage and hung at the mouth of the Thames River as a message to others. The British government wasn't exactly subtle. Kidd's body supposedly remained there for years before finally rotting away. Meanwhile, his backers suffered a bit from the scandal but in the end held on to their wealth and power."

"What a grisly tale!" I exclaimed. "But what about the buried treasure?"

"With John Gardiner's help, the British authorities unearthed some ten thousand pounds worth of gold from his island. But the other treasure—if it ever really existed—has never been found."

"Fascinating!" I was already looking forward to telling Nick the true story of Captain Kidd. I wondered if I could find a way to capture enough of the magic to tell Maggie Rose without giving her nightmares.

Glancing down, I realized I'd polished off the rest of my lunch without even realizing it. I was actually sorry that I'd run out of excuses to converse with Theo Simcox. I never would have expected he'd turn out to be such a captivating storyteller.

I only wished he'd been as forthcoming about Cassandra as he'd been about Captain Kidd.

"I suppose I should be on my way," I said reluctantly.

"Actually," he said after clearing his throat, "if you're not in a hurry, meeting you the other day reminded me that I've got a pet of my own that I've been meaning to bring to the vet. Haven't had the time, though, especially since I've been helping at the Thorndikes' vineyard. Since you're out here and all, I wonder if you could stop by and take a look at one of my greyhounds. Shiraz has had allergies since I got her. Scratching excessively, rubbing her eyes...the poor thing has had such a rough time. Her regular vet put her on a drug I believe he refers to as 'pred.' I've been giving her five milligrams a day."

"Prednisolone," I said. "It's a synthetic adrenal corticosteroid that's used to reduce inflammation."

"Shouldn't I worry about her being on a steroid like cortisone?"

"It might not be a bad idea to reevaluate," I commented. "Whenever you're dealing with a steroid, you have to consider the side effects. I have some time right now, and I'd be happy to stop over."

"I'd certainly appreciate that. Come autumn, we all get incredibly busy, just like Joan was saying the other day. Of course, my operation isn't nearly as big as the Thorndikes'. Still, sometimes it's difficult to find time for even the important things."

He grabbed the check. "I'll get this," he insisted. "And once we're paid up, you can follow me to my humble home."

• • •

Just as I had with Joan Thorndike, I followed Theo to his house. It was easy not to lose him, not only because there was little traffic but also because he drove so slowly. I wondered if that was because he was getting on in years or simply because of his old clunker of a car, a dented Dodge that was at least twelve or thirteen years old. Still, I suspected that, like his soft, well-worn shirts, it was simply something he felt comfortable in.

Our two-vehicle caravan made a sharp right turn after a large wooden sign that read *Simcox Wineries*. Unlike the Thorndikes, he lived on the same piece of land that his winery occupied, just to the east of Thorndike Vineyards. I followed him along his paved driveway, relieved that it was much shorter and smoother than the Thorndikes'. Theodore Simcox's home was a rambling if somewhat ramshackle Victorian farmhouse that was set fairly far back from the road, behind the dignified brick building that served as the vineyard's visitors' center. It had a few faded shingles and the shutters could have used a coat of paint, but it looked solid enough. Beyond the house stretched acres of farmland, planted with the now-familiar rows of grapes.

"This part of Long Island is so beautiful," I observed

as I climbed out of my van, taking in the manicured fields flanking the road. "It's hard to believe we're only seventy miles from Times Square."

"It is quite nice, isn't it?" Theodore agreed. "When people think of Long Island, they picture one housing development after another. Yet right now we could be in the Napa Valley—or in one of the wine regions of France."

"What about the wine industry here on Long Island?" I asked. "I know it's only a few decades old. How did it get started?"

"Interestingly enough, two Harvard students are responsible," Theo explained. "A married couple, Louisa and Alex Hargrave, who happened to be passionate about wine. But they were more than mere devotees. They were also true visionaries, the first to recognize that the growing conditions on Long Island's East End—the soil conditions, the climate—were just like those of France's Bordeaux region.

"In the mid-seventies, the Hargraves took a chance by planting Vitis vinifera wine grapes on their North Fork land—the same type used by French and Californian wineries. Many people thought they were fighting a losing battle. But in the end, they prevailed. These days, they're considered the founders of one of Long Island's major industries."

"Do the Hargraves still run the vineyard they created?"

Theodore shook his head. "Actually, they sold it a few years ago—to an Italian prince. But their legacy lives on. Today, there are some sixty vineyards on both the North and South Forks, a total of three thousand acres that are planted with wine grapes. And Long Island wines have become a sixty-five-million-dollar-a-year industry, producing over a million gallons of wine annually."

"That's a lot of wine," I observed, glancing at the rows of lush green grapevines alongside Theo's house with new respect.

"But what makes Long Island wines really special is the approach toward fermentation," he continued. "In one region of France—Bordeaux—wine production takes place on a tremendous scale, and special techniques have been developed to hurry the fermentation process along. But in Burgundy—Bourgogne—wineries are small enterprises with only limited production. There, the winemakers apply a much more personal touch. Fermentation takes place over months, rather than days.

"Long Island wines represent an interesting combination of those two regions of France. Smaller amounts are produced and fermentation is more complex, but those methods, the type used in Burgundy, are used on grape varieties that are popular in Bordeaux, like merlot. As a result, Long Island wines tend to have a special woody quality that the French call *sous-bois: sous* meaning *under* and *bois* meaning *woods.*"

I was about to thank him for enabling me to sound like I actually knew what I was talking about the next time someone offered me a glass of wine, when we turned the corner of the barn. Two regal greyhounds began jumping up on the wooden fence that penned them into a spacious yard, barking gleefully.

"Calm down!" Theo commanded, chuckling. Of course, the sound of his voice only fueled their excitement. It wasn't until he'd unlatched the gate and the two dogs were free to leap up on their master that the barking stopped. He crouched down and lovingly caressed their sleek heads.

"Good thing you have two hands," I observed, smiling as I watched what looked very much like the greeting I got from Max and Lou whenever I walked in the door. "One for each."

"Indeed. We don't want any sibling rivalry, do we? Let me introduce these two. This is Shiraz—and this is Buffett."

"Hey, Shiraz! Hell-o, Buffett!" I leaned over and petted their smooth heads and scratched their necks and ears. Like most greyhounds, they were friendly, gentle dogs. They eagerly focused their attention on me, pleased to make a new person's acquaintance.

"I got Shiraz first, from a greyhound-rescue organization in Connecticut," Theodore explained, running his hand along the silky fur on her back. To prove his point, he flipped back her right ear. Sure enough, a number was tattooed on the inside, indicating her date of birth and litter order. On the left, I knew, would be a five-digit registration number assigned by the National Greyhound Association. "She was originally named Valley Aspen. But it's not unusual for new owners to rename a rescued greyhound."

"She's a beautiful animal," I told him sincerely.

"I suppose I should have been content with just one. But a couple of years went by, and I decided to adopt a second." Smiling, he added, "A lot of us who 'go grey' end up doing the exact same thing. Somehow, we can't manage to stop at one. I told myself Shiraz needed the company, but I knew all along that I really got Buffett for myself.

"I got him when he was just seven weeks old. He was born at a dog-racing track in Connecticut, part of an unplanned litter. Track breeders call them 'oops litters.' When the puppies' lineage is unknown, they can't be raised to race or even to show." Smiling warmly as he stroked the dog's sleek head, he added, "Can you believe he weighed only seven pounds the first time they put him in my arms? Since then, I can't tell you how much joy he's brought me. He's named for the singer Jimmy

Buffett, of course, whose music has also brought me a lot of pleasure."

"It's wonderful that you rescued these two animals," I said. I knew the abuse that was known to go on in the racing industry was horrendous. I'd heard that in some instances the poor animals weren't given food or even water unless they'd won a race. A lot of them were constantly penned up in tiny cages, and some were muzzled almost all the time. Thousands died every year from sores they got from being muzzled or caged, parasites, heart attacks, broken legs, heat stroke... And when they lost their usefulness, they were often "disposed of" in cruel ways. Only a small percentage had the good fortune to be adopted into loving homes.

"Yet they make such wonderful pets," Theo added. "They're sweet, outgoing animals, and since they were bred by professionals, you generally don't have to worry about hereditary physical conditions or problems with temperament. Another plus is that they get so much attention from breeders and handlers while they're young that they're very sociable with people."

"When you renamed Shiraz, you named her after a wine," I observed. "Just like Beau, Cassandra's cat."

"Ah. So you two have met?"

"Cassandra's next door neighbor, Maggie Rose, introduced me to Beau. In fact, I believe I'm now his veterinarian, so I should be seeing a lot more of him."

"I see. You're right about both animals being named after wines. When it came to naming Shiraz, Cassandra inspired me." He smiled sadly. "In fact, she inspired me in all sorts of ways."

"Like a muse?" I asked.

"More like a daughter. At least, that's how I always thought of her."

I knew about that kind of relationship. It was the kind

Betty and I enjoyed. All the affection of a parent and child—without the complications.

"Then she was lucky to have you," I told him. "We can all use as many loving parents as we can get."

"Yes, it was definitely love," Theodore said vaguely. Looking startled, he added, "The fondness that Cassandra and I felt for each other, I mean."

I didn't reply. Was I correct in assuming he was talking about the kind of love between parent and child? I wondered. Or is it possible that Theodore Simcox's feelings for Cassandra Thorndike were love of a different sort?

"What about Ethan?" I asked. Not only was I anxious to change the subject; I was also curious about how this close friend of the family perceived Cassandra's baby brother.

His reaction didn't surprise me. "Sad," he said, shaking his head slowly. "Ethan Thorndike is such a complicated young man. So terribly conflicted, for reasons none of us has ever been able to understand. Poor Gordon and Joan have put so much effort into helping him find his way. Sending him to that special school—the Sewanhacky School, or whatever it's called—finding him psychologists and psychiatrists and...and even witch doctors, for all I know." He let out a deep sigh. "I don't think Ethan will ever be able to make his own way in the world. It wouldn't surprise me if he spent his entire life living in that tiny apartment above the garage."

I had to agree with his assessment of Ethan as *complicated*. And I would have bet my van on the word *conflicted* being just as accurate. In fact, Theo's comments about both Cassandra and Ethan certainly gave me something to think about. At the moment, however, it was time to concentrate on still another kind of love: the love between an animal owner and his pet.

"Let's get these two into the van so I can take a look at them," I suggested.

I checked them one at a time, examining their eyes and ears, then running my hands along their spines and checking each vertebra. Meanwhile, I asked Theo the usual questions about whether they'd been eating and drinking the normal amount, their recent activity level, and whether they'd been coughing, sneezing, vomiting, or suffering from diarrhea. I hadn't expected to find much, since they clearly had a devoted master who took excellent care of them. Sure enough, aside from Shiraz's allergies, they were both fine.

"This is the drug I've been giving her," Theo said, handing me the bottle.

"Given her weight," I said, glancing at the label, "keeping her on five milligrams a day is fine. In fact, going up to ten would be safe. But there are some other drugs you might consider. There's one called Temaril-P that dermatologists really like. Antihistamines are generally not very effective for this type of skin disease. But this medication is a combination of a little pred and a little antihistamine. So if we switch, Shiraz here would be taking a lot less cortisone.

"There's a second possibility, a drug called Atopica. It's traditionally been used in cases of human transplant rejection, and its use in veterinary medicine is relatively new. Some dermatologists rave about it, but some have reservations. My feeling is that it would probably be perfectly safe for your dog at low doses. But it's pretty expensive, and it doesn't always work. Frankly, I'm comfortable with all three options: increasing the pred to ten milligrams or trying either of the other two drugs."

"If it was your dog," Theo asked earnestly, "what would you do?"   •

"I think I have to recommend the Temaril-P. You can start tapering off, taking her off the pred and getting onto the new medication. I'll give you the schedule you should follow." I wrote out some instructions, then handed them to him along with a yellow box that contained a jarful of the drug.

"I'm very grateful, Dr. Popper," Theo said.

"Please, call me Jessie."

"In here, it's Dr. Popper."

"If you insist," I told him, laughing. "But outside this van, I hope we can be friends."

As I said those words, I couldn't help feeling a little guilty. After all, one of the main reasons I was cultivating this man's friendship was that he'd known Cassandra and the rest of her family so well.

Yet there was nothing more important to me at that point than getting Suzanne out of the nightmare she'd found herself in. If a little deception was required, it seemed a small price to pay.

So I was pleased when Theo smiled and replied, "Friends. Definitely friends."

• • •

I was still mulling over Theo Simcox's comments about Ethan Thorndike late that afternoon when I heard a car door slam outside the cottage. I glanced out the window, wondering who my unexpected visitor might be. The familiar forest-green SUV that had pulled into the driveway, right in front of my cottage, gave me my answer.

"This is a surprise," I greeted Forrester as I opened the door.

"I'm going to assume you meant to say a *pleasant* surprise," he returned, grinning. "Aren't you going to invite me in, Popper? That's what most people would do."

Most people would also call ahead to give a little warning, I thought petulantly. But I realized I was actually glad to see him. In fact, I found myself wondering if my reaction was *only* due to the fact that he might have information for me about Cassandra Thorndike's murder.

I quickly put such thoughts out of my head. After all, I was on the verge of taking my relationship with Nick to the next level. A woman in my position shouldn't even entertain such thoughts. Fortunately, I had a ready distraction, since as soon as he stepped inside, my two canines charged him, acting as if they'd both been in solitary confinement for the past week. Prometheus added to the chaos, screeching, *"Awk! Who's your daddy? Awk!"*

"I hope you like dogs," I said. "And cats. And birds. And—"

"Whoa," he replied, crouching down to give Max and Lou an energetic enough greeting to let me know he was, indeed, a dog person. "I'm almost afraid to hear the rest of the list. You don't have any crocodiles, do you?"

I laughed. "Even an animal lover has to draw the line somewhere."

"That's a relief."

By that point, Max and Lou had calmed down enough to permit Forrester to saunter around the living room. "Nice place you've got here."

"Considering that you're a writer, I would have thought you'd be able to come up with something more original."

"I told you, Popper: I'm a reporter. My concern is being accurate, not creative." He seemed to be taking in every detail of his surroundings. He reminded me of a real-estate agent who was running numbers on an invisible calculator in his head. "So this is where it all happens."

I raised my eyebrows. "What exactly do you think happens here, Forrester?"

"Your real life."

He kept glancing from side to side. I got the feeling there was something in particular he was trying to find.

"What are you looking for?" I finally asked, annoyed. "Mounds of dust bunnies that prove that my house-cleaning standards aren't very high? Some off-the-wall relative I keep stashed away in a broom closet?"

"Actually, I was looking for that boyfriend of yours. Nick, isn't it?"

"You remembered. How thoughtful."

"Actually, I feel like I'm the guy's understudy. I keep waiting for him to break a leg and get rushed to the hospital so I can fill in."

"Oh, really? And what makes you so sure you even passed the audition?"

He just smiled. Gesturing toward the kitchen with his chin, he asked, "So where is he? Or should I check that broom closet you mentioned?"

"He's at school."

"Kindergarten or first grade?"

"Actually, he's at the library, studying." Standing up a little straighter, I added, "Nick is a first-year student at the Brookside University School of Law."

"Well, I can't say I'm sorry. That I missed him, I mean."

"You did meet him once," I reminded him. "Last week, after I had my stomach pumped at North Country Hospital. He was arriving as you were leaving."

"Gee, I don't remember. That's strange," he added dryly. "I usually have such a good memory for faces."

"*Awk!* Shake your booty!" Prometheus squawked.

"What's with the X-rated parrot?" Forrester asked, sounding amused.

I shrugged. "I keep begging him to hang with a more wholesome crowd, but do you think he listens?"

Grinning, he plopped down on the couch and draped

one arm along the back. Even though he'd left me plenty of room to sit down beside him, I perched on the upholstered chair facing him.

"By the way, Forrester," I said, "I wanted to thank you."

"You're welcome. But what are you thanking me for?"

"For keeping Suzanne's name out of the newspaper."

"I don't deserve your thanks for that one. She's just one of several people the police are looking at. It's not as if she's been charged with anything."

I sighed. "I'm still hoping it never comes to that. That I can find out who really killed Cassandra before…" I let my voice trail off, not wanting to say the horrible words out loud. The image of Lieutenant Falcone loomed before me ominously. I could see him exactly the way he'd looked on the air, his face drawn into an intense expression as he promised the people of Norfolk County he was hot on the trail of Cassandra's killer.

Forrester picked up the ball. "On a lighter note," he said, "I have an ulterior motive for coming over here today, as you may have already guessed. There's something I want to talk to you about."

"I'm listening."

"At the risk of sounding clichéd, you ought to be on television."

I screwed up my face. "Not that Channel Fourteen business again."

"Hear me out, Popper. This all started because a friend of mine over there, a producer, told me she's hot to start a TV show about pet care. The station wants to expand its programming to include more local people. Local professionals who viewers would find—how did she put it?—'interesting and informative.' So I told her all about you."

I narrowed my eyes suspiciously. "What did you say, exactly?"

"That I knew an attractive, intelligent, articulate veterinarian who'd be perfect."

"But, Forrester, I have no interest in being on television. I can barely keep up with all the calls I have to make as part of my regular veterinary business, not to mention—"

"You'd be doing all of Long Island a favor by telling Channel Fourteen's viewers how they can be better pet owners. Think of all the doggies and kitties you'll help by reminding their masters how important it is for them to get regular checkups and shots and...and whatever else they need. Besides, it's a great way to help build your practice."

My head was buzzing with a hundred reasons to say no. "But...but...I've never been on TV! What would I say? How would I act? What would I wear?"

"Look, Popper. Just go over there and talk to them. Find out what they're looking for. You might not even be the type they're looking for."

" 'Type'?" I repeated, confused. Even though I wasn't even sure I wanted this gig—and in fact was pretty convinced I didn't—the fact that they might turn me down was already making me defensive. "I'm a real live veterinarian. What else do they need?"

Forrester laughed. "Poor Popper. You have so much to learn."

I *hated* it when he acted that way. In fact, it made my blood boil so fast I felt like somebody had just popped me in the microwave.

"Wait a minute," I insisted. "First of all, stop talking to me like I just rolled out of the cabbage patch. Second of all, if you're such an expert on the way the mysterious world of television works, why don't you take twenty seconds to explain it to me?"

He looked at me with amusement in his eyes. "You're so cute when you're angry."

"And you're so dumb when you're arrogant." Okay, so it wasn't my greatest line, but it was all I could come up with.

"Point taken." Grinning, he added, "Sorry. I can't resist teasing you. Somehow, you bring that out in me. It's probably sublimation. You know, taking sexual desire and turning it into something socially acceptable—"

"Frankly, I don't think being a condescending smart-ass is any more socially acceptable than what you call 'sexual desire' for someone who's living with another man—"

"And so very comfortable doing so," he interjected sarcastically.

Got me there, I thought. But I wasn't going to give him the satisfaction of knowing he'd hit a raw nerve.

"Look, Forrester. I don't know who you think you are to—"

"Knock, knock!" a high-pitched female voice called gaily. "Anybody home?"

My landlady and close friend Betty had just poked her head inside the front door.

Betty *never* opened the door without knocking.

"Hello, Jessica." Feigning surprise—and not doing a particularly good job of it—she added, "Oh, heavens! I had no idea you had someone over!"

Right, I thought. That SUV the size of a UPS truck sure is hard to miss.

"Come on in, Betty," I told her.

She floated into the living room, the image helped by her long, flowing sundress made of batik fabric splashed with bright oranges, yellows, and greens. To ward off the coolness of the early October afternoon, she had wrapped a shiny green silk shawl around her shoulders. It was covered with tiny mirrors the size of dimes and edged with gold metallic fringe. Her delicate silk slippers were elaborately decorated with colorful beads that matched the beaded earrings dangling below her smooth, white hair, worn in a neat pageboy.

As was often the case, her outfit looked like something a costume designer had dreamed up. Betty Vandervoort had moved to New York City from Altoona, Pennsylvania, decades earlier to pursue her dream of conquering Broadway. Dancing in the chorus of hits like *South Pacific* and *Oklahoma!* had been only the beginning of what I considered a fairy-tale life, even though it had been marred early on by the death of her husband, Charles. I was pleased that she'd recently returned to the theater, even though this time around she'd set her sights on community productions rather than the Great White Way. Getting back into show biz had made her already sparkly sapphire-blue eyes shine even more brightly. Of course, the recent appearance of a new beau on the scene had catapulted the sparkle to even more dazzling heights.

Lighting on the edge of the couch like a butterfly, she asked sweetly, "And who, may I ask, is this?"

"Forrester Sloan," I replied. "He writes for *Newsday*."

Betty stiffened. "Oh, yes," she said with a touch of haughtiness. "I've heard all about you."

"Only good things, I hope," Forrester returned, flashing her a grin.

"Hmm" was all she said, making no bones about the fact that she was looking him over. She also made it clear that she had no intention of going anywhere.

"Forrester is helping me find out everything I can about Cassandra Thorndike's murder."

"Oh, yes," Betty said, her eyes clouding with concern. "Jessica told me all about the predicament her poor friend is in." Her look of concern quickly turned back to coldness as she pointedly said, "I suppose that's the reason you're here, then."

Forrester cast Betty a wary glance, then stood up. "And our business is just about done, so I guess I'll get going." He reached into his pocket and handed me a business card. "Here's the person I told you about. Call her. She's expecting to hear from you."

"I'll think about it," I replied, taking the card.

After he'd left, Betty twisted around to face me. Crossing her arms, she demanded, "And what, may I ask, was all that about?"

"All what?" I asked innocently.

She drew her lips into a straight line. "Attractive young men dropping by to visit you during the day."

"Do you think he's attractive?" I asked coolly. "Actually, I always thought Forrester was kind of—"

"Jessica, you know perfectly well what I'm talking about. I wasn't born yesterday, you know. And I recognize chemistry when I see it."

"Speaking of chemistry," I said, pointedly changing the subject, "what's up with you and Winston? I've noticed he's been spending a lot of time at your place. In fact, it looks as if he's practically moved in."

Betty hesitated, as if wondering if she should go along with my obvious ploy to shift the focus from my love life to hers. "Actually, it looks as if he's going to do exactly that. Tomorrow, as a matter of fact."

My eyebrows shot up so high they practically grazed the ceiling.

"Someone is interested in buying his house," Betty went on. "It's such a lovely estate, and Old Brookbury is an extremely desirable area. The buyer is anxious for the deal to go through quickly, which would leave Winston without a place to live. He and I have been talking about making a deeper commitment to each other—"

"That was fast," I said, thinking aloud.

"People our age experience time differently, Jessica. At any rate, with him having no place to go and me rattling around that huge house all by myself...Well, we're going to try living together."

"I wish you the best," I told her sincerely. "I'm sure you'll both be extremely happy."

"Seems to me you and Nick have been considering a similar arrangement," Betty noted.

"Yes, and we've decided to give it a try," I said, noticing that my mouth was suddenly dry. "But it's mainly because his landlord is making it very clear that he can't wait for him to vacate the apartment so his daughter can move in. Besides, it's just an experiment. We've agreed on a time frame of a few months. Then, if it isn't working out..."

"Well, I couldn't be more pleased that you're finally making a commitment to Nick. You know how much I adore him, and I love the idea of the two of you going hand in hand into the sunset." Betty glanced at the front door, as if wanting to make sure Forrester had really made his way onto the other side of it. "Without anything—or anyone—getting in the way."

"Betty, Forrester and I are just friends, I assure you."

"Well, you might think that," she said. "But I can assure you that *he* doesn't."

I shrugged. "Can I help it if the guy has an overly active imagination?"

"As a matter of fact, you can." She paused to take a deep breath. "Jessica, I'll be blunt."

That's a change, I thought crossly.

"I can't help feeling that you're sending that young man signals."

"Betty," I replied, trying not to sound too exasperated, "I've reminded him that I have a boyfriend so many times that even *I'm* sick of hearing it."

"There are the things we say—and then there are the things we don't say."

I was about to point out that she sounded like a badly written fortune cookie when she added, "Just be careful, Jessica. This one isn't just flirting. This one is serious."

Chapter 8

"I've never understood why women love cats. Cats are independent, they don't listen, they don't come in when you call, they like to stay out all night, and when they're home they like to be left alone and sleep. In other words, every quality that women hate in a man, they love in a cat."

—Jay Leno

Screech. Crunch. *Bang!*

Even before I flung open the door on Tuesday morning, I knew I wasn't going to like what I found on the other side. Sure enough: There in the driveway right outside my cottage was an orange and white U-Haul truck that was only slightly smaller than my van. Harder to maneuver too, at least if the fact that it had just smashed into the low brick wall on one side of the driveway was any indication.

"Nick?" I cried as Max and Lou rushed past me, both of them barking wildly. "What are you *doing*?"

He hopped out of the passenger's side of the cab, wearing a sheepish grin. Tucked under one arm was a shoe box. "Sorry. I guess Ollie's not that great a driver."

Just then, the other door of the cab opened. A chubby

man with a complexion that would make a dead man look rosy-cheeked climbed down awkwardly. "I hope I don't have whiplash!" he whined. "I can already feel shooting pains in my neck!"

I strode over to Nick. "You let *him* drive?" I whispered hoarsely.

"It's okay. His father owns the franchise."

"That's a relief. Hopefully, Daddy will pay for damage."

Oliver J. Sturges III—Ollie, as his friends called him, assuming he had any—was a member of Nick's study group. First-year law students apparently found it helpful to get together once a week to pool their notes and share their insights—although having met the other four members, I found it hard to believe they had much of anything to offer Nick, aside from convincing him he was one of the few normal people at the Brookside University School of Law.

"Hello, Ollie," I greeted the man wearing jeans pulled up nearly to his armpits and a plaid flannel shirt that his mother had no doubt ordered for him from the L.L. Bean catalog. The shirt was still creased from being folded in the package. I just hoped the pins had been removed. "Thanks for helping."

"I forgot that you have all those...those *animals* in your house!" he rasped. "Dogs and cats and...and... Oh, my God, I forgot my inhaler. There's no *way* I'm going inside that death trap, Nick!"

"That's cool, Ollie," Nick replied patiently. "I can handle unpacking the truck. You've already done enough."

"I'll say," I muttered, checking out the huge dent that was the result of his obvious intellectual deficiency in the area of spatial relations. Turning back to Nick, I said, "I'll help you unpack."

"Thanks!" Nick leaned over and gave me a kiss.

Unfortunately, it was the kind Mike Brady used to give Carol Brady on *The Brady Bunch*.

"Hey, don't I get a real kiss?" I protested. "After all, you and I are about to start cohabitating. Shouldn't we mark that with something symbolic?"

He grinned. "Later. After Ollie's gone and I'm all settled in."

With that, he handed me the shoe box.

"What's this?"

"You mean *who's* this. Leilani. Her tank is packed up with the rest of my stuff."

Leilani was the Jackson's chameleon Nick and I had brought home from our fateful trip to Hawaii a year earlier, a trip that had almost meant the end for us. While I thought we were there to snorkel and eat shave ice, Nick had surprised me by asking me to marry him. My less-than-enthusiastic reaction had prompted us to split.

Fortunately, fate—or, more accurately, my first foray into murder investigation—had brought us back together a few weeks after we returned home. But I still thought of Leilani as the best part of that entire episode. I suspected that Nick did too. I carried the box carefully, not wanting to add to the trauma the poor creature had already endured simply from driving over. I brought her into the house, placed the shoe box on the bed, and closed the door to keep curious kitty cats away from their new housemate.

By the time I got back outside, Nick had opened up the truck. He grabbed a carton of what looked like very heavy books and began U-Hauling them toward the front door. I wandered around to the back, figuring I'd do my share of the heavy lifting—then froze.

"What's all this?" I asked, blinking in disbelief as I glanced inside.

"Just some of my stuff," Nick returned cheerfully.

I felt as if my cottage had just been selected to be the winter headquarters of the Ringling Bros. and Barnum & Bailey Circus. I checked behind me, hoping I wouldn't see a team of elephants trundling up the driveway.

No elephants, thank goodness. But plenty of clothes on hangers and in shopping bags, cardboard cartons of books and CDs, electronics with long, dangling cords, must-have housewares like a rice cooker and a juicer, boxes piled high with dress shoes and worn-out sneakers, lamps, rolled-up posters, and black Hefty bags whose contents I could only imagine.

"I guess I never realized you owned so many things," I said feebly.

Nick just laughed. "Don't worry. We'll find a way to make it fit. I'm really good at that kind of thing."

I was wondering what else I'd be learning about Nick in the days and weeks to come when I noticed Betty trotting toward me from the Big House, waving.

"So today's the big day!" she cried, her blue eyes twinkling.

"This is it," I replied hoarsely, already wondering if I'd made the biggest mistake of my life.

"How exciting! In fact, why don't you and Nick stop by tonight for a little celebration? After you've both had a chance to get settled, of course. I'm sure Winston and I can find a bottle of bubbly to mark the occasion."

"Sounds like fun," I told her.

Certainly more fun than watching my beloved little cottage being transformed into a climate-controlled room at one of those self-storage facilities.

• • •

"Isn't this nice!" Betty cooed, glancing over at me and beaming. "To think that just last week, Jessica and I were the only ones who lived here on the estate. And now we have two fine gentlemen in residence!"

I had to admit that taking a break at the Big House was a great relief. While the U-Haul was long gone—along with its whiny driver, thank goodness—my worst fantasies about Nick moving in were already being realized. We were up to our earlobes in boxes. As if that wasn't enough to induce acute claustrophobia, there was no place to sit, since cartons of books and CDs occupied all the good spots. No place to lie down either, with piles of clothes stacked on the bed and shopping bags filled with socks and belts and shoes covering the floor. As for the impossible-to-live-without rice cooker, it took up nearly all the counter space in my tiny kitchen.

Just stepping into Betty's large, clutter-free parlor had been a great relief. I was able to breathe normally for the first time all day. In fact, I felt like the four of us were making a Merchant Ivory film. The whole setting was so darned civilized: the roaring fire in the fireplace, the crystal fluted glasses filled with bubbling champagne, the recording of a string quartet playing softly in the background, and of course Winston's lovely British accent and Old World charm.

Even the dogs were on their best behavior. I'd wanted to leave them at the cottage, but Betty and Winston insisted it was high time Max and Lou made Frederick's acquaintance.

I could already see that my canines were adjusting to the sudden increase in population here at the Tallmadge estate much more easily than I was. Especially Max, who had instantly taken to Winston's wire-haired dachshund. The compact, friendly dog with fawn and tan fur was as energetic as my terrier. They bonded immediately, which I figured was due at least in part to the fact that dachshunds and West Highland whites had both originally been bred to hunt the same type of frisky critters, especially badgers.

Lou, however, was being treated a bit like the odd man out. While the two little guys romped together, sniffing and nipping each other and having a grand old time, he hovered a couple of feet away, doing his share of romping but acting more like a spectator than an active participant. I hoped that, sooner or later, they'd include him. These play dates were so difficult to orchestrate.

"It's nice that Frederick has some new friends to romp around with, right here in his own backyard," Winston observed, beaming like a proud father.

"And it's lovely that we have a new neighbor, too!" Betty was glowing as she raised her champagne glass into the air. "I propose a toast to Nick. Welcome!"

"Thanks, Betty." Nick clinked his glass against hers, then insisted that they weave their arms through each other's before drinking. She giggled like a schoolgirl.

"Now, now, you two," Winston quipped, "I hope I won't have any competition, now that there's a younger man living on the premises."

"I promise to keep him in line," I said.

"You don't have to worry," Nick added, slinging his arm around my waist. "I'm a one-woman man. Believe me, I'm smart enough to know a good thing when I've got it.

"In fact," he added, "the entire world—or at least all of Long Island—is about to discover what a star Jessie is."

"Come on, Nick," I mumbled, feeling my cheeks grow warm. "You know nothing's certain yet."

"What's this?" Winston boomed. "Sounds like you've got something exciting in the works, Jessica!"

With three pairs of eyes focused on me, I had no choice but to come clean. "I'm meeting with a television producer tomorrow to talk about the possibility of doing a weekly show on pet care. It's only Channel Fourteen—"

"That's wonderful!" Betty cried.

"Goodness, I watch Channel Fourteen all the time," Winston chimed in. "It's the best way to find out what's happening locally."

"Nothing is certain yet," I insisted. Being in the limelight—even among friends—was already making me uncomfortable. I wondered if I had what it took to be on television.

"I think that's just marvelous!" Betty exclaimed. "And, Jessica, if there's anything I can do to help—teach you makeup tricks or give you pointers on how to make an entrance—I hope you won't hesitate to ask."

"Thank you, Betty."

"How are you progressing with your other...endeavor?" she asked hesitantly.

It took me a few seconds to realize she was talking about Cassandra Thorndike. Before I had a chance to respond, Winston said, "What's this? Another foray into the arts?"

"Not exactly," I told him. "I've been investigating a murder." I filled him in on the case, especially Suzanne's involvement. Then I updated my small audience on everything I'd learned so far, leaving out any mention of my secret e-mail buddy. Nearly 48 hours had passed since I'd received that creepy anonymous communiqué. Yet every time I checked my e-mail, my heart started to pound. While I hadn't heard from him or her again, I had a feeling that, sooner or later, I would.

Still, I'd made a point of not telling Nick about it. I was feeling so frustrated by my lack of progress that the last thing I wanted was him trying to hold me back because he was worried about me. There was simply too much at stake.

"I'm sure you'll be just fine," Winston insisted heartily. "You're a very brave, resourceful young woman with a good head on her shoulders. I'm certain you'll find success in clearing your friend's name. As for any possible risks, I certainly can't imagine that someone as clear-thinking as you would ever take on anything that wasn't safe."

The look I saw Betty and Nick exchange told me they didn't quite agree.

Anxious to change the subject, I said, "Hey, I just realized we toasted Nick, but we haven't toasted Winston! We don't want him to feel left out...."

As the champagne took effect, everyone mellowed, including me. Even the dogs were lolling on the thick Oriental carpet—all three of them acting like old friends, I was relieved to see. Noting that the menfolk were absorbed in a discussion of their own, I sauntered over to Betty, who was basking in the warmth of the fireplace.

"I feel like I'm starting a brand-new chapter of my life," I commented, trying to sound brave and adventurous.

"We both are," Betty returned. "And I'm going to give you a word of advice."

I waited in silence, knowing there was no way I could stop it, even if I wanted to.

"Enjoy it, Jessica. Life's too short not to."

I just nodded. She made it sound so simple. And maybe it was.

At the very least, I could try.

• • •

Coffee.

As always, the thought that my morning shot of caffeine was just a few steps away was sufficient reason for me to drag myself out of bed. Of course, the sudden appearance of a warm wet nose in my face—Lou's, this time, reminding me that not all of us were able to benefit from indoor plumbing—was another strong incentive.

I climbed out of bed, groping my way toward the kitchen. My mind was still foggy, so much so that I'd forgotten that anything in my life had changed. It certainly felt just like any other day, what with Max getting underfoot and Lou hovering nearby and Prometheus already greeting the new day with annoying exuberance.

Until I snapped on the kitchen light and was confronted with a carton of mismatched mugs with cute sayings like, *Instant Human! Just Add Coffee,* a Tupperware container of utensils whose various purposes I couldn't begin to imagine, and the official Mr. Healthybody Super-Juicer, still in its original box.

"He'll find a way to make it fit," I muttered as I poured water into Mr. Coffee, wondering if I should start thinking of my favorite appliance as Mr. CaffeineAddictedBody. "He's really good at that kind of thing. He told me so himself."

As my beloved coffeepot began burping and sighing, I shuffled into the bathroom and launched into my usual morning routine. I grabbed my toothbrush, then opened the medicine cabinet to retrieve the toothpaste.

And instinctively ducked to protect myself from an avalanche as not one but four tubes leaped off the shelf and into the sink.

"Ni-i-ck!" I cried. "Why do we have four tubes of toothpaste?"

A few seconds later, he stuck his head in the doorway. His hair was tousled and his eyes looked as if the Tooth Fairy had sneaked into the bedroom in the middle of the night and, just for fun, glued the lids together.

"Wha-a-a, Jess?" he mumbled.

"Either our toothpaste gave birth during the night," I

replied, trying to remain calm, "or someone is guilty of the crime of hoarding oral-hygiene products."

Nick yawned loudly, meanwhile scratching his head with both hands. "Is *that* all."

Not the right answer. "I'm serious, Nick. This place is too small for four tubes of toothpaste."

"They all do different things," he explained. "See? That one's got whitener in it, and that one's for sensitive teeth. And that one's just regular old fluoride toothpaste."

"Why do we need all these different kinds?" I persisted. "Besides, doesn't some enterprising company make just one superduper toothpaste that performs all these vital functions at the same time?"

"Probably. We'll get some, okay?" He came up behind me and wrapped his arms around my waist. Looking in the mirror, I saw my reflection, except with an extra head resting on my right shoulder. "I've got a great idea. How about these two official roommates taking a shower together?"

I was about to blurt out an excuse—something like the coffee was probably ready or we didn't have enough time. Instead, I suddenly heard Betty's words of advice from the night before in my head.

"Enjoy it, Jessica," she'd said.

I had to admit, Betty was a bit older and way wiser than I was. So I figured I'd give it a try.

"Only if you promise to wash my back," I returned.

"Tell you what," Nick countered, sliding his warm hands under my T-shirt. "Just to show you what a nice guy I am, I'll wash anything you want."

"*Anything?*"

"Just point me in the right direction."

Maybe Betty's right, I thought. And figured I should at least be willing to give her the benefit of the doubt.

• • •

My morning of soapsud fun was long forgotten as I strode into the lobby of Sunshine Multimedia, the parent company of Channel 14 News, trying to exhibit a level of confidence I wasn't even close to feeling. I gave my name to the woman at the front desk and, at her request, signed in. Then I took a seat in one of the comfortable upholstered chairs that formed a circle around the giant TV dominating the waiting area. Needless to say, it was tuned to Channel 14 News.

I shouldn't have said a word about this to anyone, not even Nick, I thought, battling the butterflies that kept insisting upon doing aeronautical maneuvers in my stomach. That way, when it turns out that this doesn't go anywhere, I won't feel like—

"Dr. Popper?" an unnaturally chirpy voice broke in.

A tiny woman in a bright red blazer and a tight black skirt had marched into the lobby. The top of her long blond hair was pulled back in a barrette, making her look like a cheerleader. In one hand, she clutched a clipboard. She stuck out the other and gave me a hearty handshake.

"I'm Marlene Fitzgerald, the PA. We spoke on the phone, remember? We're so glad you were able to come in today."

"Thank you." I hesitated before adding, "What's a 'pee-ay'?"

"Production Assistant. Come on back. I'll introduce you to Patti. She's the producer. I believe you two already spoke on the phone."

At least *producer* was an actual word, and one that I recognized, instead of just initials. I was already feeling out of my element, and I hadn't even made it out of the lobby.

I followed Marlene down a hallway that looked like a corridor in any other office building. At the end was a pair of double doors painted black. A red lighting fixture was perched above the doorway.

"Whenever this light is on," Marlene said, pointing upward without breaking stride, "it means we're on the air—and that it's crucial that this door remain closed. Of course, you'll be inside while we're broadcasting, so you won't have to worry."

You mean *if* I get the job, I thought.

I was shocked when she pushed open the doors and led me into a large room that looked just like the television studios I was used to seeing in the movies.

"This is Studio A," Marlene announced. "It's, uh, our *only* studio." Quickly, she added, "Most of our spots are remotes. You know, our reporters are out in the field."

Actually, I was amazed at what a simple setup it was. Studio A consisted of a single large room, painted black, with three different sets. One was a big desk with space for two anchors to sit and look authoritative. The backdrop looked like a huge fish but was actually a map of Long Island. Ten feet away was another set, two upholstered chairs separated by a wooden table. The arrangement was ideal for face-to-face, one-on-one interviews.

The third set consisted of a high counter that was placed on a platform. Funny; I'd had a feeling that was where we were headed. Maybe the profusion of stuffed animals along the back wall tipped me off.

"This is where you'll be doing your spot," Marlene explained. "You'll start off with some introductory remarks—"

"I'll take over from here," a female voice boomed through the darkness. The woman it belonged to clip-clopped over in a pair of treacherous-looking high heels.

"This is Patti Ardsley," Marlene said. "That's Patti with an *i*."

Somehow, the *i* didn't surprise me. I wished I could say the same about the fact that the show's producer looked like she was about twelve years old. Like Marlene, she was dressed in a skirt and blazer. Only hers matched. A real suit. And her light brown hair was styled in a multi-layered pageboy, as if she were at least trying to look like a grown-up.

"Dr. Popper, we're so pleased to have you as part of the Channel Fourteen News family," Patti said, sticking out her hand and forcefully shaking mine. Even though she probably weighed in at about a hundred pounds, she had all the strength and energy of a used-car salesman. I just hoped I wasn't about to make a purchase I'd end up regretting.

She turned to her assistant. "Marlene, take Dr. Popper onto the set and help her get settled. I'll be over in a minute."

"But—" I said lamely.

"Okay, Dr. Popper," Marlene said. "We're working with two cameras. You look into whichever one has the red light on. Simple, right?"

"I guess so—"

"For the opening, the script will be right here on the teleprompter. All you have to do is read it. Got it?"

"Got it."

"Great. Forrester told us you were a quick study." She flashed me a big smile. "Okay. You'll need to show up about half an hour before the spot airs. That way, we'll have time for hair and makeup. This Friday, for the first show, you should probably come in a little earlier. And do you have any animals you could bring?"

"Excuse me?"

"Pets. Dogs, cats, that kind of thing? Animals that you could use for demonstrating...I don't know, procedures or whatever?"

"I have pets," I replied. "I suppose I could bring one or two."

Somehow, I got the feeling I was on a roller coaster that had started to roll before I had a chance to put the safety bar in place. I tried to remember how many appointments I had scheduled for Friday morning—and how much phone-calling it would take to reschedule everybody.

"Uh, excuse me," I interjected. "I thought this was a job interview, not an audition. I mean, I wasn't prepared to sit in front of—"

"You've already got the job," Patti's voice called from somewhere in the dark, sounding irritated.

Marlene leaned forward. "We're desperate," she whispered.

"But I'm not even sure I want to—"

"Let's have her run through the opening," Patti instructed. "Stand here, behind the counter."

I did as I was told, meanwhile sneaking a glance at my cohosts, the twenty or thirty stuffed animals behind me. A grinning crocodile, a zebra with multicolored stripes, a fluffy fake-fur fish . . . I felt like a guest on *Sesame Street*. I only hoped a costume with a giant animal head and big furry feet wasn't in my future.

"Okay, try sitting on the stool," Patti instructed.

Obediently, I lowered myself onto the high wooden stool behind the counter. The fur from the purple stuffed orangutan tickled the back of my neck.

"Now, smile!" Patti commanded. "Hold your head up high, but not too high. Sit up straight—that's it. And above all, look natural!"

"Whenever you're ready," Marlene prompted.

I plastered on what I hoped looked like a sincere smile, peered into the teleprompter, and opened my mouth to speak.

"Welcome to *Pet People*, the program for people who are passionate about their pets," I stopped. "You can't be serious."

Patti's face emerged from the darkness. She was scowling. "Is there a problem?"

"Don't you think the opening sounds too much like 'Peter Piper picked a peck of pickled peppers'?"

"Excuse me?"

"It's just that it's kind of a mouthful."

"You're doing fine," Patti said acidly. "Let's start again."

I took a deep breath. "Welcome to *Pet People*, the program for people who are passionate about their pets." Out of the corner of my eye, I could see her nodding approvingly. But then she held up her hand like a crossing guard in a school crosswalk.

"Wait. I had an idea."

Probably not a good thing, I thought.

"Your name is Dr. Popper, right?"

"Yes..."

"We simply have to include that in the opening. The—the—what's that thing called where everything starts with the same letter?"

"Alliteration," I said weakly. This whole thing was starting to sound like a really bad idea—and I hadn't even gotten my first scathing review.

"Right. Whatever. Let's change the opening so you say your name first. Try, 'I'm Dr. Popper. Welcome to *Pet People*'...and then the rest."

Please, *please*, don't let the phrase "Thanks for popping in" pop into her head! I thought.

"Got it," I said cheerfully, wondering if the Crocodile Hunter put up with this kind of treatment. Somehow, I couldn't picture Steve Irwin letting the Pattis of the

world push him around. Not when even six-foot crocodiles weren't allowed to do that.

"I'm Dr. Popper..." Somehow, I got through the in-
troduction. After tripping through an obstacle course of
*P*s, the rest of the script, which was written in normal
English, was a cinch.

Even Patti seemed pleased. "Good job, Dr. Popper.
Okay, so next you give your five-minute presentation.
We'll go over it before you go on the air, but basically the
content will be up to you. Then it's time for the call-in
segment of the show."

I blinked. "No one said anything about that."

Marlene nodded like a bobble head. "They're very
popular. Audience participation and all."

Patti clearly agreed. "Let's give it a try. Your opening
line is on the teleprompter. You just wait until a red light
on the phone lights up, press it, and read your line."

"Wait a sec. Exactly who are these people? The ones
who are calling in, I mean."

"Don't worry," she replied impatiently. "We screen all
the calls."

"Meaning?"

"Before we allow them to talk to you, we find out
their name, where they live, and the nature of their question. That way, we can keep the crazies from getting on
the air."

Marlene leaned forward and whispered, "We get a lot
of crazies."

"Could we cut the chitchat?" Patti barked. "Okay, Dr.
Popper. Let's see how you handle this."

"Thank you for calling *Pet People*," I said brightly,
pretending to press one of the buttons. "How can I help
you and your pet?"

"Excellent. You just listen to the caller's question and
answer it the best you can. Got it?"

"Got it."

It sounded simple enough. In fact, now that I'd gotten this far, I was pretty sure that the whole thing sounded like something I could manage.

As long as I could master the Peter Piper part of the job. If I could manage that, the rest would be a piece of—er, pie.

Chapter 9

"I wish I could write as mysterious as a cat."

—Edgar Allan Poe

How did it go?"

I'd barely made it back into my car before my cell phone jingled. I checked the Caller ID screen and saw it was Forrester. I wondered if Patti had already let him know that I'd passed the audition and was on my way to becoming a star.

"Fine," I told him, surprised by how proud I felt. "I got it."

"Far out, Popper! I knew you'd be great!"

I didn't bother to mention that, from what I'd seen, "great" wasn't one of the qualifications for the job. Breathing, yes. Able to read a teleprompter, certainly. Good at working with stuffed animals, definitely a plus.

"So when is your television debut?" he asked.

"Friday morning at ten."

"I'll be watching, even if I have to call in sick." He paused. "I hope the fact that you're skyrocketing to fame doesn't mean you've lost interest in the Thorndike case. I've got something you might find interesting."

Adrenaline was already shooting through my veins. I

felt like my dentist was prepping me for a particularly painful procedure. "News about what?"

"The three peculiar objects that were found near Cassandra's body. You remember them, right?"

"Of course."

"Get this," Forrester announced. "The only finger-prints the forensics people found on any of them were hers."

I was right! I thought. "So it *was* Cassandra who was trying to tell us something, not her killer."

"That's what it looks like."

"But are the cops any closer to figuring out what it means?"

"Nope. At least, not that I've heard."

I contemplated telling Forrester my theory about *The Scarlet Letter* referring to an affair—a real one, not the one that involved Hester Prynne and Reverend Dimmesdale. My contemplation lasted all of two seconds. I decided that there was nothing to be gained by sharing my theory with him or anyone else. At least, not until I'd found out more about Cassandra's love life.

"By the way," Forrester interjected, "I spoke to our buddy Lieutenant Falcone this morning. He's been putting together a list of the people who'd recently been in the room where Cassandra's body was found."

My heartbeat was just starting to speed up again when he added, "Don't get your hopes up. It's turning out to be a pretty long list. In fact, just about everybody she knows is on it. Seems the place was crawling with the fingerprints and hairs of the people she knew and loved."

"Like who?" I prompted.

"Let's see." I heard him rustling papers. "Okay. Gordon Thorndike, Joan Thorndike, Ethan Thorndike, family members. Robert Reese, fiancé. Jean-Luc Le Bec, pastry chef at Robert Reese's restaurant. Theo Simcox, family friend. Virginia Krupinski, neighbor. Suzanne Fox, of course." He paused. "There are quite a few more names. Should I go on?"

I sighed. "It's like you said. The list includes just about everybody she ever knew."

"I told you on day one, Popper. The answer to this one isn't in the forensics. It's in the backstory. Who Cassandra Thorndike was and what she was into."

"Thanks anyway, Forrester," I said, hating to admit that he was being a tremendous help. "It never hurts to have all the information."

"Just trying to be of assistance," he replied. "See that, Popper? I'm really not such a bad guy, once you get to know me...."

I was barely listening. Instead, I was already plotting how and when I'd return to the Scene of the Crime.

• • •

It wasn't until I pulled up in front of 254 Cliffside Lane a few hours later that I realized that a bright red Volkswagen was likely to attract as much attention as my Reigning Cats and Dogs van. So much for sneaking into Cassandra Thorndike's neighborhood. I only hoped that my nondescript outfit, which consisted of my navy-blue jacket and a pair of jeans, would make it difficult for any bystanders to pick me out of a lineup, if it ever came to that.

Besides, I told myself, there's nobody around in this quiet residential neighborhood. Not in the middle of the day. And the bright yellow crime-scene tape is gone, so there'd be no reason for anyone who happened to drive by to be suspicious.

My theory fell apart as soon as I started up the front walk that led to Cassandra Thorndike's house.

"Hi-i-i!" a high-pitched voice called.

I glanced over at the house next door and saw Maggie Rose standing on the porch, dressed in pale pink corduroy overalls and a yellow T-shirt. She gave me a big wave and an even bigger smile. "It's me, Maggie Rose. Remember?"

"Of course I remember," I replied, trying not to appear dismayed.

Not that I hadn't found Maggie Rose charming—and enjoyed our conversation, even if I was forced to admit that I'm a little weak in the lepidoptera department. But given the fact that I was trying my darnedest not to be seen, the last thing I wanted was to stand outside on the front lawn, chatting with a four-year-old.

"How's it going, Maggie Rose?" I added without breaking stride.

"Good." She drifted halfway down the front steps of her great-grandmother's house and draped herself across the banister. "You're the doctor who takes care of animals, right?"

"Right. Except butterflies." I wondered if there was any way I could ask the exuberant little girl to speak a little more softly.

"I know a story about a bunny," Maggie Rose said. "Want to hear it?"

"I wish I had time. But I'm afraid I'm kind of busy—"

"But this is a really good story. It's from a book. Cassie used to read it to me."

My ears pricked up at the little girl's use of the words *bunny* and *Cassie* in the same sentence. Still, I'd come here on a mission. If I let myself get distracted by Maggie Rose, who was no doubt desperate for a playmate who preferred telling stories to watching the Shopping Channel, I might run out of time.

Or, worse yet, lose my nerve.

"I'm afraid I can't," I told her. "At least not today. I

just stopped over for a minute to...uh, check something."

"Maggie Rose! Are you outside again?" Virginia Krupinski's voice called from inside the house. "Didn't I tell you not to go out without your sweater?"

And I bet there's one with a mean popcorn stitch that has your name on it, I thought.

"I'm not cold, Grammy!" Maggie Rose whined.

"You come back in here right now!" Virginia insisted. "Besides, it's time for your nap!"

I had a feeling it was really time for Virginia's nap, but that wasn't any of my business.

"You'd better go inside," I told Maggie Rose. "It sounds like your great-grandma means what she says."

"She *never* reads me stories!" she returned, sticking out her lower lip in an unconvincing pout. But she turned and marched up the stairs and onto the porch, not even waving good-bye before disappearing into the house.

Perfect timing, I thought, silently thanking whoever had invented naps.

After glancing around one last time to make sure no one was watching, I headed around toward the back. Sure enough, there was a cat door. Just as I remembered from the other time I'd been here. A knot immediately developed in the pit of my stomach.

Funny, I'd imagined it would be so much bigger.

I suddenly regretted helping Nick finish off those pastries Jean-Luc had forced upon me a couple of days ago. Still, I'd come this far. I had to give it the old college try, whether it turned out I could actually manage to fit through the small space or not.

I yanked off my fleece jacket, trying to minimize my resemblance to the Michelin Man. And wishing I could come up with some other ways of making myself narrower.

Here goes, I thought, crouching down and pushing the swinging door open. As I extended both legs through the square opening, a horrifying image popped into my head—one that involved me getting wedged inside the cat door at the hip, firefighters arriving on the scene with the Jaws of Life or at least large containers of cooking oil, and Lieutenant Anthony Falcone watching the whole thing with a smirk on his face and a pair of cuffs in his hands, thrilled that he'd caught me breaking and entering.

Suppressing the urge to shudder, I wriggled across the back steps, inhaling as deeply as I could. When I got to the hips, I tightened all the relevant muscles, chastising myself for never taking those "Buns of Steel" videos seriously.

True, it was a tight fit. But I made it.

So far, so good, I muttered. But the next challenge, getting my shoulders through, wasn't far behind.

It turned out that I had a lot more play with my upper body. A wrench of the arm here, a twist into an extremely uncomfortable position there, and I managed to squirm all the way through.

My heart was pounding and I felt oddly light-headed as I stood up. Whether that was from having just stuffed a round peg into a square hole or the fact that I was standing in Cassandra Thorndike's kitchen, I couldn't say.

Once I got my bearings, of course, I realized I could have simply stuck my head and one arm through and unlocked the back door.

Next time, I told myself, even as I hoped against hope there wouldn't be a next time.

What mattered for the moment was that I'd made it inside and was free to explore.

I glanced around, breathing in deeply and trying to get a feel for the woman who had lived here. Died here too, although at the moment I was more interested in discovering whatever I could about Cassandra's life than her death.

The kitchen was an excellent place to start. People's kitchens tell a lot about them. How organized they are, how much time they spend at home...and their idiosyncrasies about eating. I grabbed a dish towel and used it to open the refrigerator without leaving any fingerprints. Empty. Whether that reflected Cassandra's lifestyle or the Norfolk County Police Department's level of efficiency, I couldn't say.

The cabinets were much more revealing. From what I could see, Cassandra was not exactly what you'd call a homebody. For one thing, she didn't appear to own a complete set of anything. Three mugs, five plates, a smattering of unmatched silverware. A few staples had been shoved onto the shelves, but they didn't strike me as ingredients that went together very well: salt, honey, Nutella, tea bags, Cap'n Crunch. I bet even Jean-Luc couldn't come up with a way to combine those.

Her apparent lack of interest in creating fine cuisine at home was consistent with the rest of the room. Her collection of cooking utensils consisted of a can opener, a bottle opener, and a corkscrew. Even I own a slotted spoon.

Still, I reasoned, maybe her Spartan kitchen was simply a by-product of being a restaurateur's fiancée. After all, why make dinner at home when you could order up anything you wanted—and not even have to do the dishes afterward?

But beyond the lack of tools required to feed oneself, the kitchen had very few of the cozy little touches that typically make kitchens the most popular room in the house. There was no calendar hanging on the wall, not even one of those freebies from a local bank or supermarket. No photographs were stuck on the refrigerator, not even one of Beau. And I'd met very few pet owners who were able to resist decorating with images of their favorite living, breathing cuddly toy. Forget cute curtains or a set of matching canisters. Cassandra didn't even appear to own a drain board.

Okay, I told myself. There's nothing surprising here. The fact that Cassandra Thorndike didn't spend her Saturdays baking cookies isn't a great surprise. But you're also not finding out anything about her life that may help you figure out who killed her.

I moved on. As I stepped gingerly through the house, aware that my heart wouldn't stop pounding and that two giant wet spots were forming under my arms, I noticed cartons and shopping bags on chairs and next to dressers. Somebody—Joan Thorndike, according to Theo Simcox—was in the process of packing up Cassandra's things.

I peeked into a couple of cartons and saw they were filled with jeans and jewelry and books and CDs. But it wasn't Cassandra's possessions I was interested in; it was her home office. Not only was it the place in which she conducted her personal business and no doubt some of her job-related dealings. It was also the room in which she'd been killed.

The simple act of stepping into the smaller of the house's two bedrooms, outfitted as a home office, was sobering. This is the last place Cassandra was alive, I thought. These walls are the last thing she saw.

It was also the place in which she looked into the eyes of her murderer—most likely a person she knew, and knew well.

Cassandra's home office was as cluttered as her kitchen was bare. I estimated the room to be about eight by ten feet, yet she'd packed in an amazing amount of stuff. Wooden bookshelves lined two entire walls, and every inch was crammed with books, boxes, and file folders.

The room was dominated by a large desk, placed at an angle with the window overlooking the sea behind it. It was covered with Cassandra's possessions, just as Forrester had described it. They were in a state of complete chaos. Here, a pencil cup lay on its side, the pens and pencils and markers it had once contained splayed out like a child's game of pick-up sticks. Papers were strewn across the desk's surface, along with the manila folders that no doubt had originally held them in an orderly fashion.

There were other signs of the terrible incident that had occurred here. The rug was stained a dark red-brown, and dried blood spattered two of the walls.

I took a deep breath, trying to remain objective and forcing myself to take an inventory of the rest of the room. The trash can was nearly empty, and the plastic tray that served as an in-box contained nothing besides a coffee mug.

I moved closer to the desk and, still clutching the dish towel, gingerly opened the drawers. I found more file folders, each one labeled with the name of an East End restaurant. Thorndike Vineyards' clients, I assumed, the restaurants Cassandra had visited in her capacity as salesperson for her family's winery. I checked a few of them, noting that all the well-known eateries were there. At least, the ones I'd heard of.

I checked the rest of the drawers. A stapler and some other office supplies, a couple of packs of gum, a comb and a small mirror. Nothing too interesting.

Frustrated, I turned to the bookshelves. After all, that was probably where the copy of *The Scarlet Letter* had come from. As I perused the spines of the hardcover and paperback books crammed onto the shelves, I learned little besides the fact that Cassandra had had eclectic taste.

Her library included everything from classic novels to best-sellers to books about wine.

Then I spotted a book with a dark red leather cover stuck up on the shelf between Jonathan Kellerman and Stephen King. It didn't have a title printed on the spine.

Intrigued, I pulled it out—and saw that the cover was embossed in gold with the year.

Cassandra's date book. She'd kept it on a shelf with her other books, and the cops had missed it.

"Bingo," I muttered. If anything could help me get a feeling for how Cassandra spent her last days, it was the book I was holding in my hands—cradled in the dish towel, of course.

I began flipping through it, searching for the previous week. Unfortunately, the few entries Cassandra had made for the last week of September didn't tell me much. Most were appointments with restaurants, the same ones whose names were on the file folders. Della Marina and Barbie's and The Washroom in East Brompton, La Cuisine and Allie's in West Brompton, Cashew and Rick and Terri's in Poxabogue. There was one restaurant I didn't recognize: THOR.

I flipped back a few weeks, landing in the last week of July. *Tuesday, dentist, cleaning, 1:00. Thursday, 2:00, THOR.*

The following week she'd written, *Friday, 1:00, THOR.*

What's Thor? I wondered. Cassandra was going there too frequently for it to be a restaurant. An organization, maybe... or some local business, like a gym?

Or maybe a man?

As I skimmed through her entire year of appointments, I saw the name again and again. In fact, the name Thor was scribbled in at least once a week. Twice, sometimes.

Whatever or whoever this Thor was, I mused, he or it certainly seemed to play a large role in Cassandra's life.

"Hey!" I cried aloud when I spotted the February 12 entry. In addition to the name Thor and the time, Cassandra had scrawled a phone number. Checking the weeks before, I discovered that this was the first time Thor had been entered in her date book.

I pulled a pen and a gas station receipt out of my purse and wrote it down.

I put the book back where I'd found it, then glanced around the office one more time. At least I got something, I thought.

Now that I had, it seemed like a good time to get the heck out of there.

I headed out of the room quickly. Too quickly. As I did, I accidentally banged into the wall of shelves with my arm and managed to knock over a box of tissues, one of those cube-shaped ones with a never-ending supply popping out, one after another.

But as it fell to the floor, they all popped out at once.

"Klutz," I grumbled as I bent over to pick up the pieces and put Humpty Dumpty together again.

As I did, I realized there was a reason the wad of tissues had fallen out. The wad itself wasn't very thick, only a half inch or so. But there had been something else in the box that helped push them out.

Film. Rolls and rolls of film, each in its black cylindrical box. Seven, I counted before flipping open the lids.

Every one was exposed but undeveloped.

And hidden at the bottom of a tissue box.

The sound of a crash made me jump. The kitchen. Somebody was in the kitchen. My mind raced as fast as my pounding heart as I conjured up the most likely scenario: Somebody had been hiding in the bushes, watching me break in to the house. And then that individual had followed suit, wriggling inside exactly the way I had.

Fortunately, I had the presence of mind to slip the rolls of film into my pocket.

I let out a cry when a shadow moved across the doorway and I realized that the explanation that had run through my panicked mind was absolutely correct. Fortunately, Beau, being a cat and all, wasn't likely to turn me in.

"It's you!" I cried, half-relieved and half-accusing.

The satiny black feline just stared at me with his round, green eyes. Maybe it was my imagination, but he also looked both relieved and accusing. Still, having been found out—even by a pussycat—was a chilling reminder that I was taking a great risk. The idea of getting out while the getting was still good suddenly seemed incredibly attractive.

"The place is all yours," I told him. "Enjoy."

Beau just blinked, then trotted into the living room and leaped onto the couch, immediately settling into what I suspected had long been his favorite spot. I, too, was suddenly desperate to be in my favorite spot.

Which, at the moment, happened to be anywhere but here.

• • •

I was feeling pretty creeped out by the whole breaking-and-entering experience by the time I slid out through the cat door, wanting to keep the back door locked. The fact that the sun had dropped low in the sky and was blanketing the cliffside neighborhood in ominous-looking shadows didn't help.

As I neared my car, holding out the remote to unlock it, I happened to glance at the front seat. And nearly jumped out of my skin when I saw that somebody was sitting in the driver's seat.

At least, I thought it was somebody at first. But as I got closer, I saw that it wasn't a some*body*. It was a some*thing*.

A dummy, in fact. The horrid little wooden doll that was Ethan Thorndike's alter ego.

Chapter 10

"He lives in the halflights in secret places, free and alone, this mysterious little great being whom his mistress calls, My cat..."

—Margaret Benson

Realizing the intruder inside my car was made of wood, rather than flesh and bone, didn't do much to alleviate my discomfort. Neither did the fact that he was once again dressed like somebody's prom date instead of something threatening like a kung fu fighter or a WWF wrestler. In fact, anything at all that was related to Ethan Thorndike automatically increased a situation's creepiness factor by at least a hundred.

I opened the door and grabbed Ethan's version of Mini-Me by the armpits.

"Okay, Woody," I muttered. "I don't consider myself a violent person, but I'm beginning to harbor fantasies of turning you into a pile of toothpicks."

"I don't think he likes that," a male voice said. "Being handled so roughly, I mean."

I wasn't particularly surprised to turn around and find that Ethan was standing behind me. Uncomfortably close, as it turned out. This guy sure didn't seem to know much about boundaries. Of *any* sort.

"Then he shouldn't go around breaking into people's cars," I told him.

Ethan smiled eerily. "I was just playing around with you, Dr. Popper."

"I already figured that out."

He shrugged. "I can't help it if I happen to be good at picking locks and getting into places where I don't belong."

I was about to ask him the obvious question—why he would even *want* to break into my car and leave behind such a peculiar calling card—when he added, "Looks like that's a talent you have as well."

"I—I don't know what you mean." I could feel my cheeks getting hot, a sure sign that they were turning the same shade of red as my VW.

"Tsk-tsk," Ethan replied. "Dr. Popper, you've been such a naughty girl. Breaking and entering. Isn't that what the cops call it? Or maybe there's an even more serious charge that would apply in this situation. Something along the lines of tampering with a crime scene."

"I did no such thing!" I insisted indignantly. Instinctively I stuck my hand into my pocket, fingering the rolls of undeveloped film I'd stashed there. I hoped that Ethan's wooden dummy was the only one around here whose nose was likely to grow longer from lying.

"Speaking of tampering with a crime scene, I don't suppose you ran into Joan in there," Ethan continued. "Or as I like to call her, Step-Mommie Dearest."

Since I'd clearly been caught in the act, I didn't see any point in pretending. "There's no one inside. And I can assure you that the only reason I went into your sister's house is that I'm trying to find out who's responsible for her death."

"Then I suggest you look no further than our own close-knit, loving family," he said bitterly.

I just stared at him. "Ethan," I finally said, "I'm sure both you and your sister had a difficult childhood. It's tragic that you lost your mother at such a young age. And I know that getting used to a stepmother isn't easy for anyone. But no matter what went on while you and Cassandra were growing up, surely you don't believe Joan is capable of murder."

His expression remained hard. "Let's just say I hear things. And see things. Things other people might not be aware of, mainly because they're so busy obsessing about their own lives." With an odd smile, he added, "That happens to be one of the benefits of not having a life."

I was itching to find out more about this peculiar young man. And the most obvious question was *why* he had never chosen to develop what he so casually referred to as "a life." Somehow, a man in his twenties who was living in a tiny apartment above his parents' garage—a man who, from the looks of things, had no job, no friends, and no interests besides ventriloquism—didn't exactly impress me as somebody who was living up to his full potential.

But I couldn't resist asking a much simpler question. "By the way, where did you learn to break into cars?"

I was rewarded with another eerie smile. "I haven't spent my entire life living above a garage. I was at MIT for three and a half years. I learned a lot of useful things there."

That particular tidbit of information certainly answered the question of where he'd honed his technical abilities. Of course, it also raised more questions, like why anyone would leave college, especially such a prestigious one, with only one semester left before graduation.

But that was Ethan for you, I decided as I watched him head toward his sister's house. I didn't know him well, and I suspected that nobody else did either. I also got the feeling that was exactly how he wanted it.

• • •

As I pulled away from Cassandra's house, I contemplated Ethan's claim that to find the murderer, I didn't have to look any further than what he sarcastically referred to as his "close-knit, loving family." He certainly made no bones about his belief that his stepmother was responsible for Cassandra's murder.

Frankly, I found it impossible to take him seriously. I'd met the woman, and while she'd made it clear from the start that she and Cassandra had never been close—that, in fact, they'd been at odds pretty much during their entire relationship—I couldn't see her in the role of murderer. In fact, the only member of the Thorndike clan I could imagine being capable of such a brutal, hateful act was Ethan himself.

But there were so many other pieces of Cassandra's life I had yet to understand. I hoped the telephone number I'd found in her date book, or maybe the undeveloped film, would help.

I made a point of getting away from Captain Kidd Cove before dialing the phone number that would hopefully tell me who or what Thor was. As far as I could tell, Ethan wasn't following me. Then again, he'd already proven himself a master of sneakiness. For all I knew, he also had the ability to tap into my cell-phone calls. So just to be safe, I drove a few miles before turning into the parking lot of a 7-Eleven.

"Six-six-eight..." I muttered as I punched in the numbers, noticing that my mouth was dry. As I listened to the ringing at the other end, I didn't know what to expect. A mysterious sexy man with an exotic accent? A drug dealer who answered in single syllables? Some sleazy bar or strip club—or even an opium den?

Given my ridiculously overactive imagination, I was disappointed when a cheerful female voice answered, "The Spa at Greeley's Inn. Kristin speaking. How can I help you?"

Greeley's Inn was a combination hotel, restaurant, and spa dotting the farthermost tip of the North Fork. Seven or eight decades ago, it had opened as a rustic summer retreat for city folk in search of a little sea and sun. In recent years, however, as the North Fork became more popular with tourists and summer residents, Greeley's raised its room rates, brought in a first-rate chef from a Manhattan restaurant, and added a spa that featured treatments that, to me, sounded either painful or edible. I suspected that the only thing remotely sinister about it was the inflated price of its Seaweed Scrub.

I did some fast thinking. "Uh, I'd like to schedule an appointment...with Thor."

I held my breath, wondering what kind of response I'd get.

"Certainly," Kristin chirped. "What kind of massage do you want?"

So Thor was a massage therapist. Thinking back to all those entries in Cassandra's date book, I wondered if she was just really, really tense or if Thor had offered her something beyond the glow that undoubtedly came from reduced muscle tension and improved circulation.

Hopefully, paying a house call would help me find out.

"What kinds of massages are available?" I asked.

"Swedish, deep tissue, shiatsu, lymphatic drainage, the sports massage, the amma massage..."

This was getting complicated. "Uh, Swedish."

"Sixty-minute or ninety-minute?"

After checking my date book, I scheduled an hour

with Thor for early the following afternoon. As I hung up the phone, I was already tingling with anticipation—and Thor had yet to lay a finger on me. In fact, I'd never actually had a real, official massage, mainly because it had never occurred to me to seek one out. But now that I was, I figured getting a Swedish massage from a guy named Thor was definitely the way to go.

My next stop was a photography shop. Even though the photo service at a supermarket or drugstore would have been more convenient, I wanted the film I'd taken from Cassandra's house to be developed by professionals. I knew it was likely the pictures would turn out to be nothing more intriguing than shots from Cassandra's last vacation. But I couldn't keep myself from hoping there had been a good reason she'd gone out of her way to hide them, or at least store them in a place they weren't likely to be discovered. In fact, I was clinging desperately to the possibility that they would turn out to contain something much more revealing than which Caribbean resort or European capital she preferred.

Fortunately, there was a small shop called Photo Stop less than a mile from my home. Not only did I like the fact that the business focused in one specific area; a huge sign in the window advertised its one-hour film-developing service.

As I stepped inside, an old-fashioned bell attached to the door tinkled, announcing my arrival. However, there wasn't anything the least bit old-fashioned about the man behind the counter. He was dressed in very dark jeans, a black *Star Trek* T-shirt printed with *Beam Me Up, Scotty,* and black-framed eyeglasses so thick I doubted lasers could pass through. Even though he appeared at least thirty, his pudgy face had a youthful look—mainly because of the pimples sprinkled over his forehead, cheeks, and chin. I wondered if the thick grease that held his dark hair in place had anything to do with the unfortunate state of his skin.

Still, it wasn't his geeky appearance that irked me. It was the fact that even though he and I were the only two people in the store, he seemed much too busy rearranging boxes and straightening up piles of paper to deal with something as trivial as providing service to a customer.

"Is this a bad time?" I finally asked, not even trying to contain my sarcasm.

At least I'd shamed him into acknowledging my presence. "Yuh?" he asked, exhibiting about as much personality as I'd expected.

"I have some film I need developed," I said, placing the rolls on the counter. "You do that here, right?"

"Actually, we're Starbucks' main competitor," he returned. "We just call ourselves Photo Stop to confuse them. Latte or cappuccino?"

I forced myself to smile. I didn't want to create any bad will here. Not with the photos I'd retrieved from Cassandra Thorndike's house at stake—*retrieved* being a much nicer word than *stolen*. "These are really important," I told him.

"Aren't they all," he said, looking bored. "The new baby, the new puppy, the trip to Disney World..."

I got the feeling that none of these events had been a part of Mr. Photo Stop's full life. I wondered if he'd like to meet a guy I knew named Ethan.

"I'll have these for you tomorrow morning," he said, grabbing an envelope and a pen. "Any time after nine."

"But I thought you were a one-hour service!" I protested.

"On a *normal* day." Rolling his eyes theatrically, he added, "We get maybe three of those a year."

So much for immediate gratification, I thought, handing over the film. Or even one-hour gratification.

• • •

With nothing to do at that point but wait—not only to meet the mysterious Thor who warranted so many entries in Cassandra's date book, but also to find out what the photos she'd hidden were all about—I decided to try forgetting all about the investigation, at least for a few hours. Nick was spending the evening studying at the library, leaving my beloved cottage to me and my menagerie. Not only was I looking forward to settling in for a quiet evening of my own; as I went inside, pulled off my chukka boots, scooped up Tinkerbell, and dropped onto the couch, I realized I actually craved it.

The annoying *whoop, whoop!* of some fancy car's alarm system told me I wasn't about to enjoy such luxury.

I sat up and glanced out the window, then groaned at the sight of the familiar low-slung Corvette. Marcus Scruggs didn't exactly drop in on me every day of the week. In fact, I couldn't remember him ever coming over before. Calling me either, unless there was something he wanted.

Which was no doubt the reason for this visit. "Make it short, Marcus, whatever it is," I muttered to myself before opening the door.

"Hey, Marcus!" I said, trying to sound friendly but not too friendly. It was the same tone I used with a large dog I'd never encountered before. I wanted him to feel unthreatened, but not so welcome that he thought it was okay to jump on me.

"Glad I caught you in," he said, striding inside.

I assumed that, like most normal people, he'd sit down and tell me what was on his mind. Instead, he continued striding. Unfortunately, it was quite disconcerting, the way he kept pacing back and forth, even though my living room isn't exactly what you'd call spacious. Even my dogs seemed confused by my visitor in motion. Max trotted alongside him, happy to have an excuse to keep moving. But Lou gave him a wide berth, as if he wasn't sure what to make of this interloper who had even more pent-up energy than he did.

As he paced, Marcus's forehead was so wrinkled that he looked like the Before in a Botox ad, and he kept running his fingers over his stubby dark-blond hair. "Can I get you anything?" I offered, always the polite hostess. "Coffee? A Coke?" A couple of Valium?

"I'm good."

He looked anything *but* good. In fact, just watching him was making me tired. I sank into the upholstered chair. "Well, then," I said, the little patience I still had fading fast. "What's on your mind, Marcus?"

He finally stopped pacing and lowered himself onto the couch. Still, as he sat with his legs spread far apart, the right one jumped up and down nervously, prompting Max to venture over to investigate. Being a terrier, he felt quite comfortable with hyperactivity. "Popper, I'm about to tell you something that very few people know." He paused. "Something about me. Something *personal*."

The word set off alarms in my head. "Marcus, I really don't think—"

"I'm about to turn forty."

I involuntarily let out a sigh of relief.

"I know what you're thinking: How could a guy as young-looking, as vital, as *sexy* as the Marc Man be hitting the big four-oh? But it's true, Popper. I swear on my life."

"Actually, I figured you were around that age," I said matter-of-factly. "After all, you'd already been in practice for a couple of years back when I was just applying to vet school, so—"

"Let me tell you, it's a sobering time in a person's life," he went on. I realized I needn't have bothered to speak at all. "It makes you step back and reevaluate. I'm thinking that one day—not yet, but in the foreseeable future—I'm going to want to settle down. Maybe even have kids, a picket fence, an SUV, the whole Hallmark-card thing."

"That's great, Marcus. You and the wife must have me over for a barbecue some time." I still didn't have the slightest idea where he was going with this. Hinting around for a surprise party? Campaigning for a really great birthday present?

"And, well, that makes a guy start thinking about the kind of woman he'd like to grow old with." He swallowed, his Adam's apple bobbing up and down so hard I suddenly remembered that Halloween was only a few weeks away.

Then, slowly, I started to get it. The sensation reminded me of waking up in the middle of the night because one of those leg cramps has begun gripping your calf. You can feel it happening in slow motion, and you know what's coming, but even so there's no way you can stop it....

"Marcus, what's your point?" I demanded icily. And here I'd actually been wondering whether he was a Medium or a Large, just in case I decided to get him a T-shirt printed with a funny saying for his fortieth.

"I feel really bad about this," he went on. "But I've got to tell somebody." He drew in his breath sharply. "Popper, I want to believe Suzanne is innocent. I mean, she's everything to me. I never believed anyone could get to me the way she has."

He paused, swallowing hard as if something was stuck in his throat. I simply stared at him, hoping that something was. And that it would prove fatal. After all, you didn't have to be a mind reader to see where Marcus was going with this.

It took everything I had to keep from picking up a large, heavy object and causing him physical harm.

"Marcus," I said through clenched teeth, "if you

know anything at all about Suzanne—if you have even an *inkling* of who she is—how could you think for even a nanosecond that she could possibly be capable of murder?"

"I know, I know. That's what I keep telling myself. And I'm ninety-nine percent convinced she's innocent. It's just that there's this one tiny little part of me that can't help wondering. I mean, when you think about it, how well do any of us really know anybody? All you have to do is pick up a newspaper and you'll read some story about a guy who everybody loved, some average Joe who went to work every day and played with his kids and coached Little League . . . and then it turns out that for the past ten years he's been burying bodies underneath the rose garden." He shook his head slowly. "My point is that even though I'm nuts about Suzanne, how can I really be sure she didn't bump off her ex's fiancée?"

By this point, I could barely contain myself. In fact, I'd begun thinking some pretty murderous thoughts myself.

"Marcus," I said sharply, "I hope you have enough decency to keep your doubts to yourself, at least until Suzanne gets through this ordeal."

He blinked, looking confused for a few seconds. I realized then that the idea of taking the high road hadn't even occurred to him.

"She needs you," I went on. "Right now she's going through what's undoubtedly the most difficult part of her entire life. And for whatever reason, you're the person she's chosen to be her life partner right now."

"But—"

"Listen to me, Marcus!" I wagged a finger at him, hoping I looked like I meant what I was saying. "If you let her down, I will never forgive you. You have a job to do here. Even *you* have to recognize that! I don't care what happens after this is all over. But for now, if you possess even a single strand of moral fiber, you will be there for Suzanne!"

He looked startled. But slowly a look of comprehension came over his face. "You're right, Popper," Marcus replied. "You're absolutely one hundred percent on the money. And I'll do it. Like you say, I'll keep whatever doubts I may have to myself. I'll be a—a rock."

"Good," I said with a nod. "I'm glad you get it."

I only wished that, deep down, I believed he was capable of following through.

• • •

"Hey, I know her!" Nick exclaimed over breakfast the next morning, his face hidden behind the pages of *Newsday*. "Jessica Popper, DVM, Long Island's favorite veterinarian."

"What on earth are you talking about?" I mumbled, my mouth still half full of the English muffin that, along with a mug of coffee the size of a small bucket, constituted my own personal breakfast of champions. I was only three quarters awake, meaning one quarter of the cobwebs that had formed in my brain during the night still clouded my thought process. Besides, Nick wasn't making himself particularly easy to understand, the way he was acting as if he'd just seen something about me in the newspaper—

"Give me that!" I cried, reaching across the table and grabbing the paper out of his hand. I scanned the left-hand page, not spotting any familiar-sounding reference in any of the three different columns that covered the page. Then I glanced at the right-hand page and nearly fell off my chair.

"Leaping lizards!" I yelped.

Poor Max, fearing his beloved mistress had just had something terrible happen to her—or was perhaps initiating some new game—jumped up, gently resting his two furry little paws on my thigh. He glanced at me quizzically, his eyes bright and his wet nose pulsing as if thinking, *Are you okay? Do you want to play? Do you have any food for me?*

Any of those possibilities would have been preferable to what had really made me cry out: a full-page advertisement for Channel 14 News.

GOT PETS? the headline read. THEN *PET PEOPLE* IS FOR YOU!

The ad went on to explain that Jessica Popper, DVM, Long Island's favorite veterinarian, was debuting her new show, *Pet People,* on Friday morning at 10:00 A.M. There was even a photograph of me that looked a lot like the photo they'd insisted upon snapping on my way out in order to provide me with a Channel 14 ID card.

"Looks like you're famous," Nick commented, grinning.

"I hope Andy Warhol was right," I replied, handing him back the paper. "About it only lasting fifteen minutes, I mean."

"I don't think Andy was talking about those of you who are lucky enough to possess star quality—not to mention your very own television show. Just think: you, Barbara Walters, Oprah, Tony Danza ... Hey, you're not going to throw me over for some boy toy, are you? A surfer dude who's ten years younger ... ?"

I was in no mood for joking around. Not with enough butterflies suddenly gathering in my stomach that they'd actually become uncomfortably heavy. You wouldn't think those light little wings could add up to much, but apparently they can.

Even Max had given up on me. Having decided that there was no food coming and no game of Slimytoy in the schedule, he'd returned to floor level. He now lay under the table, chewing on his hot-pink rubber poodle, no doubt luxuriating in the sound of its relentless squeaks.

"I don't think that many people will see that, do you?" I asked Nick hopefully.

"Probably not," he returned. "Especially since it's right next to 'Dear Abby,' the gossip column, and today's horoscopes. I mean, who looks at any of those?"

The butterflies were getting even heavier. I suddenly felt as if I was getting myself into more than I'd bargained for. To be honest, I'd been so focused on Suzanne's plight that I hadn't given much thought to the new TV show Forrester had gotten me involved in. I'd simply seen it as a way to help pet owners take better care of their animals. It had never occurred to me that I was in line to become the new Crocodile Hunter.

"Anybody home?" I heard Betty call from outside.

"Come in," I yelled back, leaping out of my seat to let her in.

She beat me to it, poking her head inside. "Are you two busy? I don't want to interrupt."

"We're behaving ourselves," I assured her. "Want some coffee?"

"Thank you, Jessica, but I have no intention of disturbing you. I just wanted to congratulate you. You did see today's *Newsday*, didn't you?"

I cast Nick a wary look.

"I was checking my horoscope, the way I do every morning, and there it was, *your* picture and *your* name, plastered across this entire page...." She held up the ad, beaming. "I'm so proud of you, Jessica. And it's such a thrill to know a real celebrity!"

"I'm sure nobody else bothers to check their horoscope," Nick said, winking. "Even so, maybe you should get used to being famous. It looks like that's what's in your stars."

He stood up and planted a chaste kiss on my head. "And now I must take leave of you lovely ladies. The

Brookside University School of Law waits for no man—or woman, for that matter. I'm outta here."

Once we were alone, Betty sat down in his seat and distractedly petted Lou, who had immediately lodged his head in her lap for that very purpose. "This is certainly a homey scene," she commented. "It looks like your new living arrangements are working out well."

"How about you?" I countered. "Are things blissful over at the Big House?"

I expected a glowing report of candlelight dinners and long sessions of doing the *New York Times* crossword puzzle together. Instead, Betty's face crumpled.

"Jessica, the man is driving me absolutely crazy."

I blinked in confusion. "Wait. We're talking about Winston, right?"

"Who else? I'm absolutely beside myself! For one thing, he snores like a cartoon character. For another thing, he has the television on all the time. It's tuned to the news, but even so, the constant noise is enough to give me a headache. And he has this exercise routine he insists on doing every single morning. I hear him huffing and puffing, sounding like he's at death's door. The first time, I picked up the phone and was ready to dial 911. And you should see my kitchen! It looks like one of those health-food stores that always smells so darned funny! He stocked it with brewer's yeast and soy powder and heaven only knows what else...."

She sighed. "I'm set in my ways, Jessica. Maybe *too* set in my ways. But if that's who I am, I'm not very likely to change. I'm beginning to wonder if I'm simply destined to live out the rest of my life alone."

I opened my mouth, hoping some words of encouragement would magically make their way out. I wasn't surprised that they didn't. I was hardly in a position to start singing the praises of cohabitation. Not when I'd practically sent Nick to live in his car the moment I was assaulted by his toothpaste collection.

"So what are you going to do?" I asked, sipping the last of my coffee.

"I thought it might be good for us to get away, so Winston and I—and Frederick, of course—are taking a little trip this weekend. It's just for a few days. But I thought a romantic interlude—someplace far away from the television and the blender—might be precisely what we need. I found a bed-and-breakfast in Pennsylvania, right in the heart of Amish Country, that claims to be 'rustic but charming.' The autumn leaves should be beautiful, and I'm hoping that being in a new environment will allow us to concentrate on what we like about each other instead of the complications of day-to-day life."

"Don't tell me the honeymoon is already over," I said woefully.

"More like a case of too much too soon." Betty sighed. "I think I forgot that you can't force intimacy, Jessica. It's something that grows over time. I'm afraid that Winston and I have been so thrilled to find the closeness we've both been craving that we may have gotten carried away. For heaven's sake, I'm sharing kitchen appliances with a man I've known for less than a month!"

I wasn't quite sure that put her into the wild-and-crazy category, but I kept my observation to myself.

"Of course, you and Nick are an entirely different story," she hastened to add. "You two have known each other for years. Even so, I thought you might enjoy house-sitting while Winston and I are away. It might be good for you to have a bit of a change yourselves."

"That's a great idea," I agreed. "We can pretend we're the lord and lady of the manor."

"Then it's settled. I'll get you a set of keys. And it would probably be a good idea for you to stop over so I can explain a few things about the hot water and some of the house's other idiosyncrasies."

"Sounds like fun, Betty. Thanks for thinking of us."

As I stepped into the shower right after she left, I continued puzzling over the difficulties Betty was having as she pursued a deeper relationship with Winston, a man she'd only recently met. The way she'd put it was, "too much too soon." I had to admit that I not only understood; I was having some of the same feelings myself.

At least Betty had an excuse. But what about me? What was *my* excuse?

Chapter 11

"A cat's got her own opinion of human beings. She don't say much, but you can tell enough to make you anxious not to hear the whole of it."

—Jerome K. Jerome

As soon as I'd rinsed the soap out of my ears and pulled my damp hair back into a ponytail, I headed directly for Photo Stop. When I entered, the same cheerful bell announced my arrival. I hoped I'd find somebody else working there, maybe even somebody who was actually in the running for Employee of the Month. Unfortunately, the same uncooperative guy I'd encountered the day before stood behind the counter, his back to me.

I cleared my throat. No reaction.

"Uh, hello...?" I tried tentatively.

"Can I help you?" he mumbled without bothering to turn around.

"I'm here to pick up some photographs," I informed him. "I dropped them off yesterday."

"Name?"

"Popper," I replied.

He whirled around so quickly you'd have thought Mr. Spock himself just walked into the store.

"So *you're* Popper." Instead of the sullen look I'd had to deal with the evening before, his expression underwent a transformation so dramatic it bordered on supernatural.

"Yes..."

He picked up a cardboard envelope that had been left on top of the box of photos that were ready to go. Then he leaned across the counter, placing his elbows on the glass and resting his head in his hands. This unexpected pose put his face so close to mine that I instinctively jerked backward. He gazed at me through half-closed eyes.

"Y'like snakes?" he asked in a husky voice, stretching his mouth into a leer.

"Excuse me?"

I couldn't believe I'd heard him correctly. Snakes happen to be the one animal I've never felt comfortable around, to indulge in a bit of understatement. Since I'm a veterinarian, that happens to be pretty darned embarrassing. But beyond the weirdness of a total stranger picking up on one of my most glaring vulnerabilities, I wondered why on earth a clerk in a photo store would ask me such a bizarre question.

"Not particularly," I replied noncommittally.

A look of confusion flickered across his face. "You mean that's not you?" he asked, holding up the envelope. "In these photos?"

At least this strange conversation I'd suddenly found myself having seemed to make a little more sense. The problem was that he had me confused with someone else. Maybe somebody who'd brought in snapshots of a family trip to a reptile farm.

"Uh, no," I replied. "That's not me."

"Oh, I get it," he finally said. "You're the photographer. You took them."

"Well...no." I peered at the envelope more closely, figuring I'd point out that there had been some sort of a mix-up. But written on the top in big, bold letters was my name: POPPER.

He frowned. "So these are pictures of a friend of yours?"

I was beginning to squirm. "Actually, I, uh, just dropped these off for a casual acquaintance. I don't really know any of the people in the photographs."

He leaned backward, returning to his side of the counter as quickly as he'd crossed it. "Oh," he said dully. "Too bad." Turning to the cash register and punching some keys, he said indifferently, "That'll be forty-four twenty-seven. Cash or charge?"

By the time I got to my van, I couldn't wait to see what these photographs were all about. I settled into the driver's seat, opened the envelope, and glanced at the photograph on top.

If I hadn't put on my seat belt, I would have fallen on the floor.

The girl in the close-up was looking directly at the camera, her face drawn into an angry scowl and her tongue sticking out aggressively. Her defiant expression was made even more grotesque by all the makeup she wore. Thick black eyeliner encircled each eye, and dark blue eye shadow was smeared up to the thin, arched eyebrows drawn on her forehead. The purple streaks on each cheek resembled wounds, a look that matched her bruised-looking, thickly painted red lips. I counted no fewer than five facial piercings: two in one eyebrow, one in the other, a ring in her left nostril, and a stud in her tongue.

Her black hair, which was cut short, was streaked with blue and gelled into spikes. But there were other spikes too. Those were the ones sticking out of the black dog collar she wore around her neck.

This sure isn't anybody I know, I thought. My Trekkie friend had to have mixed up my film with somebody else's.

Yet as I studied the photograph, a chill ran through me. I realized that I did know this woman, after all. She was Cassandra Thorndike.

This Cassandra, however, was a far cry from the dewy-eyed Cassandra draped in purple velvet that I'd seen in the oil painting at Thorndike Vineyards.

I moved on to the next shot. In this one, she stood in a menacing position, as if she were about to lunge at whoever was photographing her. Most of her body was exposed, and the parts that weren't were clothed in black leather. A leather mask covered her eyes and most of her head, and a tight leather corset that was cut out in the most unlikely places hugged her torso. She wore spiked heels so high they looked positively excruciating. But that was nothing compared to the piercings she had in various unlikely parts of her body. Just imagining the pain of having them inserted made me grimace.

The next few photographs were also of Cassandra, once again dressed in garments I was pretty sure you wouldn't find at the Liz Claiborne outlet. She boldly posed in leather garter belts and fishnet stockings, peekaboo dresses made of nothing but straps, and gloves with metal talons at the fingertips. She wore wigs in many of them, ranging from a short platinum-blond pageboy to a pink net creation to long black strands that actually resembled her own. In some shots, she brandished chains, handcuffs, whips, and ropes. In others, she was deliberately inflicting pain upon herself, showing off a breast pinched in several places with clothespins or an arm with safety pins inserted into her skin. In one, she dripped melted candle wax on her thighs.

Next came a few photos in which she was completely naked, lying on the floor in an extremely provocative position. But what was even more startling was the fact that her bare flesh was smeared with something brown. Brown paint, perhaps, or maybe chocolate pudding. At least, I hoped that was what it was.

The final shots, the ones at the bottom of the stack, clued me in to why the clerk and I had had our friendly little discussion about snakes. Cassandra clearly hadn't shared my distaste for Serpentes. In fact, from the ecstatic look on her face as she writhed on the floor with two pythons, wearing nothing but a faux-leopard-skin thong, I'd have to say she felt pretty comfortable around them.

I stuck the stack of photos back into the envelope, noticing that I'd developed a gnawing stomachache. Now that the shock value had worn off, I was left feeling extremely disturbed.

Cassandra had obviously had a few secrets up her black-leather sleeve. There was a side of her that was pretty dark, which meant she may have gotten involved with some unsavory people. And given the type of toys she and her pals obviously enjoyed fooling around with, the possibility that someone had gotten carried away while playing with one of them wasn't very difficult to imagine.

• • •

After the unsettling glimpse of Cassandra Thorndike's secret world I'd gotten that morning, driving out to the end of the North Fork for my appointment at Greeley's Inn was a breath of fresh air—both literally and figuratively. After turning off the main thoroughfare, I meandered along for another half mile or so, getting closer and closer to the shoreline. At the end of the road, I spotted what had to be my destination.

Rising up from the gentle sand dunes was a complex of rough-hewn wooden buildings, a line of A-frames that were probably hotel rooms and a large structure with walkways and patios on several levels. I pulled up in front of the big building, which overlooked the waves of the Atlantic Ocean rolling onto the white-sanded beach just a few hundred yards away. A large sign above a side door read, *The Spa at Greeley's*.

I parked and went inside, passing a door that led to the pool area and inhaling enough chlorine to give my lungs a good bleaching. But as soon as I moved farther along the hall and walked through a set of double glass doors, I found myself bathed in one of those hippie scents that these days passes for aromatherapy—patchouli or frangipani or some other fragrance that only seems to exist in the hearts and minds of candle and incense manufacturers.

The reception area was decorated in the soothing colors of the seashore, the same pearly white of the sand and the rich blues and greens of the ocean that I'd just seen outside. Behind the counter stood a young woman with pale blond hair pulled back into a neat ponytail, wearing a sea-green polo shirt embroidered with the words *The Spa at Greeley's*. She gave me a welcoming smile.

"How can I help you?" she asked in a low, soothing voice.

I felt more relaxed already. "I'm here for a massage," I told her. "With, uh, Thor."

She nodded knowingly. "Thor's the best. Some women find that they actually become addicted to him."

Personally, I prefer limiting my addictions to caffeine and Ben & Jerry's. But the gleam in her eye told me she was one of the women who had fallen under Thor's spell.

"Have a seat," she instructed. "He'll be with you in a minute."

I lowered myself onto one of the two love seats, meanwhile glancing at the magazines splayed across the coffee table. While this was my big chance to catch up on the latest issues of *Yoga and You* and *The Vegan View,* I decided to use these free moments to get psyched for my first massage—and to plan a strategy for my meeting with the man whose name was scrawled all over Cassandra's date book.

It was hard not to wonder what he looked like. When I imagined a massage therapist named Thor, I pictured a true hunk—six feet tall, bulging but well-proportioned muscles, blond hair, blue eyes, perfect teeth... the whole stereotyped Scandinavian-god type.

I wasn't the least bit disappointed.

"Jessica?" a deep male voice asked.

I jerked my head up and saw Thor standing in the doorway, smiling at me. If anything, my fantasy had fallen short of the reality. He was blond, all right, with eyes as blue as the Swedish flag. He also had the muscular build I'd imagined, although I'd been a little off in the height department, since he probably stood a little over six feet tall.

Calm down, I instructed myself. You're here for a murder investigation... remember?

"Is it all right if I call you Jessica?" he asked, flashing two rows of startlingly white teeth.

"Fine," I said. Actually, I kind of chirped the word "fine," sounding a lot like Prometheus with a couple of seeds lodged in his throat.

"Great. Then follow me."

I resisted the urge to mumble something like, "To the ends of the earth." It wasn't hard, since I didn't think I'd gotten my normal voice back. My sudden throat condition wasn't helped by the fact that for some reason, Thor was wearing nothing but one of those Speedo bathing suits. One that looked about two sizes too small.

He led me into a small, windowless room with walls painted a serene shade of blue. The only piece of furniture was a massage table, covered with a white sheet. New Age music floated in from some unseen source, strange, wispy sounds that made me expect a line of druids to drift into the room any minute.

"This is the first time I'll be giving you a massage, right?" Thor asked.

I just nodded. It seemed simpler than attempting to speak.

"Great. The most important thing you need to know is that my main goal is making you feel completely comfortable."

In that case, I thought, you might consider putting on a sweatsuit.

"I'm going to leave you alone for a minute," he went on. "While I'm gone, take off everything and lie down on this table, facedown, with this sheet over you."

"Everything?" I squawked.

"Is this your first massage?"

"My first professional massage," I croaked.

"In that case, I'm honored to be the one breaking you in." He smiled, looking extremely pleased with himself.

I forced myself to think about Nick as I pulled off my clothes and lay down to wait. But at the moment, he seemed very far away.

I was already in position when I heard Thor come in and close the door.

"Okay, I see you're all set. Why don't you close your eyes and relax?" he suggested.

I managed the first part—but not before I saw the lights dim. A few seconds later, a soothing fragrance wafted into my nostrils.

"Do you like this scent?" he asked, his voice as thick and creamy as a pint of Cherry Garcia. I was beginning to understand how women could become addicted to this man. "It's very calming, a mixture of lavender, marjoram, green Mandarin...Pretty powerful stuff."

"Mm-hmm," I replied, not wanting to risk uttering any noises that would make me sound like a thirteen-year-old choir boy whose voice was changing.

"That doesn't surprise me. From the moment I saw you, you struck me as the sensual type."

Before I had a chance to wonder about the implications of that, I heard a peculiar blurping sound.

"What's that?" I demanded, ready to leap off the table.

"Relax," he replied. "It's just massage oil. To decrease friction."

"Friction?"

"Between your skin and mine. It makes the movement smoother. Nicer. More gentle." I heard what sounded like him rubbing his hands together, probably to warm the oil. And then I felt a little fluttery feeling on my back.

"Ooh, that tickles," I cried. "Is it supposed to tickle?"

"That's just the oil. I can tell you're a little tense, but you'll get used to it." Thor was silent for a few seconds before adding, "I should probably explain why I'm dressed like this."

Or undressed, I thought. But no words were forthcoming. Not when he'd already pulled the sheet down, exposing my upper back, and begun kneading my muscles with a soothing rotating motion.

"I just got off."

My eyes popped open. "Excuse me?"

"I'm only supposed to work a half day today," he continued. "That's why I took a quick dip in the pool just now, right before Kristin told me you were on the schedule. Nothing like a quick dip, don't you think?"

"No." At least I was managing to articulate words. Single-syllable words, anyway.

"But I guess I should be used to getting screwed," he continued cheerfully. His hands were moving downward, the kneading of his fingers becoming more forceful.

"What?" I croaked.

"By Kristin. She's always screwing up the schedule. But I don't mind. She keeps telling me it's because so many women insist that I be the one to give them their massage. If she's right—and she's not just messing with me—I wouldn't want to let them down." He was silent for a few minutes, working on my body as if I were a mound of pizza dough.

"You are very good at this," I murmured.

"That's what they tell me," he replied, sounding matter-of-fact.

"You're particularly good at that," I continued. "And—oooh—just a little too good at that."

"So much tension," he said. "I can really feel it right in here." He made little circles on my shoulder blades, impressing me with the strength of his thumbs.

He was silent for a while, systematically melting parts of me I hadn't even realized were frozen. A persistent voice deep inside my head kept trying to remind me that I was there for a reason, even though other, louder voices were doing their best to block it out.

"What about you?" he finally asked. "How did you hear about me?"

That lone little voice in my head gave a triumphant yell. I thought you'd never ask. "Through Cassandra Thorndike."

"Ah, Cassandra." He sighed deeply. I opened my eyes enough to see that a look of pure bliss had crossed his face. It quickly turned to one of distress. "I can't get over what happened to her. It's just too horrible. That girl was so full of life. I can't imagine who . . ." His voice trailed off, and a heavy silence hung over the room.

"I didn't know her very well," I finally volunteered. "Did you?"

"Sure," he replied. "She was a regular here. I used to give her massages once or twice a week." He hesitated before adding, "But we were also friends. Outside of her coming here, I mean. In fact, I'd kind of sneak her in a lot of the time so she didn't have to pay."

"Then I guess you were pretty upset when she and Robert got engaged."

"Oh, it wasn't like that. I mean, we never went out." He paused again. "We had the same—I guess you'd call it a hobby."

I hoped he didn't notice that my muscles immediately tensed, pretty much undoing everything he'd accomplished in the past fifteen minutes. "Really?" I asked. "What kind of hobby?"

It took him a long time to answer. As he kneaded my shoulders in silence, I hoped he wasn't about to say something like stamp collecting or bungee jumping.

"I guess you could say we were both interested in photography," he finally replied.

I decided to take a chance. "Actually, she showed me some photos she'd posed for. She even let me keep a few." I stretched out my arm, reached into my bag, and pulled out a few of the tamer shots. As I handed them to him, I turned my head so I could study his face.

"Uh-huh," he said noncommittally, barely giving them a glance.

"Cassandra looks so great in these," I went on. "Of course, the photographer also did a fabulous job."

"Thanks," he said without thinking. Then he froze. "I mean—"

"Is that how you two met? Because of your shared interest in"—I searched for the right words—"...this kind of thing?"

"Yeah," he replied. "We ran into each other at a dungeon event."

"What on earth is a dungeon event?" I blurted out before I had a chance to stop myself.

Out of the corner of my eye, I saw him smile patiently. "A dungeon is a place—a *safe* place—that's designated for S&M play. That's sadism and masochism, in case you're not familiar with the phrase."

"I see. And when exactly was this particular dungeon event?"

"Maybe a year and a half ago. Anyway," Thor continued, "we got to talking, and somehow it came up that she was interested in posing. I told her I'd done some photography. You know, fetish, S&M, cross-dressing, that kind of stuff. But artsy shots, not exploitative. Erotic photography, not pornography."

"I see. And she was interested?"

"Yeah, she was game, even though she told me this whole world was new to her." He shrugged. "At the time, Cassandra wasn't actually into anything besides vanilla sex."

"Excuse me?" I asked. "What exactly is—"

"Vanilla sex? That's a term people in the S&M world use to describe conventional sex."

"I see." My vocabulary was growing so quickly I felt like I needed flash cards.

"Anyway, it turned out she was really good at it," Thor continued. "Not only posing, but also putting together the getups. She loved going into the city and buying the clothes, and she was even up for the whole piercing thing. Cassandra was a good-looking woman, and—let's face it—she knew it. She enjoyed showing off, and this was a fun way of doing it. In fact, I wasn't surprised that we actually got some of the pictures into fetish magazines."

I guess the look on my face told him that the concept

of fetish magazines was something else I needed help understanding.

"See, there are all kinds of fetish publications," Thor explained patiently. "Spanking magazines, bondage magazines, magazines for rubberists—"

"You mean people who are into rubber?"

"Exactly. You've heard of 'looners,' haven't you?"

"Can't say I have," I admitted, thinking I'd be needing one more flash card.

"Those are people—guys, usually—who get turned on by balloons. They love the feel and the smell, and they're into blowing them up, rubbing against them—"

"I had no idea all these different magazines existed," I said quickly. I'd already heard all I needed to hear about the balloon thing. In fact, I was afraid I'd never look at a birthday party quite the same way again.

"They might even have magazines for WAMers," Thor mused. "That's 'wet and messy,' stuff like mud, paint, food—especially dessert toppings."

Which explained why Cassandra had posed lying on the floor, smeared with what I now told myself had to be chocolate pudding or perhaps even chocolate mousse. I wondered what Jean-Luc would think if he ever saw desserts treated in such an unseemly fashion.

"Which magazines published the photos you took of Cassandra?" I asked.

"We stuck to the tamer ones," Thor assured me. "See, it was all just for fun, as far as Cassandra and I were concerned. Look, I know that a lot of folks freak out over this stuff and that people who are into it are usually considered sickos. But in the psychology world, it's no longer considered pathological. They say one in ten people have experimented with it. Hey, as long as everybody follows the rules, nobody gets hurt. In fact, in S&M, the motto is 'safe, sane, and consensual.' Safe means nobody gets seriously harmed, sane means there's no tolerance for crazies, and consensual means it's only cool if everybody involved is over eighteen and into it.

"In fact, alternative sex practices are getting so mainstream that there's even a national association for people who are into them," he continued. "Ever hear of Black Rose?"

"No." I didn't even dare hope it would turn out to be a garden club.

"It's an organization for people who enjoy exploring fetishism, dominance and submission, bondage and discipline, that kind of stuff. They've been holding annual conventions for the last twenty years or so, with workshops and vendors and, of course, plenty of parties."

Of course, I thought. What's a convention without a few dungeon events?

"Me, I've pretty much gotten out of it," he continued. "Too busy, for one thing. And I guess the novelty kind of wore off after a while. But for people who are into it, there's plenty of action all the time. Like here on Long Island, you could probably find a dungeon event every night of the week. Some are at clubs, but a lot of them take place at people's houses."

Trying to sound casual, I said, "I wouldn't mind checking one out—maybe even the group you and Cassandra hung out with."

"Cool," Thor said, adding, "I could make a couple of calls, if you want."

I took a deep breath, nearly choking on lavender and marjoram. "Just tell me when and where."

• • •

Even though a massage with someone of Thor's caliber should have made me relaxed and dreamy, I left the spa feeling energized. I was finally getting closer to learning who Cassandra Thorndike really was.

I only hoped that investigating further wouldn't mean getting into more than I could handle.

In the meantime, I was well aware that while I may have been a sleuth during my off-hours, I was still a veterinarian by profession, and I launched into a full afternoon of house calls. In fact, it wasn't until that evening that I remembered that I was smack in the middle of a murder investigation. And the reminder hit me with the same force as a half-frozen snowball stuck down the back of my shirt.

Nick had already gone to bed, and I was using the quiet hours to catch up on paperwork—including my e-mail. Cat, my usual e-mail buddy, was already asleep in front of the refrigerator, and even Tinkerbell had turned in for the night. The dogs were also asleep. They lay curled up together, Lou making the little wheezing sounds that were his version of snoring, Max jerking his front legs and mumbling a soft "Woof! Woof!" every once in a while, leading me to believe he was dreaming about chasing squirrels.

All in all, it was a pretty peaceful scene. At least until I eyeballed my list of New Messages and saw there was another one from AGoodFriend.

"Shoot," I muttered. I licked my lips, which were suddenly uncomfortably dry, then clicked on the message.

Hey, Jessie, it began. Can't wait to see you on TV. You can be sure I'll be watching.

"*Watching* seems to be something you're particularly good at," I muttered.

I kept reading. Knock 'em DEAD, from your biggest fan.

And then, further down, Get it?

The sight of those few words made me feel as if all the blood in my body had just drained down to the floor.

• • •

I don't know what I should be more worried about, I thought as I pulled my VW into a visitor parking space outside the Sunshine Media office building early Friday morning with Max and Lou beside me. Being stalked via e-mail—or the fact that I'm probably about to make a complete fool of myself on television.

Intellectually, I knew my stalker should definitely be my greater concern. At the moment, however, it was the idea of walking into a real TV studio and going on the air—live, no less—that was responsible for the sick feeling in the pit of my stomach. And while bringing my two supercharged canines had seemed like a good idea at the time, watching Max bounce around the front seat as if he'd doubled up on his morning shot of cappuccino was giving me second thoughts.

"Why did I ever listen to Forrester?" I moaned, peering into the rearview mirror to at least make sure I wasn't wearing half my breakfast on my face.

But it was a little late for regrets. And I had to admit that Max and Lou looked great. They were both freshly washed and, in Max's case, fluffed. They even wore spiffy new collars, red for Lou and blue for Max. Once I glanced in the mirror one last time and determined that I, too, was more or less presentable, I headed inside.

The receptionist's face lit up when the three of us walked into the lobby. "You made it!" she cried. After glancing at my Sunshine Media ID to make sure I really was who she thought I was, she added, "And do you cute little doggies have ID too? No? Then I guess I'll just have to trust you two!"

Lou returned her kindness by sneaking behind the counter and sticking his nose in her crotch. Max, meanwhile, was sniffing underneath the couch, probably attempting to snarf up a lint-covered cough drop or some other delicacy somebody had left there months earlier.

Buzzing me inside, the receptionist added, "You can

wait in the greenroom, right down the hall. You'll see it on your left. 'Bye, doggies!"

The greenroom was easy to find because its walls were actually painted green. Like the lobby, it was furnished with tasteful upholstered furniture and a large TV tuned to Channel 14 News. As my two escorts performed reconnaissance, snuffling every square inch of the fragrance-laden carpeting, I tried to focus on a discussion of the future of education, conducted by a group of school superintendents from different districts around Long Island. But given my level of agitation, it was just as well that Marlene appeared in the doorway mere seconds after I lowered myself into a chair.

"All set, Dr. Popper?" she chirped.

Help! I was thinking. Get me out of here!

I forced myself to smile. "As ready as I'll ever be."

"And I see you brought two animals." Before I had a chance to introduce them, she eagerly asked, "What's your topic for today?"

"I already e-mailed my presentation to Patti," I told her. "She thought it looked fine. I'll be talking about how people can make their homes safe for their pets."

"Pet-proofing," Patti the Producer said as she strode through the door.

I blinked. "Excuse me?"

"It's perfect. We can call the segment 'Pet People's Pointers for Pet-Proofing Your Pad.'"

What is this woman's obsession with the letter P? I mused, wondering if it had anything to do with P being the first letter of her name.

Before I had a chance to protest, she added, "Real, live dogs," making her observation with cool objectivity. "Nice touch." She peered into my shopping bag. "What's in here?"

"I brought along some visual aids. I hope that's okay."

"That's good. Very good." Patti nodded enthusiastically. "We love visuals. Besides the dogs, I mean. What have you got?"

I'd never really thought of my Westie and my Dalmatian as visual aids before. "Just some common household items that are dangerous to pets."

"Cool. It sounds like you've got everything under control. Are you ready for makeup?"

"Actually, I put on a little lip gloss before I—"

"This way. Aldo is ready."

"But—"

"You have no idea how brutal the lights in the studio can be," she insisted. "Marlene, hold the visual aids while Dr. Popper's in makeup. Maybe you should give those two some water or something."

"But—" I protested.

"They'll be fine," Patti assured me. "Marlene is very good with children and animals and those kinds of things."

I could tell this was nonnegotiable. Besides, Lou was a sucker for perfume, and he already seemed enamored of Marlene. So I followed Patti down the hall to a small dressing room that looked just like the ones I'd seen in a hundred movies and television shows. Three swivel chairs, the kind you find in hair salons, were lined up in front of a long mirror. The counter in front of them was covered with cosmetics, hair products, and several sets of electric rollers, the mere sight of which gave me heart palpitations.

But before I had a chance to explain that I had severe reservations about being made up to look like Joan Rivers, Patti placed her hands on my shoulders and commandeered me into one of the chairs.

"I'm sure Aldo will know exactly what to do with all this—oh, good. Here he is now."

I glanced up as a slender young man with heavily gelled hair and a single earring breezed into the room.

"This is the amazing Aldo," Patti cooed after the two of them exchanged air kisses. "He works magic with hair and makeup."

"But I don't usually wear makeup," I protested. "And I think my hair looks fine. I just washed it this morning."

"Honey, you have no idea what the camera does to a person," Aldo gurgled. With a little shudder, he added, "It washes people out like high tide."

"Then maybe a *little* color wouldn't hurt," I told him, making a point of emphasizing the word *little*. "But not too much—"

The glazed look in his eyes told me he hadn't heard a word I'd said. He stood behind me, studying my reflection with his hands on his hips.

"Just *look* at her ears," Aldo said to Patti, pursing his lips disapprovingly. "They stick out like Shrek's horns."

"My ears are fine!" I insisted, covering them protectively as if I didn't want them to hear someone insulting them.

As for Aldo's ears, they seemed to be on the fritz. Either that or he was choosing to ignore me. He shook his head, still studying my reflection in the mirror. "All I can say is that it's a good thing her hair is so fluffy. She has this kind of cocker spaniel thing going."

"My hair is not fluffy!" I protested. "Well, maybe a little, at least when it's damp . . ."

Patti was nodding enthusiastically. "You're absolutely right about her hair, Aldo. We'll have to fix that, of course."

I absolutely hate it when people talk about me in the third person. It makes me feel like I'm invisible—or else four years old.

I also hate it when somebody makes me look like someone I'm not. However, this time even I had to admit that Aldo had worked something very much like magic. Thanks to some chemicals in a spray can and a blow-dryer, my hair was soon an impressively sleek mane. As for my face, Aldo masterfully wielded a blush brush, a mascara wand, and a bunch of other powders and creams, achieving surprising results.

"You're perfect!" he announced triumphantly. Leaning forward so Patti couldn't hear, he whispered, "Or at least good enough for Channel Fourteen!"

While the makeover had turned out to be an interesting distraction, by the time I got back to the greenroom, I was dealing with some pretty serious butterfly action, even with the commotion of having my dogs returned to me. So I jumped when I heard somebody call, "Hey, Popper!"

"Forrester?" I cried, surprised.

Sure enough, he was standing in the doorway. "He-e-y! If it isn't the latest media star. Can I have your autograph?"

"What are you doing here?" I demanded. I was already nervous enough without being teased.

"I'm not staying," he said, leaning over to indulge Max and Lou with a little neck-scratching. "Just thought I'd stop by to give you a little moral support." Grinning, he added, "And to find out what it feels like to be in the presence of greatness."

"Actually, you're in the presence of intense anxiety and raging regret."

"Come on. Don't tell me you're nervous about this gig."

"Not at all," I assured him. "I'm fine. In fact, it's perfectly normal for me to walk around in a cold sweat, feeling like I'm about to lose my breakfast."

He laughed. "That's the spirit. Knock 'em dead, Popper. If anybody can do it, you can." Before walking out the door, he turned. "By the way, you look fantastic.

Even better than usual—and I didn't know that was possible."

I didn't get a chance to fend off the compliment. All of a sudden, it was showtime. Perky Patti reappeared, leading me and my dogs to the studio and delivering a monologue about what I should do and not do. Not a word of it went in. I felt like a zombie, as if in addition to Aldo's magic with blow-dryers and makeup brushes, he'd also worked a little voodoo.

All I knew was that I suddenly glanced around and found myself in the same spot in which I'd auditioned, standing behind a counter with a cheering squad of stuffed animals surrounding me. Even the presence of Max and Lou, who seemed much cooler about the whole situation than I was, didn't help.

A burly dark-haired man with cigar breath appeared from out of nowhere, gruffly identified himself as Mel, and hooked a tiny microphone onto my collar. And then, suddenly, a very bright light shone in my eyes, as if somebody was about to give me the third degree. Despite the light, I could see Patti in front of me, gesturing histrionically. Just like in the movies, she counted down, "Five, four, three..." then held up two fingers, then one, while mouthing the words.

The rectangular screen of the teleprompter lit up with words. Someone whose voice sounded an awful lot like mine began reading them aloud. "I'm Dr. Popper. Welcome to *Pet People,* the program for people who are passionate about their pets."

I gradually came to realize that I was the person who was speaking. I also realized that this was turning out to be just as easy as it had been during the audition.

"Bringing home a pet for the first time is an exciting event," I continued, suddenly feeling confident and calm. "But it's also important to make sure you provide a safe environment for your new dog or cat."

I suddenly remembered that I'd brought along a couple of dogs of my own. However, Max was halfway across the studio, chewing on a thick black cable that fortunately didn't appear to be attached to anything. Lou was next to me, his backside facing the camera as he stood on his back paws so he could stick his nose into the display of stuffed animals. I turned my head in time to see him remove the fish covered in orange fake fur, gently carrying it in his jaws.

"This is Lou," I announced to the camera. "And he's just demonstrated how easy it is for a pet to get into something that could be hazardous. In this case, it's just a stuffed animal, which isn't likely to cause any harm. However, since it's not an approved dog toy and we don't know what's in it..."

I reached over and attempted to take the fish away from my Dalmatian. He, however, assumed I was initiating a game. He began to growl playfully, meanwhile twisting his head from side to side and pulling.

"Let go, Lou," I commanded.

He refused to take me seriously. "Grrrr!" he growled more ferociously, upping the excitement—at least, from his perspective. While I knew he was just kidding around, I realized that wrestling with an eighty-pound beast on the air—and losing—wasn't doing much for my credibility.

"Let go!" I insisted in a voice that sounded much sharper than I'd intended.

Lou dropped the fish, all right. But he looked at me so woefully you'd think I just committed some horribly cruel act.

"Good dog." I looked back at the camera and smiled.

"There are several things an animal owner can do to keep a new pet safe inside the home," I continued, afraid to make eye contact with Patti. "First, it's important for the members of your family to remain calm."

At that moment, I noticed that Max had moved on to a different cable. This one, however, was plugged into the teleprompter—which, in turn, was plugged into an electric socket.

"My dog!" I cried, immediately realizing I was plugged into something electrical myself and that I couldn't very well dash across the studio to rescue Max. Besides, I was supposed to be conducting a television show. "Uh, my other dog, Max, is also here in the studio today. Max, let me introduce you to the, uh, viewing public. Perhaps someone could, uh, get him away from that cable and bring him over?"

Mel, the man who'd wired me for sound, got my point. He scooped up my twenty-pound Westie and handed him to me, ducking down low to stay out of the camera's range.

"Here he is!" I said, beaming as I plopped my little doggie down in front of me. "This is Max, a West Highland white terrier. Say hello, Max."

My attempt at humor didn't go over very well. At least no one in the studio responded. I decided I'd better forget the Jay Leno routine and stick to the script.

"As I was saying," I continued, clutching Max tightly to keep him from chomping on any other potentially lethal pieces of studio equipment, "it's important to stay calm around a new pet. Moving into an unfamiliar place can be a traumatic experience. And keep in mind that kittens and puppies will want to explore, so this is a good time to pack away any breakables you own. The same holds true for medications, household chemicals like insecticides and cleaning fluids, and antifreeze, which may leak out of your car and onto the driveway—"

Suddenly, Max began emitting the low, ominous-sounding growl he makes whenever he senses danger from a threatening source like a chipmunk or a UPS delivery person.

"R-r-r-r-r-r..." came the throaty growl, not quite loud enough to drown me out but distracting enough that I kept losing my train of thought. Frantically I scanned the studio, looking for the perpetrator. Knowing Max as well as I do, I quickly realized it was the big, mean-looking camera that he'd just identified as a potential enemy. Twenty pounds and the looks of a teddy bear, yet he was ready to take on the world.

"It's okay, Max," I said in a soothing voice. I had a feeling that if I suggested that the TV folks remove the menacing camera from the studio, the answer would be no. Peering into it, I ad-libbed, "Max is kind of new to show biz. I hope you'll bear with him."

I finally mustered up the courage to glance at Patti. She didn't look at all inclined to bear with a neurotic Westie who was hell-bent on protecting me, not to mention himself, from menacing metallic monsters on tripods.

"R-R-R-R-R-R!" Max continued, his sturdy little body becoming more tense and his growl becoming louder as he realized he wasn't being a sufficiently effective watchdog. And then he broke out into loud barking. "Ruff! Ruff-ruff-ruff!"

"Uh, maybe someone should take Max," I suggested calmly. With a little chuckle, I added, "Not everyone is cut out to be in the spotlight."

Mel stepped over to retrieve him. Yet as he carted off my fierce protector, Max still wouldn't calm down. Even after the two of them left the studio, I could hear him barking indignantly from behind closed doors, no doubt furious that he hadn't had the chance to do battle with an antagonistic piece of electronic equipment twenty times his size.

Still, with Max out of the way and Lou plopped down at my side, out of the camera's range, I was free to discuss poisonous houseplants, the dangers of twist ties, plastic bags, paper clips, safety pins, rubber bands, and buttons, and foods like chocolate, coffee, onions, raisins, salt, garlic, avocados, macadamia nuts, bread dough, cigarette butts, and alcohol, all of which were capable of poisoning a dog or cat. Every now and then I emphasized what I was saying by holding up one of the items I mentioned, as if wanting to make sure everybody knew exactly what a Hershey bar and a can of Raid looked like. Wondering if I was laying on too much doom and gloom, I glanced at Patti. From the way she was beaming, I could tell I was doing just fine.

When she gave me a sign that it was time to wind down, I began to wrap up my presentation.

"Here at *Pet People*," I said, "we know how much you love your pet. So take a little time to keep your dog or cat safe!"

Just as I was beginning to wonder what would happen next, I noticed that one of the red buttons on the phone was glowing. I pounced on it gratefully.

"Ah. We have a call," I announced, pressing the button. "Thank you for calling *Pet People*," I said brightly. "How can I help you and your pet?"

"Hi...Dr. Popper?"

"You're on the air," I said brightly. "Who am I speaking with?"

"Uh, this is Fran from North Islip. I have a tip that might be helpful to some listeners. I noticed my kitten kept sticking her paw in the electric outlets around the house, so I got some of those plastic disks with prongs they sell to keep toddlers safe from electricity."

"An excellent idea!" I said, pleased that the show actually seemed to be accomplishing something. "You can also use duct tape to cover outlets. And be careful with electrical cords. If your puppy chews them, he might get electrical burns." I couldn't resist adding, "Which is why I was so concerned about Max before, when he began chewing on the electrical cables."

I'm actually having fun, I marveled. The red light went on again, indicating that I had a second caller.

"Thank you for calling *Pet People*!" I exclaimed.

"Dr. Popper, I got a question for ya," a gruff male voice said.

"That's what I'm here for," I replied. "Who am I speaking with?"

"This is Richie from Riverton."

Cute, I thought. "What can I help you with?"

"Yeah, see, I got a coupla American bulldogs. I take 'em to the vet whenever they got, like, some kinda problem. But my vet, he's tellin' me I should bring 'em in every six months or so, even if there's nothin' wrong. What is this, a way for you guys to make money?"

"An excellent question, Richie!" I replied. I hope the smile I plastered on my face didn't look as strained as it felt. "I'm glad you brought it up. It's important that pet owners bring their cats and dogs in for regular examinations at least once a year—and I have to agree with your veterinarian that every six months is even better. Trained medical professionals often catch the early signs of something that could get serious if it isn't treated in a timely manner. Tumors are a good example. But if your pet is gaining weight or has an infection, or even if there's something as routine as tartar building up on his teeth, your vet can help you deal with it. In fact, by taking care of problems at the beginning stages, your pet will probably suffer less—and you'll actually end up saving money."

"Yeah," my caller grumbled, clearly not convinced. "Whatever."

After Richie from Riverton hung up, the phone just sat there. Even though I'd been amazed at how smoothly things had gone so far, I was beginning to panic. I could see Patti in the shadows, making those "move it along" motions again.

I looked straight into the camera. "One thing that's important to remember," I said slowly, without having the slightest idea of how I was going to finish that sentence, "is that, uh..." What seemed like an hour passed, even though it couldn't have been more than a second or two. "...Nobody knows your pet as well as you do. So whenever you speak with your vet, be sure to report even minor changes in your pet's behavior or appearance that you've noticed. Something you think isn't at all meaningful could turn out to be— Great! Another call!" I pressed the red button. "Thanks for calling *Pet People*," I said. "How can I help you and your pet?"

"Dr. Popper?"

"You're on the air!" I said cheerfully. "Who am I speaking with today?"

"Is this Dr. Popper?"

"I'm Dr. Popper, and you're on *Pet People*. Who's this?"

"This is Cheryl. I'm from Metchogue."

"Go ahead, Cheryl." *Please* go ahead Cheryl, I thought. Patti was making a round-and-round motion with her hand, as in "Speed it up, already."

"I have a question. It's about...kind of a *game* I like to play with my German shepherd."

"Certainly a fun-loving breed," I said encouragingly.

"I, uh, cover my feet—well, my toes, actually—in peanut butter, and then I lie in bed while Oscar licks it off."

I didn't respond. I was too busy trying to keep my jaw from getting carpet burn.

"I know it sounds weird," Cheryl continued. "But the thing is, it feels really good." The caller hesitated. "I guess my question is, do you think it's bad for Oscar?"

I cast a desperate look at Patti. She looked like she'd just been worked over with a stun gun.

"Peanut butter isn't particularly bad for dogs," I said calmly, "although eating too much could—"

"Oh, good," Cheryl replied. "Not about the peanut butter so much. I mean, I'm thinking more like—you know, that maybe what Oscar and I are doing is kind of—kinky. Because actually, I was thinking of expanding our game. I thought it might feel good to put some peanut butter—"

"I have another call!" I exclaimed, noting that Patti was frantically making a throat-slashing gesture with her finger. "Thanks for calling, Cheryl! And good luck to Oscar!"

Pressing another button, I cried, "Thanks for calling *Pet People.* How can I help you and your pet?"

By the time I got out of there, I was exhausted. Was it possible that only fifteen minutes had passed since I'd walked onto the set?

"Dr. Popper, you were great!" Patti gushed. "They loved you. You're so good at thinking on your feet! Even the thing with that white dog and whatever he was barking at—you handled it brilliantly."

"Really?" I still couldn't quite believe I'd successfully made it through my first television appearance. But as the dogs and I headed out to the parking lot, I was already working on a topic for the following week.

As I slid into my van, my cell phone trilled. I expected it would be Forrester, gloating over having "discovered" Long Island's newest celebrity. Instead, the Caller ID screen read *Suzanne Fox.*

"Hey, Suzanne," I answered breezily. In my triumphant haze, I assumed the only reason she'd be calling would be to give me her critique of my television debut. "What's up?"

"Jessie! I'm so glad I got you." She sounded breathless. "You have to come over right now. The police just arrived with a search warrant."

I stiffened. "Okay, stay calm. I mean, it's not as if they're going to find anything, right?"

The only response I got was a long silence.

"I'll be there as soon as I can," I said, turning the key in the ignition and speeding out of the parking lot even before I had a chance to hang up.

Chapter 12

"Cats conspire to keep us at arm's length."

—Frank Perkins

'd barely hung up before my cell phone rang again.

I grabbed it and answered on the first ring. "Nick?"

"Sorry. It's Nick's rival," Forrester replied cheerfully. "I just wanted to tell you how great you are. But I've always known that."

"Thanks, Forrester," I said.

"You sound a little distracted. Everything okay?"

"Everything's fine. I'm just in a hurry. Emergency house call."

"I won't keep you, then. You're a star, Popper!"

I gritted my teeth as I careened around the entrance ramp and onto the Long Island Expressway. I told myself I hadn't exactly lied to Forrester by not telling him that at that very moment, the cops were searching Suzanne's house. It was just that having him swoop down would make things even more complicated.

Besides, I reminded myself grimly, he'll know, sooner or later. Not only that they were there, either. He'll also know if they found anything.

When my cell phone went off still one more time, I got ready to fend off Forrester again.

"Hey, Jess. It's me," Nick said cheerfully. "I've only got a minute, but I saw you on TV just now. There's one here in the student center. You were terrific!"

"Thanks," I replied. "Listen, Nick, something's—"

"Sorry, Jess. Just reached my classroom. Gotta run!"

It's just as well, I told myself. No need to involve him either. At least, not at this point. But I suddenly felt as if I were about to parachute into a disaster area with absolutely no backup.

I reached Suzanne's house in record time, making a slight detour to drop off Max and Lou at home. It cost me twenty minutes, but with no way to anticipate what I'd be dealing with, I didn't want them getting in the way—or distracting me.

It turned out to be a wise move. Even though I'd tried to prepare myself for whatever I'd find, the sight of a Norfolk County police car parked outside made my stomach wrench. Directly in front of it was a small white van. I pulled up across the street, taking deep breaths. Through the open front door, I could see two men in Suzanne's living room, picking up pillows and peering under furniture. They both wore shirts printed with the words *Crime Scene Unit* on the back, as well as hairnets and latex gloves.

Suzanne stood on the front lawn, her face puffy and her hair so limp and straggly it looked as if she hadn't washed it for days. She was wearing the same dark sweatpants and gray Purdue sweatshirt I'd seen her in the last time I'd come to her house.

"Thanks for coming, Jess," she greeted me weakly. Up close, I could see that her eyes were swollen and red.

I gave her a hug, then asked, "What are you doing out here?"

"This is where the guy from the crime-scene unit told

me to wait." Using a gruff voice to mimic him, she said, " 'Would you mind stepping outside, Ms. Fox?' "

I forced a smile. It faded quickly. "Did the police tell you what prompted them to get a search warrant?"

She bit her lip and took a breath. "One of the cops told me they found my fingerprints on the doorknob at Cassandra's house. A few other places too."

"I see," I said simply.

"And since I told them I hadn't been there—" Her voice broke off and tears pooled in her mournful blue eyes. "What do you think they're looking for?"

"The murder weapon, most likely," I said. "Or anything else incriminating. Letters, e-mails, photographs..." Quickly, I added, "So you have nothing to worry about."

She swallowed. "If they'd only let me explain—"

"Excuse me, Ms. Fox," one of the crime-scene-unit investigators interrupted. "Could I please have the keys to your car?"

"My car?" she repeated, her voice going up an octave or two. "You're going to search my car?"

"Yes, ma'am. Standard procedure."

"Uh...sure." She reached into the pocket of her sweatpants and pulled out a ring of keys with what I thought was surprising reluctance.

"Suzanne?" I asked once he was out of earshot. "The police aren't going to...find anything, are they?"

"I—I just don't trust this whole process, you know?" she stammered. "I mean, I've heard of situations where cops twist things..." Her voice trailed off uncertainly as she stared in the direction of the driveway.

I followed her gaze. All four car doors were wide open, and the investigator who'd asked for her keys was bent over the backseat, methodically sorting through the clutter.

"I can't imagine what they expect to find in there," I

said, trying to keep my voice light. "Used coffee cups, a bunch of torn maps..."

When I glanced back at Suzanne, I saw that her face had turned white.

"Are you okay?" I asked, fearful that she might pass out.

She never had a chance to answer. The crime-scene-unit investigator had returned, and this time he was holding something in his hands.

"Ms. Fox?" he said with a distinct edge to his voice. "The police are going to ask you to go with them to the station. We just found this in your car."

He held up a pink cardigan sweater embroidered with a swirling letter *S*. It was spattered with what looked very much like dried blood.

I stood and watched two uniformed officers escort Suzanne to the police car, too stunned to react.

"Come with me," she yelled over her shoulder. "Please, Jessie. And call Marcus!"

As the police car drove off with Suzanne in the back-seat, she pressed her face against the side window. From the desperate look in her eyes, her thoughts were unmistakable.

Save me!

I hopped in the car and sped after her, never losing sight of her through the rear window of the police car.

• • •

This can't be happening, I thought.

But it was. And as I waited in the lobby of the police station, sitting on a hard wooden bench beneath harsh fluorescent lights, I was completely powerless to do a thing about it.

Finally, after what seemed like a very long time, the door opened. Suzanne emerged, looking dazed.

"Suzanne!" I cried, rising to my feet.

"Where's Marcus?" she asked anxiously as she hurried over.

"I suppose he's on his way. What happened in there?"

"You called him?"

"Yes, back at the house. Did the police—"

"And he said he'd come right over to the station?"

I hesitated, wondering if honesty really was the best policy. Did she really need to know that he'd sounded more annoyed than concerned or that he'd insisted that he was *"extremely* busy" or that all he'd promised was that he'd "do his best" to get there?

"As fast as he could," I told her.

"Oh, good. I knew I could count on him." She looked so relieved—and so pleased—that I felt as if the two of us weren't doing anything more demanding than planning a dinner party.

As soon as we were outside the police station, Suzanne scanned the parking lot, searching for his car.

"Tell me!" I demanded. "How did it go in there?"

"I think it went well." She sounded surprisingly calm. "I mean, it's not like they arrested me or anything. All they did was ask me questions."

"Was your lawyer there?"

"I couldn't reach him. His secretary told me he'd taken the day off. And his cell phone's broken."

Even worse than I thought.

Frowning, she said, "Maybe Marcus misunderstood and he's waiting for me at the house."

"Probably." I glanced around, wanting to be sure we wouldn't be overheard. "Suzanne, what's the story with the sweater?"

She hesitated. "I—I dropped it while I was at Cassandra's house. It was right near where she was lying, so I guess some of her blood got on it."

"You *guess*?" I repeated.

"Okay, I noticed some of her blood got on it. But it was an accident!"

"Why was it in your car?"

"I just threw it in the backseat as I drove away. I never thought anybody would find it. Especially the police."

"Suzanne," I began, trying not to sound as exasperated—and as frightened—as I felt. "Did you finally tell them the truth about what happened that day Cassandra was...you know?"

"Yes." She cast me a woeful look. "You were right, Jessie. They weren't at all happy that I hadn't been straight with them about being at her house right around the time she was killed."

Surprise, surprise.

"But you finally told them exactly what happened, right?"

"Yes. And I explained that I had a perfectly good reason for holding back about the truth."

"Which was...?"

She looked surprised by my question. "That I didn't want them to think I had anything to do with what happened, of course!"

Of course, I thought, wishing I shared her feelings about the cops being a bunch of nice, friendly guys who were as anxious to believe she was innocent as she was to convince them. I could only imagine the field day Falcone was going to have with a sweater emblazoned with an *S*-for-Suzanne and stained with blood that would prove to be Cassandra Thorndike's.

It was time for the $64,000 question. "Did they believe you?"

"I'm not sure," she replied, her voice wavering.

I only hoped that, one day, I wouldn't be asking her the same question about a jury.

• • •

I didn't know whether to feel relief or dread when I pulled up in front of Suzanne's house and saw Marcus Scruggs's Corvette parked out front. He stood on the lawn, looking peeved—probably because he'd arrived to find no one at home yet.

Suzanne jumped out of her car and dashed over to him. "Marcus!" she cried.

I waited for the love theme from Tchaikovsky's *Romeo and Juliet* to start playing.

"Hey," he said, sounding less than enthusiastic. "What took you guys so long?"

Those homicide detectives can be so darned inconsiderate, I thought, fuming but determined to make this one of those rare occasions when I kept my mouth shut.

The focus of my emotions shifted as soon as I saw his expression. This didn't look good. Not at all.

"Oh, Marcus, thank God you're here." As Suzanne threw her arms around her soul mate, he stiffened. While he didn't actually remove her bodily, his posture made it clear he wasn't available for hugging.

"Listen, Suzanne, I know this is a tough time for you and all..."

Don't say it, I thought. Please, Marcus. If you possess even an ounce of humanity...

"...but I'm thinking maybe it would be a good idea for us to stop seeing each other for a while."

Damn you! I thought. Damn, damn, *damn*! I gave him my version of the evil eye, designed to bring on impotence, adult acne, and chronic indigestion. If I'd had a voodoo doll in my pocket, I would have whipped that baby out, too.

"You're joking, right?" Suzanne asked hopefully. She'd lowered her arms, but only halfway, as if she were waiting for her cue to resume her embrace.

"And, uh, you probably shouldn't refer your clients to me anymore," he added without looking her in the eye.

"I think we should make a clean break. Don't you think it's for the best?"

"No," Suzanne replied coldly. "I don't think any of this is 'for the best.' In fact, I can't believe you'd *abandon* me like this. Not when I'm going through the biggest *mess* of my entire life!"

I felt like crying, largely because I was thinking the exact same thing. I felt as if some villain in a monster movie had reached inside my chest and pulled my heart out. And I wasn't even the one who was being dumped—mere minutes after the police had made it clear I was definitely a murder suspect.

"Look, we can talk about this later," Marcus said, waving his hands in the air and striding toward the ridiculous phallic symbol that passed itself off as a car. "But frankly, Suzanne, this is more than I can handle. I'm sorry, but that's the way it is. I'm outta here."

Suzanne stood on the front lawn, silent as she watched him drive away. I stood next to her, ready to catch her if she fell.

But she didn't.

"Bastard," she muttered. "What was I even thinking?"

You go, girl, I thought. But I didn't say that.

I didn't say the other thing I was thinking either: You're better off without him.

• • •

By Friday evening, I was more than ready for my romantic tryst with Nick. For one thing, my appreciation of him had increased about a millionfold after witnessing Marcus's abominable behavior—especially when I related the events of the day and Nick was as outraged as I was. For another, I was at a loss as to how to proceed with trying to fix Suzanne's situation, and I welcomed the break, not to mention the chance to recharge.

I'd made some preparations for the weekend, thinking through the best way of taking advantage of this rare opportunity for a vacation—even though we'd only traveled a few hundred feet for our getaway. For one thing, I decided to leave my entire menagerie back at the cottage, stealing back a few times a day to tend to them. While I'd miss having the tykes around, I shuddered to think of Lou curled up against one of Betty's beaded silk pillows or Max gnawing on the hand-carved legs of her Louis Something end tables. Even Cat, who had been her houseguest over the years, would require constant monitoring to make sure she didn't damage any of the exquisite antiques that made the mansion feel more like a museum than a place to kick back with the remote and a bag of chips.

Besides, Betty had had just the two of us in mind when she orchestrated this romantic little interlude. I was supposed to be concentrating on Nick.

I decided to play the role to the hilt. I'd rummaged through my closet, letting out a squeal of joy when, way in back, I found a squished but still serviceable floor-length burgundy-colored velvet skirt. I'd grabbed it off a clearance rack one January, snatching it up at forty percent off its already heavily discounted price. At the time, I'd envisioned saving it for the following holiday season, harboring a vague vision of throwing a Christmas party like the one in *The Nutcracker*. My fantasy included a brass quartet softly playing carols, a big bowl of clove-and-cinnamon-scented punch, and a roaring fireplace.

At least four years had passed since that uncharacteristically romantic moment, and the tags still hung from the skirt's waistband. But the time to wear it had finally come. I even had access to a fireplace.

It turned out the skirt went a long way toward inspiring me. Martha Stewart's not the only one who can pull off this kind of thing, I thought early Friday evening as I lit the last of the string of scented candles I'd lined up on the mantelpiece. Of course, they all had different scents, since I had to work with what I had. But I hoped the Nutmeg Vanilla would turn out to be subtle enough that it wouldn't clash with the Frangipani or the white candle I'd found at the bottom of my "miscellaneous" drawer that was mysteriously labeled Winter Snow. I'd never noticed that snow even *had* a scent, so I wasn't too worried.

But the candles were just the beginning. I'd lit a fire in the tremendous marble fireplace that covered an entire wall of Betty's side parlor, a room she rarely used. I'd also put on soft music, although it was classic rock, Nick's favorite, rather than classical. I hoped James Taylor and Carole King wouldn't mind being reduced to background music, just this once.

And while brandy and caviar weren't on the menu, they were about the only things that weren't. I'd gone wild at the local gourmet market, a place I rarely set foot in. After all, this seemed like the perfect occasion to see how the other half lived—meaning those who planned far enough ahead to actually stock their refrigerators with takeout food, rather than ordering it by phone when hunger pangs made the thought of waiting for the oven to heat up unimaginable. I'd bought a little bit of everything: chicken stuffed with goat cheese and gouda, pasta salad with artichokes and sun-dried tomatoes, potato salad made with three kinds of potatoes, when I didn't even know three different kinds of potatoes existed.

I'd also picked up a couple of bottles of wine. One was from Thorndike Vineyards and one was from the Simcox Wineries. Now that I knew the owners, I was looking forward to drinking wine that came with a personal connection.

As soon as Nick walked into Betty's parlor, I knew by

the look of astonishment that crossed his face that my plan to impress him had worked.

"Wow," he said. It was more of a simple, straightforward statement than anything else.

I couldn't help grinning.

"Where'd you get that outfit?" he asked.

"This old thing?" I glanced down at the skirt and the clingy black top I'd also found at the back of the closet. It was cut pretty low, which explained why I couldn't remember having ever worn it but which didn't explain how I'd come to acquire it.

Nick was doing some grinning of his own. "This idea of staying at Betty's is looking better and better."

"Wait until you hear what I've got on the schedule."

"There's a schedule?"

"It starts with wine and appetizers in front of the fire," I told him. "Then, dinner will be served in the formal dining room. Next, we will retreat to the study for Ben & Jerry's and a video." I shrugged. "We are living in the twenty-first century, after all."

"And then?" Nick asked.

"And then we snuggle up in a four-poster that probably creaks."

"I'm already looking forward to making it creak—a *lot*." Nick came over to where I was standing and put his arms around me. He leaned forward to kiss me, then stopped.

"What's that smell?"

"What smell?" I asked nervously.

"It smells like cookies...and something flowery... and *snow*, all mixed together."

"It's a special romantic scent," I replied, doing some fast thinking. "A well-known aphrodisiac."

"Ah. Then I like it." He leaned over and gave me a long, mushy Hollywood-style kiss, the kind that was common back in our early courtin' days but that we rarely made time for these days.

"Umm," I murmured. "Nice."

"There's more where that came from," he assured me.

"But there is one rule for this weekend," I said. "No law books. In fact, nothing legal at all. We can't even watch any John Grisham DVDs."

Nick's forehead crinkled, even though he kept his arms around me. "Well...I can probably get away with one day of goofing off. But I'm afraid I've got to hit the books first thing Sunday."

At the moment, Sunday seemed far off. All that mattered was that we had thirty-six hours all to ourselves.

And we used every second of it to its fullest. We watched two movies, ate every morsel of food I'd bought, played five games of Scrabble, and put that old four-poster through some pretty heavy creaking.

By Saturday night, my veterinary practice, law school, and even Cassandra Thorndike's murder seemed very far away. Nick and I lolled on the velvet couch, watching the fire in the fireplace and sipping red wine from crystal glasses with very large globes.

"Do you know how I feel right now?" I asked.

"How do you feel right now?"

"Rich. Very rich." Waving one arm in the air dramatically, I added, "I could see living in a house like this. Think of the space we'd have for all our stuff. Besides, we could each have our own room. Lou would probably decorate his in black and white. Cat's would have a big stuffed couch with lace doilies on it, and Prometheus would model his after Elvis's Jungle Room. But mostly we'd just enjoy having all this space."

Nick poured himself another glass of wine. I couldn't remember having ever seen him drink more than a glass or two. But somehow, between the two of us, we were making our way through the Simcox merlot quite nicely.

"Do you know how *I* feel right now?" he asked.

"Nope. How?"

"Married," he replied. "I feel very, very married."

I held my breath, waiting for the feeling that someone had just closed all the windows and turned up the heat. Nothing. In fact, instead of sliding into a state of panic, I found myself contemplating Nick's statement objectively.

"Is this how being married feels?" I asked him.

"I guess so. How else would it feel?"

"I don't know. Maybe like you're under constant pressure to remember to take out the garbage and buy anniversary cards."

"Naw. I think it feels...comfortable. Easy. Just like this, you know? Hanging out with your best girl—or in your case, your best guy....I am your best guy, right?"

"Best and only. My number-one heartthrob." I stuck my hand under my shirt and did a theatrical imitation of a pounding heart.

He grinned. "I think this is going pretty well so far, don't you? You and me living together, I mean."

"Well...it's only been a few days."

"True. But I think I'm really well-suited to it." Nodding thoughtfully, he added, "I figured I'd be."

"It's different than I expected," I admitted. "You're right, it is easy. And comfortable."

"So maybe we should think about it. The thing about feeling married, I mean. Not soon. But one of these days. When I'm done with the semester. Or my first year of law school. Or even all of law school. That's three years away."

I didn't say yes, but I didn't say no. At the moment, three years sounded nice and far away.

• • • •

"Do you know what's wrong with this place?" I asked as I lolled in bed the next morning, luxuriating in what had to be the smoothest, silkiest sheets I'd ever been sandwiched between in my life.

"I can't begin to imagine," Nick replied, glancing at me without raising his head from the pillow.

"The butler service. It's much too slow."

"I wouldn't be able to reach the bell pull from here, anyway," he commented. "That is, if there was one."

"If we had a really good butler," I pointed out, "we could just yell. Something like, 'Hey, Jeeves? How about a couple of cappuccinos, when you get a chance?' "

Nick nodded solemnly. "That would work."

And then he let out a long sigh, one I suspected had nothing to do with a desire for caffeine. "I really don't want to do this," he said, "but I'm afraid that, after breakfast, I'm going to have to head over to the law library."

I groaned, pulling the covers over my head. The moment I'd been dreading had come to an end. Reality had resurfaced.

Then I realized this made it a good time to inject some reality of my own.

"Nick," I said, unexpectedly experiencing a twinge of nervousness, "that reminds me that I have something kind of... *strange* to ask you."

"I think I can handle strange."

You have no idea *how* strange, I thought. "How would you feel about going to a dungeon event?"

"It depends on how busy I am with—a *what*?"

I had to admit, I mumbled those last few words. This time, I forced myself to speak more clearly. "A dungeon event."

He frowned. "Sorry, I don't know what that is."

I could feel my cheeks growing warm. I was glad the blankets hid them. "It's kind of a party. For people who are into bondage and sadism and similar kinds of sexual behavior." Quickly, I added, "It's for the investigation. It seems Cassandra was involved in some fairly unusual things."

"That's pretty intense stuff," Nick commented matter-of-factly. "We did a case that involved BDSM a couple of weeks ago."

I sat up, suddenly as alert as if I'd actually downed one of those cappuccinos I'd been fantasizing about. "I'm talking about fetishes and leather clothing and whips and chains..."

"Right," he said. "BDSM—Bondage, Degradation, Sadism, and Masochism. Or as the medical field refers to it, paraphilia. An S&M group called the Leather Lords and Ladies sued a big hotel chain when it canceled its conference after learning what the theme was. If you want, I can grab my notes."

"Which you just happen to have brought with you?"

Looking guilty, he said, "I thought I might sneak in a little study time. But that was before I knew how much fun this weekend was going to be."

"Hmm," was all I said. But I had to admit that I was glad he'd brought along his notebook.

He retrieved it from his backpack and began thumbing through the pages. "Here it is. *Paraphilias are defined as attractions that, in the extreme, deviate from the most generally accepted forms of sexual expression. They include practices like inflicting or receiving pain, as in sadism and masochism, exhibitionism, voyeurism, and fetishes, like leather or rubber.*"

My ears pricked up at his mention of rubber. So the medical profession had the goods on those balloon-lovers, after all.

"What I learned is that, in general, the feeling is that there's nothing wrong with a little experimentation," he went on. "Or even with playing out a few fantasies. Apparently even something as innocent as adding whipped cream to a couple's sexual experience could be considered part of BDSM."

He glanced over and leered at me before continuing. "Let's see what else... *Some couples engage in spanking or tying one member up with silk scarves or handcuffs. Others enjoy dressing up and role-playing. As long as only consenting adults are involved, this type of activity isn't considered pathological.*"

"Is there any relationship between paraphilia and an inclination toward violence in other situations?" I asked.

"That's a bit more complicated," Nick said, skimming his notes. "Take exhibitionists, for example. They find it sexually stimulating to expose themselves to strangers. Yet they rarely seek out additional sexual contact and hardly ever commit rape.

"Interestingly," he continued, "the goal of acting out S&M scenarios isn't actually sex, although sexual relations do frequently follow. But the acting out is considered a reward in itself. Most people who engage in it report that they find it cathartic. In fact, many people enjoy this kind of activity primarily for its value as an escape. It gives them a chance to let go of their identity and become someone else, at least for a little while. They find it an effective way of reducing stress."

Even I had to admit that dressing up in leather and chains didn't have the side effects of wolfing down a pint of Chunky Monkey.

"Yet there's an interesting contradiction in the BDSM world," Nick continued, impressing me with how much useful information he'd picked up in only a few short weeks of law school. "The world of S&M has its own set of strict rules. A 'frame,' as it's called, is a set of parameters that participants substitute for reality. As long as they remain inside that frame, they experience a freedom to do and say and even feel in ways they might not be able to in their real lives."

"All this makes the BDSM thing sound pretty innocent," I observed.

"For the most part, I think it is. However, at the other extreme are behaviors that can be considerably more harmful, psychosexual disorders that may include rape and pedophilia. And any sexual activity that involves sadism and masochism certainly has the potential to get out of hand. One of the most common problems occurs when one person chokes another to enhance the sexual experience by decreasing the amount of oxygen that reaches the brain. From time to time, someone estimates wrong, resulting in death.

"But things can also get out of hand psychologically," Nick went on. "For some people, engaging in paraphilism, especially masochistic behaviors like being spanked, can feed into their sense of low self-esteem. They may be attracted to situations in which they're abused because they think they deserve it. Others have trouble limiting the experience, bringing either masochism or sadism into other aspects of their lives, where it's inappropriate or even destructive."

Interesting, I thought. And not quite as innocuous as Thor made the whole scene out to be. While before I'd been disturbed by what Cassandra Thorndike had been into while she was still alive, I now wondered just how much it had had to do with her death.

"So does everything you learned about BDSM make you more inclined to be my date at a dungeon event—or should I start reading the personal ads?"

"I'm in." Nick sighed. "After all, it sounds like we have no choice. Not if it might help get Suzanne out of this situation." Frowning, he said, "There's only one problem."

"What?" I asked nervously.

"I haven't got a *thing* to wear."

• • •

"The worst thing about getting away from it all," I announced as Nick and I tromped across the wooded area surrounding the Big House, back to the cottage, "is that when it's over, you have get *back* to it all."

Still, as I neared the front door, I had to admit that I was kind of looking forward to returning to my real life. There was something to be said for having your own coffeepot—not to mention being able to find the milk and sugar without sending out a search party.

Even more important was my menagerie. I'd missed having them around, even though I'd stopped in at least five times the day before to feed them, check their water bowls, walk them, scratch their necks or smooth their feathers, and play a few rounds of Slimytoy.

"I must be nuts, but I'm actually looking forward to spending the day studying," Nick said. "I think I'll just—*oomph!*"

The *oomph* came from the fact that he'd just walked into me. And that was because as soon as I opened the door and stepped inside the cottage, I froze.

Something was wrong. Very wrong.

While I wasn't the most conscientious housekeeper in the world, I knew immediately that there was no way I was responsible for the chaotic condition of the living room. Even though I'd rushed in and out several times the day before—and was now viewing it with a fresh outlook—this level of disarray could only mean one thing.

"The place has been ransacked!" I cried, my voice a hoarse whisper.

Nick stood beside me in silence as we both took in the

scene before us. The cushions had been pulled off the couch and the upholstered chair, and the stuffing from one of the throw pillows had been torn out in handfuls and strewn across the floor. The veterinary journals I'd left stacked on the coffee table had also been tossed to the ground. My CDs were dumped on the rug, mixed in with the junk mail that had been piling up on the table that served as both a desk and a place to eat.

"My animals!" I cried, my eyes darting around as I frantically attempted to spot them. Prometheus stood on his perch, looking a little agitated but otherwise fine. Leilani was in her tank, undisturbed, blinking at me lazily.

As for the others, the yelps and scratching sounds coming from the bedroom clued me in to their whereabouts. I just hoped the vile intruder who had done this hadn't harmed a single piece of fur on any of them....

I stifled a sob as I strode quickly through the room, feeling too overwhelmed to take it all in. Glancing into the kitchen, I noted that everything in there seemed to be in its proper place.

The bedroom was another matter entirely.

As I expected, Max and Lou sprang into action the moment I opened the door, leaping up on me excitedly. Catherine the Great blinked at us from her comfortable position on a throw rug, while Tinkerbell leaped around excitedly like Baryshnikov on speed. Aside from the inconvenience of all four of them being forced to bunk together, they didn't look the least bit ruffled—or hurt.

"Thank God you guys are okay!" I cried, running my hands over each one of them and looking into their eyes, just to make sure. "If only you could tell me what happened!"

Looking around the room gave me some inkling. Clothes that had been pulled out of drawers and yanked off hangers lay across the bed and floor like the remains of a ticker-tape parade.

Nick joined me in the doorway. "Glad I left most of my notes in the car," he said grimly.

The dogs had immediately dashed over to him, anxious to give him a warm enough welcome that he wouldn't feel left out. Tinkerbell, meanwhile, had already trotted over to her water dish, while Cat looked as if she wasn't going anywhere.

I did have one pet who was capable of speaking, more or less. I went back into the living room to interrogate him.

"Who was in here, Prometheus?" I asked my parrot.

"*Awk!*" he cried. "Happy birthday to you!"

Nick followed, distractedly pushing the hair out of his eyes. He watched my futile interaction with my bird, then shook his head and asked the same question.

"Jessie, who the hell could have done this?"

I couldn't say for certain. But I'd just spotted something lying on the ground that gave me a pretty good idea.

Chapter 13

"If animals could speak,
the dog would be a blundering outspoken fellow,
but the cat would have the rare grace
of never saying a word too much."

—Mark Twain

I bent over and picked up the red object.

"What is that?" Nick asked, sounding confused.

"A bow tie." I fought to keep my voice even. "The kind that's worn with a tuxedo."

"What does that mean? That our intruder was a runaway groom?"

"I can't be certain," I replied, "but it does suggest one person in particular. Ethan Thorndike. Cassandra's brother." I couldn't resist adding, "He's kind of strange."

"But why would he come here—especially if he was on his way to a formal event?" Nick asked. "Do you think he was looking for something?"

I shook my head. "First of all, he's not the one who would have been wearing this. It was more likely worn by the ventriloquist's dummy he carries around with him like a large and not very subtle security blanket. Second, I doubt that this tie just fell off. It's much more likely that

Ethan is trying to send me a message. One that says 'Mind your own business,' loud and clear."

"But our cars and your van are parked right outside," Nick pointed out. "Last night or early this morning, whenever he was here, it must have looked like we were home."

"Not if he broke in last evening. There were no lights on here in the cottage." Sighing, I added, "There isn't much to that lock on the front door. I usually feel so safe here that it never even occurred to me to get a stronger one."

Nick frowned. "This might be a good time to take care of that." Pulling his cell phone out of his pocket, he added, "After I call the police, how about if I call a good locksmith?"

It was a good plan, and I turned on my laptop to find the number of someone local. But there was also something else I wanted to research online.

"I think it's time for me to get to know the murder victim's baby brother a little better," I told Nick as my computer booted up. "Seems to me it wouldn't be a bad idea for Lieutenant Falcone to do the same. In fact, I think I'll suggest it to him when I call him to tell him that somebody broke into my house, clearly to scare me. Maybe this will convince him that Suzanne had nothing to do with Cassandra's murder—and that he'd be better off focusing on finding the person who did."

A startled look crossed his face. "Don't tell me you're going to ask this Ethan character over for dinner."

"Don't worry," I assured him. "I'm much more creative than that."

• • •

While I waited for the police, I logged on to *Newsday*'s Web site to check the day's headlines. It was a good thing I braced myself, since a wave of dizziness swept over me as I read the words splashed across the screen: *Ex-Wife Questioned in Thorndike Murder*. The article's byline, Forrester Sloan, didn't make me feel any better.

As I started reading, things quickly went from bad to worse.

A new suspect has emerged in the murder of Cassandra Thorndike, a sales representative for her family's winery, Thorndike Vineyards in Cuttituck.

On Friday, Norfolk County police questioned Suzanne Fox, the ex-wife of Thorndike's fiancé, after investigators discovered a bloody sweater in Fox's car during a search of her home and vehicle.

"Fox is someone we are looking at closely, along with several other individuals," Lieutenant Anthony Falcone, Norfolk County chief of homicide, said at a news conference yesterday. Falcone indicated that police are close to making an arrest in the case. According to police, several witnesses described a person fitting Fox's description leaving the murder scene shortly before Thorndike's body was discovered on October 3.

When questioned by authorities, Fox, a veterinarian in Poxabogue, first denied being at the home at 254 Cliffside Lane, but later reversed her story when detectives discovered her fingerprints at the residence, police said.

Thorndike, 29, was found stabbed in her Cuttituck home office. Police discovered the body while following up on a telephone call from her next-door neighbor, Virginia Krupinski.

The victim's fiancé, Robert Reese, owner of the restaurant Granite in East Brompton, told police that his ex-wife was "upset" when she learned that he intended to remarry.

"Oh, boy," I breathed. I had to admit that Forrester had written the article very objectively, stating the facts and only the facts. Still, seeing Suzanne's name in print, along with Falcone's claim that the police were looking at her closely, was chilling.

The clock I could hear ticking in my head suddenly seemed very loud.

I was actually relieved when a pulsing red light flashed through the front windows. I dashed over in time to see a uniformed police officer climb out of a blue-and-white car with the Norfolk County Police Department insignia on the side.

Nick joined me at the window. "Anyone you know from your P.I. days?" I asked.

"No," he replied. "Unfortunately. We'd probably get better service if it was."

We opened the door to a large, beefy man with light brown hair and a ruddy complexion. I instructed Lou to "stay" in no uncertain terms, then picked up Max and held him under one arm like a furry white football. "I'm Officer Malloy," he greeted us. "I understand there was a break-in."

"That's right."

After taking down our names, the time frame in which we believed the incident occurred, and other basic information, he asked, "What was taken?" He stood with his pen poised above his pad expectantly.

I glanced at Nick before answering, "Nothing."

"Nothing was taken?" he repeated, as if he wanted to make sure he was getting this right.

"Well, no."

The corners of his mouth drooped downward. "In that case, what was damaged? Any broken furniture, computers, other personal items? Any spray paint or other types of vandalism?"

"Just the lock," I replied, pointing to the front door. "That's the only thing that got broken."

He cast me a strange look before he went over and

studied it. "Not much of a lock," he observed. "Any other signs of forced entry? Broken windows? Scratches on the door?"

"No," I said.

He glanced at Nick, who shook his head in agreement. "Okay, then anybody hurt?" Gesturing toward Max, he added, "Your animals, for example?"

"No, they're all fine."

The police officer narrowed his eyes. "So exactly what did you find?"

"Just look at this mess!" I exclaimed, throwing out my arms to indicate the entire room. "Clothes were pulled out of drawers—and the drawers were left open. Cushions were thrown off the couch, and—and the stuffing was pulled out of one of my pillows."

"That's it?"

This time, I let Nick answer. "Pretty much."

Officer Malloy flipped his pad closed. I had a feeling that wasn't the only thing that was closed. "Know what I suggest? That you get a better lock."

"Look, someone broke in here," Nick insisted. "Maybe they didn't actually steal anything or break anything, but there was a break-in."

"And I think I know who did it," I added. "I also think I know why."

I explained the whole scenario to him as briefly as I could—Cassandra's murder, Suzanne becoming a suspect, my attempts to find out who the real killer was, Ethan's odd behavior, and the red bow tie I found after the break-in.

He listened patiently. But I could see the skepticism in his eyes.

"Look," he finally said. "You could be right that this friend of yours with the dummy is responsible. But frankly, there's not much we can do aside from filing a report, since nothing was taken and nothing was destroyed. You should be glad. Compared to a lot of people, you got off easy."

"That was a waste of time," I grumbled as soon as he left.

"At least there's a police report on file," Nick said, sounding as dejected as I felt. "For what it's worth."

As I turned back to my computer, it occurred to me that Lieutenant Falcone's reaction wasn't likely to be much different from Officer Malloy's. With no real damage done aside from a traumatized throw pillow, he might even think I'd fabricated the whole incident to try to convince him that somebody other than Suzanne was guilty. And after our trial run with this cop, I had to admit that my version of what had happened came off sounding pretty weak.

I was back to my original position: trying to find out for myself who had killed Cassandra Thorndike. But my suspicions about who that was were stronger than ever.

And I had a plan: learning more about Ethan Thorndike by talking to other people who had known him. And thanks to Theo Simcox, I knew the perfect place to start.

I scooped up Tinkerbell and dropped her into my lap, figuring it wouldn't hurt to have the company of someone warm and fuzzy. And then my fingers began flying across the keyboard, supercharged by the adrenaline surging through my veins.

"S-E-W-A..." As I typed the most likely spelling of *Sewanhacky School* into my favorite search engine, I said each letter aloud, as if somehow that would help me get it right. Of course, that possibility went out the window when Tinkerbell added *xxxxxxxxcccccaaa* with her tiny soft paws. Even Google wasn't clever enough to figure that one out.

"Arrgh!" I cried in frustration. Nuzzling her sweet, fuzzy little head, I said, "You think everybody should be online, huh, Tink? Even kitty cats?"

I tried again, this time managing to accomplish my goal without any feline editorializing. I held my breath as I waited for my computer to do its thing. I was afraid Ethan Thorndike's alma mater would turn out to be located in some distant state—or worse yet, that it would have gone out of business.

"Bingo!" I cried as I saw from the first listing that this "highly regarded school for children who may be facing exceptional challenges" was located in Laurel Bay, less than half an hour's drive from Joshua's Hollow. And as I began reading its mission statement, I knew in my gut that I'd found the right place.

Some students follow the same path that thousands of young people before them have followed. Others need to make their own way, struggling through the dense foliage of childhood without a compass or a map. At the Sewanhacky School, we provide such individuals with the tools they need to forge their own personal pathway.

I just hope those tools don't include machetes, I thought. At least, not with kids like Ethan.

I read on.

Our mission includes much more than teaching the 3 Rs—reading, writing, and arithmetic. More importantly, we also teach the 3 Ss—self-determination, self-confidence, and satisfaction. At Sewanhacky, students aged 10 to 18 are invited to explore both the Outer World and their own private and personal Inner World. With a flexible curriculum and few daily demands, our young wayfarers evolve into independent young adults. Maintaining open communication among students, parents, faculty, and staff furthers our goal of helping each member of the Sewanhacky community fully achieve his or her potential. Meanwhile, the creative environment that surrounds each and every one of our students nurtures both the intellect and the spirit, making the journey to adulthood an exciting and unique adventure.

"Sounds good to me," I told Tinkerbell. She, however, had lost interest in technology, having decided the piece of fuzz clinging to my sweater was much more fascinating. I clicked around the Sewanhacky School's Web site, trying to get a handle on what the place was all about. On the Academics page, I learned that the institution did, indeed, teach the 3 Rs. It also taught Introduction to Zen Buddhism, Rakku Pottery, and The Films of Keanu Reeves. In addition to nurturing the intellect and the spirit, it appeared to have a pretty solid physical-education program. With classes in sailing, polo, and crew, this fine educational institution clearly didn't cater to the hoi polloi.

I just hoped its open-communication policy included busybodies like me who had absolutely no good reason to be there, poking around the creative environment and asking a lot of questions about one young wayfarer in particular.

• • •

First thing Monday morning, as soon as I'd worked out my story, I put a call in to the headmaster's office. The woman who answered the phone seemed to accept my claim that I was looking for just the right school for my daughter. I guess I managed to sound pretty desperate, because she squeezed me in at three o'clock that afternoon, a time that meshed pretty well with my schedule.

I packed up my best outfit to bring along with me on the day's calls. I figured it wouldn't hurt to look authoritative, or at least like a grown-up, during my visit to the Sewanhacky School. If my tasteful wool blazer and real leather shoes that actually had heels didn't fool them, nothing would.

Thanks to my trusty Hagstrom map, I maneuvered my way through the winding back roads of the North Shore with ease. Still, when I reached what was supposed to be the right spot, I wasn't completely certain I hadn't taken a wrong turn somewhere.

It was the tall iron fence surrounding the property that threw me off. Or, to be more precise, the fact that at the top of each rail was what looked like a scalloped arrowhead. Or a barbed arrowhead, depending on how you looked at it. But a small, discreet sign reading *Sewanhacky School* stood next to the gate, assuring me I'd reached my destination.

"The fence is probably just to keep the riffraff out," I muttered, hoping that didn't mean me.

It wasn't until I passed through the gate and caught sight of the school itself that I wondered if maybe that scary-looking fence had been built to keep the riffraff *in*. It was a cloudy day, and the huge, Gothic gray stone structure looming up ahead looked like something out of an Alfred Hitchcock movie. It even had a tower, with a single row of tiny windows encircling the top. I wondered if the kids who forgot to do their Keanu Reeves homework ended up locked in there.

I parked my van in the Visitors' Parking area, noticing how out of place its shiny, bright white surface looked amid all the doom and gloom of the Sewanhacky School campus. I slipped on my blazer and my dressy shoes,

glad I'd thought to bring them. As I hobbled up the uneven cobblestone walkway that led to the door marked
Main Entrance, I half-expected to hear bats screeching
overhead. Or vultures.

Inside, the décor pretty much matched the building's
exterior. A marble table just inside the entryway held a
huge bouquet of flowers, but they were dried flowers.
Even though the lighting was dim, I could see that this
had once been a gracious mansion. The floors were marble, the chandeliers were ornate, and the heavy-looking
couches and chairs looked as if giving them a hard swat
would cause a cloud of dust to rise over them. While I
supposed it might have been fun to attend a masked ball
here, it didn't impress me as being all that well suited to
nurturing young people's creative spirits, or whatever it
was that the school's mission statement promised.

I was startled to discover that the receptionist I encountered just inside the building was actually pleasant.

"You must be Dr. Popper," she greeted me, glancing
up from her computer and smiling at me warmly. She
wore a pale gray sweater set with a string of pearls. I
wondered if the outfit was her own or if it had been supplied to her, like a school uniform.

"That's right," I replied. "Jessica Popper."

"I'll tell Mr. Stickley you're here. Why don't you have
a seat?"

I lowered myself onto one of the burgundy velvet
chairs that lined one wall, hoping I hadn't tracked any
dirt onto the Oriental carpet. It was that kind of place.

I'd barely had a chance to glance through the glossy
Sewanhacky School booklets neatly stacked up on the
table beside me, filled with photographs of teenagers
peering into test tubes and strolling across green lawns
with piles of books in their arms, when the receptionist
said, "Mr. Stickley will see you now."

I immediately got a sinking feeling in my stomach, as

if being called into the headmaster's office had to mean trouble. I quickly reminded myself that I was pretending to be a paying customer—or at least a potential paying customer—and was suddenly my usual self again.

At least, until I came face-to-face with the headmaster of this fine institution.

"Mr. Stickley?" I said, boldly sticking out my hand.

I imagined the man standing in the doorway was doing his best to look welcoming, but he wasn't doing that great a job. Part of the problem was his appearance, which I knew he couldn't help. He was well over six feet tall, yet so thin I could probably have taken him in a wrestling match. He wore a dark suit and a thin tie that might have looked just fine on somebody else but somehow managed to give him the look of a funeral director. Of course, his pallid skin didn't help—even though that tended to be a characteristic of such an establishment's clients, rather than its owner.

But superficialities aside, he was one of those people who simply didn't seem comfortable with himself. He didn't know where to put his hands, at least if the way he kept shoving them into his pockets and taking them out again was any indication, and his attempt at smiling looked so painful I was tempted to tell him not to bother on my account.

"Thank—thank you for coming in today," he said, stiffly walking back to his desk and sitting down. He gestured toward the chair opposite me, indicating that I should do the same.

"So. What brings—what brings you in today?"

"I'm trying to learn more about your school," I replied, taking care not to repeat any of the words that came out of my mouth. "For my daughter. It certainly has an intriguing name. Sewanhacky—that's a Native American word, isn't it?"

Mr. Stickley looked impressed. At least, if the little tic

in his left cheek was any indication. "I see you know your Long Island history."

Actually, I didn't. It was just a lucky guess.

"*Sewanhacky* was the—the Algonquian name for Long Island," he continued. "It's used in the early Dutch settlers' records of land purchases. Historians believe *sewan* means *purple shell* and *hacky* means *place*. The natives in this area were known for the fine quality of their wampum."

Gee, I thought, I've only been at the Sewanhacky School for ten minutes and I already learned something.

Of course, unlike the young wayfarers, I'd pretty much got my path all cut and paved. Heck, I'd even put in a few handrails.

"Tell me about your daughter." Mr. Stickley was clearly ready to get down to business. "What did you say her name was?"

I drew a blank. Desperately, I ran through the names of my pets, the closest thing to my children. Tinkerbell, Prometheus... "Max," I blurted out. "Uh, Maxine. I call her Max." I couldn't resist adding, "I think giving a child an affectionate nickname helps build self-esteem, don't you?"

"Absolutely. And how old is Maxine?"

"She's, uh, ten. Just turned ten."

He nodded. "The Sewanhacky School may well be just the right place for her," he told me solemnly. "You know, some students—some students have no trouble following a traditional path. But we specialize in children who need to make their own way, struggling through the dense foliage of childhood without a compass or a map."

The man didn't seem to realize I happened to own a computer—and that I was one of those few million people who had access to the Internet. Either that, or he couldn't help eating, sleeping, and breathing this stuff.

"Max definitely falls into that category," I told him, thinking about all the chair legs and bedroom slippers my fake daughter's namesake had torn to shreds. "And you may be right about Sewanhacky being the best place for her. In fact, the school came highly recommended to me by friends of mine. The Thorndikes? Their son, Ethan, was a student here."

His eyes clouded. "The Thorndikes told you . . . good things about the Sewanhacky School?"

"Yes. They were very enthusiastic." I tried to sound brave, but the tight feeling in the pit of my stomach told me I'd just said the wrong thing.

"Interesting, considering the fact that Ethan Thorndike was one of the school's few failures. In fact, he was one of only two students in our twenty-seven-year history who was asked to leave." His lip twitched, just a little, as he added, "The last I heard, the other young man was serving eight to ten."

I decided it was time to try some open communication of my own.

"Mr. Stickley, I'm going to lay all my cards on the table," I told him, even though I intended to keep one or two tucked away inside my sleeve. "You may not have heard about this, but Ethan Thorndike's sister, Cassandra, was recently murdered. I'm trying to learn as much as I can about the entire family in order to help find out who was responsible."

Mr. Stickley raised one eyebrow about a millimeter. I had a feeling that, for him, it was a shameless show of emotion. "So you work for the police."

I took a deep breath. "It's more like I work *with* the police." Okay, so a few more cards managed to find their way inside my blazer.

However, Mr. Stickley suddenly looked as if a curtain had been drawn across his face. Something told me this was turning out to be one of those occasions when honesty was *not* the best policy. "In that case, Dr. Popper, you should know that an educational institution is not authorized to give out any information about any student without explicit permission from the individual in question."

I sat up straighter, doing my best to look indignant. "Mr. Stickley, since this is a situation that involves murder, I just assumed that you would be anxious to be as helpful as you possibly could. In fact, I'm surprised that—"

"I'm afraid I'm going to have to ask you to leave," Mr. Stickley interrupted, standing up abruptly. "And frankly, I don't at all appreciate you coming in here this way. Especially since you tried to deceive me about your true purpose in requesting a meeting with me."

I was about to argue that I really did have a Max at home who was sorely in need of guidance. However, my Max was a he, not a she—and the kind of help he needed had mainly to do with learning that sit, stay, and get down were commands, not suggestions.

I, too, stood up. But that didn't mean I wasn't about to give it one last try. "Mr. Stickley," I said, "please let me assure you that—"

"And that comment I made about the other boy who was thrown out serving eight to ten?"

I nodded.

"That was a joke. I was just kidding."

Somehow, Mr. Stickley didn't impress me as much of a kidder. But he was clearly serious about getting me out of there. Before I had a chance to comment, I found myself on the wrong side of the door.

• • •

"Did you and Mr. Stickley have a nice chat?" the receptionist asked in a kind voice, even though the creases in her forehead told me she knew exactly what kind of chat we'd had.

"Uh, I think I'll be leaving now," I told her. "But if you don't mind, I'd like to use the restroom first. To compose myself."

I guess she could see I needed composing pretty badly, because her expression softened to one of sympathy.

"Of course. It's right down that hall."

"Thank you." I cast her a grateful smile and headed in the direction she'd indicated.

I found one of those impersonal-looking restrooms with three wooden stalls, a chipped tile floor, and an empty paper-towel dispenser. I splashed cold water on my face, took a few deep breaths, and exited. By that point, I'd had more than enough of the Sewanhacky School and I couldn't wait to get out of there.

In fact, I was making a beeline for the door when I heard, "Pssst!"

At least, I thought that was what I heard. The soft whistle could have come from a door swinging shut or even a radiator. Still, I glanced around.

"Over here!"

I turned, my eyes darting from side to side. I had to admit, I'd never met either a door or a radiator that was capable of forming complete sentences.

Sure enough, there was a man with a grizzled beard and a hairdo that made Albert Einstein look like a Pantene model, sticking his head out of a doorway with a sign that read *Maintenance*. He wore a pale gray jumpsuit that matched the receptionist's outfit. Instead of pearls, however, he'd accessorized with the name *Mr. Waylan* embroidered on the pocket in red.

"Yes?" I asked, still puzzled.

"I heard you just before, talkin' to Mr. Stick-in-the-Mud Stickley."

"Really?" I was genuinely surprised. The old-fashioned

wooden doors looked thick enough to keep out the Spartan army. How could this man have possibly overheard our conversation?

He answered the question for me. "Through them air vents," he said, pointing upward.

I tried listening. "I don't hear anything."

"That's 'cause you gotta stand on a bench."

"I see." So he hadn't exactly overheard. It was more like he considered part of his job description to be testing the strength of the building's air vents by making sure they carried sound waves effectively.

Mr. Waylan gave a loud snort that sounded like a noise a horse would make. A horse with a very bad chest cold.

"Damn rich kids. You wanna know what screws 'em up?"

I half-expected him to start quoting Carl Jung. Instead, he continued, "Having too damn much money, that's what. They're all damn spoiled!"

I couldn't completely disagree with him, at least in part.

"You been askin' questions about that Thorndike boy, right?"

"That's right." Trying not to scare him off by sounding too interested, I added lightly, "I don't suppose you knew him."

Mr. Waylan let out the same equine snort. "Sure I did. Everybody knew 'im. Boy like that, one of them peeculiar types, is the kind of kid everybody talks about."

"Peculiar...how?" I asked, as if I hadn't made a few observations of my own.

The maintenance man looked from right to left. Then, peering at me from underneath his bushy eyebrows, he said, "I noticed Stickley didn't say nothin' about the time the Thorndike kid stuck a pair of scissors in that girl's hand over and over."

"No," I replied, impressed by how matter-of-fact I managed to sound. "I don't believe he mentioned that particular incident."

He snorted again, making me wish I'd brought along a wad of tissues. But I quickly forgot about Mr. Waylan's revolting personal habits when he said, "He was all set to call in the police and everythin', but then the kid's father, the one that owns that big winemaking operation out east, he comes in and starts makin' a fuss."

Somehow, I found it difficult to picture Gordon Thorndike making a fuss about anything. Then again, I hadn't exactly seen him under the most usual conditions.

"So Stick-in-the-Mud decides he's just gonna expel the kid, without callin' in the authorities. Y'ask me, kid like that should be locked up. And they should throw away the key. Kid like the Thorndike boy ain't nothin' but trouble."

As repulsed as I was by this gentleman, I couldn't resist picking his brain—such as it was—just a little bit more. "How badly was the girl hurt, exactly?"

"Ha!" Another snort. This time, at least, I was quick enough to jerk backward before any bodily fluids hit me. "How'd you feel if you got a pair of scissors stuck into your hand more'n a dozen times?"

"Probably not that great," I admitted. "Had Ethan and this girl had an argument?"

"Kid like that don't need no real reason t'go around hurtin' folks. He was just...weird, y'know? Probably the kinda kid that enjoys that kinda thing. Good riddance, I say. Maybe they didn't lock 'im up, way they should, but at least they got him outta here."

"Well. Thank you," I said. "For your insights, I mean."

He just shook his head in disgust, then leaned over to pick up a large metal pail. I expected him to move away, but he stepped inside the maintenance closet and closed the door. For all I knew, Mr. Stickley had another appointment on the schedule and he wanted to be sure to position himself so he wouldn't miss a single word.

By this point, I'd really had enough of the Sewanhacky School, even though I had a feeling the short conversation I'd just had could well have made the entire trip worthwhile.

As I moved toward the front door, the receptionist called, "Dr. Popper?"

I was surprised to see that she'd followed me into the entryway. I was about to ask if I'd left behind my umbrella or something when, in a loud whisper, she said, "Don't listen to what Mr. Waylan says. I knew Ethan Thorndike. And I thought he was a perfectly nice boy. A little eccentric, perhaps, but a lot of the kids who come here are. In fact, I never believed that that incident with the scissors was his fault. There was something strange about the whole thing. I think Mr. Stickley was wrong to expel him." She'd barely gotten the words out before she glanced over her shoulder nervously. "Of course, I'd never let him know that."

I stared at her for a few seconds, as surprised by her interest in clearing the name of one of the school's students as I was pleased to get a second opinion of the young Ethan Thorndike.

"Thank you," I told her sincerely. "I appreciate your honesty. It's true that I came here to find out whatever I could about the boy, but it's only because his sister was killed. Anything I can learn about her family is bound to help."

"In that case," she said, "I hope I've been of some assistance."

She hurried back to her desk before I had a chance to tell her that she had. It was probably just as well that I didn't have the opportunity to mention that her comment about Ethan Thorndike was the first positive thing I'd heard about him.

But one thing was certain: Whoever's version of the pen incident was more accurate—the janitor's or the receptionist's—it was definitely worth further investigation.

I was still ruminating about the two radically different portraits of the ventriloquist as a young man I'd just gotten as my van came into sight. I slowed my pace, my heartbeat quickening at the sight of a dark shadow in the front seat. At first glance, the round shape looked like the silhouette of a person. I could feel the adrenaline surging through my body. I glanced around, hoping to spot a friendly stranger or two. But it was late afternoon by now, and the lot was almost empty. There were no other vehicles in the Visitors' Parking section, and most of the spaces in the Faculty area were vacant.

I must be seeing things, I told myself. No one could break into my van. Besides, who would want to?

Cautiously I walked closer, telling myself I'd probably just thrown a sweater over the back of the seat, or maybe the lengthening shadows were playing tricks with me. Then a beam of sunlight reflected off something shiny, and I knew that was no sweater.

As I neared the van, I let out a little cry. Someone was waiting for me in the front seat, all right.

Or at least some*thing*, I thought, realizing in a split second what was going on.

Once again, Ethan's dummy sat propped up in the driver's seat in what had been my locked van.

Not again, I thought, unsure of whether to be relieved or frightened. That is, until I noticed that the shiny object that had caught the light was a scalpel stuck into his chest.

Instinctively I stuck my hands into my pockets, searching for something that could serve as a weapon. Quickly realizing that a crumpled tissue and a half-melted cough drop weren't going to do the trick, I did a mental inventory of the contents of my purse. While I remembered that I had a couple of pens, I wasn't exactly what I'd consider adequately armed.

I glanced around, remaining as silent as I could as I listened for the sound of a footstep or even someone breathing. Nothing. I stood still for what seemed an eternity, finally concluding that once Ethan had delivered his calling card, he'd left the premises.

This time, it appeared, he wasn't looking for a face-to-face confrontation. Instead, there were two simple facts he wanted me know.

The first was that he was aware that I'd visited his alma mater to ask questions about him.

The second was that he wasn't happy about it.

• • •

"Out of the front seat, Mr. Ed," I muttered as I gingerly lifted the dummy and stashed it in the back of the van, taking care not to displace the scalpel or add any fingerprints. For all I know, I thought grimly, Dollface here could end up as Exhibit A at Cassandra Thorndike's murder trial.

Then I hightailed it out of there. As if it wasn't disturbing enough driving around with that thing in my vehicle, I had another peculiar errand to run. I just hoped the Arthritis Foundation's thrift shop in Elmwood still had that rack of leather castoffs I remembered seeing there once or twice.

By the following evening, I still hadn't mentioned my unexpected driving partner to Nick. I'd decided that, like my mysterious e-mail pal, I was better off keeping Ethan's disturbing little communiqués a secret. In addition to the fact that I was already inclined to keep the details of my efforts at investigating Cassandra's murder to myself, the last thing I wanted was to creep Nick out. I needed him to be my date at tonight's dungeon event, and I didn't want him having a change of heart before I managed to push him out the door.

As he and I got dressed after dinner, I noticed he was taking an awfully long time. He'd also holed up in the bathroom, which was unusual for somebody like him, who wasn't exactly the modest type.

When he finally shuffled out of the bathroom, wearing nothing but the pair of gently used black leather pants I'd been thrilled to pick up for ten bucks, he didn't look happy.

"Hey, not bad!" I cried, trying to build up some enthusiasm.

"These pants are too loose," Nick grumbled.

"Better than the alternative," I pointed out.

"But they make my butt look big!"

"How do you think I feel?" I demanded, standing up straighter to show off my low-cut black leather halter top, fishnet stockings, and a black leather skirt that was so mini I knew I'd have to remain standing the entire evening.

"Actually, I kind of like it," he said. "Although you might want to put a few tears in those stockings."

"This is as far as I'm going," I countered. "I already feel like I'm dressed up for a costume party. And frankly, I'm having a hard time believing that you and I aren't going to be the only ones at this party who actually have the nerve to dress up like this."

The fact that the house in which my friendly, local dungeon event was being held looked surprisingly ordinary from the outside didn't help. Even though most of the other guests had parked along the street, I pulled into the driveway, figuring we wouldn't be staying long enough to box anyone in. Besides, this way, we could make a quick getaway if we had to.

We sat in silence for a few moments, just staring at the house.

"It looks like any other house," I finally commented.

"You sound disappointed," Nick replied. "What were you expecting, whips and chains decorating the mailbox? A *Beware of the Dungeon Master* sign on the doghouse? Leather curtains hanging in the kitchen window, with—"

"Okay, okay," I told him through clenched teeth. "I'm already nervous enough, thank you."

"Just pretend it's already Halloween," he suggested, "and your Snow White costume is at the cleaners."

"Ha-ha," I returned unconvincingly.

"Besides, once you go inside and see how nice and friendly everyone is, you'll be tossing around those whips like a pro."

That wasn't exactly what happened. In fact, the moment Nick and I walked through the front door, I sensed that he was just as stunned as I was. I stood frozen, scanning the masses of people crowded into the living room, dining room, kitchen, and even the den, which was outfitted with two desktop computers and a flat-screen TV. Some people stood in small groups, chatting as if they were at a corporate cocktail party. Others were dancing to the loud music blaring in the den, while others swarmed around the dining-room table, stuffing themselves with the usual chip-and-dip, cheese-and-cracker-type party snacks.

It would have looked like any other suburban party except for the fact that every single guest was dressed in an outfit composed entirely of black leather, scary-looking metal, and a great deal of flesh. I saw so many thongs, garter belts, face masks, and bustiers made of black leather that I wondered how I'd gotten this far in life without ever owning anything made of the stuff besides shoes. One man wore a headdress comprised of what looked like snakes, although even I could tell they were rubber. A few had tattoos covering most of their skin, and many had multiple body piercings, including several in places that made me cringe. And quite a few were only partially dressed, revealing body parts that wouldn't even be shown in the Abercrombie & Fitch catalog.

I heard Nick gulp loudly. "I have a feeling nobody's going to be paying much attention to my butt tonight."

I had to agree. Just then, an attractive young woman with long black hair, thick black eye makeup, and a large ring in each nipple, linked together with a pair of handcuffs, walked by.

Nick's eyes widened. "I had no idea this kind of thing really went on," he whispered. "*Especially* on a school night!"

At the moment, however, I was unable to speak. I was too astonished by something in the den that had caught my eye.

I'd braced myself for the various accoutrements of the BDSM world. I was prepared to confront more leather than the last time I'd ventured into the Shoe Warehouse. I even expected to witness behaviors that a vanilla-sex person like me was bound to find shocking.

What I *hadn't* expected was to run into someone I knew.

Chapter 14

"My kittens look at me like little angels—and always after doing something especially devilish."

—Jamie Ann Hunt

Nick," I whispered, "whatever you do, don't look over there."

"Over where?" Nick's head swiveled like an office chair.

"I told you not to look!"

His head swiveled right back. "Okay, then tell me what I'm not looking at."

I, of course, was completely unable to keep my eyes off precisely what I'd told Nick not to gape at. The man standing less than ten feet away from me was Jean-Luc Le Bec. I was certain I recognized him, despite the fact that I'd only met Robert Reese's short, plump, baby-faced pastry chef once, despite the fact that he and I had spent less than ten minutes together, dishing about Robert and Cassandra's less-than-perfect relationship—and despite the leather.

Not a *lot* of leather. In fact, Jean-Luc was completely naked except for what could best be described as a G-string. Even though the straps that encircled hips and a butt both the color and texture of large-curd cottage cheese were narrow, the leather pouch in front was huge. In fact, it was oversize to the point of being ridiculous. The garment's various pieces were held together with enough buckles and studs to send an airport metal detector into overdrive.

His only other attire was also constructed of black leather. It was a mask that covered his entire head, made of crisscrossing straps that made him look like he was peering out a window. Or a dungeon.

Still, I could see enough of his face to be ninety-nine percent certain it was the mousse master himself.

"Earth to Jessie," Nick said impatiently.

"Sorry. Remember the pastry chef who gave me all those goodies I brought home?"

"Of course. He has a soft spot in my heart for eternity."

"You might not find his confections quite as appetizing after you see him in this getup. Especially since it looks like he stuffed a few éclairs in his thong."

This time, there was no way I could keep Nick from looking. As soon as I heard him gasp, I knew he'd zeroed in on the gentleman in question.

"That's *him*?" he cried.

"Afraid so."

"You're right," he muttered. "I'm swearing off sweets as of this second."

Frankly, I was much less interested in how Jean-Luc spent his free moments while his soufflés were rising than in the fact that he clearly traveled in the same circles that Cassandra had once frequented. In fact, I was so fixated on his outfit—as well as his pathetic attempt at doing a dance that seemed to be a cross between the monkey and the hora—that I didn't bother to look very far beyond.

At least, not until Nick said, "Check out his dancing partner, the guy with the two-tone hair."

The term *two-tone hair* should have been enough to tip me off. But it wasn't until I studied the herd of sweating, undulating bodies and finally figured out which one Jean-Luc was do-si-do'ing with that I let out a cry. And it wasn't the black-leather garter belt, or even the neat rows of needles piercing the flesh of both arms, that was responsible.

"That's Preston DeVane!" I exclaimed.

"Who?" Nick asked distractedly.

"The owner of—I'll explain later. But you and I have to get out of here." I grabbed his arm, figuring the worst thing I could do was let Jean-Luc and Preston spot me. Something was going on—between them, obviously, but also between Jean-Luc and me.

"But we just got here!" Nick protested.

I opened my mouth to explain that while he thought all he was seeing was two men who could have used a session with the fashionista from *Queer Eye for the Straight Guy*, I was seeing proof that Jean-Luc had lied to me about his relationship with his boss's number-one competitor. His insistence that he and the owner of G were archenemies was clearly a ruse. The question was, why was he trying so hard to fool me?

But I quickly snapped my mouth shut, realizing that trying to explain the relevance of what I was seeing with my own eyes was much too complicated.

Besides, I had an idea.

"You know, Nick, you're right," I said. "How about if—wait, let's find a quiet corner somewhere." A quiet *dark* corner, I thought, where it's much less likely the two foodies will realize I'm on to them.

"Okay," he agreed.

As we moved away, I heard Jean-Luc shriek, "Who's ya daddy?" with one of the strongest New York accents I'd heard since the last time I'd watched a Martin Scorsese movie.

He's not even French! I thought. And he accused *Preston* of being a fraud!

"Nick," I said breathlessly once we'd moved away from the dance floor, "I need a favor."

"Sure, anything." He glanced around the room and frowned. "Wait a minute. Maybe you'd better tell me what it is before I agree."

"I just want you to stay at this party a while longer, alone."

"But—"

"I can't let Jean-Luc see me!" I went on. "Now that I know he lied to me, I have to consider him a suspect. If he realizes I'm on to him, it might be dangerous. But he doesn't know you. Could you just mingle a little and see if you can learn anything about him? He obviously feels comfortable with this crowd. Somebody here might be able to tell you something useful."

"Jessie, if it was anyplace else—"

"We went to all this trouble, with the leather pants and all . . . and you really do look like you fit right in."

As soon as I said those words, I regretted them. Fortunately, Nick is a good sport. Either that, or deep down he was as committed to doing whatever it took to get Suzanne off the hook as I was.

"Half an hour, okay? After that, I'm outta here."

"Thanks, Nick! I owe you!"

The look he shot me told me he was perfectly aware of that—and that he wasn't about to let me forget it.

No sooner had I moved away from him toward the door than a sweet young thing with a tattoo of a skull on her left bicep shot across the room like a heat-seeking missile. She would have looked like an extra in a horror movie if it weren't for the fact that she was tall, slender, and ridiculously pretty, even with a small hypodermic needle stuck through one nostril. She also happened to be wearing nothing besides a peekaboo thong, cut out in a deep V-shape in front, the two sides held together by a silver chain, and a black bra with two revealing circles cut out.

"You're new here, aren't you?" I heard her coo as she sidled up to Nick. "At least, I haven't seen you before. I know I would have remembered."

Maybe her outfit qualified her to be a pinup girl for the Hell's Angels, but she sounded as sweet and flirty as a Southern belle. I bet that if she hadn't had half a pound of eye makeup on, she'd have batted her lashes at him.

I gritted my teeth and headed out the door. "Nick had better find out something important," I muttered to myself. "And I'm not talking about Needle-nose's phone number either."

I headed out to the car, slumping down in the front seat so no one would notice me. I also opened the window a couple of inches, hoping to overhear an incriminating piece of someone else's conversation as they left the party. Something like, "The metal studs on Jean-Luc's G-string were certainly shiny tonight, weren't they? Considering that he just murdered Cassandra Thorndike and all."

No such luck. In fact, there was very little activity out here. It was incredibly boring, sitting in a cold, dark car, checking my watch every two minutes. Even after that half hour we'd agreed upon passed, there was no sign of Nick. Thirty-five minutes passed. Then forty.

Don't tell me he's actually having fun in there, I thought. It did occur to me that he might be in some kind of trouble. But if he was, I had a feeling it wasn't the kind I was in a position to help him with.

Finally, I couldn't resist getting out of the car and creeping over to a window. It took me a minute or two to locate Nick. When everyone's wearing pretty much the same color—black—it's hard to pick out one particular person in the crowd.

When I did spot him, I almost wished I hadn't. He was standing in a corner, although whether it was voluntary or he'd been cornered by the two women monopolizing him, I couldn't tell. What I could tell was that they were both pretty attractive, if you looked past their clothing. The one wearing the thong and the medical equipment kept giggling like a nervous teenager on her first date. The other one, whose entire body was smeared with something dark brown, had the thick blond hair and innocent face of a Miss America contestant.

Even though I felt a twinge of something that seemed very much like jealousy, I had to admit that Nick was doing exactly what I'd asked him to do: mingle. I just wished he didn't look like he was enjoying it so much.

I went back to my car—and waited. Another ten or fifteen minutes passed. When a shadow finally crossed the front seat and the door on the passenger side opened, I let out a loud sigh of relief.

"Finally!" I cried as Nick slid in. "I was beginning to think you'd fallen into the punch bowl! Or maybe even the snake pit."

"No snakes—at least, not until next week," he replied pleasantly. "That's when they're having the Snake Festival."

"Oh, really? I hope you paid your annual dues so you won't have to miss it."

Nick cast me an odd look. "Am I wrong, or did you not specifically ask me to stay in there to see if I could find out anything?"

"You're right. I did. It's just that when I see you cavorting with tall, gorgeous women who are dressed as if they only had time to put on half their Halloween costume, I tend to get a little edgy."

"I was hardly cavorting," Nick insisted. "Besides, they both turned out to be pretty nice."

I bet, I thought. And they probably didn't think those pants make your butt look even *close* to big.

"That woman who came up to me as you were leaving—the tall, gorgeous one, as you described her? She works in an assisted-living facility. Anyway, Princess Hellfire—that's her name—introduced me to Betty Boob, and the three of us just hit it off."

My eyebrows jumped up so high they nearly popped off my head. "Those are their names?"

"Not their real names," Nick replied impatiently. "It's part of the persona they take on when they come to dungeon events."

My boyfriend suddenly seemed very much at home in this world. I wasn't sure I liked that, even if it was for such a good cause.

I was about to ask him if he'd remembered he was there on assignment, rather than simply to make new friends, when he volunteered, "I found out something I think you'll be interested in hearing about."

"Shoot."

"According to Betty and the Princess, Cassandra was gloating the last time the group got together."

"I'm impressed," I commented dryly. "It sounds as if those two told you quite a bit about her."

"Cassandra Thorndike inspired a lot of jealousy, at least among some of the females who knew her. It seems she wasn't above bragging about her good fortune, whether it related to her skyrocketing career in the glamorous wine industry or modeling for kinky magazines or hanging out with some guy named Thor they told me was 'a real hunk.'" Turning to face me, he announced, "Apparently Cassandra was pretty excited about some new venture she was about to undertake."

"What kind of venture?" I felt a familiar pounding in my chest, my usual reaction to learning something that might get me a step or two closer to figuring out what a murder victim had been up to in the days or weeks before he or she was killed.

"They didn't say," Nick replied. "But it must have had something to do with her father, because according to Betty Boob, Cassandra made a sly comment about how she had her daddy wrapped around her little finger. At least, that's how Betty remembers it."

"Interesting." And perfectly true, I thought, at least according to Joan Thorndike, who was certainly in a position to know. But if these leatherettes were to be believed, it sounded as if this exciting new endeavor of Cassandra's had something to do with her father.

Which meant he was likely to know about the new twist Cassandra's life was about to take.

Suddenly another thought struck me. "Good work, Nick... but I don't suppose you asked them about Jean-Luc and Preston DeVane."

"As a matter of fact, I did," he replied, looking quite pleased with himself. "The two of them are regulars at this Tuesday night dungeon event. They've been showing up together for months. They're pretty tight too."

"*Very* good work," I told him.

In fact, I was still trying to digest all the interesting new information I'd learned about Cassandra and her entourage this evening when Nick said, "By the way, Jess, we're not coming back again next week, are we?"

I just stared at him for a few moments before I collected myself enough to say, "No-o-o."

"I didn't think so." He hesitated. "It's just that I agreed to be on the refreshments committee. I signed up to bring a cake or cookies or something. Since we're not coming, maybe I should go back and tell Princess Hellfire—"

"I think they'll manage fine without us," I assured him, turning the key in the ignition. "Besides, from what

I saw, it looked like the chocolate-pudding committee had things pretty well under control."

●　●　●

First thing the next morning, after Nick had left for school and I was finishing my coffee, I made a dozen phone calls and, as I hoped, managed to reschedule enough appointments to fit in an *unscheduled* visit to the North Fork late that afternoon.

I was scribbling in my date book, crossing out David and Marty Dauwalder and their cockapoo Wally in Port Townsend and writing them in for the next day as Cat lay contentedly in my lap, when a knock at the door startled me. For some reason, I immediately pictured my visitor as someone dressed in a black leather hood, brandishing a thick chain. So I was relieved when I peeked through the window and saw Betty standing outside.

"Betty!" I cried as I flung open the front door, understanding why Max and Lou hadn't done anything more threatening than wag their tails and whine a little. I felt both relieved and guilty, the latter because I'd been so busy thinking about Cassandra over the past few days that I'd forgotten all about Betty's romantic R&R with Winston. "How was your getaway?"

She thrust a white box at me. "Shoofly pie," she explained. "A Pennsylvania Dutch specialty. I swear, you can't drive ten feet through Amish Country without running into one of these."

"Great!" I said, taking it from her and setting it down on the coffee table. "Lately, Nick and I have been developing quite a sweet tooth—hey, get away from that, Lou! That's people food!"

As Betty settled into the upholstered chair, giving Max the enthusiastic welcome he always insisted upon, something about her smile struck me as forced.

"Was your trip as wonderful as you'd hoped?" I asked, plopping down on the couch.

Her smile faded. "First, there was so much traffic between here and Lancaster, Pennsylvania, you'd have thought they were offering free land in Oklahoma again. Second, our 'rustic yet charming' bed-and-breakfast was such a bare-bones operation I thought I'd become Amish myself. Third, if I look at one more quilt, I might begin to shriek hysterically."

She let out a deep sigh. "To tell you the truth, Jessica, home sweet home has never felt quite this good."

"What about Winston? Did you two . . . you know, rekindle the old spark?"

"Turns out he snores just as loudly in Pennsylvania as he does in New York. And that he brings a lot of his other quirks with him on the road too. And those include his brewer's yeast and his soy powder."

Shaking her head slowly, she added, "I know I'm not perfect either. In fact, he did mention—in a very *nice* way, of course—that I have a few annoying idiosyncrasies of my own. I guess the bottom line is that Winston and I just have to get used to each other—and to living with another person too. It's never an easy thing, of course, and when you've been living on your own the way each of us has—and for as long as each of us has—it's even harder. But one good thing did come out of our trip."

"What's that?" I asked hopefully. Frankly, I was surprised by how hard I was rooting for them.

"Winston and I had a long heart-to-heart conversation on the Belt Parkway, coming home. And since they closed two of the three lanes, I can assure you that we had plenty of time to talk. He and I agreed that we have really strong feelings for each other, and that no matter how difficult it is, we're going to keep trying. I guess he's as much of a romantic as I am, but he believes as strongly as I do that what we have is special—and worth fighting for."

"Wow," I breathed. I felt like I was watching the ending of a really romantic movie, the kind that makes my eyes sting.

"How about you and Nick?" she asked, the look in her eyes going from dreamy to bright. "I hope you two made the best of your romantic getaway, even though you didn't get very far away."

I couldn't help glancing around the cottage, suddenly worried that maybe I hadn't put everything back in order—at least enough so that it looked like my normal level of chaos, instead of the scene of a ransacking. The last thing I wanted was for Betty to worry. Even though the unsettling incident had occurred on her property, I was utterly convinced it had nothing to do with her.

"It was lovely," I assured her. And as I said the words, I realized that it really had been lovely. Nick and I were lucky enough to have that same special connection that she and Winston had—and, like them, we were lucky enough to recognize how valuable it was. "Thanks for letting us use your place, Betty. It was a great chance to step out of our regular day-to-day life and really appreciate each other."

"Good!" she cried. "In that case, I say we put on the teakettle and break into the shoofly pie." In response to my look of astonishment, she added, "I said they were everywhere in Amish Country, but I didn't say I wasn't crazy about them!"

• • •

The good mood our impromptu tea party created didn't last long. As I turned off Route 35 and into the Thorndikes' driveway later that day, a feeling of dread came over me. While I'd been excited by Nick's discovery that Cassandra was about to embark on some sort of new venture, I found the prospect of talking to the victim's father about it pretty unsavory.

As I got out of the car, the place seemed unusually quiet. That didn't mean Ethan wasn't lurking in some dark corner somewhere, I realized, waiting to pounce on me when I least expected it. I kept an eye out for him as I knocked on the back door. There was no response, from either him or his stepmother.

Next I tried the barn out back, a dilapidated building I'd noticed but hadn't ventured into before. The sounds of something being slid and dropped, over and over, told me I might have found the man I was looking for.

Sure enough, when I peeked inside, I saw Gordon pulling cardboard cartons of wine off a dolly and loading them into the garage.

"Mr. Thorndike?" I called softly, not wanting to startle him.

He turned around, barely gave me a glance, and went back to what he was doing.

"I don't want to bother you," I began, "and I can see you're busy—"

"I remember you," he said without looking back at me. "You're that veterinarian."

"That's right."

I took a deep breath. "Mr. Thorndike, first let me say how terribly sorry I am about your daughter. I can imagine how devastated you must feel."

"Thank you." For the first time since I'd walked in, he stopped shoving boxes around and looked me squarely in the face. "Somehow, I have a feeling that's not what you came here to say."

"No." I took a deep breath. "Last night, I spoke with some of Cassandra's friends." My voice cracked as I uttered that last word.

Still, I'd gotten her father's attention. "Go on," he prompted.

Maybe it was the emotion in my voice, or maybe he

also had questions about her "friends," but he suddenly seemed extremely interested in what I had to say.

I took another deep breath. "One of them said something about Cassandra being excited about a new venture she was about to undertake. And she mentioned that Cassandra's father had something to do with it." My heart felt like it had leaped out of my chest and become lodged in my throat as I added, "Do you have any idea what she might have been talking about?"

"Well, sure. That'd be the new winery."

I blinked. I hadn't expected this to be easy, yet Cassandra's father seemed to know exactly what I was talking about. "What new winery?"

"Look, Cassie was one of those kids who took a while to find herself. You know, to figure out what to do with her life." He shook his head slowly. "That girl tried a lot of different things. Art, acting...even modeling, from what I understand."

Let's hope you never really do, I thought.

"But lately she'd developed an interest in the wine business," he went on. His eyes shone, as if someone had turned on a light. "Of course, I couldn't have been more pleased that she wanted to follow in her old dad's footsteps. A couple of years ago, she started learning the business by working in sales. You know, going around to East End restaurants, trying to convince them to serve our wines. She took to it better than I ever expected. Began asking a lot of questions, too, showing a real interest in the process. I was only too happy to teach her everything I know. Only too happy to help her get started, too."

"Do you mean started in sales?" I asked, confused.

"I mean started with her own winery. She'd certainly learned enough about the sales and marketing end of things to give it a go. True, she had a ways to go in terms of learning how to actually run a vineyard, but I figured I could help her as she went along."

A soft look had come into his blue-green eyes, as if he was seeing the scenario play out—at least, the way he'd originally envisioned it. "I was looking forward to working side by side with her. I'm getting on in years, so I figured this was a good way to make sure Cassie had a secure future. After all, she was going to inherit all this eventually, anyway. Why not start making it hers *now*?"

I just nodded. Suddenly another thought popped into my mind: the age-old issue of sibling rivalry.

"What about Ethan?" I asked. "Did he ever show an interest in the wine business?"

"Ethan? Nah. He's not stable enough to take on something that ambitious. Besides, he's much more of a loner than Cassie ever was.

"Interestingly, it was Joan who was against the idea," Gordon continued, almost as if he was talking to himself.

"Joan?" I repeated, surprised. "Why? Wasn't she pleased that Cassandra had found something she was excited about?"

Yet even as I asked the question, I already knew the answer. Joan probably knew Cassandra Thorndike better than anyone else, including her own father. And like so many of the other people who knew the beautiful but flighty young woman, Joan had no illusions about who Cassandra was—and who she wasn't. Maybe Gordon Thorndike was convinced that his daughter was ready to take on the role of effective businesswoman, but I could imagine Cassandra's stepmother thinking otherwise.

"Joan was convinced this would turn out to be another dead end," Gordon replied, as if he'd read my thoughts. "She insisted that I was fooling myself. She kept telling me that sooner or later Cassandra would lose interest. In fact, Joan and I got into quite an argument about it, just a couple days before..."

He shook his head thoughtfully. "I know she's sorry now. I'm sorry, too, that she's got this weighing her down. Sometimes I think Joan doesn't really understand how much she means to me. And how grateful I am for all the work she's done, helping me raise those two kids. I can't imagine a more thankless job, given how difficult they could both be.

"But this time, I'm sure Cassie was going to follow through. I'd never seen her so excited about anything. She was so full of plans for this new venture the two of us cooked up! Why, she talked about it nonstop." Chuckling, he added, "Practically drove us all crazy the last few weeks. Babbling on and on about getting distribution all over the country and planning special promotions.... She had a lot of good ideas, that girl. It would have really been something, sitting back and watching her succeed."

The soft look had faded from his eyes. Instead, I saw the same dead look I'd seen the first time I met him, when he'd wandered around the kitchen, dazed.

"Thank you for telling me all this," I told him, realizing it was time for me to go. "I know how difficult it must be."

He'd already turned away, and I suspected that the words I was saying weren't really going in. I mumbled good-bye, then slipped out of the barn and headed back to my van.

Once I was alone, the windows rolled down and the fresh air flying into my face, I didn't know whether to feel exhilarated or defeated. Deep in my gut, I had a feeling I'd just found a major piece of the puzzle. Yet I didn't begin to have a sense of how it fit in with all the rest of the pieces.

The fact that Cassandra had been murdered as she

was about to embark upon an exciting new venture—starting her own winery—only made the whole thing that much more tragic.

I was contemplating calling Forrester to get his take on my discovery about the new path Cassandra Thorndike was about to follow when my cell phone rang. I pulled over to the side of the road and answered without bothering to check the Caller ID.

"Dr. Popper," I answered crisply.

"Jessica? I'm glad I got you. Listen, I was wondering if you and I could talk."

Even though I hadn't checked to see who my caller was, I recognized the voice immediately. I tried not to sound surprised as I answered, even though this was the last person in the universe I expected to hear from.

Chapter 15

"I've met many thinkers and many cats, but the wisdom of cats is infinitely superior."

—Hippolyte Taine

Robert Reese had called me from his restaurant on the South Fork, which was less than a half hour's drive from the Thorndikes' home on the North Fork. Still, the ride seemed endless as I agonized over his reason for getting in touch with me.

The possibility that he'd come up with a piece of evidence that pointed to his ex as Cassandra's murderer put a knot in my stomach the size of one of Jean-Luc's espresso-flavored crème brûlées.

I tried to act matter-of-fact as I strolled inside. I found him sitting at one of the front tables with a cup of coffee in front of him. It appeared to be untouched.

"Robert?" I said gently, not sure if he'd heard me come in.

"Thanks for coming, Jessica," he said dully, glancing up only for a moment. "Especially since our last conversation wasn't exactly the most congenial."

"This is a difficult time for all of us," I replied, telling myself to stop fantasizing about slugging him in the head with a Starsky and Hutch lunch box. Instead, I pulled out the chair opposite him and sat down.

"I'm not sure I trust you enough to talk to you about this." He was silent for a few moments before adding, "But I don't know who else to talk to. Look, I know you're on Suzanne's side. I understand that the two of you have been friends for years and that you're trying to do what's best for her."

I simply nodded.

"Besides," he went on pensively, "I don't see how Suzanne could have anything to do with this."

"With what?" I asked.

He took a deep breath, as if he wanted to brace himself for what he was about to say. "Someone's been sabotaging the restaurant."

I gasped. "Sabotaging Granite? How?"

Robert shook his head, as if in disbelief. "At first, I thought I was just imagining it. Or that the things that were happening were simply mistakes. Like that night last August, when one by one the customers starting spitting out their coffee, so outraged they practically stormed out of the restaurant. I tasted some myself and realized somebody had mixed cayenne pepper in with the grounds.

"I apologized profusely, passed out a round of free desserts, and put the incident behind me. But then, a few nights later, something else happened. Peculiar things kept turning up in the salad. The top of a ballpoint pen, a piece of someone's credit-card receipt...Not only the kind of thing that upsets the Board of Health, but also instantly loses customers."

Robert's face sagged, as if the mere act of relating these unsettling events was aging him. "I started keeping an eye out for strange occurrences," he continued. "And I noticed they were getting more and more commonplace. One night I got complaints that the pasta was too salty. I tasted it, and even I nearly spit it out. It was as if it had been boiled in water with an entire cup of salt in it. Another time, all the seafood in the refrigerators just vanished! Bay scallops from right here in Meconic Bay, local oysters and clams, flounder, striped bass—it all disappeared just before we opened for dinner. The financial loss was nothing compared to the fact that we disappointed one customer after another.

"It was amazing how quickly we started losing business. Nothing too significant at first, but I've noticed that over the past eight or ten weeks we're down nearly fifteen percent compared to this season last year."

"Have you spoken to your staff?" I asked.

"Sure. I brought each of them into my office, one at a time. Everybody from the busboys up. I like to think I'm pretty good at reading people. But I couldn't get anything out of any of them."

"What about the police?"

Robert shook his head. "First of all, no real crimes have been committed, at least nothing I can prove. But even more important, if I can't get to the bottom of it, I can't expect some outsider to figure out what's happening here.

"At first I thought maybe somebody was playing a series of practical jokes," he continued. "That maybe some members of the kitchen staff were just goofing around, or maybe up to something more onerous like trying to get somebody fired. But I'm starting to think it's something much more serious. That somebody is out to ruin Granite."

He looked at me expectantly, as if it were my turn to speak. But I was at a loss for words. In fact, I still hadn't figured out why he was telling *me* all this.

Then he leaned forward. In a low, earnest tone, he said, "I saw you talking to Jean-Luc the first time you came in here. Did he say anything to make you believe he secretly has it out for me—or maybe even has some other reason for wanting to see the restaurant fail?"

My mind raced as I debated whether or not it was in my best interest to be completely honest with Robert. My first priority was finding Cassandra Thorndike's murderer—and absolving Suzanne of guilt. I wasn't particularly interested in solving the mystery of who was trying to grind Granite to dust, unless it had something to do with finding the killer.

On top of all that, I still didn't know who I could trust. Was Robert the enemy? Was Jean-Luc? For all I knew, both of them had been involved in Cassandra's murder.

"No." I finally said, deciding to keep what I'd learned about the Jean-Luc-and-Preston connection to myself. "Not that I recall."

"I hate to think anything ill of the guy," Robert said thoughtfully. "I mean, Jean-Luc's been with me since the beginning. I trust him like a brother—and I know him as well as I know myself."

Bet you don't, I thought. But I remained silent.

In fact, I'd actually begun to feel a little sorry for Robert. Someone was clearly trying to ruin his business, and I had a pretty good idea who that someone was. I also suspected that the jovial pastry chef who secretly loved whips as much as he loved whipped cream wasn't acting alone. My theory was that Jean-Luc and Preston were working together to destroy Granite, for reasons I could only guess at but which I suspected were either monetary gain, personal satisfaction, or both.

"I'm sorry I can't be more helpful," I told him. "But I barely know Jean-Luc—and I don't know anyone else on your staff at all."

"I knew it was a long shot," he said. "But if you find out anything, you'll let me know, right?"

"Of course," I told him, thinking, Around the same time I learn to make perfect puff pastry.

As I left the restaurant, I pondered all I'd learned about Jean-Luc's duplicity. He had lied about so many things. Pretending to be as French as a *tarte tatin* when he was as American as apple pie—or a slice of New York cheesecake. Claiming to despise Preston DeVane, his employer's number-one competitor, when the two of them were as tight as a leather thong. And now this: the revelation that he was doing his darnedest to destroy the business of a man who considered him a loyal friend.

He certainly was turning out to be a complicated man. But did that mean he was capable of murder?

• • •

Jean-Luc wasn't the only complicated man I'd encountered since this whole episode had begun. I hadn't forgotten about the scissors incident that got Ethan Thorndike thrown out of the Sewanhacky School or my determination to find out more about it. Glancing at my appointment book, I decided I had time to squeeze in at least one more stop—even if going back to the North Fork from the South would take me a bit out of the way.

I made it to Theo Simcox's house in record time. I knew he was at home, because his car was parked in the driveway.

As I peered through the screen of the back door, I could see him sitting at a laptop computer he had set up on his kitchen table. On the screen was a picture of a sleek, brand-new sedan.

So he's finally decided to unload that tired old jalopy, I thought with satisfaction. Good. A man his age needs a reliable car.

"Mr. Simcox? Theo?" I called through the screen.

He turned around, looking surprised to have a visitor.

"Dr. Popper," he said warmly. "You caught me indulging in one of my vices: wasting time on the Internet."

"Something many of us are guilty of these days," I commented, smiling.

"I'm thinking it's finally time to get myself a new car," he explained, closing his laptop. "My Dodge wouldn't start this morning. Again. It's a big investment, but I guess I've got to bite the bullet."

"Sounds like a wise decision." I hesitated, wondering if we'd spent enough time making idle chitchat, then said, "If you have a moment, there's something I'd like to ask you about."

"Of course. Come on in. You don't mind if I don't get up, do you? Seems the annoying arthritis in my knees is acting up a bit today."

After I'd sat down opposite him at the kitchen table and refused his offer of coffee or a cold drink, I got right down to business.

"Theo," I began, "I know you've been friends with the Thorndikes for a long time. Do you know anything about an incident Ethan was involved in while he was at the Sewanhacky School?"

Frowning, he replied, "You must mean him piercing that girl's hand with the scissors. Her name was Lisa or Liza—something like that."

I nodded. Since Theo was such a close friend of the Thorndikes, I wasn't surprised that Gordon and Joan had been open with him about what must have been a devastating episode. "How bad was it?" I asked. "Was it just two kids playing a game that got out of control or something more serious?"

He stared at me for a few moments, as if debating just how forthright to be. "The girl was stabbed thirteen times. She ended up getting something like twenty stitches."

"And Ethan was responsible?"

"Yes. He came right out and admitted that he'd done

it. Practically bragged about it, in fact. But to be fair, Ethan has come a long way since then," Theo insisted. "He does pretty well as long as he takes his medication."

He hesitated, then added, "Of course, when he doesn't take it, there's no telling what he'll do."

"I didn't know about the medication," I said, more to myself than to Theo. "Or that he's not consistent about taking it."

"That's why Joan and Gordon keep him close to home. They feel responsible. Not only to make sure he's safe, but to make sure he doesn't hurt anybody else."

"I understand Ethan was thrown out of Sewanhacky after that," I said.

"He certainly was. But he finished up at the local public school. Ethan may have his problems, but the boy is smart as a whip."

"He went to MIT afterward, right?"

"Almost graduated, too. And from what I understand, he was an outstanding student, at least in the subjects he was interested in. But for some reason, in the middle of his senior year, he just left. Nobody ever knew the whole story."

"And what about the girl?" I asked. "Do you know what happened to her?"

He was silent for a long time before answering. "She's dead."

"Dead?" I repeated, not sure I'd heard him correctly.

"That's right. She fell down a long staircase a few weeks after the incident with Ethan." He paused. "Either that or she was pushed. It was never clear."

My heart pounded as I wondered if I dared ask the obvious question. "Was Ethan anywhere near her when she fell?"

"As a matter of fact," Theo said with a definite edge to his voice, "Ethan was spotted leaving the house shortly before the poor girl was discovered. The girl's parents knew all about him being there. But for some reason, they didn't pursue it. In fact, they never stopped insisting that her death was an accident."

Another stabbing. This time, it was a young woman's hand, rather than her torso, but the *modus operandi* was the same. And according to Theo, Ethan had come right out and admitted he was responsible.

The similarity between what had happened to the girl at Ethan's school and what happened to Cassandra wasn't wasted on me. And even though it was hardly enough to conclude that Ethan Thorndike was responsible for his sister's death, it suddenly seemed extremely important to hear his side of it.

● ● ●

Fortunately, I had the perfect excuse to pay Ethan Thorndike a social call. Ever since my visit to the Sewanhacky School on Monday, I'd been driving around with Mr. Ed in my van. The grinning guy in the red bow tie gave me the creeps under the best of circumstances, and with a scalpel stuck in his chest, the mere sight of him practically made me break out in a rash. As a result, I'd been keeping him stuffed in back. Now it was time to see him—or, rather, *it*—home.

For the second time that day, I drove onto the Thorndike property. As I crunched along the driveway, I found the place quiet. This time, even Gordon didn't appear to be around. Even though I wasn't exactly looking forward to confronting Ethan, I desperately hoped I'd find him holed up in his tiny apartment above the garage.

I drove up to the sagging white building and stepped out of my van, clutching the dummy under my arm like a sack of wooden potatoes. There was no movement or sound anywhere on the property, aside from the rustling of leaves in the cool autumn breeze. Yet rather than seeming serene, my desolate surroundings struck me as eerie.

In fact, as I opened the side door and stepped into the garage, my heart pounded so furiously that I hoped it wouldn't set off any of the car alarms.

So I leaped about six feet into the air when something suddenly flew in front of me from out of nowhere, letting out a screech that made even the hairs on my toes stand on end.

"Yaaah!" I yelped, or something that sounded an awful lot like it. And then: "It's *you*!"

I was beyond relieved to discover that the spooky monster that had just scared the so-called living daylights out of me was only Jenny, Ethan's calico cat.

But I hadn't forgotten that the soft mass of gray, white, and orange fur wasn't very friendly when it came to veterinarians. In fact, she glared at me, making it clear that she didn't think dropping in like this unannounced was a good idea *at all*.

"Don't worry, Jenny," I told her, keeping my distance. "I won't be staying long."

But I *would* be staying. Jenny apparently wasn't the only one lurking in the shadows of the creaky garage. From upstairs, I could hear footsteps, meaning Ethan was home.

I crept up a flight of wobbly wooden stairs that creaked so loudly I figured there'd be no need to knock. Just as well, since when I reached the top, the wooden door leading to the second-floor apartment was wide open.

Almost as if he'd been expecting me.

"Ethan?" I called as I ventured a few feet inside through a small, dimly lit hallway. That silly heart of mine was still pounding, mainly because I didn't know what I'd find. I braced myself for anything from the laboratory of a crazed scientist in a sci-fi flick to the climax of *The Silence of the Lambs.*

So I was relieved to find that Ethan's apartment was actually fairly ordinary. I stepped farther inside. Beyond the hallway I could see a cluster of small but immaculate rooms that were painted white. Pale gray wall-to-wall carpeting gave the stark space a softer look. The furnishings were simple, wooden pieces that looked straight out of the showroom of IKEA. There were a few designer-type touches like brightly colored throw pillows and a pot of sunny yellow chrysanthemums on the living-room windowsill that had Joan Thorndike written all over them.

But Ethan had superimposed his own signature over the place as well. A bookshelf was crammed with the works of dark writers like Dostoevsky and Kafka and Sartre, along with a few oversize art books featuring the gloomy paintings of the German Expressionist movement. On the wall were several framed black-and-white photographs, which looked like tasteful accents from a distance but up close contained some disconcerting elements—like the stunning stylized portrait of a naked woman that on closer inspection turned out to be a naked man.

Since I was holding Mr. Ed in my arms, I knew that at least I wouldn't be caught off guard by the dummy's sudden appearance. But that didn't mean I didn't jump at least a foot in the air when Ethan suddenly leaped out from behind a doorway.

"Did I scare you?" he asked eagerly, his eyes bright.

"Not at all," I insisted, not wanting to give him the satisfaction of knowing he'd just taken several months, if not actual years, off my life. Boldly, I strode into the middle of the boxy living room. "Sorry to drop in unannounced like this, but I wanted to return something I believe belongs to you. I know this dummy is yours—and I imagine the scalpel is too."

"I suppose I should thank you," he said begrudgingly, taking the dummy from me. I noticed he left the scalpel in place. "But somehow Red always finds his way home."

"Red?" I repeated, puzzled.

"Red, Mr. Red..." Ethan shrugged. "I've got a few different names for this guy, most of them based on his bow tie. Makes him look pretty dapper, don't you think?"

I didn't respond. I was too busy saying, "Mr. Ed, Mr. Red," in my head, surprised that I'd managed to get the name of Ethan's alter ego wrong.

"I hope you didn't take my practical joke the wrong way," Ethan said, scrutinizing my face.

"Not at all. I enjoy a chuckle as much as the next person." I wasn't about to go for the bait. Not when I had something much more important than Ethan's fondness for ghoulish antics to attend to.

"There's another reason I wanted to see you," I said, my sudden breathlessness betraying my discomfort. "I'm curious about an incident I understand you were involved in while you were at the Sewanhacky School. The one that you ended up being expelled for."

His steady gaze flickered. "Liza Ackerman," he said in a strained voice. "The scissors."

"That's right. I was hoping you'd tell me your version of what happened."

"There's not much to tell," he said, his blue-green eyes clouding. "Liza ended up in the hospital with multiple stab wounds in her hand. Ten or twelve, I think. They stitched her up and sent her home."

"I heard from a couple of people that you admitted you were responsible."

"Sure, I admitted it," he replied with a shrug.

"So you're the one who stabbed her?"

"No," Ethan said, looking at me as if he couldn't believe how naive I was. "She did it."

"She did it to herself?"

"That's right. I was covering for her."

"Why?"

"Because we were friends. Because I really cared about her."

"I don't understand."

"Liza used to cut herself."

I blinked. "On purpose?"

"That's right," he replied. "Some people see it as a way of easing the extreme emotional pain in their lives. By comparison, the physical pain they inflict on themselves seems like a relief. For them, it's a way of getting through the tough periods."

Sure, I'd heard about people, usually teenage girls, who deliberately injured themselves with razor blades, knives, or anything else with a point or a sharp edge. But I'd never come into contact with anyone who actually did it.

"She did it all the time," Ethan continued, "but usually in places people didn't see, like the inside of her thighs. She hardly told anybody, but I knew. She even showed me her wounds. But she made me swear I wouldn't tell anybody. Especially her parents."

"But how could her own parents not know she was that unhappy?"

He laughed coldly. "Most of the time, parents only see what they want to see. And Liza's were the worst. They insisted their daughter was perfect. And she tried really hard to be just that. She got all As, she was in every club you can imagine... But her mother and father were so self-centered that they barely noticed how great she was, much less how disturbed she was.

"Not that it would have mattered," he added bitterly. "They were the type who never would have been able to bring themselves to face the fact that there was anything wrong with a daughter of theirs. After all," he added sarcastically, "it would have looked bad."

Maybe Mr. Waylan, the janitor, was wrong about the problem with these kids being that they had too much money, I thought. From the way it sounded, the real problem may have been that their parents had too much money.

"Ethan, I realize you were just a kid yourself. But did you ever think that maybe you'd be helping her by telling someone other than her parents? Maybe someone at the school?"

"Sure I thought of it. But Liza begged me not to. She was afraid that if anybody knew, she'd get stuck in some mental institution. Although maybe that wouldn't have been such a bad idea, given what happened a few weeks later." He swallowed hard. "She killed herself."

"Were you there when it happened?" I asked softly.

He nodded. "I'd gone over to her house when nobody else was home. Her parents had flown to Cancun or the Riviera or someplace like that for the weekend. They were really rich, and they lived in a huge mansion. That place was like a palace. I knew she didn't like being there by herself, so when she called me up and asked me to keep her company, I went over.

"I figured we'd play video games or watch a movie or something. But as soon as I walked in the door, I could see something was wrong. She seemed...crazed I guess is the word. She was talking really fast and she sounded practically hysterical. And she couldn't sit still. I don't know if she was on something or what. But she kept thanking me over and over for being her friend, telling me how much it meant to her.

"I didn't know what to do, but I figured just being there was enough. Then she asked me to go upstairs and find this CD she really liked. She said it was in her room somewhere and that I should just look for it. Her room was a mess. I'd been up there for less than five minutes when I heard this loud crashing sound. I came running out and saw her sprawled out on the marble floor of the foyer. See, when you walked into the house, there was this tremendous entryway with ceilings that were two or three stories high and one of those big staircases, the kind you see in the movies.

"Liza was lying at the bottom of the staircase with her neck broken. Dead. It took the police two days to locate her parents. When they finally came home, they insisted it was an accident. The last I heard, they sold that house and bought another, one that was even bigger."

"Ethan," I said, "did you ever tell all this to anyone else?"

"Sure. I told Liza's parents. At least, I tried to. But they just insisted I was lying, that it was all an accident. Like I told you, they didn't want to believe their daughter was anything less than perfect.

"Besides," he continued, "what difference would it have made if the truth came out? Liza was dead. And I'd already been thrown out of Sewanhacky. It wasn't like I cared about going back there or anything."

"But didn't you want your parents to know what really happened?"

He shrugged. "People believe what they want to believe."

The version Ethan was telling me was certainly different from what almost everyone else who knew about the incident seemed to believe—not only Theo, but the girl's parents. Yet somehow it all sounded plausible.

As I turned to leave, I noticed something I hadn't seen on my way in. Pictures of Cassandra were tacked up along the cramped, dimly lit hallway. Not one or two, but dozens of photographs covered one entire wall. Cassandra as a little girl romping with a big furry black dog. Cassandra in a school play, probably in junior high, dressed like Juliet. Cassandra staring into the camera moodily, her look of utter disdain so convincing it was impossible to tell if she was sincere or simply posing.

"Wow. You sure have a lot of pictures of your sister," I commented, not knowing what to say but figuring I couldn't go too far wrong by stating the obvious.

Ethan surveyed the collection for a few seconds before saying, "Even this many pictures can't begin to capture who she was. There were so many sides to her. Frankly, she could be pretty nutty, and we spent most of our childhood at odds with each other. But she was also the sweetest person I ever knew. Like when we were kids? I had a really hard time falling asleep, so she used to read to me every night. My mother never had the patience. She always said she was too tired, making it sound like *I* was the one who'd made her so tired. But Cassie never said no. In a lot of ways, she was like a mother to me, especially since I was pretty young when our real mother died."

Glancing at the wall of photographs one more time, he added, "So when Cassie was killed, I held my own private memorial service. Thing is, once it was over, I still couldn't let her go."

My heart wrenched. For the first time since I'd met Ethan Thorndike, I realized how painful it must have been for him to lose his sister. Maybe he wasn't exactly your average man on the street, but of course he must be devastated by such a tragedy.

Only a teensy-weensy voice somewhere deep inside me dared to venture a single cynical comment: How do you know it's not an act?

In fact, as I climbed back down the rickety stairs, I realized that while I'd come to Ethan's apartment to confront him head-on, hoping to determine once and for all whether he was a demon or just a poor, lost boy, I still didn't have the slightest idea what to believe about Ethan Thorndike.

•　•　•

Thursday turned out to be such a busy day that I didn't have a moment to devote to Suzanne's predicament. But even as I drove all around Long Island, putting in a long day of making house calls, the details of Cassandra's life kept nagging at me.

Part of me felt I was tantalizingly close to figuring out which of the different conflicts she'd been embroiled in had culminated in her murder. I'd met so many people who could have killed her, even though I wasn't yet one hundred percent clear on what each person's motivation might have been. From the start, I'd had to suspect the members of her family—at least her stepmother, Joan, her creepy brother, Ethan, and her fiancé, Robert. But she'd also been enmeshed in a battle that was being fought in the highly competitive Bromptons restaurant scene, one that involved not only Robert but also his competitor Preston and his supposedly loyal pastry chef Jean-Luc—even though I had yet to figure out exactly who was on whose side.

Then there was Cassandra's dalliance with the S&M set. What Nick had learned was that people with a proclivity for violence in their fantasy lives sometimes let things get out of hand in their real lives. That scenario pointed not only to both Jean-Luc and Preston once again but also to Thor and any number of others I couldn't name but had seen at the BDSM party I'd attended with Nick.

Having identified all those strong possibilities, it wasn't surprising that I felt pretty darn close to solving the case. Of course, another part of me felt I wasn't even in the right galaxy. Sure, I'd uncovered many of the threads that had comprised Cassandra Thorndike's life.

But I was still struggling to untangle all the loose ends—complex intrigues, secrets, and lies that had led to one of them unraveling.

Friday morning, as I drove to Sunshine Media's television studio, I promised myself that I'd dedicate the next few days to Cassandra Thorndike's murder. By this point, I was desperate to help Suzanne put this whole ugly episode behind her. Especially since Lieutenant Falcone was hot on her trail, anxious to prove to his adoring public what a great job he was doing.

But for now, I had to put all that out of my mind and focus on perfecting my performance for *Pet People*. It was showtime.

The second time around was easy, compared to the first. For one thing, I now knew that while Max and Lou were stars in my eyes, they simply weren't cut out for the celebrity life. My instincts told me Tinkerbell was equally likely to use her fifteen minutes of fame to commit acts that were better off not being televised. As for Cat, subjecting her to the studio's bright lights and strange sounds, not to mention all that moving around, would cause her too much discomfort. So this time, I'd brought along my least mobile loved ones: Prometheus and Leilani.

Now that I was an old hand at this, I was able to find my own way to the greenroom, then sit patiently while Aldo performed his subtle but effective magic. I walked confidently into the studio, secure in the knowledge that my lips were sufficiently glossy and my cocker-spaniel hair concealed my unsightly ears. As soon as Patti pantomimed the countdown, I launched into my intro.

"I'm Dr. Popper," I began, feeling oddly at home amid a set that not long before had struck me as positively bizarre. "Welcome to *Pet People*, the program for people who are passionate about their pets.

"Today I brought along two of my own pets for you

to meet. The first one is Prometheus, a blue and gold macaw." I raised the hand holding my exquisite bird up in front of the camera so everyone in TV land could admire him. "Parrots make terrific pets. They're not only beautiful; they're also extremely intelligent. They can be taught to speak and to play games, and they'll quickly learn to recognize different members of your family.

"However, anyone who's thinking about getting a parrot should be aware that they require a great deal of care—in many ways even more than a dog or a cat. It's important to provide them with social interaction, as well as some time outdoors whenever possible."

"*Awk!*" Prometheus screeched. "I'm gonna give you my love!"

I cringed. My lovely, graceful parrot had chosen this moment to treat the viewing audience to his rendition of a well-known Led Zeppelin song. One that wasn't particularly suited to daytime television.

"Uh, as you can see," I continued in a much less confident voice, "one of the fun aspects of parrots is their ability to repeat anything they hear. Prometheus probably heard this song on the radio—"

"Every inch of my love!" Prometheus shrieked.

"The problem, of course," I said through gritted teeth, "is monitoring what they hear in order to limit the words and phrases they learn." I made a point of avoiding eye contact with Patti.

"Every inch!" he squawked. "*Awk!*"

"Uh, I think this may be a good time to move on to Jackson's chameleons," I said, desperately eyeing Mel. Mainly because they're blessedly silent.

Fortunately, Mel took the hint. He slunk across the studio and, ducking down out of the camera's range, reached for Prometheus with his ham-hock-size hands.

Unfortunately, Mel didn't know the first thing about handling birds.

"Ow!" he yelped. While his face might have been out of the camera range, the microphone picked up his gravelly voice loud and clear. "The little bastard bit me! I'm *bleedin'*!"

"Hey, don't call Prometheus names!" I shot back without thinking. "He wouldn't have bitten you if you'd handled him correctly! He's only trying to protect himself!"

"Listen, dealing with birds ain't in my job description!" Mel returned gruffly. "Who's cockamamy idea was it to put a stupid talking bird on the air in the first place?"

I finally dared to look over at Patti. From the agonized expression on her face, anyone would have assumed that *she* was the one who had just had her skin pierced by a bird's sharp beak.

But she had the presence of mind to start making the "move it along" rolling motion with her hands. Always the professional.

"Maybe we'll bring Prometheus back another time," I said. Then I caught sight of the latest expression on Patti's face. "Or...maybe not. Anyway, let's talk chameleons. While Jackson's chameleons are native to East Africa, in the early 1970s a pet-store owner in Hawaii began importing them. The first of them arrived so sickly and so dehydrated that he let them loose in his backyard for what was supposed to be a short time. However, they escaped and started reproducing..."

I kept that segment short and sweet, then breezed through my presentation on Keeping Halloween Safe for Your Pet. Patti nodded enthusiastically all the way through, letting me know how relieved she was that we were back to putting on a G-rated show.

I finished with a warning about feeding dogs chocolate, since one of its ingredients, theobromine, is toxic and may be fatal. By that point, I felt relaxed and confident and pretty much ready for anything.

Even quirky phone calls.

"Thank you for calling *Pet People*!" I told my first caller. "This is Dr. Popper. How can I help you and your pet?"

"Dr. Popper? My name is Maria. I live in, uh, Brompton Bay?"

"Good morning, Maria. What's on your mind?"

"I just got a cat, and even though I've had cats my whole life, I've never seen one act like this. When he walks, it's almost like he's marching? And I don't know if this is related, but whenever he tries to jump up on the couch or go upstairs, he falls. My husband keeps telling me he's just a klutz, but I'm wondering if there's something wrong with him."

Oh, good, I thought. An easy question.

"I suspect you're right, Maria," I said. "It sounds as if your cat has a neurological problem. There are several ways this could have happened. He might have gotten a head injury, or he might have even gotten an infection while he was still a kitten. But if he's doing all right otherwise, he's probably fine. Still, you might feel better if you have your vet check him out, just to be sure."

"Thanks! I told my husband he was wrong. See, he always acts like he's the only person in the world who—"

"And thank *you* for calling, Maria. I see we have another caller." Pressing the glowing red button, I breezily answered, "Thanks for calling *Pet People*. How can I help you and your pet?"

"I know what you're doing," the caller said in a hoarse whisper.

He spoke so softly, in fact, that I wasn't sure I'd heard him correctly. I blinked, not knowing how to respond to something I didn't really understand.

"This is Dr. Popper at *Pet People*," I said, nervously

glancing at Patti. She just looked confused. "How can I help?"

"I know what you're doing," the caller said again, speaking in the same peculiar voice. "I'm watching you. And I'm warning you."

My mind raced and I suddenly felt nauseated. At least I had the presence of mind to push another button. But there was no need to cut off the call. He'd already hung up.

"Uh, it's, uh, always nice to hear from a fan," I stuttered, looking into the camera and trying to smile. "And now, uh, let's take another call..."

As soon as the show was over and the studio lights went out, I stormed over to Marlene.

"I thought you were screening all the calls that came in!" I cried.

"We are," she insisted, looking stricken. "Honestly, I asked him all the usual questions: his name, where he lives, what his question was about—"

"And what were his answers?" I demanded.

Anxiously she scanned her clipboard. "He said his name was Jesse and that he lived in Joshua's Hollow. He has two dogs, a Westie named Max and a Dalmatian named Lou, and two cats named Tinkerbell and Cat—wait, did I get that right?"

"Oh, you got it right," I assured her, my stomach tightening into a painful knot.

I did too. At first, the mysterious person who called himself AGoodFriend had wanted to tell me he knew what I was doing.

Now he was making it clear he wanted me to stop.

I had to admit, I was frightened. My secret pal had no qualms about intruding into my life, whether it was by sending me creepy e-mails or breaking into my house and messing up my possessions.

But there was something that frightened me even

more: the possibility of him getting away with killing Cassandra while my real pal, Suzanne, paid for the crime. And so rather than scaring me off the case, the idea that the murderer thought he had even a chance of getting away with what he'd done only fueled my determination.

As I headed out of the studio and into the parking lot, I found myself ruminating about something Ethan had said when I saw him two days before. His reminiscence about his sister reading to him when he was a kid had struck me as familiar at the time, but it wasn't until now that I made the connection.

Maggie Rose had also told me that Cassandra read to her. In my head, I could hear her high-pitched voice. "I know a story about a bunny," Maggie Rose had told me. "Cassie used to read it to me."

Books were obviously important to Cassandra. And the one she repeatedly read to her next-door neighbor featured a bunny—which might possibly have something to do with the stuffed rabbit she had struggled so hard to leave behind.

It was a real long shot, I knew. But without much else to cling to, it suddenly seemed like my last chance.

Chapter 16

"Do not attempt to teach your cats tricks—
They already know every trick there is."

—Sidra Malik

Late Friday afternoon, as soon as I'd finished my last call, I trekked out to the North Fork once again. I was determined to follow up on the one path I had yet to follow, even though the trail marker was nothing more than a sweet voice that continued to echo through my head.

I knew that the possibility that Maggie Rose, of all people, might be able to provide me with some information that would turn out to be helpful was a long shot. Yet her persistent attempts at telling me about the book Cassandra used to read to her echoed through my head. I kept berating myself for not having paid more attention to them sooner. It wasn't until Ethan mentioned his sister reading to him that I'd taken them seriously.

Calm down, I scolded myself as I trundled along Route 35, barely glancing at the flat, green fields stretching out on both sides of the road. You're acting on a hunch. Nevertheless, I couldn't stop thinking about the stuffed bunny Cassandra had put so much effort into leaving behind the day she was killed.

As I turned onto Cliffside Lane, my heart was pounding so hard I was practically dizzy. By that point, I'd become so focused on learning exactly what Maggie Rose's bunny story was all about that I half-expected the little girl to be standing on the front lawn, waiting for me. But as I pulled up in front of Virginia Krupinski's house, neither she nor her great-granddaughter were in sight.

Still, Virginia had told me herself she rarely went anywhere while the little girl was in her care. I climbed the steps to the front porch and knocked on the screen door.

"Mrs. Krupinski? Are you home?"

I knew she had to be, since from inside I could hear the blaring television. I noticed she kept the volume turned way up. Between the loud TV and her aging ears, it was no wonder she hadn't heard anything the day Cassie was murdered. Since knocking wasn't getting me anywhere, I tried pounding.

"Mrs. Krupinski?" I yelled, peering through the screen. "It's Jessica Popper. Hello? Anybody home?"

"Grammy," I finally heard Maggie Rose say, "somebody's at the door."

The volume of the TV immediately went way down and I heard footsteps.

"Goodness, girl, you got to make a little more noise if you expect me to hear you," Virginia scolded as she scurried toward the door, pulling her bulky sweater more closely around her.

"I'm sorry to bother you," I told her. "I just wanted to ask Maggie Rose a question. She mentioned something about Cassie that I think might be important."

Virginia glanced down at Maggie Rose protectively. "Now, I don't want you getting her upset that her friend Cassie's moved away and all."

"I won't, I promise."

Virginia eyed me warily before finally opening the door and gesturing for me to come in. Then, standing in the same spot—as if making it clear she fully intended to sit in on any interrogation her young charge was subjected to—she said, "Maggie Rose, Dr. Popper here has a question for you. You answer it as best you can, okay?"

The little girl nodded uncertainly.

"Maggie Rose," I said in a gentle voice, "you told me Cassie used to read you a story about bunnies. Do you remember that?"

She nodded again, this time with complete certainty. My heart resumed its frenetic pounding, even though I kept telling myself it was unlikely that a four-year-old girl would provide me with the critical information I needed to figure out what Cassandra had been trying to tell us during her last few minutes of life.

"Could I see the book, please?" I asked.

This time, she shook her head.

"Why not?" I asked, fighting a feeling of defeat.

"Don't have it. It was Cassie's. She said it was her favorite book when she was a little girl, so it must have been really old."

Old enough to be out of print? I wondered.

"Do you remember what the story was about?" By this point, keeping my tone of voice matter-of-fact was a struggle.

"Sure. It was all about a bunny named Red Rabbit, who got lost and couldn't find his way home. So he asked all his animal friends for help...."

I stopped listening. I was too busy listening to the sirens that were going off in my head. *Red Rabbit.* The wheels were turning. Was it possible that *red* matched up with *scarlet*—as in *The Scarlet Letter*—and *rabbit* with the stuffed bunny? Or was my increasing desperation causing me to get carried away?

While it was tempting to go with the second possibility, it seemed worth exploring the idea that whatever Cassandra had been trying to tell us had something to do with the children's book she'd loved so much that she shared it with the little girl next door. I couldn't let go of the notion that some element of the story, or perhaps one of the characters, could have been related to her murder—or her murderer.

"Thank you, Maggie Rose," I told the little girl sincerely. "It sounds like a wonderful story. And I'll tell you what: Even though it's probably a very old book, if I find a copy, I'll give it to you, okay?"

Staring up at me with her huge brown eyes, she asked, "Will you read it to me?"

"Of course." Suddenly, another thought occurred to me. Turning back, I glanced at Virginia, then asked, "Maggie Rose, do you remember the last days Cassie was still living in the house next door?"

She nodded.

"Did you ever hear loud voices coming from her house? People laughing or playing a game . . . or arguing?"

I held my breath, watching her screw up her face as she pondered my question.

Virginia answered for her. "Maggie Rose takes a nap in the afternoon. And she's a deep sleeper. She probably wouldn't have heard anything. That is, if there was anything to hear in the first place."

"Thank you both," I said. "You've been really helpful. Especially you, Maggie Rose."

She grinned shyly. "Don't forget to bring me that book," she said. "I really liked the pictures. Especially the ones of Red Rabbit."

"You got it."

I got back into my van and headed toward town, energized by the likelihood that the story about Red Rabbit contained the answer to why Cassandra had been murdered—and by whom. I couldn't believe it was nothing more than a coincidence that its main character had a name that was comprised of two of the three clues she'd left behind. For all I knew, the character routinely wore sneakers, tying in the third clue.

Somehow, I had to get ahold of that book.

• • •

Bonnie's Bookery was an old-fashioned bookstore, the kind that was becoming more and more of a rarity these days. It occupied a small storefront nestled between an antiques shop and a real-estate office. As I walked inside, a little bell tinkled. I paused to inhale the friendly, slightly musty smell of paper and paste, then glanced around.

I was instantly charmed. One entire wall was red brick, which gave the intimate space a relaxed, homey feeling. The other walls were lined with wooden shelves that ran from floor to ceiling and were covered with books. Even though the single room was compact, I spotted comfortable places to sit, including a deep-blue velvet couch in the Romance section and a leather-covered chair in the Business section. A recording of a string quartet played classical music in the background.

The requisite cat lay curled up at one end of the velvet couch. The smoky-gray feline glanced up and blinked lazily, as if saying, "I suppose you can come in . . . but you don't mind if I don't get up to greet you, do you?" A second cat, this one black, peeked out at me from behind a stack of books, then meowed "Hello."

But Bonnie's Bookery was an equal-opportunity employer. A large golden retriever lay next to the counter, wagging her tail but also remaining in place. I figured she'd been taught that not all customers would welcome the enthusiastic greeting the breed was famous for.

"Hello," the smiling woman with short, dark-red hair behind the counter greeted me. The name *Bonnie* was printed on the plastic tag she wore on her blouse. "Is there anything I can help you with?"

"Actually, I'm looking for a children's book."

"We have an excellent children's section, right over here." She pointed to the back corner, where the walls were painted bright yellow and large stuffed animals sprawled across tiny chairs or sat on shelves. Most of them held books in their paws.

"There's a particular book I'm trying to find," I began. I noticed a little flutter of anxiety in my stomach now that I was confronted with the possibility that the book didn't really exist—or that even if it did, I wouldn't be able to find it. "It's a book about a red rabbit," I went on, studying her face and bracing myself for a blank look. "He makes friends with all kinds of animals—"

"That sounds like *Red Rabbit Comes Home*," she said. "Is that the one?"

"I don't know. I mean, it could be. All I know is that it's about a red rabbit."

"This is a classic," Bonnie told me, going over to a shelf and pulling off a single slim volume. Sure enough, as she handed it to me, I saw that its cover featured a whimsical drawing of a cute bunny rabbit with bright red fur. "I can never keep it in stock for more than a few days, yet it must have come out at least twenty-five or thirty years ago."

Around the same time Cassandra Thorndike was a little girl, I thought.

I opened the book greedily, as if the answer to the riddle of her murder would leap out of the pages. Instead, I saw only illustrations of the rabbit hopping around a farm and talking to other animals like a horse and a cow and a chicken, all of them a most unlikely color.

"What age group is this for?" I asked.

"Preschool," Bonnie replied. "It's a very sweet story about a bunny who gets lost, so he asks all his animal friends how to find the way home. Dotted Dog tells him to follow the smell of cookies baking, Green Goose says he should look for the place with flowers in the window box...in other words, everybody has their own idea of what makes a home. Children love it. In fact, preschool teachers often use it as a way to get a discussion going of what home means to each of us."

"I can see why it would appeal to kids," I commented. However, I had no clue about how it could be tied to Cassandra's murder.

I paid for the book, then said, "Would you mind if I sat here and read it?"

"Of course not!" Bonnie replied. "Just be careful not to trip over our resident pets. That's Virginia Woof," she said, gesturing toward the retriever. "Or Ginny, as we call her. And the cats are Dot and Dash, after Dorothy L. Sayers and Dashiell Hammett. Needless to say, only pets with literary names are allowed in a bookstore!"

I laughed. "No problem. I've been told I have a way with animals."

I sat down in the first suitable place I found, a comfortable upholstered chair that reminded me of Papa Bear's chair. My mouth was dry as I turned to the first page and began to read.

I turned page after page, glancing at the pictures and reading the simple but important story of a red rabbit who finally made his way home by getting advice from all kinds of other animals. At the end of the book, he invited them all over to his house for tea and cookies.

Yet as I read the last page and closed the book, a feeling of disappointment swept over me. While I'd been afraid that I'd be on a wild-goose chase, either not finding the book or learning that it had never even existed in the first place, I now realized there was one more possible outcome I'd neglected to consider. And that was the possibility that I'd find the book, read it, and not know any more about what Cassandra was trying to tell us than I did before.

I let out a loud sigh, causing Virginia Woof to glance up at me. She sighed in return.

If this book really is a clue about the murder, I thought, distractedly petting her head, I have to dig a little deeper. I have to figure out exactly what it meant to Cassandra.

That meant talking to someone who'd known her as a little girl. The good news was that the one person I had in mind also happened to be the only person in her life I felt I could trust.

• • •

As I bumped along the Thorndikes' driveway, I noticed that, as usual, the place seemed oddly quiet. While there were cars parked on the property, there were no actual signs of life. The silence gave me an eerie feeling. Then again, I had to admit that these days I creeped out pretty easily.

I pulled up along the side of the house and got out. As I walked toward the back door, I noticed it was open.

Peering through the screen door, I could see the back of someone's arm and shoulder.

"Mr. Thorndike?" I called, knocking on the wooden frame. "It's Jessie Popper."

"Jessie?" I heard Joan Thorndike say. I thought I heard a note of alarm in her voice but decided she was just surprised by my unexpected visit. "Dr. Popper! What are you doing here?"

"I'm looking for Gordon."

"Come in, Jessie," she said.

As I entered, she glanced up at me from the kitchen

table and smiled. But I noticed she looked flustered. Quickly, she gathered up the haphazard array of papers spread across the table, putting them into a pile. Then she stretched her arm across them, as if she was trying to cover them up. She did a good job, too, since I couldn't see anything aside from the fact that the pages in front of her were legal-size. "I wasn't expecting anybody."

"Sorry to bother you." I craned my neck, trying to get a better look at what she was attempting to hide. No such luck. From what I could tell, the white pages could have been a legal document—or a long, chatty letter or even a bunch of recipes. "Is Gordon home? It's really important that I speak to him."

"He's at the winery," she told me.

"Thanks." I hesitated. "Joan, is everything all right?"

"Of course," she answered quickly. "Why wouldn't it be?"

"You seem a little distracted, that's all."

"It's been a difficult couple of weeks," she said. This time, the sad smile she offered up seemed sincere.

As I left the house and got back into my van, I wondered if I'd simply imagined that she was trying to conceal the papers on the kitchen table from me. After all, she wasn't exactly exaggerating about this being a tough couple of weeks for her and her husband.

Besides, the only person who'd cast any suspicion whatsoever on Joan was Ethan. And I didn't exactly consider him the last word in trustworthiness.

That dummy of his either.

• • •

As I made the turn into Thorndike Vineyards, the sun was low in the sky and the chill of autumn electrified the air. Usually, I love that feeling of crispness. This evening, however, I found myself wishing I'd brought along something warmer than my polyester fleece jacket.

There were only one or two cars in the parking lot. I pulled my van into a space near the main building, then checked my watch as I hurried to the front door. It was 5:30.

My heart sank as I glanced at the sign posted next to the door. *HOURS: Monday through Friday, 10:00 to 5:00.*

I tried the door anyway—and was relieved when it opened.

"Hello?" I called as I walked into the cool, somber building. Just like at the house, there were no signs of life. At least, not that I could see. But somebody had to be around, I figured, or else the door would have been locked.

I wandered through the gift shop and back toward the offices. As I slid past the *Employees Only* sign, I saw Cassandra Thorndike staring down at me from her life-size portrait. For a fraction of a second, I got the feeling she was trying to communicate something to me. But paintings were like animals. They never came right out and told you the things you needed to know.

"Hello?" I called. "Mr. Thorndike? Gordon? Anybody here?" As I made my way along the short hallway, I tried all the doors, rattling their knobs but finding every single one locked.

Finally, at the end, I found one last door. It was different from the others. There was no plaque hanging on it, for one thing, to identify the person whose office it was.

But what made it even more distinctive was that it was made of heavy, rough-hewn wood, rather than the same sleek, polished veneer as all the others. Thinking, What the heck, I tried that one too.

Surprisingly, this time the knob turned. In keeping with the same what-the-heck mentality, I pushed the door open. Even though the light was dim, I could see a long flight of stone stairs that appeared to lead down to the basement.

"Hello?" I called. "Anybody here?"

For a few seconds, there was nothing but silence. Then, from somewhere behind me, I heard a footstep.

I was about to turn when I felt a forceful shove against my back.

I let out a yelp, but it was too late. Before I could grab on to the rickety wooden railing, I plummeted forward, watching in horror as the stone steps grew closer and crying out again as my head slammed against something hard.

Chapter 17

"The cat has complete emotional honesty—an attribute not often found in humans."

—Ernest Hemingway

U h-h-h..."

I let out a dull groan as I dragged myself to a sitting position on the cold stone floor. My head was spinning, not only from the fall but from the collision it had had with the wooden handrail that had specifically been put there to keep people from tumbling down the stairs. But I forced myself to take a quick physical inventory to figure out which body parts actually hurt.

My butt, for one thing. My ribs and the side of my left thigh too, which had borne the brunt of my slide down the sharp edges of the stone steps. My left cheek stung, telling me that one of those rough edges had sliced through the skin. Still, nothing seemed to be broken.

I stood up slowly, bracing myself against the craggy stone wall and blinking hard as I tried to adjust to the dim light.

Where am I? I wondered.

The hundreds of bottles of wine lining the wall gave me my answer.

Okay, I'm in the Thorndike Vineyards' wine cellar, I thought, feeling moderately encouraged. In fact, some people would consider this a dream come true.

But not me. Especially given the way I'd gotten there. I only hoped I wouldn't have too much trouble getting out.

I glanced up the staircase I'd just wrestled with and saw that the heavy wooden door was shut tight. Probably locked, I figured grimly, certain that whoever had pushed me down all those steps had made sure of that.

Still, I climbed back up, just to check. I moved as silently as I could, not wanting to give anyone who might be poised on the other side of the door any information about my activities—or my condition.

Gently I laid my hand on the knob, grasping it tightly in my fingers. I tried to turn it.

It didn't move.

Just as I thought, I reflected, swallowing hard. I'm locked in.

I crept back down the stairs, wondering if my attacker was standing on the other side, listening.

Now what? I thought, trying to remain calm. Rather than focusing on being locked in, I tried to concentrate on the fact that the place in which I was being held prisoner wasn't exactly terrible.

Still, I figured that finding a good hiding place was probably a wise move. I wandered through the cool, dimly lit maze of rooms. From what I could see, they'd been constructed with no obvious plan. Some opened into other rooms, while some of them were dead ends. Most of them had no windows—and the few I spotted were very high up, with very thick glass.

My chances of escape were looking slim.

It could be days before anyone comes down here, I thought woefully. I immediately reminded myself that October was the busiest time of year at the wineries, and that tomorrow was Saturday. The usual hordes of tourists would undoubtedly come pouring into this part of the island and into Thorndike Vineyards. Surely somebody would come down soon to look for a particular bottle of wine or to restock the gift-shop shelves.

At the moment, however, there were no creaking floors or footsteps from the level above. The gift shop and the tasting room were closed, and the tours were done for the day. I figured I shouldn't expect anyone to come down until the following morning.

Except, perhaps, the person who'd locked me in here in the first place.

That thought not only quickened my heartbeat; it sharpened my senses. I noticed how cool it was down here and was glad I'd brought along my jacket.

I also noticed I was getting hungry.

Great, just great, I thought. I'd probably be spending the night down here. Maybe even longer, depending on how long it took before somebody came down here looking for a few bottles of 1985 merlot—or a nosy veterinarian who'd mysteriously vanished.

I couldn't even help myself to a relaxing glass of wine. While I was surrounded by hundreds of bottles of the stuff, I didn't have a corkscrew.

Water, water, everywhere, I thought wryly.

I didn't really mind. Keeping a clear head seemed like a good idea, since somebody was obviously upset enough with me and my investigation of Cassandra's murder that he or she saw fit to push me down an entire flight of hard, stone stairs and lock me in a wine cellar for who knew how long.

What I did mind was knowing that, right upstairs, countless boxes of crisp crackers and hunks of weird-smelling cheese lay in wait. Just then, my stomach let out a loud grumble.

"Quiet, you," I muttered.

Telling myself that resisting the body's cravings built character, I continued wandering. I was actually finding it kind of interesting, seeing what a real live wine cellar looked like.

Until I heard a loud crash.

I froze. It sounded like glass smashing against something hard, like brick or stone.

But it wasn't the fact that something had broken that bothered me. It was the realization that I wasn't alone.

My heart pounded so loudly I was afraid whoever was down here with me could hear it. So much for keeping my whereabouts concealed. I crept along the wall, glad, for the first time, that the cellar was dark—and getting darker by the moment as the sun dropped lower and lower in the sky, by this point casting only minimal light through the few high windows.

When I reached a doorway, I hesitated, trying to figure out a way to get across it without being seen. Impossible, I knew. I was just going to have to take a chance that whoever it was would be looking away. Either that, or stay where I was. That option was sounding better and better. True, I was in full view—but only if the person down here with me in this labyrinth of rooms happened to wander into my little corner of the basement.

I jumped when I heard another crash. By now, the urge to look was irresistible. I moved my head—just a little—so that I could peer through the doorway, into the room to the right, with my right eye...

"It's you!" I cried aloud. And nearly burst out laughing with relief.

The mysterious stranger who was stalking me—and had accidentally given away her presence by breaking a couple of bottles of wine—was standing just a few feet away, staring at me with unblinking eyes. Next to her was a puddle of wine, pooling around jagged-edged shards of broken glass.

I hoped she hadn't cut her paws.

"Come here, Coco," I said gently. "Hey, remember me? I'm the one who took care of that nasty bladder infection."

She came over and rubbed against my leg, purring as if she were as grateful as I was to find out that the other being who was stuck down here was a friend.

Then I realized something important: *She* wasn't stuck down here. Coco hadn't been pushed down the stairs, the way I had. Which meant she'd either come down here earlier, while the door was open—or there was another way of getting in and out.

"How did you get in here?" I asked, scooping her up and looking into her eyes. She just blinked, proving to be no more helpful than Cassandra's portrait. Okay, so animals can't talk. But at least they could answer direct questions some other way, like pointing to a picture with a paw or mewing or barking when they heard the correct answer.

I knew she wasn't about to tell me anything. Still, that didn't mean she couldn't show me.

"Let's get out of here, Coco," I told her. "Show me the way. Please!"

She looked at me with her intense green eyes, then turned abruptly. Something told me that, somehow, she'd understood.

Sure enough, she led me through that room and into the next, then over to a small window I hadn't noticed before. It wasn't exactly large, but at least it was bigger than the others. It was hinged on the bottom and opened inward. At the moment, it was open a few inches, just enough for a cat to slink through.

But not a person. At least, not unless that person took something hard and used it to smash the glass.

I glanced around anxiously, desperately hoping to find

a hammer or a piece of metal. No luck. In fact, pretty much all I could see was wine.

I grabbed one of the bottles, hoping it wasn't one of those rare, extremely valuable wines that people spend thousands of dollars on.

Sorry, Gordon, I thought. I never meant to damage your property. But I'll reimburse you for the window. Besides, I think we'll both agree that it's a small price to pay for me getting out of here and fingering your daughter's killer.

I wrapped up my right hand with my fleece jacket, covered my face with my left arm, and smashed the window.

I let out a yelp of victory when I saw I'd created a hole big enough for me to crawl through. I knew I'd have to expect a few cuts and scrapes from the jagged edges that remained inside the frame, either to my skin or my clothes. At the moment, that didn't seem to matter very much.

I climbed up the wooden shelves that housed the wine, hoping I wouldn't end up pulling an entire wall of bottles down. Fortunately, they turned out to be stronger than they looked. I stuck my head through the broken window and wriggled through. Much to my surprise, Coco was waiting for me outside.

"Thanks, pussycat," I told her. "I owe you."

I planned to make it up to her too. There were definitely some chicken livers in this feline's future.

At the moment, however, I had more important things to do—like find Gordon and ask him about the meaning of the Red Rabbit book in his daughter's life.

And I had to get to him quickly. Since the very beginning of this wrenching ordeal, the clock had been ticking. Now, it seemed to be doing double-time.

• • •

I found Gordon Thorndike in the building out back, the one that contained the temperature-controlled "tax room" I'd learned about during my winery tour. He was in a small storage room right behind it. Just like last time, he was surrounded by cardboard cartons. Only instead of moving them around, he was sealing them up with packing tape.

"Mr. Thorndike?" I said softly, not wanting to startle him.

He only glanced up for a moment. "Dr. Popper," he said, immediately going back to what he was doing.

"I don't want to bother you, but this is important." I swallowed hard, thinking, Important enough for somebody to lock me in a dungeon as a warning.

Trying to sound calm and matter-of-fact, I asked, "This might sound like a strange question, but do you have any idea what the book *Red Rabbit Comes Home* might have meant to Cassie?"

He glanced up again, looking at me blankly. At first, I assumed that was a bad sign. But then his face softened into a smile.

"Of course. That was one of Cassie's favorite books back when she was a little girl. I used to read it to her all the time. I'd be trying to get her to go to sleep, but she'd insist that I read it again...." His voice trailed off and he shook his head sadly. "Even then, that girl wasn't about to take no for an answer. If she wanted something, she'd just storm ahead, doing whatever it took to get it."

"But what about as an adult?" I asked, careful not to let my impatience show. "Did that book have any significance to her lately?"

He seemed surprised by my question. But this time his expression told me it was because I didn't already know the answer.

"That's the name she picked," he said with a little shrug.

"Picked . . . for what?" I asked.

"For her winery." He reached into one of the cartons next to him and pulled out a roll of what looked like stickers. "Look. These are the labels I had printed up for her. They were supposed to be a surprise. A birthday present. You probably didn't know she was about to turn thirty, in just a few more weeks." He held out the roll, which I could now see contained both front and back labels, alternating on a strip of waxy white paper. "See? I had an artist design labels with the name of what was going to be her winery. She chose the name back when she first started talking about doing it."

As soon as I took the thick roll from him, I felt all the blood rush out of my body, down toward my toes. I opened my mouth to breathe more deeply, vaguely aware that I was feeling light-headed.

"That was so much like Cassie," Gordon went on, too wrapped up in his own world to notice that I was having difficulty catching my breath. "Planning to name her winery after some book she'd loved when she was a kid. She never let go of that little-girl innocence, you know? It's like part of her was still a kid, filled with awe and wonder about the world."

I blinked, still trying to take in what I had just learned from the labels Gordon Thorndike had had designed for his daughter's brand-new winery.

Each was comprised of bright red letters against a black background. Centered on the front label was the silhouette of a rabbit, also printed in red. Above it was the name she had chosen.

Looking at it sent a chill down my spine as palpable as if someone had tossed an ice cube down my shirt.

Red Rabbit Run.

The name perfectly matched the three objects she'd left behind as she was dying.

Red, as in *The Scarlet Letter.*

Rabbit, as in the stuffed bunny.

Run, as in the running shoe.

She had been murdered because of her vineyard, and she wanted us to know it.

"Where was Cassandra going to start her winery?" I asked in a strained voice. "Here on Long Island?"

"Of course. Right on my property, in fact. I was going to give her some of my land. Twenty acres bordering Theo Simcox's property. That was going to be part of her birthday present too." He let out a long, deep sigh. "But now I'll go back to my original plan, since I can't even bear to look at it anymore."

"What was your original plan?"

"Selling it."

"To whom?" I asked. My mouth had become strangely dry.

"Theo," Gordon replied with a little shrug.

The significance of what he'd just said hit me like a magnum of champagne.

"I suppose he plans to expand his winery," he continued, seemingly oblivious to my reaction. "I can't imagine what else he'd do with that extra piece of land. In fact, Joan was just looking over the legal papers earlier this afternoon. She has a much better head for that kind of thing than I do. We've been trying to keep the sale of the land quiet, since we both feel kind of bad about moving on so quickly when it was supposed to be Cassandra's." His voice thickened as he added, "But that's the whole point. Now it will never be hers."

I was only half-listening, since my head was spinning too quickly for me to concentrate.

Gordon had planned to sell those twenty acres to Theo, then decided to give them to Cassandra instead so she could create her own vineyard, Red Rabbit Run. Now that she's gone, he'll get them after all.

My head throbbed with the realization that Theo

Simcox was the one person who had something to lose by the establishment of Red Rabbit Run Vineyards—something he could only get back through her death.

That was what Cassandra was trying to tell us with the clues she left behind.

But would Theo really consider the chance to acquire more land a reason to kill? I asked myself, wanting to be sure I wasn't jumping to conclusions. After all, he'd told me himself that when it came to the wine business, he'd never had what he called "Gordon's magic touch."

Then I remembered something else he had said. "There's treasure out here, all right," he had insisted. *"The land."*

And then an image flashed into my mind of Theo gazing at his computer monitor, shopping for cars on the Internet. When I'd caught him at it, I'd been heartened by the thought that he was finally going to get himself a reliable car.

Now, replaying that moment in my head, I realized there had been something on the screen that caught my eye but hadn't registered at the time: a small silver circle with an inverted Y inside.

The symbol for Mercedes-Benz. The car that the seemingly mild-mannered, nearly doddering old man in the torn flannel shirts was shopping for wasn't exactly a reasonably priced day-to-day errand car that most people would consider a replacement for an ancient Dodge. It just didn't jibe with a man who referred to dining regularly at a restaurant that charged eight bucks for a three-course dinner as his "one indulgence."

Unless he saw getting that land from the Thorndikes as a means of getting rich.

All of a sudden, the pieces of the puzzle fit together so perfectly I could practically hear a snap. And I could almost see Cassandra nodding her head approvingly. Theo Simcox had killed her because it was the only way he could get those twenty acres. It was greed that had brought about the young woman's death. Not her dalliance with the dark side of her sexuality, not her involvement in the cutthroat restaurant business, not her petulant fiancé or her frustrated stepmother—and not her unbalanced brother. Greed. Pure, simple greed.

But I was also filled with dread. While I'd been thinking all along that the really hard part was figuring it all out, I knew I still had something even more difficult ahead of me. And that was convincing Lieutenant Falcone that it was Theo Simcox, not Suzanne, who had murdered Cassandra Thorndike.

• • •

As I sat in my van less than five minutes later, my head was still spinning like a merry-go-round gone berserk. But despite feeling both excited and sickened by having finally solved the puzzle of Cassandra's murder, I had to act—and to act fast.

I grabbed my cell phone and dialed Falcone.

"Homicide," a male voice at the other end answered.

"I need to speak to Lieutenant Falcone," I said, forcing myself to talk slowly enough to be understood.

"He's not here," the man replied, sounding as if he didn't care in the slightest. "I can give you his voice mail."

"No, thanks. Wait—yes, give me his voice mail."

"You have reached the desk of Lieutenant Anthony Falcone..."

"Come on, come on," I muttered. When I finally heard the beep, I began to babble.

"Lieutenant Falcone, this is Jessica Popper. It's vital that you call me as soon as you get this message. I know who killed Cassandra Thorndike. If you'll just give me two minutes to explain everything—please call me back!" I recited my cell-phone number, then clicked off.

When my cell phone warbled just a few seconds later, I grabbed it on the first ring, grateful that he'd returned my call so quickly.

"Lieutenant Falcone? I'm so glad you called! I figured out what—"

"Dr. Popper?" The squeaky, uncertain voice I heard wasn't even close to matching Anthony Falcone's.

It only took me a few seconds to place it. "Mrs. Krupinski?"

"Dr. Popper! I'm so glad I got you. Something's wrong with Beau."

"I'm afraid I—"

"Cassie's cat? The one Maggie Rose has been taking care of?"

"Yes, of course I remember Beau."

"He's really sick all of a sudden. He keeps throwing up, and he's starting to look really weak. I wouldn't bother you, but Maggie Rose is beside herself. I offered to bring Beau to a vet around here, but she insisted you were the only animal doctor she wanted around her precious pussycat."

My mind raced. Until Falcone called me back, there wasn't much I could do. Besides, I was only a couple of miles away from Virginia Krupinski's house, so stopping in to take a look at Beau wouldn't take me very far out of my way.

"I guess I could stop off at your house. I'm nearby, in fact."

"Oh, good! It will mean so much to Maggie Rose. She's really grown attached to her little kitty cat."

"I'll be there as fast as I can."

•   •   •

I made it to Virginia Krupinski's house in record time, then dashed up the wooden stairs. Which made it all the more frustrating that, once again, I stood on the front porch for what seemed like a very long time, knocking and yelling and ringing the bell.

"Mrs. Krupinski?" I called over the blaring television. "Virginia? Anybody home? Maggie Rose, are you in there?"

Finally, I simply opened the unlocked door and walked in. Even over the shopping-channel hostess's claim that only four of these unique Halloween vests were still available at the unbelievable price of $39.99, I could hear banging and clanking from the kitchen. I walked to the back of the house and found Virginia standing at the counter with her back to me.

"Mrs. Krupinski?" I tried one more time.

She finally turned. "Dr. Popper! Thanks for coming by. Beau's out back with Maggie Rose. Her mom is due to pick her up any minute, but in the meantime she's playing nursemaid to her kitty."

Sure enough, as soon as I stepped outside, I spotted Maggie Rose in the backyard, crouching on the grass beside Beau. He did look weak—too weak, in fact, to put the energy that would be required into running away from his concerned owner.

"Hey, Maggie Rose. What's up with Beau?"

She looked up at me with her large brown eyes. "Beau's sick," she said forlornly. "He keeps throwing up."

"That's what your great-grandma told me—and that's why I'm here," I told her gently. "Tell you what: Let me take him into my van over there, and I'll try to figure out what's going on. Okay?"

She just nodded, then watched as I carried away her beloved pet.

Inside the van, I checked Beau's throat for some kind of obstruction and palpated his abdomen to see if he was in pain or had an inflamed intestine. So far, so good. Then I took his temperature. It was 101.5 degrees Fahrenheit, normal for a cat. Checking his gums, I saw that he wasn't dehydrated. In fact, aside from the vomiting, I couldn't find anything wrong with him.

When I carried him out again, I found Virginia hovering in the driveway, holding Maggie Rose's hand. They both looked at me expectantly.

"He doesn't seem to be seriously ill, but we'll need to keep an eye on him," I told them. "Beau could be vomiting because of something he ate—or even from having eaten too much. It could be from anxiety or it could be a sign of something more serious, although it doesn't look that way. I'm going to recommend that you keep him off food and on nothing but clear fluids for the next forty-eight hours. At that point, we'll see how he's doing."

"See that, Maggie Rose?" Virginia told her tiny charge. "Just like I said. It's probably just something poor little Beau ate. The doc here says he should be fine."

"The vomiting can actually be a good thing if it's helping Beau get rid of something bad he ate," I added, handing the cat back to Virginia. "But let's be cautious. Don't hesitate to call me if the vomiting doesn't stop in a few hours or if you see him developing any other symptoms."

"Thanks, Dr. Popper," Virginia told me, looking sincerely grateful. "As for you, Maggie Rose, you've had enough excitement for one day. It's time for you to pack up your toys— Oh, look. Your mommy's here. Hurry out to the car, now. Don't make her wait." Glancing at me wearily, she added, "It's been a long, trying day for me."

For me too, I thought.

I stopped in the bathroom to wash my hands, then warded off Virginia's effusive thanks. Even I noticed how much quieter the house seemed with Maggie Rose gone—even though, as usual, the TV was turned way up.

As I stepped out onto the front porch, I welcomed the blast of crisp autumn air that assaulted me, even though I saw it was turning out to be one of those oddly dark nights with only a pale moon and not a star in the sky. It was at that point that I realized just how tired I was. But the fact that my day had been at least as long and trying as Virginia Krupinski's didn't matter at all, given the fact that I'd finally solved the mystery of who had killed Cassandra Thorndike.

Now I'd found myself back at the scene of the crime. This time, just glancing over at Cassandra's house sent a chill running through me. I could picture the entire incident exactly as it must have happened, right inside that building. And her murderer finally had a face.

Still feeling shaken, I went down the steps and along the walkway outside Virginia Krupinski's house. But I froze when I noticed an odd shadow through the windshield of my van, feeling as if my heart had just been clamped in a vise.

Something—or someone—was sitting in the front seat.

But this time, it was no dummy. It was Cassandra's killer.

Chapter 18

"A cat is a puzzle for which there is no solution."

—Hazel Nicholson

I whipped my head around, desperately searching for a place to run. But it was too late. Theo had spotted me. In fact, he'd already opened the door of the van, slid out, and was heading toward me with a spring in his step I'd never seen before—with or without his supposed arthritis.

As he got closer, I saw that underneath his blue plaid flannel shirt, the same threadbare one he'd been wearing the day I met him, was a gun.

"I've been expecting you," Theo said in a low, calm voice. "I knew the dedicated Dr. Popper would never be able to resist helping a sick animal. Even if she'd just escaped from a locked wine cellar."

"How—how did you know Beau was sick?" I asked. My mind suddenly felt horribly muddled.

He let out an odd little laugh. "Because I'm the one who made him that way. Oh, don't worry. It was nothing but a healthy dose of syrup of ipecac, delivered with an eyedropper. Cassandra's cat will be fine."

This Theo Simcox appeared to be the younger brother

of the Theo Simcox I'd gotten to know. Not only did he move with more assurance; his posture was no longer stooped and his eyes had a brightness I'd never seen before.

"W-what are you doing with that gun?" I asked.

He laughed coldly. "You're about to find out. And we can begin by walking around the house so you can smash the glass window on the back door."

"Why would I do that?" I asked, partly stalling for time and partly genuinely confused.

"Because I want there to be signs that you broke into Cassandra's house," he replied matter-of-factly. "A forced entry through the back door, your fingerprints on the knobs throughout the house . . . maybe a muddy footprint would be a nice touch. Not that anything that dramatic will really be necessary. Even without it, the police should have no trouble piecing together what happened."

"Why do you want the police to think I broke into Cassandra's house?" I asked, even though I suspected I already knew the answer.

"I'll explain once we're inside," he insisted. And just for good measure, he jabbed me with the barrel of his gun.

I swiveled my head toward Virginia Krupinski's house, hoping that, somehow, she'd hear what was going on. I knew immediately that that wasn't about to happen.

So I shuffled around to the back of Cassandra's house with Theo right behind me.

"Now break the glass in the door, then reach inside and unlock the door from the inside," he instructed, keeping the gun pointed at my head in case I lacked motivation.

"Someone might hear us," I tried hopefully.

He just laughed. "With the TV blaring next door? I don't think so."

I did exactly as I was told. Sure enough, not a creature stirred at the sound of a glass window being smashed. Once we were inside, he stabbed me in the back with the barrel of his gun again. "Go on," he urged. "Walk around. Touch things. Knock things over."

"Can I at least turn on a light? I can hardly see in here!" I cried, hoping I still might manage to pique some neighbor's interest.

"I'm sure you can manage," Theo snapped. "Now start making it look like you broke in and were looking for something of value to steal."

I made a halfhearted attempt at doing what he told me to do. Frankly, it wasn't in my nature to break things or make a mess, so I settled for throwing a dish towel onto the floor, then following up with a couple of spoons.

"You're not very good at this, are you?" he complained.

"I'm doing my best!" I assured him, not bothering to explain that on the few occasions I'd sneaked into a place I didn't belong, my goal had been leaving as few signs that I'd been there as I could.

"All right, all right, I can take care of this later," he growled. "At least the window is broken and your prints are on the knob."

"Mr. Simcox—Theo—there has to be a better way out of this," I said, boldly turning to face him. I ran my tongue around the inside of my mouth, not wanting to let on how dry it had gotten. My mind, however, was becoming increasingly clear, thanks to all the adrenaline rushing around inside my body. Keep him talking, I thought. "I—I only wanted to find out who killed Cassandra."

Even in the darkness of the shadowy kitchen, I saw him give a little shrug. "And now you have. Despite my efforts at discouraging you, I might add. I could see from the start that my e-mails weren't enough to frighten you away. My phone call to the television station either, or ransacking your house. Even pushing you down the stairs at the Thorndikes' and locking you in the wine cellar didn't do it.

"You really are a stubborn woman, aren't you? Stubborn enough that you weren't about to give up investigating Cassandra's murder, no matter what. I knew it was only a question of time before you found out who really killed her. So you can see why I had no choice but to force you to give up. For me, it's the only way out."

"At least let me make sure I understand what happened," I pleaded. "After all, I helped Shiraz with her allergies. You owe me that much."

He just uttered a begrudging "harrumph."

"So you killed Cassandra to get the twenty acres Gordon had originally promised to sell you," I said, still not able to believe that someone who had painted himself as a family friend for years could actually be capable of such a heinous act.

"At a very good price, I might add, thanks to the fact that Gordon is a bit of an innocent." He smiled indulgently, as if he were talking about a child. "True to form, he never realized its true value. To land developers, I mean."

"Developers? You mean the kind who put up four hundred ugly condos overnight?" I couldn't resist blurting out.

Theo shrugged. "What they use the land for is not my concern. The only thing I'm interested in is how much they're willing to pay for it."

So *that* was what the land deal was really about, I thought. Theo had no intention of expanding his winery, the way Gordon assumed. He was going to let some developer cram it with town houses—at a hefty profit.

"In case you haven't noticed," he continued, "I'm at a

point in my life when I'm starting to think about slowing down and enjoying my 'golden years.' My wine business has been only moderately successful. As I already told you, we haven't all had the benefit of starting out as financially comfortable as Gordon. And I've never had his knack for making wine. A strong woman like Joan either, someone to help with sales and marketing, not to mention running the place.

"From the beginning, I've had to struggle to keep my little vineyard in the black. It's been hard work, let me tell you. Maybe it looks glamorous, but that's because people outside the industry don't know about the day-to-day difficulties like weather and insects and government bureaucracy. I'm damn tired and I'm getting ready to retire. That won't be easy without a hefty influx of cash. Hence, my plan."

Even though his face was blanketed in shadow, I saw him smile coldly. "See, Dr. Popper? I was absolutely right about there being treasure out here on the North Fork—and that it's the land itself. Captain Kidd's entire chestful of jewels and doubloons wouldn't hold a candle to the amount I'm going to get from the developer I've struck a deal with, now that Cassandra is out of the way. And something I hadn't even anticipated is that since Gordon is beside himself with grief, he's so upset that he even reduced the price, just to get rid of it. He actually believes I'm doing him a favor by taking that land off his hands, since he'd already come to think of it as Cassandra's property. He wants no part of what was supposed to be the site of Red Rabbit Run Vineyards."

"So in the end, you got what you wanted," I said, trying my best to sound as matter-of-fact about all this as he was. "So why don't we just leave it at that? I'll just walk away, and you can go ahead with—"

He laughed. But I got the feeling that it wasn't over anything I was likely to think was even remotely funny.

"Surely you're not serious," he said. "Why on earth would the bighearted Dr. Popper risk having her good friend take the blame for a crime someone else committed? Especially murder?"

I didn't have a good answer for that one. So instead I tried, "You're not really going to shoot me, are you?"

"Actually, shooting you is Plan B. But I'm hoping Plan A will work."

"And what exactly is Plan A?" My mouth was so dry I could barely get the words out.

"Now that it's obvious you broke into Cassandra's house, it wouldn't be that much of a stretch for the police to believe that as you attempted to run away, you accidentally plunged down the bluffs behind Cassandra's house, tragically falling to your death." Theo Simcox spoke so calmly that it took a few seconds for the meaning of his words to register. "I'm hoping you'll be somewhat cooperative. If not, that's where taking care of this matter the old-fashioned way—by shooting you—comes in."

"You can't shoot me! The police would easily catch you! The neighbors would hear the shot, you've left all kinds of physical evidence behind..."

"True, Plan B would launch a considerably more complicated scenario. But I've already worked out my story. I'll simply claim that I came to Cassandra's house one last time, just to say good-bye to the lovely young woman I thought of as the daughter I never had. And that while I was here, an intruder undid the lock and sneaked inside. Fearing for my life and the sanctity of a dead woman's house, I simply panicked and fired the gun in what I believed to be self-defense."

Waving the gun in the air, he added, "I could actually make you seem even more menacing, in fact. It would be easy enough to plant some ordinary object on you that could also serve as a weapon. A knife, or some heavy object—after all, you're young and strong, and I'm just a frail old man." Theo shrugged. "In the end, Dr. Popper, it's your choice."

I lowered my eyes to the gun he had pointed at me. It seemed very, very close—and he seemed very, very serious.

Buy yourself time, a voice inside my head commanded. There's still a chance that someone will see you...or hear you.

Given how dark it was outside, and given the fact that it was cold enough that not many people were likely to be out enjoying the evening air, neither possibility sounded very likely. But I wasn't about to give in.

Especially since I had at least a chance of getting away if I could get out of the house.

"I guess I prefer Plan A," I told him in an uneven voice.

As soon as I got the words out, I wondered if I'd just walked right into a trap. For all I knew, he was going to go ahead with whichever "plan" I *didn't* choose.

At least he was true to his word.

"Fair enough." With his gun, he gestured toward the back door. "After you, Dr. Popper."

I turned around and headed out the way I'd just come in. I couldn't resist the instinctive urge to check over my shoulder every few seconds. Not a very good feeling, being followed by some guy who has a gun aimed at your back.

Outside, the brisk autumn air hit me in the face like a slap. It was another harsh reminder that it wasn't very likely anyone else would be in the area, enjoying the chilly October air. Not when this was a night better suited to relaxing in front of a roaring fire, sipping hot mulled cider, than taking a stroll.

"Keep walking," Theo prompted.

It was dark enough that I couldn't see him very well. Yet I could tell he was right on my heels, the thud of his footsteps menacingly close as he trod across the hard ground behind me.

We walked a hundred feet or so out behind Cassandra's house. If I'd felt like he and I were the only two people around before, at this point I felt as if we were the only two people in the entire world. Even the moon wasn't very good company, emitting only a feeble light against the dark, starless sky.

"And now, Dr. Popper, you're about to meet with a most unfortunate accident," he finally announced. "Rather than the two of us getting into a struggle, I suggest that you simply jump."

Even though I'd known all along that that was Plan A, peering over the edge of the craggy bluff made my heart leap up somewhere around my ears. True, the drop wasn't that far, maybe forty or fifty feet. But that was far enough, even with the waters of Long Island Sound waiting below like the monster at the bottom of the pit. They simply weren't deep enough to break a fall.

Not exactly my idea of taking a pleasant dip at the seashore.

I stood there for a few seconds, my mind racing as I tried to come up with a way to escape. And then I heard a slight rustling in the bushes—and a black shape rushed by.

"Look out!" I cried in a panicked voice.

I instantly realized it was only Beau darting past us. But I also knew that Theo wasn't likely to figure that out, at least not for a few seconds. Behind me, I heard him gasp, reacting to the unexpected movement just a few feet off to the side.

I reacted fast, taking advantage of the distraction. I glanced down, desperately searching for something— anything—that could serve as a weapon. All I spotted was a tree branch. It wasn't thick enough to cause much damage, and the few twigs that protruded from it didn't look capable of doing much more than making a few superficial scratches on the skin. But it would have to do.

With one smooth motion, I swooped down, picked it up, and turned to face him. I half-expected the gun to go off. But I didn't exactly have a lot of choice.

Fortunately, he hadn't been expecting this crafty little maneuver. As I swung the branch in his face, thinking I might take out an eye or two and not caring a bit, I let out an angry yell, the kind of sound an angry pirate might have made.

"Aargh!"

I don't know if it scared him, but at least it surprised him. Theo stumbled backward, dropping his gun. It flew in a diagonal direction, landing a few feet in front of him.

"Damn you!" he cried, lunging toward it.

As he did, he underestimated the distance—maybe because of the darkness, maybe just because of the heat of the moment. At any rate, before I understood what was happening, the sandy soil at the edge of the bluff crumbled beneath him, sending him plunging down to the beach.

Without waiting to see the results, I turned and ran back toward the house. I charged through the open back door and grabbed my cell phone out of my purse, punching in numbers as I ran toward the safety of my van.

• • •

I never in a million years would have thought I'd actually be glad to see Lieutenant Falcone. But I guess you just never know where life will take you.

"Slow down, Dr. Popper," he growled. "You're talkin' so fast I can hardly understand you."

"I'll start at the beginning," I said, pausing to take a deep breath. He and I stood in Cassandra's backyard, surrounded by the cops and paramedics who were swarming around her property.

I proceeded to relate everything that had happened since I'd escaped from the Thorndikes' wine cellar and come to Virginia Krupinski's house to treat her cat—including every word Theo Simcox had said to me. I hadn't expected to remember it all so clearly, but it turns out that having somebody point a gun at you can do wonderful things for the memory.

When I'd finished, Falcone smiled sardonically. "So, Dr. Popper, you're telling me that Theodore Simcox confessed to Cassandra Thorndike's murder. But aside from your word, you don't have any proof. You have no witnesses—"

"As a matter of fact, she does."

I don't know which one of us was more surprised to turn around and see Virginia Krupinski standing at Cassandra's back door, peering out at us and pulling her puffy hand-knit sweater around her more tightly.

You could have knocked me over with a knitting needle.

"I was in the house the whole time," she announced. "I heard him confess."

"You were in the house?" Falcone repeated, incredulous.

"That's right." Virginia folded her arms across her chest and stuck her chin in the air defiantly. "What, you think old people can't be sneaky?"

"And were you being sneaky?" he asked.

"I guess you could say that. I live right next door. See?" she added, pointing as she made her way down the steps. "Right in that house over there."

"I remember where you live," he said impatiently.

"Now, that's a surprise," Virginia replied, "since you didn't seem to think I was anybody important enough to consider as part of a murder investigation, just because I happen to have a few years on you. And it's true that I'm a little hard of hearing. But that doesn't mean I don't know what goes on."

"I get your point," Falcone returned, his mouth drooping downward. "So what were you doing inside Cassandra Thorndike's house?"

"If you'll give me a chance to explain," she said haughtily, glancing over at me.

I gave her an encouraging smile.

"See, Cassie was always nice to me, bringing me little treats like desserts and candy from her job," Virginia explained. "There was one chocolate candy in particular that was my favorite, and I was pretty sure she'd said something about the sales rep who was always giving them to her just piling it on the last time she saw him. She said something about how he'd practically filled the trunk of her car with them candies, and how she was gonna need my help to finish them off.

"That was just a few days before—well, you know, before she was killed. So this evening I decided I'd go over to Cassandra's house to see if I could find them. I went as soon as Dr. Popper left. In fact, I was heading out the back door as she was going out the front. I'd only been inside for a minute or two when I heard the window breaking and somebody coming in—that horrid man and Dr. Popper, it turned out. I wasn't about to let on that I was in the house, standing right there in the dining room. After all, stealing candy from a dead person isn't exactly the most honorable thing to be doing, I suppose. But you can't get those chocolates anywhere else. Believe me, I've looked. See, they have these swirls of this truffle stuff inside, with different flavors like coffee and raspberry—"

"How did you get inside?" Falcone demanded.

"With a key, of course," Virginia replied, clearly indignant over having been asked such a silly question.

"Cassandra gave me a spare when she first moved in. In case she ever lost hers and got locked out."

"And what exactly did you hear Theo Simcox say," Falcone interrupted, "while you were sneaking around Cassandra Thorndike's house, looking for candy to steal?"

Virginia stood up a little straighter. "No need to try to make me feel bad about what I was doing," she shot back. "Not when I'm turning out to be your star witness. Along with Dr. Popper here, that is."

I noticed that his shoulders sagged, just a little. And then Virginia proceeded to give Falcone the exact same report I'd given, repeating everything Theo Simcox had said, practically word for word.

When she'd finished, Falcone cast me a look of disbelief.

"I guess you're telling the truth," he told her. "You really did hear Simcox's whole confession."

"Well, of course I did!" Virginia said archly. "In fact, I was about to rush back to my own house to call the police myself when I heard that horrible commotion. First Dr. Popper yelling, then that nasty man screaming... then I heard Dr. Popper on her cell phone, calling 911. So I just stayed where I was, figuring I'd sneak back home once the coast was clear."

"Mrs. Krupinski," Falcone said wearily, "I'll need you to come down to the station and make a formal statement." Turning to me, he added, "You too, Dr. Popper."

"I'd be happy to."

"Mrs. Krupinski, let me explain a couple things about what happens next..."

"Hey, Popper," I heard someone behind me say, "I hear you wield a mean tree branch. You got a license to handle foliage?"

I turned to see Forrester grinning at me.

For a change, I was actually happy to see him, too.

Funny what euphoria can do. "I actually have Beau to thank for getting me out of that one," I told him. "Cassandra's cat saved the day. And they say having a black cat cross your path is bad luck!"

"Hey, whatever it takes!"

"What are you doing here, anyway?"

"Falcone called me. An exciting new development like this warrants a trip out to the North Fork. Seems like the cops finally got their man.

"As for the courageous and ingenious Dr. Popper," he went on breezily, "it looks like you've got another notch in your belt. One of these days, Falcone's going to have to put you on the payroll."

"Thanks, but I already have a job," I replied. "Besides, I've had enough of murder investigations for a while."

"This wasn't exactly your average investigation," he observed. "This time around, you saved your pal Suzanne's butt."

"And found out who really killed poor Cassandra." I sighed. "So it wasn't her adventurous life that killed her, after all," I mused. "It was her desire to give it all up, once and for all, and do something meaningful with the rest of her life."

"Unfortunately, that's not in the stars for Theo Simcox," Forrester observed. "Looks like he's going to be trading a view of the vineyards for a view of the prison yard."

"So he survived the fall onto the beach?" I asked.

"He's tougher than he looks, especially since he snagged his pant leg on a shrub, which slowed him down. That paramedic over there told me he broke his leg and smashed a couple of ribs but that he's fine otherwise. Certainly in good enough shape to stand trial."

Forrester and I headed to the front of Cassandra Thorndike's house, then stood together and watched the parade of vehicles go by. First, the ambulance carrying Theo Simcox off to the hospital, his leg in a splint and his hands in cuffs. Next, Lieutenant Falcone, speeding off in his dark-blue Crown Victoria, his jaw set firmly and his expression hard. Finally, a blue-and-white Norfolk County police car with Virginia Krupinski sitting in back, her eyes bright as she talked the ear off the officer who was driving.

It was over. By that point, I couldn't tell if I felt exhilarated or just exhausted. But one thing was clear: I suddenly couldn't wait to call Nick and tell him what had happened.

However, there was something else I needed to do first.

"If you'll excuse me," I told Forrester, "I have an important phone call to make."

I couldn't help grinning as, for the second time in less than half an hour, I rummaged through my purse and pulled out my cell phone. Only this time, I punched in Suzanne's number.

• • •

"I've thrown my share of parties," I told Nick. "But finding Cassandra's killer and clearing Suzanne's name has got to be one of the best reasons ever for a celebration."

I glanced around my small cottage, which I'd decorated with so many crepe-paper streamers I felt like I was hosting a school dance. I guess I'd gotten kind of carried away in terms of the bouquets of flowers too, but I figured this was one of those special occasions when there was no such thing as over the top.

The same went for the food. Even though the impromptu little gathering I'd thrown together had only a small, select guest list, I'd decided not to skimp.

"Definitely cause for a celebration," Nick agreed. "And nothing says 'party' like ice cream. In fact, I've got enough here for an entire summer camp." He began unpacking the three brown-paper shopping bags he'd just lugged in from the car. "Five—count 'em, *five*—flavors of Ben & Jerry's. And nuts, sprinkles, chocolate syrup..."

Okay, so Nick and I hadn't really lost our taste for sweets, despite learning that at least one well-regarded pastry chef had his hand in a lot more than pastry dough. And indulging in build-it-yourself ice cream sundaes seemed like the ideal theme for a Saturday afternoon get-together.

"Are we too early?" Betty called gaily, peeking through my open front door. She was wearing a strapless red satin party dress that hugged every curve and carrying a big white bakery box. Winston was right behind her, decked out in a yellow-and-white polka-dot bow tie that made him look extremely spiffy.

"You're right on time," I told them as Max and Lou skidded across the room to welcome them officially, falling over each other like clowns.

"I suppose that explains why the guest of honor is right behind us," Winston commented, patting Lou on the head even though the Dalmatian suddenly seemed much more interested in sniffing whatever was in Betty's bakery box than in cementing friendships.

"Suzanne?" I called.

"Jessie!" Suzanne exclaimed. She charged inside and immediately threw her arms around me. From the way she collapsed against me, I couldn't tell if she was hugging me or just needed a way to keep from falling over.

"How can I begin to thank you?" she cried breathlessly once she finally let go. "There's so much I want to say to you! First of all—"

And then she burst into tears.

"You don't have to say anything," I assured her, grinning and squeezing her shoulders. "I feel the exact same way."

Betty glanced around. "Where's that boyfriend of yours? Marcus, isn't that his name?"

Kicking myself for forgetting to brief Betty, I glanced at Suzanne nervously. Much to my relief, she made a face.

"Good riddance to bad rubbish," she said cheerfully, smiling through her tears. "That's what my mom used to say, and she was right." More to herself than to us, she added, "The same goes for Robert, too. I am *so* over him."

"Here's another old saying," Betty added. Her long, dangling earrings, strings of tiny red stones so brilliant they had to be rubies, swayed from side to side. "Men are like streetcars. If you miss one, there'll be another one coming along soon." She frowned. "Oh, dear. I suppose they don't have streetcars anymore, do they?"

Leaning over, Nick said softly, "So good old Marcus really meant it when he dumped Suzanne at the lowest point in her life. He didn't even give her the satisfaction of dumping *him* after she realized what a jerk he was." Frowning, he added, "I guess what they say is true: When the going gets tough, the wimps take off."

"I'm sure it was really hard on Suzanne at first," I replied, "especially given his timing. But at least she finally saw him for what he is."

"She definitely deserves better," Nick agreed. "And she'll find better."

"How about finding the best," I said, only half-teasing, "the way I did?"

"Dr. Popper?" I heard someone call through all the babble.

"Virginia!" I cried, pleased to see that she'd made it. And standing beside her—actually half-hidden behind her—was Maggie Rose. "Come in! You too, Maggie Rose. Thank you both so much for coming."

"You have a cat," Maggie Rose announced. She pointed at Cat, who had crept into the room to see what all the commotion was but was crouched underneath a chair, choosing to spectate rather than participate.

"I have two," I informed her. "I have a feeling you're really going to enjoy playing with the other one. She's only a kitten. And she's just about your size."

At the moment, however, the little girl was too busy fighting off an affectionate Westie and a love-starved Dalmatian, both of them acting like it had been days, not mere seconds, since Winston had given them both a professional-caliber neck-scratching. It wasn't long before their persistence became too much for her, forcing her to give in to their demands. Fortunately, she giggled all the way through.

I turned to Suzanne. "I'm really pleased to introduce these two people. They're the ones you should be thanking. Suzanne, this is Virginia and this is Maggie Rose."

"I'm really happy to meet you, Maggie Rose," Suzanne said, crouching down so she was at eye level with her. "One of the reasons is that I understand you really like animals."

Maggie Rose nodded earnestly. "I have a new cat. His name is Beau."

"You're so lucky. Cats are such great pets. But there's definitely something to be said for dogs, don't you think?"

Maggie Rose nodded wisely, meanwhile hugging Max, who, for a change, was acting like the teddy bear he so closely resembled.

"Tell you what," Suzanne offered. "How about coming to my animal hospital sometime to play with some of the animals we're taking care of while their owners are away on trips? Sometimes we have ferrets, guinea pigs... even cute little potbelly pigs."

"Can I pet them?" Maggie Rose asked seriously, wanting to make sure she fully understood the deal before making a commitment. "*All* of them?"

tip to box and forced the stroke to make a small explosion of light . . . that was gone as soon as it appeared.

A frustrated moan popped in her throat and she swallowed it. She needed to stay calm. She lowered her forehead to the tops of her outstretched arms to gather herself and then began once more from the beginning, closing her eyes to concentrate, to pray . . . to arrive at the same result.

Her head shot up suddenly, like an alert rabbit. She heard a new whirring sound, a not-wind drone coming her way, getting closer. A look back at beams of light coming up the road shot electricity to the tips of her toes and out her fingers—made her muscles spastic as she scrambled to get to her feet. Could she make it to the pavement in time to flag it down? Her first step brought her down with a cry and shout. "No, no, no!" Her feet were tied up in the sweater. "No, no, no. I'm here. I'm here." Bag and sweater were off in a flash. "Help! Help me! I'm here." She made it to her feet in time for its approach; to jump waving and screaming and to stagger into snow before it passed her by without slowing down.

Natalie stood, stunned and confounded. What now? The question circled in her mind until her feet were shrieking in pain and instinct alone had her back-stepping to the mat. Hardly aware of it, she searched the dark for the towel and went about the business of surviving.

She discovered that cupping her hands around the box provided marginal protection from the wind—but marginal wasn't enough. She made a mini-dome with a hamburger wrapper—another blowout. But when a second attempt produced more than a spark, an actual flare, she gave it two more chances before moving on to option four—matchstick nine—which was to dig a small hole, a tiny fire pit of sorts.

With fewer matches in the box it became easier to count them—there were four left.

Looking up, she was startled to see . . . to be able to see, actually. The ambient light from the gray skies reflected off the white snow making it almost as bright as day. That which had been hidden from her in darkness had come to light. Trees and bushes had magically materialized while her attention had been elsewhere. Trees heavy with snow, balancing inches of snow on tiny limbs; the car at the road, a snow-topped boulder a few yards away; the road and the fields beyond—empty and stretching for miles—it all glistened as if littered with millions and billions of tiny diamonds.

If she wasn't so cold or so terrified it might have been exquisite—as it was: "It's a good sign."

Putting the box back in her pocket for safekeeping, she took some time to scrape away as much of the frozen ground that a dull stick would allow and used more leaves and papers from the trash to build up the walls around it; tugged the paper canopy into place. Blindly, she skimmed stiff fingers over her handiwork and when she was sure she could do no better, she went for the matchbox once more.

Match four was impressive but three looked, for a whole second, as if it might catch—charring the edge of a leaf. It was worth another try . . . but proved another failure.

She squeezed tears from her eyes and clutched the matchbox, and the last of its contents, tight in the palm of her hand. The near-constant shivering was taking a toll on her strength; she was fatiguing. Even the choice to use or to save the last match was an extraordinary chore . . . until she came to understand that she wasn't going to get any warmer, that conditions weren't going to get any better than they were at that moment. There might not be a later in which to use it.

"I've never been much of a saver anyway."

Sluggishly she came to the decision that, no, no better preparations could be made—what's more, she didn't have the energy. This time the lighting ceremony held more desperation than expectation; much less faith in the outcome. And when it was over, it was something of an odd relief.

She'd done her best. She had fought . . . fought the young man, fought the cold and the night. She hadn't given up . . . not on herself, not on her hope of surviving . . . not on her dream of being with Miles. She still hadn't. As long as her heart beat there was always a chance—she truly believed that, with every molecule in every cell in her body. She believed. The thing was, she simply didn't know what else she could do. She was too tired to walk; she wouldn't make it to the road. The last best thing she could do was to stay as dry and as warm as she could for as long as she could, and wait, and trust that help would come before sleep.

The mat had snow on it now, and while brushing it off still gave her some protection from the moisture of the snow, it had become a conductor of its freezing temperature. Wrapped in plastic and pieces of cotton and wool, she settled the least amount of her body mass on the mat as possible— the poorly covered soles of her feet and the base of her spine, with her back against the small slumbering tree.

All that remained was the time it would take for her body to exhaust itself and stop shivering.

"It'll be all right," she said, though it didn't sound any more convincing out loud than it did in her head.

Gently, slowly, and cherishing each one, she began to sort through memories of love and laughter, recalled friends both old and new. She prized her accomplishments and the gifts she'd received from others—her lids grew heavy and a warm, calm contentment spread through her at simply having known Miles.

One corner of her mouth tipped upward and her heavy-lidded gaze lifted to the sky. The radiance, the soft lighting of the sky that she'd noticed earlier was . . . *more*, she thought, fancying that the once solid mass of heavy cloud cover that had unburdened itself of its snow was now pulling apart, separating and plumping up. Small patches of star-studded sky spread slowly as she watched through air so clear and crisp it all but crackled.

As a matter of fact, everything around her was shimmering, shining . . . the word *heavenly* came to mind. Her lazy gaze fixed on two particular stars, low in the sky, moving, coming closer, and . . . no, not stars. Headlights registered.

A car traveling in the far lane, on the other side of the median toward Beaumont . . . too far away to see her . . . too far away . . .

"I'm still here." The words floated from her in a cloud of warm air and were just as audible.

In a trance, she tracked the vehicle with her eyes between slow, long blinks—until it drove into what looked like a spotlight on a stage—a curio that penetrated her groggy awareness.

Once again, her vision turned aloft. Her lips, stiff and cracked, bowed at the sight of brilliant crepuscular rays streaming from the heavens. God rays. But not from the sun . . . not even from a full moon.

More and more of the comet's tail appeared before the last of the clouds broke away to reveal its true magnificence— a staggering light in a moonless night sky with a gloriously long, luminous tail.

"The Christmas Comet."

She'd never seen anything like it. No one alive had seen it before—racing along on its epic orbit around the sun; pulling and rolling and shifting the molecules in the air, trailing ancient and magical dust in its wake.

She'd read about it, seen pictures of other comets . . . There were those who believed ISON was the return of what was named the Star of Bethlehem—that it was this brilliant comet the magi followed so very, very long ago. And who knew, maybe it was.

All Natalie knew, for sure and for certain, was that anything so extraordinary and beautiful was a singularity—a miraculous event. A miracle.

"It just has to be . . ."

CHAPTER EIGHT

⦿

"I couldn't believe it." Miles wasn't sure how many times he'd said it in the last three days but he *still* couldn't believe it. "There she was, sitting under a tree, sound asleep. I couldn't believe it."

See?

Having made it through the worst of her ordeal, Natalie was now stable—all she had to do was wake up.

"What made you turn around and go back?" asked Special Agent Palmer, sitting casually in the chair at the end of her hospital bed. He'd arrived several hours earlier on an assignment to first check on her condition and then give her some good news.

"When I found her car at the side of the road, out of gas, with her not in it, I wanted to wring her neck. She knew better than to get out . . . and to stay in one place so we could find her. God, I was so mad." Instantly, his remembered anger bubbled in his veins, but it didn't belong to Natalie anymore. "The best I could hope was that she'd set out for town, not too far, a few miles—I thought I'd catch her on the way in. Maybe she thought she could hitch a ride . . .

"The first thing I found was an open convenience store with a couple police cruisers parked outside. Turns out two kids—a girl and a boy—did hitch a ride into town and when the driver stopped there for gas they took off in his van . . . with the gas he hadn't paid for yet, which is what caught the attendant's notice and why he called the cops so quick. By some miracle there was a patrol in the vicinity. They were collared inside twenty minutes. The kids and the van were then brought back for identification and that's when I rolled up. When the driver said he'd picked 'em up a couple miles outside town, that they'd run out of gas, I asked him to describe the car. It was Natalie's."

Agent Palmer chuckled and nodded. "So the kid didn't really slip on the ice, land on his face, and break his own nose." It wasn't a question.

Miles shook his head once and clenched his still sore fist. "Technically, I suppose, he slipped *after* his nose was broken." He looked back into Palmer's face, saw no judgment, and knew the infinitesimal dollop of guilt he felt was all his. "I haven't hit anyone since I got out of the army thirteen years ago."

"So then you went back to her car," said the DEA agent, leaping over the subject with ease, needing no further explanation.

"I went back to *their* car where they'd left her."

"That's when you saw her."

He nodded, perplexed. "I don't know why I didn't see it the first time I passed by. The storm was over." Again he shook his head in wonder. "There she was, plain as day. I couldn't believe it."

"Well, you weren't the only one out looking . . . or the only one who missed seeing her. We were watching for her, too. We took that same road—we even saw the car, slowed down. It looked abandoned. Kills me to think she was only a few yards away." His gaze shifted toward the bed. "She's good people."

Miles sighed and went back to watching her breathe. She was more than just a good person to him.

After a short time the Posers returned from the cafeteria with coffee for both Miles and the agent, and once they'd extracted a promise to be notified when Natalie woke up, they left for the night. A little while after that, Palmer got up to stretch his legs and went down the hall to the visitors' lounge to check in with his office and call his wife.

Miles leaned forward to take up Natalie's hand. He'd always liked the way she talked with her hands; they were almost as expressive as her face. Gloveless, they'd been nearly purple when he found her—in fact, everyone had marveled at how well she'd pinked up and had sustained no frostbite at all. The words *amazing* and *miraculous* and *most uncommon* were repeated often, in wonder and speculation.

Miles smiled. He'd often used the same words, in the same way, just watching her ladle soup or pester a man to go to the free clinic or slip a burner phone to a kid to call home with when she thought no one else was looking . ... or simply walking down the street, done-in and ready for sleep.

Come to think of it, he was dead on his feet, too. Bouncing high and low like a hard rubber ball for the last few days was taking its toll. After that night at her apartment he soared so far above the ground he could have painted the sky blue by hand, which made his fall into hell when she didn't arrive at the church all the more violent and chaotic. Elated when he found her, knocked down by her condition, and back to overjoyed when she was out of the woods was a monster roller-coaster ride unlike any he'd taken before—but there was no one in the world he'd rather take it with than her.

"Ruined." At least that was the word her murmur sounded like.

"What?" He leaned closer, waiting for her to speak again. "Natalie?"

Eyes closed, she drew her chapped lower lip into her mouth to wet it, then tried again. "It's ruined."

"What's ruined?"

"My dress."

His chuckle was silent. "That's okay," he said, sympathetically. "You're going to need a completely different one for our reception, anyway."

She frowned, confused enough to blink her eyes open several times before they came to focus on him. Her immediate smile was warm and affectionate—and then it drooped as she took in the space over his shoulder, the strange bed, the TV on the wall, the tray table, the out-of-place hotel picture on the wall . . . Her gaze came back to and clung to the one thing in the room she recognized: Miles.

He smiled, caressed her face without touching it—then realized he could, and did. "I can't believe you stood me up on our very first date."

The furrow between her brows deepened. Gradually, as she glanced away and recalled *why*, her expression relaxed and her gaze met his. "Car trouble."

His eyes opened wide; he grinned and nodded at the understatement.

They might have been smiling at one another but the current between them was spiked with fear and relief: It conveyed the terror and panic they'd each endured, the hope they had stretched to its limits, and the love that had driven them to this moment.

She turned her hand over so they were palm to palm and she could clasp his tighter. Softly and sincerely, she said, "I'm so sorry."

He knew it wasn't for missing their date or for ignoring his repeated advice to be cautious or for being herself and doing what came natural to her: helping those in need. Her only regret was having caused him distress and the pain that accompanied it.

"Well, you're here and you're safe," he said, then attempted a grudge. "I'll forgive you this time."

"Even if I can't promise there won't be a next time?"

He sobered and answered seriously. "Yes, even if . . . though I hope you won't test me." In her expression he saw that she knew she was no longer alone, that her life and his life were one life now, and what one did the other would

feel. But he also saw *her*, and he smiled. "And I can't promise I'll be this nice about it next time, so keep that in mind
when you do."

She laughed, then hissed at the stiff pain on the left side
of her face and reached for it.

"A couple of minor scratches there . . . and one hell of a
shiner," Miles said, his voice easy and light despite his tense
expression. "A few other bruises, too. You got off easy."

"Better than you, I think." She reached up to palm his
cheek. "I don't think I've ever seen you unshaven." She
grinned at him. "You're a mess."

There was a noise at the door and they both looked
that way.

"Good. You're back," Miles said to the dark-haired man
in blue jeans and winter jacket standing mostly in the hall.
"Come in. She's awake."

NATALIE WAS CURIOUS ABOUT THE MAN, OF COURSE, BUT
even more intrigued by the sudden rush of excitement rolling off Miles.

"Natalie, this is Special Agent Palmer from the DEA.
He has a story to tell you."

"Please don't." Not too curious and not at all apologetic,
she said, "I'm sorry, Agent Palmer. No offense. I do sometimes wish I could help you guys out. I do. But I can't risk
getting between you and the dealers and the addicts who
might come to me for help. They need to be able to trust
me." She chuckled, hoping to take some of the sting and
insult out of her rejection. "Plus, I just promised Miles I'd
try to stay out of trouble for a while."

The agent had a nice smile. "Good. And I'm glad you're
feeling better. You had us worried." He skipped a beat. "And
I'm not here to ask for your help. You've already helped us
more than you know, without even knowing it."

"Oh no."

"Without anyone knowing it," he said quickly. "Except
for those you helped. And they are extremely grateful."

Okay. Now she was curious. "So grateful they've asked us to help set up a rather large trust in your name so that you can start up your soup kitchen and . . . well, whatever else you want to do with it to continue to help people, like you helped them."

"Who?"

Again, he smiled. "Aldene and the children?"

"Aldene? She has money for a trust?"

"A big trust. And her name isn't Aldene."

"What is it?"

He shook his head. "For your safety I can't tell you who she was and I can't tell you who she is today because she and the rest of the family are in protective custody with the DOJ and I don't know. But I can tell you that the man that you met, Luis Pena—also not his real name—is her father and his sons are her brothers."

"Okay." Still family, though why they'd lie about the order of it was still confusing. "I never asked about a husband. I guess I just assumed he'd passed away or . . . or was off somewhere looking for work or . . . I try not to pry too much."

He nodded, aware that her friendship and help had been unconditional. "He's why they fled Mexico." He sat, took a breath, and began the story. "Wealthy people in Mexico, affluent families that have lived there for generations, are prime targets for kidnapping and ransom by the drug cartels. They pay street taxes to leave their homes and spend fortunes on bribes and protection for their families. And for the most part, if they don't get in the way or cause any trouble, they manage to keep what is theirs and stay in the country they love.

"I can't get specific about the Pena family, but Aldene's husband, her oldest son—"

"Arturo . . . not his real name, right?"

He nodded. "Also one of her brothers . . . they were out together and witnessed a cartel execution. He sent the boys running in one direction and took off the other way. He was captured and killed. The man, Luis, gathered his entire family and smuggled them over the border that night and didn't stop running until he got here and could safely contact the authorities. We were called in first and they were given temporary S-5 permits—for witnesses and informants in criminal or terrorists cases. We, and certain people in the Mexican government, have been after these guys for years.

"Turns out the kid, Arturo, didn't see the actual murder but his young uncle did and he was willing to testify in exchange for witness protection for himself and his family." He looked away briefly. "*But* sometimes risking your life isn't enough, and somewhere between the DEA, the DOJ, and Homeland Security, it was decided that a legal and permanent residence—and *then* witness protection—was going to require an EB-5 visa." There was an angry tick in his cheek when he paused to gather an explanation. "EB-5s are what you might call a rich man's visa that gets their wheels greased to the front of the line by investing five hundred thousand dollars or more in American business projects— what they call economic growth projects for rural and high unemployment areas. *Or* a million for projects outside those areas." He hesitated, rethinking what he was about to say, and then tipped his head regrettably to say, "Money."

She could see he didn't approve of the deal Aldene and her family had to make to stay safe for doing the right thing . . . to stay alive. She liked him for it.

"Anyway, Luis apparently didn't feel secure without a solid deal in place so he used some connections he had to slip away and drop out of sight until the financial arrangements could be made. *Way* out of sight, because by the time we found his connection he'd stashed the kids and he was the only one making periodic contact with them." He shook his head. "Considering the long fingers of the cartels in this country, it's hard to believe he felt safer on the streets than in a temporary safe house . . . but he said that was exactly why he thought it was best to be able to separate and move around than to sit all together in one place." He shrugged.

"Who knows? Scared is scared and you do what you do to keep your family safe. And with the money thing . . . ? Hard to tell who you can trust when money's involved."

"I like money . . . and I never have any. How'd they know I wouldn't sell them out? I mean, if I somehow found them out."

Agent Palmer's gaze shifted to Miles, who then grinned at her. "You're as well known for being a soft touch as you are for your soup, sweetheart. And, apparently, you *can* do discreet better than I gave you credit for, because the father was keeping his ear to the ground. He knew his daughter and grandchildren were safe with you as long as he didn't hear anything about them, or get wind of anyone staying with you."

"See?" She played proud, but only to cover the deep gratification she felt in having been a part—albeit unknowingly—of the family's escape from danger.

"Don't get cocky," he said with a loving frown. "It was still risky and dangerous."

"It was," the agent agreed, and shifted his weight in the chair he was sitting in. "Which is why, when we finally connected with the family again, we thought it would be safer if you never knew who they were and they simply disappeared. Aldene told her father you were trying to get them into a shelter so we accelerated that process a little . . . and it would have worked out perfectly except she knew you were behind in your rent and working extra jobs to make ends meet. She and her father, as I said, are extremely grateful to you for helping them—and with no ulterior motive." Yet another disparaging reference to the special visa—she *really* liked him for it.

"Long story a little shorter, they insisted that they wanted to give you money . . . outside of that entailed by their EB-5. For your dreams, they said. They planned to send you a fortune anonymously through the mail." He chuckled. "We explained how conspicuous and possibly hazardous that might be for you, and a little about taxes and all that, and they finally agreed to let us arrange for a trust to be set up in your name. It has its own background and cover story and can't be traced to them."

He stood and pulled a long white envelope from a pocket inside his jacket. Stepping around to the side of the bed opposite Miles, he handed it to her. His expression was serious but his eyes were twinkling with goodwill.

He cleared his throat and began to recite: "*On behalf of the Pena family*—not their real names—*please accept this token of their gratitude and friendship. They will never forget you or your kindness to them*." He smiled and reached back into his jacket. "And neither will I. Please, take my card. If you ever need me for anything, I want you to call. I get the position you're in but you never know—having a friend in the DEA might come in handy someday."

She took his card; they all shook hands and then he was gone.

For one entire minute, Miles and Natalie stared at the white envelope on her lap.

"Aren't you going to open it?" he asked finally. She turned her head and scrutinized him until he became a little uncomfortable. "What?"

"What sort of reception?"

He was surprised into laughter, but didn't hesitate to answer. "Our wedding reception."

Her brows rose over sparkling eyes. "Aren't you getting a little ahead of yourself?"

"No. I'm way behind where I should be with you. I should have asked you to marry me three years ago, about a week after I met you, when I first realized I was hopelessly in love with you."

"It took you a whole week?" For her it was that first night when he'd helped her, all battered and bruised, out of the back of his police car and then, needlessly, he'd picked her up in his arms and carried her into the ER. Literally, he'd swept her off her feet.

"Only to realize it . . . and then that night, the night I finally asked you out . . . that's when I realized you felt the same. That look on your face? I'd seen it so often, waited for it, worked for it, hoped it would be there every time I saw you. It just didn't occur to me, until then, what it meant." Suddenly, he was so overcome with emotion she thought he might cry. She reached to smooth her hand over the side of his face, through his hair, and to rest on the back of his neck. He smiled and leaned into it. "The other night, shortly before I found you . . . I was a little bit out of my mind, but life was never so clear to me. It's short. Way too short. I vowed then and there that if I found you alive I wouldn't live another second without you. I'd marry you and we'd live happily ever after." He leaned in, mere inches from her face. "Please marry me."

"Tonight?" she asked, being facetious.

"Yes. Tomorrow at the latest."

"Okay."

The kiss they shared was everything she knew it would be—soft and demanding; conquering and offering; rousing and freeing—it fused her soul to his.

At last, Miles smiled between sweet, sipping kisses and pulled away to say, "I can't wait to start bragging about my wife's survival skills."

She nodded, dubious. "My luck is fantastic, but I don't think luck is a skill."

"Trust me, building a fire like that in the middle of a snowstorm isn't just luck."

"Fire?"

"I couldn't have built it on my best day in the army. It had clearly been burning for a while. I couldn't believe it— the broken branches and twigs still burning in the pit, the embers red hot. I was amazed by the heat it was putting off."

"What fire?"

"The one you built to stay warm . . . also a good signal fire, by the way. It was so bright I couldn't believe I missed—"

"I used up all my matches . . ."

"I'm not surprised. It couldn't have been easy."

"No. I mean, I didn't . . . It didn't . . . I . . ."

She saw it again. That staggering light in a moonless night sky with a gloriously long, luminous tail crossed her mind in all its true magnificence. So unique, so powerful and moving. So unearthly and magical.

"What is it?" Miles asked, watching as clarity lit her expression.

Accepting the fire as real, she looked down at the unopened envelope on the bed and back at Miles.

Life, purpose, and love—all she'd ever wished for.

"The Christmas Comet."

AUTHOR'S NOTE

Originally I chose Hans Christian Andersen's *The Little Match Girl* as my fairy tale for this novella. However, while most fairy tales are not exactly funny and upbeat, most, in their most common versions, don't end quite so grimly or without a happy ending. I soon discovered that the Brothers Grimm had also been inspired to write a story about an impoverished little girl in *The Star Money* that ends on a much lighter note. Inspired by both, my story is a mix of the two.

P.S. Comet ISON is real and should be visible from Earth from approximately November 2013 through about February 2014. Watch for it. And if it passes through your part of the sky, make a wish.

STROKE OF MIDNIGHT

R. C. RYAN

To my daughter-in-law Maureen,
whose generous heart makes all who meet her fall in love.

And in memory of my Tom,
who forever owns my heart.

PROLOGUE

"Sydney." Margot stared in surprise at her sixteen-year-old stepdaughter, dressed in her school uniform, carrying an armload of textbooks. "What are you doing home from school so early?"

"I told you we were having a half-day for teacher conferences." Sydney watched, wide-eyed, as workers swarmed over the barn her father had converted into his artist studio, efficiently wrapping dozens of his paintings. "What are they doing?"

"Preparing them for shipment."

"Shipment? Where? Why?"

"We've been over this, Sydney. With your father dead, we have no use for this big farmhouse and this barn"—Margot waved her hands to indicate the cavernous surroundings—"where your father used to hide away for hours on end. Not only was I fortunate to find a buyer for this place, but someone who obviously has more money than brains offered a fabulous sum for the entire collection of your father's art. I was hoping to have it out of here before you got home."

Sydney turned away to hide the tears that sprang to her eyes. She hated the way the grief could sneak up on her and make her weep at the worst possible time. "But Dad promised me they would all belong to me one day."

"He said no such thing to me." Margot's hand shot out, grabbing the girl by her shoulder, her fingers gripping painfully. The woman's eyes flashed the way they always did when she was challenged. "As your father's widow, I don't need your permission. I'm free to dispose of his estate as I choose. I have to think about the future. It was hard enough when I had only my own two daughters to worry about. Now, thanks to your father's untimely death, I have one more to feed and clothe and educate." She gave a dismissive look at the girl's prim navy jumper and white blouse. "There will be no more private schools for you. Not with Hester and Hilda ready for college and all the expense that will entail. I told your father he was spoiling you, but he was determined to make it up to you because you'd lost your mother at such a tender age. Now that I'm in charge, there'll be no more of such pampering. You're old enough to be exposed to the realities of life. The money from your father's paintings will allow me a comfortable lifestyle, but money can't be stretched forever. We'll move to the city where you can walk to school, and Hester and Hilda can pursue their dreams of careers in fashion in New York City."

"Dad said . . ."

"Enough." Margot lifted her hand in a dismissive gesture. "I know your father fancied himself a true man of the earth while painting all those pastoral scenes. He made it plain that he wanted you to grow up in the country as he had. That life is gone now, Sydney." Margot narrowed her eyes on the girl. "It's time to stop mourning our loss and move on. Thank heavens some foolish collector thought those paintings were worth more than the paint and canvas, though I must say, your father was such a dreamer, I was afraid we'd all be left destitute." Her tone sharpened. "The buyer of this farm wants to take possession by the end of the month. I've already contacted your school to let them know you won't be back for the next term."

She turned away with a swish of skirts. "Pack only what you absolutely must have. Since your sisters will be living on campus in the fall, you and I will make do with something much smaller and more manageable."

When she was gone, Sydney walked among the remaining unwrapped paintings, allowing her fingers to trace her father's familiar signature at the lower right-hand corner of each canvas.

How she'd loved being here, working alongside her father, learning the craft from a master. He'd patiently taught her how to mix the paints to make the sky that perfect shade of blue, the meadows so green and lush, she could imagine herself lying in the grass, watching the clouds overhead turning into castles and carriages and kings. While they'd worked, he'd spoken lovingly about his happy childhood in the tiny town of Innismere, in the west of Ireland, where he'd honed his craft along the lovely river Glass, which meandered across his beloved valley.

She could hear his voice, as clearly as though he were still here beside her. "I'll take you there one day, Sydney, and we'll walk the hills and forest glades, and you'll see that marvelous light that shines down on Ireland in a way that it shines nowhere else on Earth. I want you to feel the peace and the love that I knew in that sweet, magical place."

"Oh, Da, I can't wait." She ran a hand along the scarred old table that held his tools and cans and rags, and breathed in the familiar scents of paint and turpentine that were forever imprinted on her mind and heart.

Feeling the press of that familiar hand on her shoulder, she paused. As though moved by invisible strings, she picked up a small framed photo of her father that she'd taken one day here in his studio. He was wearing a paint-smeared shirt, his hair mussed, his smile bright as he worked on one of his many canvases. He'd loved the photo so much he'd had it framed.

"Take it, Sydney. Keep it close and think of me often. And remember this, darlin': Believe."

Had the words been spoken aloud, or had she merely heard them in her mind?

No matter. Whether or not she could see or hear her father, she knew he was here beside her, watching out for her, keeping her safe. She could hear his voice inside her head and feel the gentle touch of his hand on her shoulder.

Wrapping the picture in one of his paint-stained rags, she tucked it in her pocket.

Margot had said to pack only the important things. This was all Sydney needed. For the rest of her days, this little memento would keep her father close, and hopefully, one day help mend her broken heart.

CHAPTER ONE

"I've finished, Sydney. Take a look." Kamal, one of the students in Sydney's evening community center art class, paused to dip his brush in turpentine before wiping it on a rag.

Sydney stepped up beside the solemn, dark-haired man to study his completed canvas.

As usual, Kamal had ignored the still life she'd set on a table, consisting of an empty wine bottle, a bunch of grapes, and a wedge of cheese on a pretty plate, and had instead chosen to paint a waterfall. Kamal was obsessed with waterfalls. Throughout the entire year he had painted half a dozen of them, explaining that it made him happy to look at them.

"Well, as waterfalls go, I think this is one of your better ones."

His smile was radiant. "Thank you, Sydney. I think so, too. I'm going to give it to my wife."

"Sydney, what do you think of this?" Mrs. Martinez motioned for Sydney to come closer.

"Very nice, Mrs. Martinez." Sydney paused beside the

white-haired woman who was wider than she was tall. "But why did you paint the grapes red?"

"I didn't want grapes in my picture, so I made them hot chili peppers. See?" The old woman pointed to the blobs of red paint bleeding into the orange cheese. "My grandchildren love red hot chili peppers."

"Very nice. But maybe they love the music group more than the vegetables."

"I don't understand," the older woman said.

"A little joke, Mrs. Martinez." Sydney was grateful when the bell sounded, signaling the end of the evening's class. "I'll see all of you next week."

She picked up her bulging backpack and headed toward the little flat above Colosanti's Deli. During her college days, she'd worked two jobs because Margot had said more money was needed for Hester and Hilda as they established themselves in their new careers. Now she continued working two jobs, teaching second grade while also teaching art at the community center five evenings a week, just so that she could afford to live alone. Though it was small and cramped, it was her very own private space. Heaven, she thought. Sheer heaven to be finally free of Margot's controlling nature and angry, hurtful words.

"Ah, Sydney." Mr. Colosanti greeted her outside his deli. He stood less than five feet tall, with sharp, blackbird eyes and a head covered with gray curly hair that reminded Sydney of steel wool. His white apron fell to his ankles. "Look what I have for you." He picked up a perfect ripe peach and rubbed it on his sleeve before handing it to her. "I've been saving this one just for you."

"You sweetie." She accepted the peach and brushed a kiss over his weathered cheek, causing him to blush clear to the tips of his ears.

As she turned he added, "You have a visitor." He lowered his voice. "Your stepmama. She insisted that I let her in."

Sydney had to fight to keep her smile in place. Everyone in the neighborhood was aware of Margot's sarcasm, and most had sampled it a time or two. "It's all right. I know you had no choice. Thanks for the warning, Mr. Colosanti."

She climbed the steps to her flat and pushed open the door.

Margot stopped her pacing to turn and glare. "How can you bear this dreary place?" She wrinkled her nose and pointed to the fat brown guinea pig in a cage by the window. "It smells like a barnyard in here because of that . . ."

"Gus. The class guinea pig. Nguyn was supposed to have him this week, but his mother is out of town, so I offered to keep him until she got back."

"Of course you did. Just like you used to offer to keep all the stray puppies and kittens that you claimed 'followed you home from school' all those years ago. You still can't resist taking in every stray you meet. I'm surprised you didn't offer to take Nguyn home with you while his mother was away."

"I did. But his aunt is with him."

Margot rolled her eyes. "I swear, Sydney, this place is so depressing."

"I'm sorry you feel that way, Margot. I like it. It's close enough to walk to work in the mornings, and look at my bonus." Sydney held up the peach. "Mr. Colosanti always saves me a piece of fruit. And sometimes, when a customer doesn't pick up a deli order, he lets me have it for my supper."

"And well he ought to, considering the rent he charges for this dump. He should be ashamed of himself. And you. Look at how you spend your days. Teaching second graders who can barely speak English, and then wasting your evenings teaching art to senior citizens."

"They're not all seniors. It's the community center, Margot. Some of my students are young. And you'd be amazed at their talent."

"I don't care if they're all Picassos. You're never going to be anything more than a second-rate, old-maid teacher if you persist in this foolishness."

"I'm single by choice. And I happen to love my job, Margot."

"Do you hear yourself? It's a job, Sydney, not a career. How can you hope to ever meet anyone of substance here? Take Hester, for instance. Since going to work for that new fashion designer, she's been introduced to several famous actors and musicians. She told me that a drummer who plays with the Hot Hunks asked her to meet him for drinks after his band's concert next week. The Hot Hunks. Their music is topping the charts. And my beautiful Hilda is dating Anthony Bellair, the star of that new police drama on TV."

"I believe he's married, Margot."

"He's divorcing. And he's hinted that Hilda could become wife number two."

"That would be number three. He was married briefly to that pretty blond model that he dumped for . . ."

"Whatever." Margot waved off her remark with a quick lift of her hand. "At least Hester and Hilda are putting themselves out there to find men worthy of consideration. How are you ever going to improve your life if you stay in this garbage pit?"

"I didn't realize my life needed improving. I like my life. In fact, I love it."

"Of course you do. Doesn't everyone yearn for a cheap upper flat in a run-down, dreary neighborhood? Doesn't every young woman hope to grow old alone, surrounded by immigrants and losers?"

Margot shot Sydney that icy stare that always managed to freeze Sydney's heart. At least it always had when she was young. These days she was working very hard to move beyond her childish fears of her stepmother, though in truth, she found herself reacting much the same way as she had when she was that frightened child who'd first met the woman and her two angry daughters who would share her life with her father. Deep inside, a lump of fear lodged like a stone in the pit of Sydney's stomach. And though she knew the things Margot said were untrue, she was helpless to fight them. Each insult hurled, each cruel word spoken, grew like an insidious seed in Sydney's soul.

Sydney's best friend, Melanie, called it Margot's venom.

Once unleashed, that snakebite poison rendered the unlucky recipient unable to think or act rationally as they recoiled from the attack.

Sydney had to blink back tears. "Do you enjoy saying cruel things, Margot?"

"I say them because someone has to remind you to grow up and be sensible. Just look at you. You may as well wear a sign that says, *Take advantage of me. I'm gullible.*"

"I'm not . . ."

"Oh, please. Don't deny the obvious. Mark my words. The first down-on-his-luck guy who gives you the time of day will have you wrapped around his finger before you can blink. You'll be bringing him home and feeding him like . . ." She turned toward the cage. "Like your guinea pig there. And if he turns out to be a gigolo, you won't even know what hit you until he's taken your time, your money, and your virtue. When that happens, don't come running to me for help."

"I wouldn't think of asking you to help me." Stung by Margo's cruel words, Sydney crossed her arms over her chest. "I'm sure you had some reason for this visit."

"Two reasons, actually. I'm moving again."

"To a better neighborhood?"

"As a matter of fact, I am. Unlike you, I won't be satisfied until I'm at the very top. I've been packing, and I found a couple of dusty boxes in storage." She pointed to the boxes she'd dumped unceremoniously just inside the door. "I don't know how they survived my first move, since they belonged to your father and I'd thought I had already tossed everything of his. I don't have time to deal with them, so I was hoping you'd set them out with your trash."

"Do Da's things mean so little to you, Margot?"

"They're tattered and torn and filthy." Margot gave one of her famous phony, teeth-baring smiles. "But if you'd like to keep them, for sentimental reasons, be my guest."

She walked to the door, eager to escape what she considered little more than a dungeon. "Maybe after I'm settled we can meet at Hester and Hilda's town house. It has a magnificent view of the river. I'm sure they could introduce you to some of the important people they know. There must be someone who can add a little luster to your drab little life."

When the door closed behind Margot, Sydney dropped down onto a chair, feeling drained and useless, her typical reaction to Margot's litany of petty complaints.

Deciding to forgo supper, Sydney set the kettle on the stove while she nibbled on the peach. Making a cup of tea, she carried it to the coffee table and opened the dusty boxes. Inside was a pile of her father's paint-stained shirts and pants, dull and faded from years of storage. They were too damaged to consider giving to a charity. Though it caused a pain around her heart, she knew she would have to dispose of them with the trash, as Margot had so coldly suggested.

Feeling tears welling in her eyes, she gathered a handful of her father's shirts to her face, wishing she could still smell him. Hearing the faint rustle of paper, she fumbled in the folds and found an envelope in one of the shirt pockets. Inside the envelope she found a fat roll of hundred-dollar bills and a note, written in her father's distinct script.

With eyes brimming, she read the note.

My darling Sydney,

My greatest wish is that you will one day visit my birthplace and discover the love I feel for it. The little village of Innismere is a magical place, as is all of Ireland. Each time I sell one of my paintings, I intend to put a percentage into this special hiding place, the pocket of my favorite shirt, which you gave me. My hope is that, by the time you've grown into a woman, there will be enough for you to travel to that grand country in style and to stay as long as you choose. While you're there, darlin', feel the magic. And believe.

Sydney studied the shirt. It was the one he'd worn in the photograph she still prized above all else. With a smile she unfolded the bills and counted them out. Five thousand dollars. Compared with her meager salary, it was a fortune.

She thought of her stepmother's hurtful words. This was enough to change her life if she chose to. Enough to move to a more modern apartment. To take time away from her job to apply for something more challenging, more glamorous.

If she chose to.

The thought came to her with absolute certainty. She knew without a doubt what she would do with this windfall.

Instead of being sensible, as Margot had suggested, she would throw caution to the wind. She would follow her father's dream and go to Ireland. To Innismere. To find the love that had shone through her father's eyes every time he had spoken of that grand old place. She would sit beside the river Glass and sketch, just as her father had in his youth. And she would feel her father's presence there beside her.

A brief visit to Ireland may not change her life, but it would enable her to store up some glorious memories to warm her heart during the long years to come.

It may be a foolish waste of money in Margot's eyes, but Sydney would have the satisfaction of knowing that she was using the money as her father had wished.

And really, wasn't that worth any price?

CHAPTER TWO

"Welcome aboard Allied America's Flight Two Twenty-seven bound for Ireland."

As Sydney settled into her seat, the flight attendant's voice began the preflight welcome. Sydney fidgeted with her seat belt and then took out the laminated sheet of instructions to follow along in case of an emergency.

When the voice faded, Sydney sat back and took a deep breath. Minutes later, as the plane began to taxi along the runway, she white-knuckled the armrests.

The passenger beside her chuckled. "I've tried that. It never works, you know."

She turned to him with a puzzled frown.

"Trying to lift the plane with the sheer force of your determination." He shot her a rogue's grin. "Half the passengers aboard are doing the same. But it's all up to the pilot now, you see."

She gave a quick laugh, as much at his brogue as that devilish smile, and very deliberately released her death grip on the armrests, folding her hands in her lap. "I didn't realize I was so transparent."

"Oh, it's natural enough. I've done it myself a time or two. But the more I travel, the more I've begun to realize that once I strap myself into one of these big birds, I've given up the control to someone else."

He was wearing torn jeans and a faded tee beneath a rumpled plaid shirt. He was badly in need of a shave and a haircut. Thick, dark hair spilled over the collar of his shirt. The rough stubble of beard added to his shabby appearance. His eyes were a smoky gray, and at the moment they sparkled with unspoken humor.

Sydney found herself drawn to those deep, soulful eyes, while ignoring his unkempt appearance. It was a result of her years of tutoring. At the community center, some of her most talented pupils turned out to be those who least looked the part.

He patted her hand and indicated the sea of puffy clouds outside their window. "You see? We're already airborne."

It was a jolt to Sydney's system to realize the truth of what he'd said. Now that they were high in the air, her fears began to subside. She let out the breath she'd been holding and opened the folder containing the various tours she was considering at the end of her flight.

Seeing them, her seatmate smiled. "Your first trip to Ireland?"

She nodded. "How about you?"

"I'm headed home after two weeks of holiday spent biking, hiking, and touring your lovely land."

She heard the pleasure in his voice. "Your first time here?"

He shook his head, sending shaggy hair dancing. "I've been a time or two. But this time I pushed myself to the limits, climbing higher, biking until I thought my legs would fall off. I can honestly say that the best thing about a holiday is looking forward to soaking my aching muscles once I get home."

"I've heard grand things about your home."

"Have you now? And who's been bragging about Ireland?"

"My father was born there. When I was little, he used to tell me stories about his wonderful, carefree childhood to cheer me up. He used to say he couldn't wait to show me his birthplace."

"Ah. And are you meeting him there?"

Sydney's smile faltered, the grief a sudden, sharp pain around her heart. "He died when I was a teen. But I've never forgotten the joy he felt whenever he talked about Ireland."

"And you're going alone?"

Sydney nodded. "Well, not exactly alone." She indicated her travel bag. "I carry my da's photo tucked away in a little pocket of my purse. I suppose it sounds silly, but I feel like a little part of him is with me."

Her seatmate nodded. "Not silly at all." He lifted a silver chain he wore around his neck. On it dangled a small silver locket. "This was worn by my grandfather, and then my father. Wearing it makes me feel close to both of them."

"That's nice. Are they still living?"

He shook his head. "My grandparents died when I was twelve. My parents when I was in my teens. I miss them still."

"I know what you mean. Even after a lifetime, I'll be able to see my da's face and hear his voice."

"Though you're American, there's a hint of the Irish in your voice, especially when you speak of your da."

Sydney smiled. "I know I should say Daddy or Dad, but it just seems right to call him Da."

The brogue beside her softened. "Mine were Da and Mum. And Granda and DeeDee."

"That's sweet." She leaned her head back and felt her nerves begin to subside until she was pleasantly drifting. Not only had the liftoff gone smoothly, but her seatmate was turning out to be a charming distraction. A distraction that was badly needed at the moment. She was still reeling from her out-of-the-blue decision to leave home, so uncharacteristic for the usually conservative young woman, and from the blistering anger when her stepmother had learned of her plans.

It had been, as always, an ugly scene. But now, she would

put aside all the unpleasantness and just think about what was to come.

It was her last coherent thought before she slept.

"ENJOY YOUR NAP?"

At the deep voice beside her, Sydney's head came up sharply.

She glanced down at the blanket covering her lap. "Did you do this?"

Her seatmate's smile had her heart doing a slow somersault. "I asked the flight attendant to fetch a blanket. They have the air blasting in here."

"Thank you." She sat up straighter. "I can't believe I slept so soundly. I guess I was more tense than I realized."

"Traveling can be stressful."

Especially if your family members call you a fool for even thinking about taking a trip. Though Sydney thought the words, she didn't speak them. It was too personal, too painful, to say aloud. Perhaps because she wasn't at all certain whether Margot had been right or wrong.

"My name is Cullen." Her seatmate offered a handshake.

"Sydney." She felt her hand enfolded in his big palm.

"No ring, I see." He glanced down at her hand, still firmly held in his. "Does that mean no husband?"

"No husband. Are you married, Cullen?"

"I'm afraid I haven't found that special one, yet."

"I'm sure there will be a lovely Irish colleen who will suit you perfectly."

"Someday." He shrugged. "Do you live in New York, Sydney?"

"Yes."

"And what do you do there?"

It was all the push Sydney needed to begin telling him about the children she taught, and the fascinating countries they'd lived in before coming to America, and the harrowing tales they told about their struggles to begin a new life so far away from the troubles and turmoil they left behind.

While she talked, he caught the glow that came into her eyes. "You love your work."

"I do. Is it that obvious?"

"It is, yes. And how do you fill your nights after teaching second graders all day?"

"I teach art at our local community center."

"You're an artist?"

"Not much of one. My da was a gifted artist. I wish I could be like him. But I'm afraid I'm better at teaching than doing."

"But you love teaching others?"

She blushed. "Guilty as charged."

"Don't make light of it. I think teaching is a wonderful gift."

Feeling a wave of self-consciousness, she tried to divert attention away from herself. "Do you live in Dublin, Cullen?"

"I do when I'm working. But my home is in Innismere."

She knew her jaw had dropped. But she was so startled, all she could do was gasp.

Cullen arched a brow. "Have I said something wrong?"

"No. It's just that . . ." She gave a toss of her head. "That's where I'm headed. Innismere. That's where my da was born."

His smile deepened. "Now what are the odds of such a coincidence?"

As the flight attendant began preparing the passengers for their descent into Dublin's Shannon Airport, Cullen laid a hand over Sydney's. "As long as we're both heading in the same direction, why don't you let me drive you to Innismere?"

"I thought you worked in Dublin."

"I do. But for now, I'm still on holiday. Since this is your first time in Ireland, I'd love to show you around. I have a car at the airport," he added. "It would save you the cost of hiring a car and driver. And I promise to deliver you right to the door of your inn. I assume you're staying at the Inn of Innismere, since it's the only decent place in town."

"I am."

"Well then. What do you say?"

She bit her lip. This man was a stranger, after all. Did she risk riding with a stranger for an hour or more?

She knew all the reasons why she ought to refuse. But there was something about this charming stranger that had her warming to him, despite all the little warning bells that were going off in her head.

Sydney shrugged. "Thank you for the offer, Cullen. I'd love to ride with you to Innismere. But only if you let me pay for the gas."

She saw the look of surprise that came into his eyes.

"Now why would you do that?"

"You said yourself you'd be saving me the cost of a car and driver. The least I can do is pay for the gas, since you're providing the car."

He took a moment to consider before the smile returned. "All right. If you insist."

"I do."

And then she was fetching her carry-on and following Cullen from the plane. She pushed aside the nagging little worry that her rumpled seatmate had charmed her into breaking her first rule—to take on no more strays. But after all, she did need a ride, and he was going to the very same town where she was headed. It made perfect sense to pool their resources. And he certainly looked as though he could use the gas money.

Still, she'd broken her first rule.

And to think she'd done it before even setting foot on Ireland's soil.

Tomorrow was another day. A clean slate. Tomorrow was soon enough to swear off strays. Both the two-legged and four-legged variety.

CHAPTER THREE

They drove along narrow ribbons of highway, past ancient ruins, and sailed through pretty little towns and villages with their church steeples gleaming in the sunlight. Everywhere Sydney looked, there were people walking and shopkeepers chatting. They drove by fields of sleek cattle or leggy horses, and Sydney exclaimed over the acres of glorious flowers that grew alongside the roads.

"There's so much to see. And all of it so grand."

Cullen smiled and nodded. "I love traveling the world. But best of all, I love coming home."

"How could you not?" She pointed to the tumble of giant stones in a pasture. "Think about the hundreds of years that have passed, and still those stones remain to let us know that someone once lived there, and made it their home."

"And fell in love there, and married and raised their children. It's easy to forget the very real people who lived and loved, just as people have from the beginning of time."

Sydney sighed. "When you say it like that, it all sounds so romantic."

"Not to spoil your illusions, but people fought and died here, too. Our people were forced to go to war on this very land. We Irish have a bloody history."

"But you endured. You remain. And you thrive."

"We do indeed."

Cullen drove up a long, curving driveway and came to a halt in front of the steps of a charming old two-story inn. The walls were covered with ivy. Flowers of deep purple and palest pink spilled from urns that lined the long front porch and wide steps—a porch dotted with several cushioned rocking chairs.

"Here we are." Cullen popped the trunk and a white-haired man with a ruddy complexion, wearing a fisherman's knit sweater and charcoal cords, opened Sydney's passenger-side door and offered his hand.

When she stepped out, the older man called, "Welcome to the Inn of Innismere, miss. I'm Sean McCarthy. My wife, Bridget, and I manage the inn."

"Thank you, Sean. It's nice to meet you. I can't wait to see the inside of your lovely inn."

Before the man could remove her suitcase, Cullen was there first, hauling it out and carrying it up the steps where he set it down.

"Thank you, Cullen." Sean clapped a hand on the young man's shoulder. "Home from your latest jaunt, are ye, lad?"

"I am."

"Bridget and I have missed you."

Cullen winked at the old man. "Then I'll have to make it up to you by spending more time here." He turned to Sydney. "I'll leave you here to settle in. You're in good hands with Sean and Bridget. If you'd like, I could come by in the morning and show you around the town."

"You're just being polite. I'm sure you have better things to do than act as tour guide for me."

"Nothing would make me happier than to show you my town."

Sydney hesitated for only a moment. "If you're sure you can spare the time, I'd like that. Where shall we meet?"

His smile was quick and easy. "I'll pick you up right here at nine."

Whatever doubt she was entertaining was forgotten under the spell of that smile. "Nine it is." She removed some bills from her wallet. When he tried to refuse them she closed his fingers around them. "A deal is a deal." She offered her hand. "Thank you for driving me here, Cullen."

Seeing the arched brow of the old man, Cullen shot her a wicked grin and a wink before accepting her money and her handshake.

"It was my pleasure."

Sydney felt the quick tingle along her arm, like magic fingers brushing her skin, and she was forced to absorb a rush of heat before he released her hand.

"I'll see you in the morning." With a jaunty salute to them both, Cullen turned and settled himself behind the wheel and was gone before Sean managed to climb the steps and hold the door for her.

If she had any concern about her unexpected agreement to spend more time with a man who was still a perfect stranger, it was swept away by the business of signing in, examining her room, unpacking, and going down to a light supper before finally falling into bed and drifting into a sound, dreamless sleep.

"AH, GOOD MORNING, SYDNEY." THE INNKEEPER, BRIDGET McCarthy, wore a fashionably tailored navy dress and pearls at her throat and ears. Her white hair, short and neat, bobbed at her shoulders. She had the sunniest smile Sydney had ever seen, and a comforting warmth that seemed to radiate from her in waves.

Sydney felt drawn in by that warmth.

"I hope you found your rooms comfortable."

"More than comfortable, thank you, Bridget. They're lovely. I especially love the view from my window."

"Ah, yes. The courtyard. You're here at the best time of year to appreciate it. The gardens are always lovely, but I was just saying to Sean that this year they seem to be at their very best. 'Tis as though pixie dust was scattered over all of Innismere, turning it from pretty to picture perfect." The innkeeper pointed to the front steps, where Cullen stood talking to Bridget's husband. "I believe you have company, Sydney."

"Cullen." Sydney turned hopeful eyes to Bridget. "Do you know him?"

"Know him?" The woman gave a delighted laugh. "Sean and I are his godparents. We've known him from the day he was born. But that's true of most everyone here. Innismere is a small enough town that everyone knows everyone."

"What can you tell me about him, Bridget?"

"Tell you?"

"About Cullen. About his family."

"Why . . ." The woman blinked and seemed to search for something to say to fill the sudden silence. "Why, I can tell you what I'd say about all our young people. Cullen's a fine man who makes us all proud. But then, I'm sure the same could be said about you and yours." She began fussing with the papers on her desk. "Isn't that so?"

"Yes. Of course." Sydney couldn't decide if the innkeeper was flustered or merely being polite. She seemed clearly at a loss for words.

"Will you be joining him now, Sydney?"

"Yes. Thank you." Sydney walked out the door and the two men, who'd been conversing in low tones, abruptly looked up before turning to greet her.

Cullen stepped up beside her. "Ready for your grand tour of Innismere?"

"More than ready." Her heart gave a sudden hitch, and she blamed it on the fact that she was actually here in Ireland, and about to see her father's birthplace. It wasn't, she told herself, because of her handsome tour guide, or the fact that his lips curved in a fascinating smile that reminded her of a rogue. And though he'd shaved, and had exchanged his torn denims for a fresh pair of faded khaki pants and a soft knit shirt, those smoky eyes and killer smile still gave him the look of a dashing hero of one of her favorite romantic novels.

He put a hand beneath her elbow. Instead of guiding her toward his car, he turned toward the ribbon of sidewalk. "I thought we'd walk through the village first, and I can show you a few of my favorite places. Would you like that?"

She'd seen the price of gas, and understood completely. She was glad now that she'd chosen comfortable shoes over stylish ones. "I'd love it, as long as we can stop and eat along the way. I slept in and didn't bother with breakfast."

"I know the perfect place." He kept his hand at her elbow and moved along beside her as they headed toward the heart of town.

It was pleasant, Sydney thought, having this man as her own personal tour guide. His charming brogue, his warm laughter, and those strong fingers brushing her skin were a lovely bonus.

"This is Kelly's Bakery." They paused to return the smile of a young girl placing a pretty platter of cupcakes in the display window. "Mary Francis Kelly bakes the finest barmbrack."

At her questioning look he chuckled. "You aren't familiar with barmbrack?"

"I never heard of it."

"It's a sort of tea cake, with bits of fruit that are soaked in a pot of tea overnight."

"It sounds . . . interesting," Sydney said with a very doubtful look.

"Oh, you of little faith. I can see that you'll have to give barmbrack a try another day. Mrs. Kelly's is the finest in the county. And she's passing her skill along to her three lovely granddaughters." Cullen lifted a hand to the older woman behind the counter, who waved back. "We'll stop by later and indulge ourselves."

They walked on, strolling leisurely, as though they hadn't a care in the world. And, thought Sydney, she didn't. Right this moment, there was nothing more pressing than a walk through her father's hometown. And wasn't that grand indeed? For a person who'd known nothing but hard, demanding work since she'd been a teen, it was a particularly pleasant feeling.

"This is Brennan's beauty shop."

Three women in smocks seated in chairs while their hair was being cut or colored or permed waved their hands, and both Cullen and Sydney waved back.

"Is everyone always so friendly?" Sydney avoided a dip in the sidewalk and Cullen's hand was instantly there beneath her elbow to keep her steady.

"And why not? They know everyone who passes them on the street, unless"—he turned to her with a grin—"'tis a visitor like yourself, in which case they'll make it a point to get to know you soon enough." His eyes danced with laughter. "Could you say the same about New York?"

She chuckled. "Don't be fooled by the throngs of people. New York's not as big and impersonal as you may think. Though there are a lot more strangers walking the streets of my city, those of us who live there have formed our own sort of bond. Take Mr. Colosanti, who rents me the flat above his deli. It's a comfort to know that he looks out for me. And though he doesn't say much, he takes care of me in his own fashion."

"And why wouldn't he?" Cullen looked her up and down. "I'm sure there are any number of men in New York who'd be wanting to look out for the likes of you."

She nudged his shoulder. "I don't think you mean that in the same way I do."

"Trust me." He caught her hand. "If I were your neighbor, I'd be looking out for you, Sydney."

It seemed the most natural thing in the world for him to continue holding her hand as they walked along, talking and laughing. She found herself telling him about the special fruit Mr. Colosanti always saved for her, and the way he offered her any leftover deli orders, especially when she'd arrived home too late to think about fixing dinner.

"Does he charge you extra for the food?"

"He wouldn't think of doing such a thing."

"Well, I've heard that big-city businessmen often take their customers for all they can."

"Mr. Colosanti isn't like that. He's more like my uncle or grandfather than my landlord."

"I see." He smoothly changed the subject. "It's glad I am to be sharing this visit with you."

As they rounded a corner they breathed in the wonderful fragrance of freshly ground coffee that drifted on the breeze.

"I promised you breakfast," Cullen said. "And it doesn't get any better than Riley's. Will Riley's brother, Frank, has a farm just outside of town, which guarantees that the eggs are fresh, as is the bread his wife bakes every morning."

Instead of going inside the small restaurant, Cullen indicated a pretty arrangement of tables and chairs in a small courtyard. The minute they were seated, a young girl hurried over carrying a tray containing cups and carafes, one of coffee and one of tea. After taking their orders, she disappeared inside, leaving them alone.

"Good timing." Cullen sipped his tea. "With the workers already at their offices, and lunch still hours away, we have the place to ourselves."

"It's such a clean, pretty town." Sydney looked around with interest. "And everyone so friendly and cheerful."

They enjoyed a leisurely breakfast in the sunlight, and laughed at the antics of a bird determined to snatch a few crumbs from beside Sydney's chair. Hunger overcame fear and the bird stayed until every last crumb had been devoured.

When the waitress brought their bill, Sydney snatched it off the table and set some money on it.

Cullen shook his head. "Have you forgotten? I invited you to breakfast."

"But it's my vacation. I came here fully prepared to pay my own way."

"And now you're paying mine, too."

She laughed. "You had an egg and some toast. I don't think it will break the bank. I'll let you buy next time."

"Promise?" He laid a hand over hers.

"Promise." She looked up into his laughing eyes and felt the curl of heat all the way to her toes.

If there were a photograph of charm in the dictionary, it would be a picture of Cullen at this moment, Sydney thought. He could melt her heart with nothing more than the touch of his hand and that wonderful, heart-tugging grin.

If she weren't careful she'd start to believe in silly fairy tales, and happily-ever-after endings. But in truth, everyone knew that vacation romances were like wisps of fog, evaporating into the air without a trace. Vacation romances lasted for a few days or weeks, and then ended in strained good-byes.

"Well." She got to her feet and reluctantly took leave of the little restaurant. "It's been a lovely tour, Cullen."

He caught her hand. Squeezed. "The tour has only just begun. The best part is yet to come."

CHAPTER FOUR

·◯·

"Now you'll see the rest of Innismere," Cullen said with a smile. "All three square miles of it."

"It may be small, but the streets are so clean." Sydney studied the scene before her. It was a busy, bustling little town. Windows of shops sparkled. People smiled as they greeted one another.

Cullen paused to pick up a torn brown paper bag that had blown across the sidewalk in the breeze.

As he tucked it into his pocket, Sydney laughed. "Do you always pick up litter?"

At her question he arched a brow. "Doesn't everyone?"

Sydney thought about his remark as they continued along. No wonder the little town looked so clean. If everyone did as he did, there would be no litter. Not just in a small town like this, but everywhere.

Such a simple thing, but she found herself admiring him for it.

She looked up at the church on the hill, its ancient silver cross gleaming in the sunlight. To one side was a low building.

Before she could ask a question, Cullen explained. "Classrooms."

"Ah. A school for the parishioners."

"Not at all. This school is available to all the children." At Sydney's look of surprise Cullen added, "Some years ago the church and the city fathers agreed that it would be a better use of money if the church would donate the school to the town. Before that, students who wanted a public-school education had to take a tram to nearby Kerryville. Now they can remain in their own town and simply walk to school."

"Their parents must be thrilled."

"Indeed. As are the teachers."

Sydney pointed. "What's on the opposite side of the church, in that little fenced enclosure?"

"Come on. I'll show you." Keeping her hand tucked in his, Cullen led the way up the hill. As he swung open a gate, Sydney could see that they were in a little cemetery. Rows and rows of old and new grave markers were neatly spaced in a lovely area beside the church, on a sliver of land that looked out to the water.

Letting go of Cullen's hand, Sydney moved eagerly among the gravestones, searching for her father's family plot. When she found it, she dropped to her knees and stared hungrily at the names and dates of her father's ancestors.

Cullen stood a little away, allowing her some privacy.

She glanced over her shoulder. "I'll never be able to remember all these names and dates."

He pulled some papers from his pocket and produced a pencil. "Hold this over the engravings, scribble with the pencil, and you'll have a perfect replica."

She did as he suggested, and held the papers up, reading the names and dates of birth and death as clearly as if they'd been photographed.

"Oh, Cullen. What a fine idea. I'd have never thought of this."

He made a grand bow. "Happy to be of service. Now you have the names of your ancestors, and their dates of birth and death."

Her eyes brightened as she got to her feet and tucked the papers in her pocket. "Tell me about the river below."

"'Tis the river Glass."

She nodded. "My father used to tell me stories about it. How he loved sitting along the banks of that very river and sketching all the lovely sights that caught his eye."

"And now you're here and you can do the same, if you've a mind to."

She hung her head as a wave of sadness washed over her. "I'd always hoped to do it with my da beside me."

He put a hand beneath her chin, lifting her face to his. "You said yourself his picture holds him close. Who's to say he won't be right there with you as you sketch?"

He could see her mood beginning to lighten once more.

"Come on." He caught her hand, swinging it as they turned back toward the town. "I believe I promised you some of Mary Francis Kelly's barmbrack."

"Yes, you did."

"And I'm known to one and all as a man of my word."

Long before they reached the heart of town Cullen had her laughing at the silly stories he told her about his antics as a child.

"It sounds as though you were a handful for your parents."

"They were up to the challenge. I'm told my own father was a wee bit wild, until my mother tamed him." He looked at their joined hands. "How about you? Did you ever drive your parents to despair? Or were you always the perfect child?"

"Perfect?" That had Sydney laughing and shaking her head. "According to Margot, I'm a perfect failure."

"Who is Margot?"

"My stepmother. My mother died when I was five, and my father told me he was overwhelmed with grief and guilt, thinking he'd never be able to do all the things a mother should do. When he met Margot, she had twin daughters who were older than I, and he was convinced that by marrying Margot, I would be surrounded by, not one, but three substitute mothers."

"That sounds like the perfect solution to a motherless child."

Sydney shrugged. "You know what they say. Man makes plans while the universe laughs."

He arched a brow. "Trouble in paradise?"

She struggled to shake off the sad mood that always seemed to grip her when she thought about her relationship with her stepmother. "Something like that." She took in a deep breath. "Bridget McCarthy told me that she's your godmother."

"That she is. She claims she put a hand on my wee head in church and vowed to see me safely through this world. I'll tell you this. She's worked tirelessly to keep that vow."

"It must be wonderful to have someone so devoted to you."

"It's grand. She was a dear friend of my parents, and I've always considered her a second mother." Cullen looked up. "Ah, here we are."

Seeing the sign outside the bakery, they paused before stepping inside.

The room smelled of bread baking, and the wonderful fragrance of cookies and cakes.

"I've been expecting you." Before they could say a word, Mrs. Kelly reached across the counter. On a small crystal plate were two slices of what appeared to be some sort of fruitcake.

Cullen shot her a wicked grin. "I haven't said what I wanted yet."

"No need," she said with a laugh. "It's always the barmbrack for you, Cullen."

"So it is. Mrs. Kelly, I'd like you to meet a visitor to our town. Sydney, this is Mary Francis Kelly."

"It's so nice to meet you, Mrs. Kelly. Cullen's been teasing me all day with promises of your excellent baking."

"That's so like our Cullen. 'Tis lovely to meet you, Sydney. Welcome to Innismere."

Sydney accepted a small slice of cake from the plate and,

as she bit into it, couldn't stop her sigh of pure pleasure. "Oh, this is delicious. It absolutely melts in my mouth."

"Thank you. I needn't ask Cullen what he thinks. He samples one every time he stops in."

"I don't think one slice will be enough today, Mrs. Kelly. You'd better give us three or four, at least. And two cups of your special herbal tea in those carryout cups."

When she'd filled a pretty little handled bag with two lidded cups of tea and several slices of barmbrack, Cullen accepted the bag. Before he could reach into his pocket, Mrs. Kelly stopped him. "Not a penny, Cullen. Now be on your way, the two of you."

She turned to Sydney. "I hope you'll come back often while you're a guest in our town."

As Cullen held the door, Sydney called over her shoulder, "You can count on it, Mrs. Kelly."

Cullen caught Sydney's hand and led her toward a small park overlooking the river. Seated on an old stone bench, they sipped steaming tea and nibbled their cake, tossing the crumbs to the birds that darted about their feet.

"Do you come here often, Cullen?"

"Every chance I have. Whenever I'm in town, I find myself drawn to the park and the river."

"My father had such fond memories of this town."

"Did he tell you why he left?"

Sydney shrugged. "He used to tell me that as much as he loved it here, he was driven to seek fame and fortune in America."

"It drove so many of our fine citizens to leave their beloved homeland. And did he find what he was seeking?"

Sydney looked away. "I think, after my mother died, he lost that drive to succeed. He took solace in his work, and I know that he loved being with me as much as I loved being with him. But nothing was the same after her death. It was as though he was simply marking time until he could be with her again."

Cullen took her hand, his thumb running lightly over her wrist. "Theirs must have been a great love."

"It was. Though I've forgotten so much about my mother, I can still see the way she glowed when my father walked in the door. And I can hear the catch in his voice when he called her his special angel."

Cullen picked up the last slice of cake and held it to her mouth. "Take the first bite. We'll share."

She did as he asked, and watched as he popped the rest in his mouth.

"I guess this means it's time to head back to the inn. I'm sure Bridget and Sean will be wondering if you're ever coming back."

"I hope they're not worried."

"They know you're safe with me."

Something in the way he said it had Sydney glancing up at his face. He merely smiled down at her before taking her hand and leading her back along the curving sidewalk, regaling her with tales of his teen years in town.

At the door to the inn, Cullen paused. "I wish I could join you for dinner here tonight. Bridget's pot roast is the finest in town. But I have an appointment."

"You don't need to apologize. You've given me an entire day. And for that I thank you. But I'm sure you have better things to do. It's time you got back to your busy life."

His grin was quick. "My busy life can wait. I can't think of a better way to spend my time than with you, Sydney."

Before she had time to realize what he was planning on doing, he lowered his head and brushed her mouth with his. It was the merest touch of lips to lips, and yet she felt the heat of it all the way to her toes.

Caught off guard, her eyes went wide as she clutched his waist.

His eyes remained steady on hers as his arms came around her and he drew her closer, covering her mouth in a kiss so hot, so hungry, she felt all her breath backing up in her throat. A sizzle of pure energy rippled through her, heating her blood, speeding up her heartbeat until it was throbbing at her temples.

As she returned his kiss, she had the strangest sensation.

As though she'd found home in this man's arms. A haven in his kiss.

Very slowly he lifted his head and stared down at her with a probing, almost fierce look in his eyes.

With her head still swimming, she heard the deep timbre of his voice. "Spend tomorrow with me."

"You have a life . . ."

He touched a finger to her lips to still her protest. At once she felt another quick rush of heat and stepped back, lifting her face to his.

"How about a picnic on the banks of the river Glass? You can bring along your paints and canvas, and you can sit and sketch, just as your father did."

"Oh, Cullen. I can't think of anything I'd rather do."

"Good." He lifted a hand to brush a strand of her hair from her eyes. At that simple touch, his eyes narrowed on her, and she felt certain he was going to kiss her again.

She wanted him to. Wanted that tingle of warmth, that feeling of belonging in his arms.

Instead he took a step back. "Tomorrow then. I'll be here around ten."

"I'll be ready."

She watched him walk away, wondering at the way her heart was thundering.

How would she ever be able to wait until ten o'clock to see him again?

How had she lived so long without a warm, vital, exciting companion such as this?

Fanciful, she thought, with a hand to her heart. Hadn't she always been too much of a dreamer?

Now she was seeing way too much in a man who was simply being generous to a visitor to his town.

Still, a girl could dream, couldn't she?

CHAPTER FIVE

•⬭•

"Ah, there you are. Good morning, Sydney." Bridget Mc-Carthy, wearing a fresh red and white polka-dotted dress and her ever-present pearls at her throat, greeted Sydney as she descended the stairs. "There's breakfast in the dining room."

"Thank you, Bridget." Sydney followed the wonderful fragrance of coffee to a sunny room, where the table was set with fine crystal and lace, and a sideboard displayed bacon, omelets, toast, and an assortment of jams.

As Sydney filled her plate, Bridget called, "With the weather so fresh, feel free to take your meal out to the court-yard if you'd like. We've a lovely old table and chairs set up amidst the gardens."

Sydney couldn't resist the offer, and found herself sitting on a cushioned chair, breathing in the wonderful perfume of flowers as she enjoyed steaming coffee and a breakfast fit for a queen. A cheese and spinach omelet, with strips of thick, crisp bacon, and cinnamon toast slathered with strawberry preserves. It all seemed so rich and decadent, considering her usual breakfast consisted of an apple or occasionally a slice of toast with peanut butter, eaten on the run.

As a fountain splashed nearby, she sat back. What if she had resisted the urge to follow her heart and come to her father's home? What if she'd done as Margot suggested and used the money for something practical? She would have never known such a beautiful, magical place as this existed. She would have missed this amazing adventure.

Amazing? It was priceless. And there was no denying that Cullen added to the magic. Without him she would have never stepped into Mary Francis Kelly's bakery and sampled her marvelous barmbrack. Without Cullen she may have missed the tiny church cemetery where her ancestors were buried.

And today . . . Her heart skipped a beat at the promise of a picnic along the banks of the river Glass. That tantalizing thought had kept her awake for hours last night. Or had it been something . . . or someone . . . else that had robbed her of sleep?

She glanced at her watch and hurriedly finished her breakfast. It was because of her nerves that she'd overslept again this morning. Of course, she could blame her sleep pattern on the distance she'd traveled, and the time change. But in her heart, she knew the truth. Her interrupted sleep was the fault of her very handsome, attentive guide who'd begun to haunt even her dreams.

She carried her dishes indoors, then hurried up to her room to fetch her paints and canvas. With everything packed neatly in a handled carryall, she descended the stairs to find Cullen conversing easily with Bridget and Sean.

He looked over with a quick smile. "Right on time. Ready?"

"I am." She turned to Bridget. "Did Cullen explain that I won't be back in time for lunch?"

"That he did."

Sydney arched a brow, but Cullen merely smiled and offered his arm. On the porch he paused to pick up a large wicker basket. And then, hand in hand, they left the inn and walked along the curving walkway until they came to a stone path leading down to the river.

Cullen guided her down the steep slope. "Did your father tell you how the river came by its name?"

Sydney nodded. "He said the river is so named because it's always clear as glass. Even in the deepest part of the river, you can see clear to the bottom."

"That's so." When they reached the river's banks, Cullen pointed, and Sydney paused to study a jumble of silvery pebbles at the very bottom of the river. As she watched, a school of fish, swimming by in perfect symmetry, caught sight of her shadow and broke ranks to dart in different directions. The sight of them, nervously flitting about, had her laughing.

She set her carryall in the grass and knelt alongside the water.

Cullen was watching her. "Did your father tell you about the river Glass's famous Slipper Rock?"

"Only that it's so named because it's shaped like a lady's slipper. Is there more?"

"Much more." Cullen stared into the distance. "The light shining through the waterfall gives the rock the look of crystal. But up close, it's made of natural granite, with bits of quartz and mica that add the shimmer of jewels. Slipper Rock stands guard in the middle of the river, and has for as long as the town has been here. Many here believe it possesses magical powers."

"Magic?" Sydney was instantly intrigued. "What sort of powers?"

"For one, it's said that when lovers are touched by the light shining through Slipper Rock, they remain true to that love for all time."

"Do you know of any such lovers?" Intrigued, her eyes widened.

"I do indeed. Both my parents and grandparents claimed to have been blessed by the light. Of course, that's true of many of our good citizens. But the story took on greater importance several generations ago." Cullen's voice lowered. "People still talk about the beautiful young maiden in our town who wed the great love of her life. Within days of their marriage, her young husband went off to war, leaving her with his babe growing within her. On that sad day he promised that one day he would return and look for her on the banks of the river Glass. She gave him her word that she would wait for him here. And so she waited, day after day, month after endless month, until at last her wee babe was born."

"Did her husband ever come back?"

"He did. Gravely wounded, he saw his love swimming in the river and, heedless of his wounds, called out to her, tore off his bloody tunic, and leapt into the water, eager to join her. She, in turn, began swimming toward him. By the time they came together in the deep, he'd lost so much blood 'tis said the river ran red with it, and Slipper Rock reflected that same bloodred hue from the setting sun. The young husband was too weak to continue. And though his wife made a valiant effort to get him to shore, the weight of his dead body dragged her down to the depths. They were found the following morning, still locked in one another's arms."

Sydney looked stricken. "How sad to think, after waiting so long, they had no time to be together."

Cullen arched a brow. "When you think of all the lovers torn apart by war, these were the lucky ones, for they died together, and together they remain for all eternity."

"At least there's that." Sydney thought about it for a moment. "What about their baby?"

"My grandfather? He was raised by some good villagers and lived a long and productive life."

"Your grandfather!" Sydney's hand flew to her mouth to stifle her little cry. "What an amazing story. And what good friends and neighbors." She glanced at the sparkling water. "Do you believe the lovers are still here?"

"I believe their spirits remain."

"What makes you believe? Have you ever seen them?"

"I haven't. No. But there are many who claim to have seen them on a moonlit night. And they say that whoever is lucky enough to see them feels a sense of peace and quiet joy that soothes even the most broken heart and soul."

"What a sad and lovely story." Sydney held a hand to her

eyes to shade the sunlight glinting off Slipper Rock. "Is that a waterfall?"

"It is." Cullen offered his hand. "If you'd like, we can cross the bridge and get a better view from the other side."

Sydney took his hand and walked with him across a lovely old wooden bridge that spanned the river at its narrowest point.

"Oh, my." She drew in a breath at the spectacular view from this side of the river, with the town and its church spire up on a hill reflected in the still, quiet waters. Slipper Rock, gleaming in the sunlight, appeared to be made of spun glass.

"I really have to paint Slipper Rock from here. With the light just so, and the water shimmering around it."

"All right." Cullen watched as she began setting up her easel and opening her paints. "If you've no need of me, I'll leave you to it."

A short time later Sydney glanced around to see Cullen lying in the shade of a tree, hands beneath his head, eyes closed, peacefully sleeping. He looked, for all the world, like a man who hadn't a care.

Was that why she was so drawn to him? Was it the fact that he wasn't driven to spend all his time charging full-speed ahead, eager for more and more success, like most of the men she knew?

She couldn't think of another man who would be willing to spend his days in the company of someone he'd just met on a plane, content to show her around his town instead of getting back to his own life.

She'd expected to feel self-conscious having him around while she painted. But as she began to sketch Slipper Rock, and then apply paint to canvas, she was soon so absorbed in her work, she completely forgot about the man dozing in the shade of a tree. But his grandfather's story would remain in her heart forever.

FROM BENEATH HALF-CLOSED LIDS, CULLEN WATCHED SYDney as she lost herself in her work. The sun bathed her in a halo of light, turning the ends of her hair to burnished flame. She was slender as a willow, her head tilted at an angle as she studied the scene before her. There was an ease, an unhurried rhythm to her movements that fascinated him as she sought to capture the flow of the river, the shimmering rock, and the trees that lined the shore.

She was born to paint. It was obvious in the dreamy smile that played on her lips, the joy that danced in her eyes. This was no weekend artist, hoping to take home a memento of her trip to a new land. This was a woman whose entire being was focused on capturing the scene before her.

Though he could hardly wait to see the finished product, he forced himself to remain where he was, pretending to sleep. A gifted artist like Sydney needed her own space, her own time, to fulfill her creation.

He thought about the strange twists and turns his life had taken. His trip to America had been a spontaneous decision, spurred by the urging of his friends. But he hadn't realized how much he needed to get away until he'd been gone for over a week, and found himself hiking trails that challenged him as nothing had before.

He'd needed that. Not only the challenge, but the time spent in the wilderness, clearing his mind of all but the essentials. He felt he was returning home with a clear sense of purpose.

And then he'd met Sydney. Sweet, innocent, generous Sydney.

He was a firm believer that there were no accidents in life.

His lips split into a warm smile as he drifted on a cloud of contentment.

SYDNEY SET ASIDE HER BRUSHES AND STRETCHED HER arms over her head.

The motion had Cullen sitting up abruptly.

She turned to him. "Sorry. I woke you."

"I had a lovely nap. Have you finished?"

"Yes. Would you like to see?"

He stood and walked close, studying the painting with a critical eye.

"You've captured it perfectly."

For someone like Sydney, who had spent a lifetime being criticized for her attempts to emulate her father's craft, Cullen's words wrapped around her heart like a warm hug. "Thank you."

"You're welcome. Hungry?"

She nodded.

"Good. While you clean your brushes, I'll prepare our picnic."

From the hamper Cullen removed a blanket, which he spread beneath the tree.

While he worked, Sydney kicked off her shoes and sat on the bank of the river while she cleaned her brushes, and then her hands.

As soon as her fingers touched the water, it began to ripple and shift, as though a boat had passed by. She looked up, but there was nothing and no one around. Still, the water rolled and tumbled on shore, directed by some unseen source.

Sydney watched as the images that had been reflected in the river changed. Instead of the trees, the bridge, and Slipper Rock, the reflection became a blue sky and clouds that shifted and changed until they resembled old-fashioned robe-clad figures that reminded Sydney of characters from her childhood stories about kings and queens, knights and maidens.

She looked across the river, expecting to see the town and the church, with its steeple. What she saw was a lovely castle shimmering in the sunlight.

"Cullen."

Hearing the urgency in her voice he hurried over. "Something wrong?"

"No. I just want to know the name of that castle."

She pointed to the hill.

Cullen gave her a gentle smile. "I see it's true what they say about an artist's imagination."

"Are you telling me you don't see the . . . ?" She blinked and looked again, only to see nothing but the church and the town.

"Come on." Laughing, Cullen caught her hand. "Your picnic awaits you, m'lady."

She joined in the laughter and allowed him to lead her to the shade.

When she dropped down on the blanket, he handed her a stem glass.

"Champagne?" Her laughter faded. "Is this a special occasion?"

"It is. Didn't I tell you?" He touched his glass to hers. "Just being with you has made this day special, Sydney."

As she sipped the bubbly champagne, she felt her heart do a little hitch. Though his words were spoken lightly enough, she'd seen something in his eyes. Something smoldering that had her blood heating, and her pulse racing.

Even though he'd given her no reason to think otherwise, she had the most overwhelming sensation that this was about to become, indeed, a very special day for both of them.

CHAPTER SIX

Sydney sipped the champagne, loving the feel of it, like bubbly liquid silver on her tongue.

Seeing the dreamy smile on her lips, Cullen paused. "You've had champagne before, haven't you?"

She shrugged. "Once, on my twenty-first birthday. But I don't remember it being this smooth." She stifled a laugh. "Or this fizzy."

Cullen uncovered a plate of tender chicken, and another of freshly baked croissants.

Sydney's eyes widened. "I think I see the handiwork of Mrs. Kelly's bake shop."

"Busted. I guess I won't try to take credit for any of this." He shot her a wicked grin. "I told her I wanted to impress a very special person, and she promised to take care of everything."

A very special person.

At his words, Sydney felt her heart do a little dance. Had that been a slip of the tongue? Was he aware of what he'd revealed?

She held the words close to her heart. Cullen thought she was a very special person.

Cullen lifted yet another lid. "Let's just see what else she made for us."

Sydney gave a laugh of delight. "Surprise. Barmbrack."

"I'd have been very disappointed if she hadn't tucked a few slices of it in the basket." He opened a covered container and held up two perfect peaches. "I suppose these are here to make us feel healthy."

"This is an absolute feast." Sydney dug into her chicken and sighed with pleasure as she buttered a croissant.

Beside her, Cullen enjoyed the meal before sitting back, sipping champagne, and nibbling his favorite treat. "I'm so glad I had this chance to show you some of my town."

Their eyes met over the rims of their glasses, and Sydney's heart took a quick, hard bounce at the look in Cullen's eyes.

"I'm glad, too. I can't think of a better tour guide."

"The tour's not over yet. Have you had enough food?"

At her nod, he gathered up the remains of their picnic and returned it to the hamper. Setting it at the base of the tree, he caught her hand. As she got to her feet, a man stepped from the woods, leading two horses.

"Just in time, Patrick." Cullen hurried forward and exchanged a few words with the man before accepting the reins of the two horses and leading them toward Sydney.

He indicated a white mare with streaming mane and tale, bearing a fancy saddle trimmed in silver and gold braid. "This is Princess."

Sydney reached up to rub the mare's forelock. "She looks like a princess."

"And has the regal bearing of one, as well. I hope you can ride."

"I grew up in the country. Margot used to refer to my father as a gentleman farmer."

"My kind of man." Cullen offered his hand and Sydney easily pulled herself into the saddle.

Beside her, Cullen mounted a roan stallion. "And this is Prince."

"I should have known. He looks every bit a prince."

Cullen leaned over and caught Sydney's hand. "I thought you'd enjoy seeing parts of my village that most tourists never get to see. The terrain is rough, but the horses are surefooted, and I promise you, the view is worth the effort. Are you game?"

She squeezed his hand. "I wouldn't miss it for the world."

Cullen wheeled his mount and Sydney did the same. With Prince leading the way, Princess easily followed as they disappeared into the cool darkness of the woods.

As she followed along, Sydney had a sudden memory of her favorite childhood dream. She was a princess, riding a white steed beside her prince in their magical kingdom. Though she knew it was just a fantasy, she couldn't shake the feeling that this day had become more than special. It was, in fact, a magical day.

The trail climbed up and up until at last the hills leveled off and the dense wall of trees thinned, giving way to a spectacular view of the land far below.

They dismounted, and Cullen tethered the horses to a small sapling before leading her to a flat, rocky promontory overlooking the valley.

Sydney's voice was hushed, as though in a sacred place. "Look at the waterfall below. And see the way the sunlight sparkles on Slipper Rock. It looks as though it's made of glass. Oh, and there." She pointed. "Your village looks like a beautiful miniature under a Christmas tree." She touched a hand to his sleeve. "Oh, Cullen, what a wonderful place. It's all so lovely, it takes my breath away."

Cullen closed a hand over hers and turned to look directly into her eyes. "It isn't the only thing that takes my breath away."

When she started to draw back he lifted his hand to her cheek. Just a touch, but she couldn't move. Could hardly dare to breathe, as he lowered his face to hers and covered her mouth with his.

This kiss wasn't at all like the first time. The heat, the fire, was instantaneous and so all-consuming it had them both trembling with need.

The hands at her shoulders were strong as she was drawn against a solid chest. The mouth moving on hers was warm and seductive, making it impossible for her to resist. Not that she thought about resisting. From the moment Cullen touched her, she found herself wanting more.

With a sigh, she wrapped her arms around his waist and gave herself up to the pure pleasure of his touch.

He framed her face with his big hands and pressed soft, moist kisses over her forehead, her cheek, the corner of her mouth. When he moved lower to her throat, she nearly purred with pleasure.

"Sydney." His fingers tangled in her hair and he drew her face up while he stared down into her eyes. "What am I going to do about you?"

She smiled. "You make me sound like a problem to be solved."

He lowered his hands to her shoulders, holding her a little away. With a puzzled frown he muttered, "Or an unexpected treasure to be cherished."

She reached a finger to the frown line on his forehead. "I don't think a treasure would bring a look like this."

"That's just it. You are a treasure. One that deserves only the best." He surprised her by tugging on her hand. "Come on."

"What about the horses?"

"Patrick will return them to their stable. I want you to see my secret place."

A secret place. Sydney was so excited by his words she found herself speechless.

Without a word, she allowed herself to be led deep into the woods.

He led her along a steeply curving trail through low-hanging branches of flowering trees and across a field of waist-high wildflowers until they stepped out into a meadow lush with grass. Far below was the river Glass, and shining like a clear-crystal sculpture was Slipper Rock. All were bathed in the most amazing light.

Sydney caught her breath. "Oh, Cullen. This is an artist's paradise. I have to come back here one day with my supplies and paint that scene."

"I'll bring you whenever you'd like. For now, come and see this." Cullen pointed to a spot a short distance away. It was a small, circular ancient stone ruin.

She turned to him with shining eyes. "I wonder how old this is."

"Ancient. I've always considered it holy ground."

"Do you know anything about its history?"

He shook his head. "Only that whenever I'm here, I feel as though I'm in another world."

"Is that what makes this your secret place?"

He shrugged. "Ever since I was a boy I've been drawn to this spot. I used to climb here whenever I could." He led her toward a low, flat rock and settled himself beside her. "I'd sit here and wonder what my life would be like when I was all grown up."

"And now, here you are." She wrapped her arms around her drawn-up knees and smiled at him. "Is your life everything you'd hoped it would be?"

"It is, yes. And now that you're here, it's even better than I'd hoped." He lifted a hand to her face, tucking a stray strand of hair behind her ear.

She plucked a shamrock that had grown up the side of the rock, and then a second and a third. "I used to make daisy chains when I was a little girl. I believe I'll make a shamrock chain for you."

She braided the vines and twisted them about Cullen's wrist.

"I love it. Thank you." He touched his palm to her cheek and smiled down into her eyes.

When she returned his smile, he leaned close and brushed her mouth with his. Suddenly he drew back as though burned and got abruptly to his feet.

Sydney was startled by his sudden mood shift. "What's wrong?"

"This isn't wise." He took a step back. "Every time we're together, I tell myself to take care. But whenever I get too close to you, all my good intentions go out the window."

"And you think being here with me is wrong? Are you afraid of a little thing like a kiss?"

"If you think a kiss is a little thing, you're wrong." His frown grew. "What I'm thinking, what I want, would shock you. And a fine woman like you deserves better. We'll go now."

She stood her ground and touched a finger to the frown line that marred his brow. "What if I want the same thing you want, Cullen?"

He shook his head in denial. "That's the champagne talking."

She caught his arm when he started to turn away. "The champagne hasn't affected me. My head is every bit as clear as the air up here."

"Sydney . . ."

She placed her hand over his mouth. "How can I convince you of what I want?"

Her eyes sparkled with humor as she lifted herself on tiptoe to brush her lips over his. At once her smile dissolved as his arms came around her, crushing her to his chest.

His mouth moved over hers with such hunger, all she could do was return his kisses with the same urgency.

When at last they came up for air, his eyes narrowed on her. "Now do you understand? This isn't a game, Sydney. If you insist on staying here, you know where this will lead. Is that what you want?"

Because she couldn't seem to find her voice, she merely nodded.

"I'm giving you a chance to refuse." His words were little more than a whisper. "I want you to be sure, Sydney. For once we cross this line, we can never go back."

"I'm sure."

He framed her face with his big hands, staring into her eyes. When at last he lowered his face to hers, Sydney anticipated the heat that always accompanied his kiss. What she hadn't counted on was the sudden shocking sexual jolt that had her body trembling with need.

As he drew out the kiss, her fingers tightened around the front of his shirt, drawing him ever closer, needing desperately to feel his body against hers.

"You taste like ripe peach," he whispered inside her mouth.

"And you taste . . ." Like sin, she thought, as he took the kiss deeper, causing her mind to go blank.

His hands moved over her, bringing the most amazing heat. She could feel her flesh growing hot, her blood flowing like fire through her veins. Even her breath felt too hot, burning her lungs, causing her to gasp for air.

"I want you, Sydney." His words were a growl against her throat, causing her heartbeat to roar in her temples. "Only you."

She thought of all the things she wanted to say to him, but her thoughts disappeared like wisps of fog when he began nibbling kisses in the little hollow between her neck and shoulder. And when his mouth moved lower, to her breast, she was incapable of any thought at all. All that was left to her was need. This grinding, primitive need that had her arms wrapping around his neck while she offered him everything.

Greedy, desperate, they dropped to the soft cushion of the meadow and lost themselves in the wonder of their unleashed feelings. Like two starving wanderers, they feasted. And like two lost souls they came together, filling up all the lonely places inside themselves.

His kisses were by turn soft and seductive, and then, without warning, fierce and demanding. His hands—those big, clever hands—moved over her, bringing her the most amazing pleasure. And still, she wanted more. She wanted everything he had to give.

"I've known," he whispered against her throat, "since I first met you, that I would have to have you. But I want you to know that I fought it. I wanted this to be your choice."

"It's what I want, Cullen. You're what I want. Only you."

Her voice, choked with emotion, nearly broke on a sob as he took her up and over the first peak.

There was no time to catch her breath before he took her again, up and up until she clutched at him, desperate for release.

As he entered her she went very still, and for a moment the only sound was their breathing, as he stared down into her eyes with a look of such passion, such desperate longing, it pierced her heart.

"Come with me, Sydney. Stay with me. Love me."

She did. Moving with him, climbing with him, as they scaled a high, steep mountain peak until their lungs burned from the effort. And when at last they reached the very pinnacle, they seemed to step back for the space of a heartbeat, savoring the intense pleasure that was building until it was almost pain. Then, unable to hold back a moment longer, they stepped over the very edge. And soared.

THEY LAY TOGETHER IN A TANGLED HEAP OF ARMS AND legs, breathing labored, heartbeats ragged.

"That was . . ." Cullen leaned up on his elbow and reached a hand to the damp hair at her neck. "Incredible."

She managed a dry laugh. "Did the earth move?"

"It did. Yes. I felt it."

"Good. At least I'm not the only one."

"Ah, but you are the only one, my love. The only one who has ever touched my heart like this."

In the silence that followed, he looked down at her. "Am I heavy?"

Instead of waiting for her reply, he rolled to one side, drawing her into the circle of his arms.

She lay perfectly still, absorbing the feel of being held in his embrace. She could hear the strong, steady beat of his heart inside her own chest, keeping perfect time to hers. His warm breath feathered the hair at her temple.

She could lie just so forever. The thought was so comforting, she let out a long, low sigh.

He laid a big palm on her cheek. "Are you weary after such a day? Do you want to go?"

"No. Do you?"

"What I want . . ." He smiled before brushing his mouth over hers. "Is you, love. Just you."

And then, without a word, his kisses became more urgent, as did his touch, as he led her down and down to a deep, dark cavern of sensual delight, to the most exquisite secret place of all. A place where only lovers can go.

CHAPTER SEVEN

•❍•

"When I was a lad, I hiked all these fields." Cullen held Sydney's hand in his as they followed the trail back to the spot beside the river where they'd left the picnic hamper.

She liked having her hand held. Liked the easy way he'd caught it, and then continued holding it, even swinging their hands as they walked. In fact, she liked everything about being with him. "It's fun to think about you out here, doing all the things kids do, Cullen. It's such a peaceful place. But so rugged. Did you ever get lost?"

"Never. How could I, with the river Glass to show me the way back?" At the bank of the river he paused to pick up the hamper before leading her across the bridge.

As they headed toward town, Sydney turned for a last look at the majestic river, meandering about the countryside like a shiny ribbon. Slipper Rock gleamed in the setting sun, a beacon of light as dusk began settling over the land. "I know what you mean. My father said he could follow the river for miles and never feel as though he'd left home." She sighed. "I felt that way about the farm when I was young. When Margot sold everything and we moved to the city, I wandered around feeling like a lost soul for such a long time."

"What happened to finally make the city feel like home?"

She thought about it. "The friends I made. Gradually they took the place of my family. And the big city that I'd found so overwhelming eventually narrowed down to a few blocks of shops and apartments. My neighbors, my students, became the family I craved."

Cullen nodded. "It was the same for me. When I lost my parents, I knew I could always count on the good people of Innismere to fill the hole in my heart, the same way they'd once cared for my grandfather."

"How did your parents die?"

"In a plane crash over Scotland."

"How awful."

He nodded. "But it comforted me to know they'd gone together. It had always been their wish to be together for all time. And now, they are."

"That's such a lovely thought. And the townspeople watched over you after you lost your parents?"

He nodded. "They were my aunts and uncles, cousins and godparents. My family and my friends." He squeezed her hand. "But friends can only do so much. They can't ever replace that special someone every heart craves."

Sydney felt a tingle of warmth all the way to her toes. Could she be that someone for him? Could he be that someone for her?

As they passed beneath a wooden pub sign, Cullen paused. "How about a pint at O'Malley's?"

Sydney laughed. "If you'd like."

He led her through a rowdy crowd, pausing at every table to call out a greeting, and to introduce Sydney to one and all. After a few minutes it became impossible for her to remember so many smiling faces, so many happy people, and all of them like old friends, so warm and easy with both her and Cullen.

They managed to squeeze into a small, cramped booth near the kitchen. As a pretty blonde in a bright green apron passed by, Cullen held up two fingers, and within minutes she set down two frosty bottles. In the space of half an hour, nearly every patron of the pub had stopped by to joke with Cullen, and to give his pretty date a few lingering looks.

"They approve," he whispered.

"Of what?"

"Not what. Who. You, of course."

"Oh." She managed to blush. "And here I thought maybe I had grass in my hair, or a piece of chicken stuck in my teeth."

"Well, you do." He rubbed his thumb over her lips and saw her eyes widen before her laughter returned. "But I still say they were looking over my lady."

My lady. The phrase did something strange to her heart.

"Here you are." A giant of a man, with red hair and a smile that turned his craggy boxer's face from stern to that of a jovial pixie, caught Cullen's hand in a death grip and squeezed. "Annie said she'd seen you come in with"—he turned to Sydney—"a rare beauty. And my Annie doesn't lie."

"Sydney, this is . . ."

"O'Malley," the giant said. "Welcome to my pub."

"Thank you. It's wonderful."

Seeing their bottles empty, the man signaled for a waitress. "Will you have another?"

"Sorry. One's my limit." Cullen got to his feet and reached for Sydney's hand.

As he dug his hand in his pocket, O'Malley closed a hand over his arm. "Not on your life. Your money's no good here." He reached around Cullen to offer a handshake. "It was lovely meeting you, Sydney. I hope you'll come back again often."

"Thank you. I'd like that."

As they maneuvered their way through the crowd, there were shouts and calls of good-bye.

After the wall of sound inside the pub, the silence of the evening was a welcome relief.

They walked through the town, smiling and answering those who called out a greeting. It was, Sydney realized, so pleasant to feel like a part of the ebb and flow of this pretty little country village.

I could easily make this town my home.

The thought caught her by surprise, though she couldn't say why. But then, after all, this had been her father's home. Why couldn't it be hers, as well?

She was so deep in thought she was caught by surprise when she found herself outside the inn.

Cullen released her hand and set down the picnic basket before retrieving her art supplies.

He studied the painting of Slipper Rock before asking, "Would you mind if I kept this?"

She arched a brow in question.

He merely gave her a devilish smile that wrapped itself around her heart and squeezed until she could hardly breathe. "A memento of this very special day. Do you mind?"

That had her blushing furiously. "Not at all. If you'd really like it, it's yours."

He brushed a quick kiss over her mouth just as Sean stepped through the door.

The old man looked from Cullen to Sydney. "Well, here you are. Bridget and I were just wondering when you'd be home."

Home. Sydney couldn't help smiling. After only a few days, wasn't that exactly how this lovely inn was beginning to feel?

Cullen gave the old man a wink. "I knew I'd better get her back before you and Bridget sent out a search party."

Sean chuckled. "We knew she was in good hands with you, lad." He turned to Sydney. "Bridget has tea and scones, if you've a mind to join her."

"Thank you. I'd like that." Sydney glanced at Cullen, feeling suddenly shy. "How about you?"

He shook his head. "I'll be leaving now." With Sean watching, he leaned close to drop a quick kiss on her cheek.

Swinging the hamper in one hand, he lifted the other in a jaunty wave before walking away.

Sydney stayed where she was, staring after him until she realized that Sean was watching her a little too closely. Her cheeks felt suddenly hot. Lifting her hand to her face, she turned away and strode into the inn.

"SO, YOU SPENT THE DAY AT THE RIVER?" BRIDGET FILLED A lovely china cup with tea and passed it across the table to Sydney, before indicating the plate of scones. "Did it cast its spell?"

"Spell?" Sydney looked up from her tea in surprise.

"Most first-time visitors to our town find the river Glass one of our most intriguing points of interest. Not only because of the lovely bridge, which offers a very different view from the other side, but the river itself, which has the most calming influence on people. It's especially appealing to people from big cities who hear only automobile horns and sirens and voices raised in anger."

Sydney smiled. "I can relate. And to tell you the truth, I thought the river did cast a spell over me." Her smile grew. "I thought I saw a castle instead of the church on the hill, and robed women and men coming down out of the clouds."

Bridget took her time selecting a scone. "Did you tell Cullen what you thought you saw?"

Sydney nodded. "We shared quite a laugh at my artist's imagination."

"Ah, yes. You're an artist." Intrigued, Bridget set aside her tea. "Tell me what you painted."

Sydney shrugged, feeling suddenly self-conscious. "I'd intended to paint everything. The river, the trees reflected in its water, even the town up on the hill. But in the end, all I found myself drawn to was Slipper Rock."

"You painted our rock? May I see it?"

Again that self-conscious shrug. "Cullen asked if he could keep it. He said he wanted it as a memento of our day together."

Bridget was fairly beaming. "Why, I think that's quite romantic."

Sydney relaxed. "I'm glad you think so." She blushed furiously. "I mean . . . I thought so, too, but I was afraid I was just being silly."

"Romance is never silly." Bridget gave her a gentle smile. "Why don't we take our tea out on the patio, where we can sit and watch the setting sun?"

Sydney followed the older woman outside, grateful for the shifting shadows that would cover the range of emotions she knew were visible in her eyes.

This entire day had been like a lovely dream. She only wished she and Cullen could have spent the night together, as well.

Later, as she made her way up to her room, she shivered with anticipation. There was always tomorrow.

IT WAS EARLY MORNING WHEN CULLEN PACED THE BACK room of the gallery while an old man sat at a table peering at a canvas through a lighted magnifier. Cullen had wanted to come by the previous night, but he'd known it was too late for his old friend to be up. And so he'd waited, and counted the hours until he'd felt it safe to assume that Paddy would be up and dressed and would have finished his morning tea.

Now he counted the tiles on the floor, and then the overly loud tick-tock of the clock on the far wall. It was the only sound he could hear. The room, like the old man, had gone eerily silent.

When at last the old man looked up, his lips curved into a wide smile. His eyes behind the thick lenses of his spectacles glinted with unrestrained excitement.

"It's as you thought, lad."

Cullen released the breath he'd been holding. "You've no doubt, Paddy?"

"None at all, lad."

The two shook hands before Cullen plucked the now-framed canvas from the worktable and tucked it under his arm. "Thank you, Paddy."

"You're welcome, lad. Shall we begin the celebrations?"

"It's a bit premature for that, Paddy. I haven't said a word to her."

"Then ye'd better get crackin', lad. Yer father and grandfather would've never taken this long."

At the mention of his father and grandfather, Cullen touched a hand to the gold locket tucked beneath his shirt and felt the warm shimmer of heat in his palm. Just the mere thought of those two old scoundrels had him sweating.

"You're right, Paddy. But Sydney's not like any other woman I've known. Despite the fact that she's been on her own for some time now, there's something very shy and sweet about her."

Just thinking about her had him smiling broadly. She was such a contradiction. Independent, yet somehow sheltered. So smart and sure of herself, and yet it was obvious that her stepmother still managed to exert a great deal of control over her life. Cullen sensed that this journey to her father's place of birth was her first halting step toward a declaration of independence. But a woman like Sydney needed time.

"If I move too quickly, she may run like a rabbit."

"I say go for it, lad. Ye could always sugarcoat it with a bit of romance. Women just can't deny that need for a romantic interlude, especially while on vacation in a foreign land. Hearing a man declare his love shouldn't cause a lass to bolt now, should it?"

The two shared a laugh.

"You're right, Paddy. I've been so focused on taking this one step at a time, I almost overlooked the obvious. After yesterday, I'm pretty certain that she could be persuaded. Especially if I remember the romance."

"Then stop wasting time with an old man like me and get yerself back to the lass before ye lose her altogether."

With a light heart Cullen let himself out of the gallery and drove away from town and out into the wild Irish countryside.

When he arrived at his home he carefully set the painting on the mantel and stepped back to study Sydney's work.

Hadn't she perfectly captured Slipper Rock, right down to the way the iridescent light shimmered through the bits of stone, making it appear as though made of glass?

He stood, hands in his pockets, gaze centered on the painting. It fit. It all fit. If he'd had any doubts before, there were none left.

Suddenly he turned away and headed out the door.

He'd spent most of the night tossing, turning, and finally pacing his room. Before dawn he'd been up and about, seeing to mundane things until he was sure Paddy would be available. All these hours he'd been too anxious to think about eating. He'd barely paused to shower and dress before heading to the gallery. Now he couldn't think of a thing except this need to see Sydney.

He'd wanted to tell her what he suspected yesterday, but something had held him back.

No more hesitation, he thought resolutely. He would tell her now.

And then he would ask her the question.

Her answer would definitely change both their lives forever.

CHAPTER EIGHT

◦⬯◦

"What are we to make of this weather?" Bridget cleared the glass-topped patio table, setting their empty breakfast dishes on a silver tray before refilling Sydney's cup with steaming tea. "It's as though you brought endless sunshine with you." She settled herself across the table and glanced at the lush flowers in her gardens. "I've never seen my planters looking so fine."

"Just admit that you have a green thumb." Sydney nibbled a scone, wondering if Cullen would call.

"I'd like to take all the credit, for I dearly love to garden. But I've never seen them looking like this before." The older woman peered at Sydney over the rim of her cup. "Are you sure you haven't brought some sort of enchantment?"

"I feel like I'm the one who's been enchanted." At Sydney's confession, the two shared a laugh.

"So." Bridget picked up the thread of their conversation from the previous night. "You're an artist like your father."

"Oh, how I wish that were true. I'm afraid I'm much better suited to teaching than to actually painting a masterpiece."

"And what makes you think that?" Bridget looked up sharply.

"My stepmother, Margot, never lets me forget it. She constantly reminds me that artists and teachers don't earn as much as tradesmen, and that my father's pursuit of his dream denied her the life she deserved. She said if my father had been a truly gifted artist, they would have lived like the rich and famous, instead of spending a lifetime on a farm in upstate New York."

"Is your stepmother poor then?"

That had Sydney chuckling. "Not by most standards, but then, nothing is ever enough for Margot. To hear her tell it . . ."

Sydney's words trailed off as Cullen came charging out the back door of the inn looking like a man on fire.

He descended the steps and halted in front of Sydney, struggling to catch his breath.

"Well, look at you . . ." Bridget fell silent when she realized that Cullen wasn't even aware of her presence. His fierce gaze was fixed on Sydney as though she were the only person left on Earth.

"I'll just take these dishes out of your way." Bridget picked up a tray laden with the remains of Sydney's breakfast and let herself into the kitchen.

Once there she summoned Sean, and the two of them remained by the open window, unconcerned about the fact that they were blatantly eavesdropping.

SYDNEY'S FIRST REACTION WAS A SENSE OF ALARM. THE fierce look in Cullen's eyes, and the fact that he was breathing heavily, had her hand going to her throat. "What's happened, Cullen? Tell me what's wrong."

"Wrong?" He blinked, and in that instant, his frown gradually turned into a smile. "Oh, there's nothing wrong, Sydney. Everything is so right."

"You're not making any sense."

He walked closer and caught her hands in his. "What

would you say if I told you that you're a very gifted artist, Sydney?"

"I'd say you were crazy."

"I am. Crazy for you. A friend of mine who is an art critic looked at your work. He called it brilliant. I know now that you're the one."

"The . . . one?"

He nodded. "The one I've been waiting for."

"Cullen . . ."

He touched a finger to her lips to silence her protest. "Just listen, Sydney. I need to say this. All of it. Before I lose my nerve." He took in a deep breath. "When I met you on the plane, I sensed there was something special about you. I tried to dismiss it, but each time I was with you after that, the feeling became stronger. Your kindness. Your generosity. Especially your generosity. And then yesterday . . ." He shook his head, remembering. "Yesterday convinced me. Please believe me when I tell you that I really wanted to wait until I could make this as special as you deserve. But I've been up all night thinking about you, about us, and I couldn't wait another hour. So . . ." Still holding her hands he dropped to his knees on the stone patio. "Sydney, will you do me the honor of being my wife?"

"Wife?" The word came out in a whoosh of air, as though at any moment she would stop breathing altogether. "We've only just met. We barely know one another."

"I know everything I need to know about you, Sydney. Please say yes."

"You . . . want to marry me?"

"I do. More than anything in this world."

"Cullen." Sweet heaven. She felt her eyes fill with tears, and found that she couldn't speak a word over the sudden lump in her throat.

He got to his feet and gathered her close. "I've made you cry."

"It's all right." Her words were muffled against his chest. "They're . . . happy tears."

"Truly?" He lifted her face to his and stared into her eyes. "Then you won't reject me out-of-hand like some crazy man? Even though I've caught you by surprise, you'll consider my proposal?"

"Consider it?" She sniffed and felt more tears springing up. "Oh, Cullen." She wrapped her arms around his neck and held on fiercely. "Yes. Oh, yes." Against his cheek she whispered, "If you're crazy, then so am I. Of course I'll marry you. I'll marry you any time, any place you say."

"Oh, my darling girl." His hands encircled her waist and he swung her around and around before setting her once more on her feet and kissing her soundly. "You've made me the happiest man . . ."

The ringing of his cell phone had him looking startled, until he suddenly reached into his pocket and stared at the number. "No. Oh no. Not Dublin. Oh my sweet Sydney, in all the excitement, I forgot about one of the most important meetings of the year. I can't afford to miss this."

He turned away slightly to say into his phone, "Sorry. Running late. I'll be there in an hour."

He pocketed the phone. "I had it on my calendar. I should have waited. But I was so blinded by . . ." He dug into his shirt pocket, looking puzzled. "Not this, too. I've left it on the dresser."

"It?"

He framed her face with his hands. "The ring. Actually my grandmother's ring, and then my mother's. And soon to be yours." He leaned close and brushed his mouth over hers.

They came together in a blaze of passion, kissing, clinging, until at last they moved slightly apart, both laughing like children. Both struggling for breath.

Cullen pressed his forehead to Sydney's. "I have to leave, but only for a few hours. When I get back, I swear I'll do this the right way. I'll make it up to you. It will be as romantic as you deserve. We'll marry at the city offices today."

"Today? You want to marry today? So soon? Is that even possible?"

"Of course." He nodded. "Now that I've found you, I'm not about to let you get away. And if we don't wed today, we'll have to wait the entire weekend, until they open again on Monday." He had a sudden thought. "But if you'd like to have your family witness our wedding, we could have a second wedding, a church wedding, later. Would you like that?"

She gave a breathless little laugh. "This is all happening so fast, I can't think." She brought his hand to her heart. "Feel what you've done to me."

At the wild beating he lifted her hand to his heart. "Listen to mine. It's thundering even harder."

"That's from running."

"All right. It's from running. But it's also because of you, my love. You've made me the happiest man in the world, Sydney."

He started to turn away, then turned back with a look of horror. "The ring wasn't the only thing I forgot. In my excitement, I left my wallet at home, too, along with all my money. I'll never make it to Dublin and back with half a tank of gas. I'll have to go back . . ."

"Here." Sydney reached into the pocket of her skirt and peeled off a number of bills. "This should do it."

He was already shaking his head. "I can't accept . . ."

"You have no choice. You said yourself you're already late. Go ahead, Cullen. If we're about to get married, my money is yours anyway."

He laughed and accepted the money before lifting her hand to his lips. "Not only are you the sweetest woman in the world, but you're the most generous, too." He started away, calling over his shoulder, "No matter how late I get back, we'll make it official. And then, if you'd like, we'll celebrate with the entire town."

He turned back and rushed to her side. "I just had a thought. Here." He slipped the wilted shamrock chain from his wrist and placed it on Sydney's. "Wear this to remind you of me until I can replace it with diamonds and rubies."

And then he was gone, racing around the side entrance of the inn as though the very devil himself were after him.

Minutes later Sydney heard the roar of his engine. And then there was only silence.

BRIDGET AND SEAN TURNED TO ONE ANOTHER WITH matching looks of astonishment.

Before her husband could say a word, Bridget touched a finger to his lips. Her words were a hushed whisper. "Not a word of this to anyone. 'Tis none of our business. Not until Cullen chooses to make it public."

The old man nodded, before turning away and going off to find something that would keep him so busy he wouldn't have time to enjoy a bit of gossip with his neighbors.

SYDNEY DANCED UP THE STEPS AND LET HERSELF INTO THE inn. Seeing no one around, she felt a tiny twinge of disappointment. She would burst if she didn't soon share her news with someone.

Her family. However distant Margot and her daughters were, they were all the family Sydney had. And at the moment, she needed to tell someone about Cullen.

In her room she dialed her cell phone, seeing Cullen's dear face before her. He'd been so happy, so eager when she'd accepted his proposal.

And why wouldn't she accept? Hadn't she known, almost from the beginning, that he was a very special man? Every moment spent with him had become magical. He made her laugh. Made her feel as though she were the only woman in his world. And yesterday her heart had been overflowing with love for him.

To think that he returned that love. It was almost more than she could take in.

"Yes. Hello."

At the sound of Margot's voice, Sydney was forced to swallow before she could say, "Margot, it's Sydney."

"I can read my caller ID. You sound out of breath. Are you in some kind of trouble?"

"Trouble? Oh, no. In fact, I called to tell you my good news. I'm in love. His name is Cullen. And he's asked me to marry him."

For the space of several seconds there was an ominous silence.

"Did you hear . . . ?"

Margot's tone was sharper than usual. "I suppose this Cullen is a native?"

"Native? You make him sound like some sort of savage."

"He lives there? In Ireland?"

"He does. In Innismere."

"I see. Your father's sleepy little hometown. I suppose that would make him seem all the more attractive to you."

"What's that supposed to mean?"

"You can't deny that you've spent a lifetime fantasizing about visiting your father's birthplace. I would think any man living there would seem . . . a larger-than-life romantic figure."

"That isn't what attracted me to him."

"Really? Is it his success then? What does this Cullen do for a living?"

Sydney stared up at the ceiling, wondering just how to respond. "I'm not sure. He works in Dublin."

"As a banker? A lawyer?"

"He didn't say."

"He didn't say?" Margot's tone hardened. "You're about to marry a man and you don't even know what he does for a living. What about his family? Do they approve?"

"I . . . don't know. His parents are dead."

"Any siblings? Aunts? Uncles? Cousins?"

"I'm not . . ."

"I certainly hope you've met at least some of his family and friends."

"I haven't, but . . ."

"Wait. You've met nobody important in his life?"

"Well, Bridget, the innkeeper here, is his godmother."

"Would that be a fairy godmother?" Margot's tone grew

more sarcastic by the word. "You've done it again, haven't you? You've taken in a stray, and now you can't part with it."

"Stop that, Margot. Don't be so cruel. Cullen is no stray. He's a lovely man who . . ."

"Just tell me this, and I'll be convinced, Sydney. Tell me that he's spent a fortune taking you to the finest restaurants and clubs."

"I'm not interested in such things."

"All right. Has he presented you with an engagement ring fit for a queen?"

Sydney lifted her wrist, to examine the wilted shamrock chain around her wrist. "Margot . . ."

The voice on the other end of the line sucked in a deep breath. The voice was pained. "And above all, please don't tell me that you gave him money."

"Well, I . . ." Sydney's words came out in a rush, eager to explain. "Maybe a little. But I was the one who insisted. He didn't want . . ."

"Stop right there. You've said enough. Let me finish the story for you. He made romantic overtures, but never happened to have any money when the bill came, so you insisted on paying. Maybe you've even loaned him more money for one reason or another, whenever he had another sad story. And all you got from this man was an empty promise. Can you deny any of this?"

"I can't, but . . ."

"No buts, Sydney. I'm betting that he even suggested that you rush into a quick marriage, so that he can claim half of everything you own."

At the silence that followed that statement, Margot's voice grew ominous. "Don't you see? He has you pegged for a rich tourist, who won't miss a few hundred dollars here or there. All he has to do is give you a few hours of his time, and take you to some local places that don't cost him anything, and you're hooked. And now he's even coaxed you into considering marrying him. It's the oldest scam in the world and you've fallen for it. Didn't I warn you before you left? You're so easy to read. You may as well have 'sucker' tattooed on your forehead. My advice to you is to get out of there as quickly as possible, before this gigolo relieves you of the rest of your money."

"He's not like that at all. He's not what you think, Margot."

"Isn't he? What's Cullen's last name, Sydney?"

At the silence that followed, Margot's tone seemed to lower a full octave. "I see. Another detail you can't supply. You're such a silly, romantic, love-starved fool. Go ahead, Sydney. Stay there in that fabled hometown of your father's. Marry your Prince Charming, who will turn out to be a fortune hunter. But don't come running home to me when you wake up alone and humiliated, without a penny to your name."

"You don't understand . . ." Sydney's only thought was to defend Cullen, and to defend herself. But even as the words formed in her mind, she couldn't speak them aloud. All of them sounded pale and empty beside the rich, ripe, colorful accusations Margot had just hurled. "It isn't like that at all, Margot. It's just . . . Oh, how can I make you see . . ."

With tears streaming down her cheeks, she struggled to find the words to convince her stepmother. It was several minutes before Sydney realized the line had already gone dead.

But not as dead as her poor heart.

She dropped the phone and sank to the edge of the bed, sobbing into her hands as Margot's hateful words played over and over in her mind.

CHAPTER NINE

Once the seed of mistrust had been sown in Sydney's mind, it began to grow and fester like a poisonous weed until it took over everything good and beautiful. It became impossible for Sydney to think about anything else. All the sweet and wonderful things she'd found so lovable about Cullen were swept aside by the venom of Margot's words.

Margot's questions demanded answers. Answers that had Sydney inwardly wincing.

Had she ever seen Cullen actually pay for anything?

At Mrs. Kelly's bake shop, that sweet woman had refused his offer to pay for his barmbrack. Why? She appeared to be a successful businesswoman. It was her job to accept pay for her work. How could she make any money if she gave away her pastries? Unless, of course, she already knew that Cullen couldn't afford to pay.

What about the lovely picnic basket? Had that good woman provided that free of charge as well? Or had he suggested that he would pay her later, when he came into some money?

And then again at O'Malley's Pub. Cullen had appeared

to make an effort to pay, but the owner had stopped him. Why? What was going on here?

Now that she thought about it, other than the picnic, and O'Malley's and Riley's, Cullen hadn't taken her anywhere. At least no place where she could actually meet his friends and have a conversation.

She'd begun their relationship by insisting on paying for his gas, and he'd appeared to grudgingly accept. Had it all been an act to set a trap for an unsuspecting tourist?

Since arriving in Innismere, they had walked everywhere. Not that she'd minded. She couldn't fault Cullen for that. It had been her wish to see her father's town. And what better way than on foot?

She'd thought it all sweet and charming.

Now, Margot's words gave her no peace.

She knew absolutely nothing about the man who had asked her to be his wife. Not his last name, nor what he did for a living, or even where or how he lived. And hadn't she felt as though his godmother, Bridget McCarthy, had been keeping secrets about him? She never gave Sydney a direct answer to even the simplest question about Cullen.

Did everyone in this town know him to be a con man? Had they been watching his latest conquest while secretly laughing behind the silly tourist's back?

And on top of everything else, there was his insistence that they marry quickly. Was that designed to keep her from asking any questions?

Shattered beyond belief, Sydney suddenly scrolled through her cell phone until she found the number for the airline. Minutes later she had booked a flight home, even though it would cost a fortune to change her ticket from the original scheduled return.

She glanced at her watch. She had just enough time to pack and get to the airport in Dublin.

Dublin. For a moment her poor heart stopped beating. Dublin was where Cullen had told her he was going. Had that been a lie, as well? And all that business about forgetting his wallet. Forgetting his grandmother's ring.

Lie, upon lie, upon lie. And she had willingly believed every word of it. In fact, she'd lapped it up like a starving housecat.

Or a love-starved fool.

She absorbed the pain around her heart and pressed a hand to the spot.

Then, taking a deep breath, she reached for her suitcase and began hastily tossing her belongings inside.

When the suitcase was closed, she again scrolled through her phone menu and called for a car to drive her to Dublin.

Giving a last look around the lovely room, she opened the door and descended the stairs.

Seeing no one around, she left a note on the closed guest book, saying she was departing at once and was leaving for Shannon Airport in order to catch the evening flight home.

Bridget had her credit card information. Sydney hoped the woman was honest enough to refuse to charge her for the time she hadn't spent there. Of course, she had every right to charge Sydney the full amount. Whatever Bridget's decision, Sydney decided that it would be worth any price just to have this humiliating scene behind her.

A car pulled up to the curb and Sydney climbed into the backseat.

"Dublin, please. Shannon Airport."

"Yes, miss."

As they drove through the town, Sydney found her gaze drawn to the old church on the hill, seeing in her mind's eye the simple cemetery and the neat rows of headstones, many of them bearing the names of her ancestors.

She had nearly shamed all of them. Thank heaven Margot had brought her to her senses in time to spare her any further humiliation.

She blinked, seeing again the lovely old castle of her dreams, and the robed men and women looking like kings and queens riding across the sky on winged clouds.

She would have to do something to curb her wild imagination.

She leaned her head back and closed her eyes, trying to

blot out all the images that began playing through her mind. Images of a tall, handsome rogue with the most wonderful smile and that charming sense of humor that never failed to touch her heart.

No wonder he'd been so charming. It had all been a well-rehearsed act. And all of it designed to steal the heart of some pathetic, love-starved tourist, just ripe for a summer romance.

SHANNON AIRPORT WAS BUSTLING WITH PEOPLE, AND ALL of them in a hurry.

Sydney made her way to the assigned terminal and was surprised to find the passengers already boarding. Grateful that she'd made it in the nick of time, she stepped into line and presented her ticket to the agent before following the others aboard the plane.

Once seated, she leaned her head back and closed her eyes against the sting of tears that threatened. She'd had such hopes for this journey to her father's birthplace. She'd spent all of his hard-earned money for her own selfish gratification. And what did she have to show for it? A few days in Ireland. A visit to her ancestors' gravesites. And . . . she felt the hot sting of embarrassment . . . a romantic whirlwind, designed to dupe anyone foolish enough to believe in love at first sight and happily ever after.

At least she'd managed to escape before the final humiliation. How would she have ever explained marriage to a complete stranger after she woke up to find herself alone and penniless in a foreign land?

"Oh, Da." With a sigh she opened her purse and took out the familiar photograph. Just the sight of her father, shirt rumpled and stained, that wonderful smile on his handsome face, had her pain of embarrassment growing deeper. "I'm so sorry. I should have listened to Margot's warning. I almost fell for the oldest trick in the world."

"Love is no trick."

She looked around, wondering at the sound of her father's voice, spoken aloud.

The seat beside her was empty.

She studied the photograph, seeing her father's face, his wise, loving eyes. "Cullen doesn't love me. Like Margot said, it was all a con. Why, we only knew each other for a couple of days."

She closed her eyes, recalling her father's words, spoken so often after they'd lost her mother. "I knew, the moment I saw her, that she was the one for me. Love, true love, doesn't need time. Nor rhyme or reason. With true love, the heart knows."

Sydney sighed aloud. "I thought I knew. But, as Margot said, I was an easy mark."

"How could Margot know, Sydney? Only those caught in the grip of love can know what's truly in the heart."

"I can't trust my heart, Da."

"If not your heart, what can you trust?"

Sydney stared at the photograph, and would have sworn that her father winked.

"Da . . ."

His words were like a soft, gentle breeze, whispering across her face. "Believe, Sydney. Listen to your heart and believe what it tells you."

As his words washed over her, she unbuckled her seat belt and started up the aisle.

The flight attendant stopped her with a hand to her arm. "You'll need to be seated, miss. We're about to depart."

"I've changed my plans. I need to get off the plane now."

"Sorry. Once the cabin door is sealed, we can't allow anyone to leave. You'll have to take your seat. Hurry now."

"But . . ."

"Now," the attendant said sternly. "Or I'll be forced to call security."

Hearing the roar of engines, Sydney made her way back to her designated seat and fastened her belt. As the plane started along the runway, she could no longer hold back the tears. They streamed down her face as she pressed her father's photo to her heart and whispered, "Oh, Da, I've made a horrible mistake. And now, Cullen will never know why I left him without a word. Oh, what have I done? Da, I do believe in love. I do believe what my heart is telling me, but it's too late. Unless there's a miracle, Cullen will never know."

Choking back sobs, she buried her face in her hands.

She felt a gentle touch to her shoulder, and her father's voice whispering, "Believe."

A voice came over the intercom. "This is your captain speaking. Due to a mechanical failure, I'm afraid we must return to the terminal. I'm sorry for this inconvenience, but the safety of our passengers is always our primary concern."

Stunned, Sydney lifted her head and watched as the plane made a slow turn and retraced the route to the terminal, where the passengers were ordered to deplane and await transfer to another, later plane.

As she followed the others past a throng of interested bystanders, one man separated himself from the crowd and started toward her.

His eyes showed the strain of tension as he caught hold of her upper arms and drew her close, burying his face in her hair.

"Sydney. I thought I'd lost you."

"Cullen." She took in a breath, wondering where to begin.

Before she could say a word, he gathered her close. "When Bridget told me you'd checked out, I drove like a maniac, desperate to get here in time. When I realized I was too late, I fell to my knees in despair. And then, just as I'd lost hope, I felt someone touch my shoulder and I heard a man's voice say, 'Believe.' I looked around, but there was no one near. And then I experienced this strange sense of peace, and I knew without a doubt that you would return to me. In almost that same instant I heard the announcement that your plane was returning to the terminal, and I knew in my heart that everything would be all right."

She lifted her head to meet his eyes. Her own swam with

tears. "It was the same for me. One minute I was filled with despair, and the next I heard the captain speaking and knew that I'd been given a second chance to make things right." She touched a hand to his face. "I need to explain why . . ."

He closed a hand over hers. "Not now, love. There are no words needed. Just come with me. Please," he added when she arched a brow. "And I promise you'll soon have the answers to all your heart's questions."

CHAPTER TEN

◦⬯◦

The drive from Dublin to Innismere seemed to take no more than a moment in time. No sooner had Sydney leaned her head back and closed her eyes than Cullen was taking her hand and helping her from his car.

She looked around in surprise. "Where are we?"

"This building houses our town hall and courthouse." He led her up the steps.

Once inside they crossed to a pair of ornate double doors. Cullen held the door for Sydney, and she looked up to see a man in judicial robes just stepping into the chambers.

"Ah. So this is the one?" the stranger said to Cullen.

"Indeed. Thank you for taking care of this on such short notice."

The white-haired judge winked. "Always happy to be on Cupid's side. Especially when Cupid is assisting the history of our fine town." He turned to Sydney. "Do you have any questions?"

"Dozens of them." She nodded. "But first, shouldn't I fill out some forms?"

He held up a handful of documents. "So you have."

When she looked at them, she could see her own hand-writing.

The judge smiled. "I must ask if you are here of your own choice."

Believe. The word played through her mind.

She glanced at Cullen before saying softly, "I am."

"And you, Cullen? This is what you desire above all else?"

"With all my heart."

"Let us begin." The judge picked up a book and began reading in a strange language.

"Gaelic," Cullen whispered.

Sydney's eyes widened as she heard her name spoken, and then Cullen's, before the judge returned to the ancient tongue.

When he had finished, he closed the book and held it out to them. "Will you swear upon all that is holy that you will abide by the laws of the land as you begin your journey together as husband and wife?"

Sydney and Cullen placed their hands on the book while raising their right hands and agreeing.

The judge produced a magnificent ruby and diamond ring. "Bridget McCarthy brought this to me. I remember your mother and grandmother wearing this very ring on their wedding days. It is more than a ring. It is a symbol of hope for all in this town."

"I'm in Bridget's debt," Cullen whispered as he placed it on Sydney's finger before lifting her hand to his lips.

Seeing the braided shamrock bracelet still on her wrist brought a smile to his eyes. "But this lovely vine means more to me than precious jewels."

Before Sydney could respond, the judge said, "Blessings on the two of you." He glanced at his watch. "Just in time. 'Tis the stroke of midnight. A minute more and I'd have turned into a wise old owl."

Adjusting his glasses, he turned away and disappeared into his chambers, while Sydney turned to Cullen with a look of alarm. "Was he joking?"

"You'll have to ask him the next time you see him." With

a wink, Cullen caught Sydney's hand and the two of them dashed out of the courthouse.

Despite the late hour, the street was alive with people holding candles who began clapping and cheering as the couple made their way to Cullen's car.

Once inside he turned to her with a smile. "Wave to all the good people."

She did as he'd said, and was surprised by the roar of approval that assaulted her ears. "They make me feel like royalty. Do they do this for every couple who marry in your town?"

His eyes, his smile, were full of mischief. "Not every couple, though I know they're particularly happy for me. I had planned on celebrating here, with the good people of Innismere. But after all this excitement, I think we could both use some quiet time. I'll let them know through Bridget that they can plan a proper celebration for tomorrow." He put the car in gear. "For now, why don't we go to my home?"

Sydney nodded. "Maybe that's best. This has all happened so quickly, my head is spinning."

As he started the car's engine, he caught her hand. "I'm sorry for all the confusion, Sydney. I hope I can make it up to you."

When she said nothing, he lifted her hand to his lips. At once she felt the warmth spreading through her veins. His simple touch was like a potent drug, putting her at ease and erasing all her doubts and fears.

"Sydney, you should know that I've been distracted ever since we met on the plane. I knew there was something special about you. And the more time I spent with you, the more convinced I was that our meeting was no accident. We were meant to meet and fall in love. It was fated from the beginning of time."

She looked away. "How many times have you said those very words to someone, Cullen?"

"Never before." When she turned to him, his smile was dazzling. "You're the first, Sydney. You'll be the last. You are the only one."

Her smile came slowly. "I ran away because of Margot's warning that I'd been taken in by your charm. She called you Prince Charming."

"Your stepmother makes that sound like a bad thing." He squeezed her hand. "I hope it's true. Are you charmed?"

"Completely."

He threw back his head and laughed. "That makes two of us. You're the most amazing, delightful woman I've ever known."

"I've always thought of myself as ordinary."

"Sydney, you're the most extraordinary woman in the world. I'm completely dazzled by you."

They drove through the darkened countryside, past pretty farmhouses with lights aglow, and Sydney began watching, wondering if she'd be able to spy Cullen's house.

The road began climbing past tall hedgerows that blotted out the twinkling stars, past lovely meandering rock walls with brightly painted doors, until they came up over a rise and drew near a magnificent manor house that resembled the castle of Sydney's vision. Every window was ablaze with light.

Cullen drove to the front door and stepped out. Rounding the car, he opened Sydney's door and caught her hand.

Before she could ask a single question, ornate double doors were thrown open and a silver-haired man in a black suit made a grand bow before saying, "Welcome home, sir."

"Thank you, Egan. This is my lovely bride, Sydney."

"Welcome to Eventide." The old man stood aside as they stepped into the elegant foyer. "Mrs. Maguire is conferring with Cook about the wedding supper you requested, sir."

"Thank you, Egan." Cullen caught Sydney's hand and led her up the wide, curving stairs to the second story.

Once inside, she stared around the elegant sitting room where a fire burned on the hearth. A white marble surround with a wide matching mantel gleamed in the firelight. Above the mantel hung two paintings.

Sydney stared in openmouthed surprise. "Is one of those mine?"

Cullen nodded. "It is, yes. I had it framed so it could hang beside its mate."

Sydney stared at a painting from her childhood hanging beside her own. She stepped closer, before turning to Cullen in stunned disbelief. "Is this my father's? How can this be?"

"My family bought it."

"Your family! When?"

"Years ago. As soon as your father's paintings were offered for sale, our solicitor was told to bid on the entire collection."

"You bought them from my stepmother?"

He nodded. "From her representative, actually. We never dealt with her directly."

Sydney's eyes filled with tears as she stared hungrily at her father's painting of Slipper Rock. "Why did you want this?"

"It belongs here. Your father's talent brought a sense of pride to our town. His early paintings were all about the familiar landmarks of Innismere. And even when he left his home, and painted the lovely scenes around the countryside of his new land, they seemed to speak of his home here."

Sydney glanced around. "Where are the rest of his paintings?"

Cullen caught her hand. "Come. I'll show you."

The majestic hallway was lined with paintings, and every one of them had been painted by her father's hand. Just seeing them, she was transported back to her childhood, and all the joyful hours she'd spent in her father's company.

She touched a hand to each painting, feeling again the dips and curves of her father's scrawled signature.

Beneath a huge skylight rested her father's finest creation. This one was a scene of the river Glass from the far shore. On the hill, instead of the church, her father had painted this castle. In the clouds above were robed figures of a king and queen.

Sydney's hand flew to her mouth. "Look, Cullen. It's the vision I described to you."

He was smiling. "So it is."

She shook her head. "I know this canvas bears my father's signature, but I never saw him paint this castle, or those royal figures."

Cullen's smile grew. "That's because this was commissioned by my grandfather when your father was just a lad. Even at a young age, he shared the magic of this place, for he'd seen it with his own eyes."

He caught her hand and led her back to his suite of rooms, where he urged her to sit beside him on a white sofa. "I owe you an explanation. You've been so patient with me, Sydney. But now, it's time I told you everything."

She clasped her hands together, wondering what he was about to reveal. Though she'd gone this far with him on faith, there was still that tiny seed of doubt that Margot had planted.

"There's much about this town, and its people, that is never revealed to outsiders."

"Am I an outsider?"

"You never were, Sydney, thanks to your father. But until we were certain, we did our best to keep our secrets to ourselves."

"And now?"

"I owe you the truth. My ancestors are direct descendants of ancient Irish lords. At one time they were considered royalty. Through the generations they've protected the land either as warriors, or, in more peaceful times, as elected officials. I've been asked to run for Parliament, or at least to be mayor of Innismere, but I choose instead to simply run my software company, which employs hundreds of people both here and in Dublin, and a few thousand more employees abroad."

Sydney's jaw dropped. "You're a successful businessman?"

"You seem surprised."

She nodded. "You never seemed to work. And you never had any money. Mrs. Kelly wouldn't take your money. Neither would O'Malley. So I thought . . ." Seeing the laughter in his eyes, her words trailed off.

"You thought I was unemployed?"

She shrugged. "Worse."

"Worse?" As the realization dawned, he burst into laughter. "You thought I was using you?"

She looked away. "Not at first, but when I told Margot that I was in love with you, she persuaded me that you were a con artist who was playing me for a fool."

"Sydney, the reason Mary Francis Kelly and O'Malley wouldn't take money from me is because, when they were about to be foreclosed, I loaned them enough to pay off their mortgages to the bank."

"Oh, I'm so relieved. You'll never know . . ."

They both looked up as a plump woman in a black dress, her cheeks bright pink, eyes alight with curiosity, charged into the room and nearly skidded to a halt.

"Ye're home then." She seemed delighted. "I was in the kitchen, and telling Cook that ye wanted yer wedding supper up in yer rooms. Little did I know ye were already here until Egan found us gossiping and told me ye needed me."

"Mrs. Maguire, I'd like you to meet my bride, Sydney."

"Sydney. Of course." The older woman seemed absolutely delighted as she stepped closer and offered her a handshake. "It's very welcome indeed ye are to Eventide, Mrs. Rella."

"Rella?" Sydney shot a sideways glance at Cullen. "When the judge officiated at our wedding, he called you something else."

Cullen chuckled. "In Gaelic, it's an ancient and noble name, and folks in Innismere prefer the Gaelic to the English translation."

"I'll be fetching that wedding supper now," the old woman said as she fairly danced from the room.

Sydney glanced at her beloved father's painting, and then at her own. The two were identical.

Seeing the direction of her gaze, Cullen said, "It all fit, you see."

"Fit?"

"The things you'd seen. Only a chosen few have ever had

the vision of our ancestors. The castle. The royal figures. And, of course, there's your painting of Slipper Rock. That fit perfectly."

"I don't understand."

He took her hand and lifted it to his lips. "Your painting exactly matched one your father painted when he was a lad, when it had been commissioned by my grandfather. A seer, who was an advisor to my ancestors, said that Slipper Rock had magical powers. He assured my family that one day, a slipper would fit an amazing woman who would become the great love of my life. I took his prediction literally, and thought I ought to try fitting a slipper on your foot. But then you chose to paint Slipper Rock, and I knew at once what he really meant. Your painting has been measured against the one painted by your father. An expert has examined and measured, centimeter by centimeter, to be certain that it fit. For, you see, once the slipper fit, I knew I'd found my one and only true love."

Sydney's eyes widened with sudden knowledge. "Are you suggesting that this is like some sort of fairy tale? The handsome, charming son of royalty? His godmother, who runs the inn? The slipper that fits? It's all . . . magic?"

"I'll leave that for you to decide, my beautiful bride. I know only that I've waited a lifetime for you. Your love has rescued me from a life that was empty and meaningless. Even though I have a good life here, with many friends, I yearned for that one special person who would mean more to me than life itself."

That lovely rogue smile lit all his features as he leaned close to brush her mouth with his, sending a tingle of warmth along her spine. "And because you're American, I'll say this in your tongue. Welcome home, my lovely Sydney Rella."

"Of course. Sydney Rella. Sydney Rella." She was up and dancing around like a girl, clapping her hands as the final piece of the puzzle fell into place.

And then she was in Cullen's arms, laughing and crying as the truth dawned.

"You love me. Truly love me. And I love you. And we really are going to live happily ever after, aren't we?"

Cullen didn't bother to answer. He was too busy kissing her, and showing her, in the way of lovers from the beginning of time, the true magic of love.